VICTIMS & VILLAINS

BARBIE AND KEN MEET SHERLOCK HOLMES

Victims & Villains

Barbie and Ken Meet Sherlock Holmes

Curated by Derham Groves

Dolls by 3rd year architecture students from the University of Melbourne

Photographs by Lee McRae

Stories by Sir Arthur Conan Doyle

RAMBLE HOUSE

Cover designed by Huey Groves

ISBN 13: 978-1-60543-338-7

ISBN 10: 1-60543-338-1

Edited by Fender Tucker

Published 2009 by Ramble House

CONTENTS

Barbie, Ken . . . and Blaine?

Astrid Britt Krautschneider

I'm not afraid to confess openly that I love Barbie. As a small child I think it was something to do with that (so predictable) girlish love for all things miniature and all things pink; I remember being obsessed with Barbie's myriad accessories—those gorgeous little dresses, those tiny handbags and shoes, that fabulous Dream House, her beautiful silky-haired dog that even came with a special comb to brush him with . . . sigh. My mother, however, never let me have a Barbie of my own, citing all sorts of logical reasons (insert whatever logical reason you like here), which of course were totally lost on a smitten 8 year-old. I had to indulge my passion vicariously through my friends, all of whom seemed to possess Barbies and thus, obviously, far more sensible mothers than mine.

What my childish imagination could not have even begun to conceive was that, much later in life, I would witness my precious Barbie in a spate of murders most foul. In February 2008, over a long lunch at the University of Melbourne staff club, Dr. Derham Groves told me about his idea for a forthcoming exhibition to be held in the University Library gallery. Given his oft-articulated passion for the crime genre, I was unsurprised to find that this proposed exhibition would draw upon the University of Melbourne's extensive collection of twentieth century Australian crime fiction. Yes, I thought, this could be quite interesting. The colourful covers of the books alone, fairly bursting with juicy pop culture references, would be a fun topic to explore in an exhibition.

Then came the twist. With Derham, you must understand, there is almost always a twist. His third-year architecture students, he explained, were to be given the task this semester of designing a centre for the study of Australian crime fiction. Before his students went ahead with their projects, though, Derham intended to make them prove they had a handle on crime by setting them the unusual task of a) reading a Sherlock Holmes story and b) depicting the victim or villain of that story using a Barbie or Ken doll. He had also succeeded in convincing a colleague Dr. Andrew Saniga to set a crime fiction theme as a base for his landscape architecture students' design studio projects. Examples from the work of both classes would be displayed in the exhibition.

I found it a little difficult to envisage at the time, exactly how all this was going to work in relation to the exhibition layout, design and interpretation, especially since—apart from the books themselves—none of the items to be showcased in the exhibition were even created yet (indeed, even as the moment of installation drew near, some unfortunate students were still frantically completing their projects). So I decided to simply place my trust in Derham's amazing ability to make perfect sense out of seemingly disparate concepts and pronounced myself delighted to work with him on the exhibition, which we titled *Murderous Melbourne: A Celebration of Australian Crime Fiction and Place.*

While I waited for the university semester to take its course, I worked on other aspects of the exhibition, but found that my mind couldn't help drifting, every so often, to thoughts of Barbie and Sherlock Holmes. While it is rare to hear these two names mentioned in the same sentence, there is no denying that both Barbie and Holmes are household words; both indisputably huge twentieth century pop culture icons.

Sir Arthur Conan Doyle's Sherlock Holmes and his trusty sidekick Dr. Watson must be among the most enduring characters in all English literature. Their London flat has even managed to take on a life of its own and cross from fiction into reality, for it now truly exists at 221B Baker Street. There is any number of Sherlock Holmes societies around the planet to choose from, and there is an almost endless array of memorabilia (or Sherlockiana) available for his hoards of adoring fans to collect.

And the fact that Barbie has just celebrated her fiftieth birthday and is still going strong, which in itself speaks volumes. Like Holmes, she too has transgressed the boundaries between make-believe and the real world: she now has a real Dream House in Malibu, been outfitted by real fashion designers (including Vera Wang and Christian Dior), she even has her own blog—on which I was mildly intrigued to read that she and Ken are back together. I was unaware that they had ever split up, although, come to think of it, I do have vague recollections of a rumour involving Barbie and an Australian surfer called Blaine.

Partiality to Barbie aside, I am also an avid reader of Sherlock Holmes stories. Conan Doyle was a master at describing in incredibly visual (or perhaps visceral) detail, all the gory circumstances surrounding the death or disfigurement of his victims. There is, quite possibly, nothing more enjoyable than curling up on the couch on a cold winter afternoon with a good Holmesian crime setting to revel in. For example, in *The Sign of the Four* (1890), Bartholomew Sholto is found killed by a poisoned thorn inside his locked study; his features set in a horrible grimace and his whole body 'twisted and turned in the most fantastic fashion'. And I particularly love the scene in *The Hound of the Baskervilles* (1902) that sees poor Beryl Stapleton discovered alive, but shrouded by sheets and gagged, covered in bloody whiplashes and bound to a post in a butterfly museum. The 'cruel-hearted' perpetrator of this crime, Beryl's scheming husband Jack, later disappears forever, deduced to have sunk into the 'foul slime' of the Grimpen Mire.

It was with some excitement then that I finally received several box loads of extensively mutilated Barbie and Ken dolls (sorry, I mean villains and victims from Sherlock Holmes' stories) into my office for arranging, identifying and labelling in preparation for display. Like Lee McCrae, the photographer who had been entrusted with the dolls before me, I was delighted with them. Derham's architecture students had transformed their Barbie and Kens (likely there were some Blaines in there as well—hard to tell—the dolls were all rendered so completely unrecognisable and I don't know what Blaine looks like anyway) into what I can only describe as 'murder maquettes' done almost precisely to scale. Bartholomew Sholto at scale 1:6, if you like.

It probably goes without saying that the dolls stole the show in our *Murderous Melbourne* exhibition. If readers get even half as much pleasure out of reading this book as I did working with Derham, Andrew and Lee on the exhibition last year, then our work is complete. The images and stories are evocative and intriguingly captivating. Like any good Conan Doyle narrative, I not only urge you to enjoy, but dare you to put this down . . .

Biography

Astrid Britt Krautschneider is co-curator of the Grainger Museum. She has a Masters degree in Art Curatorship from the University of Melbourne and wrote her thesis on the collection of Napoleonic memorabilia owned by Melbourne society doyenne Dame Mabel Brookes.

Victims and Villains:

Barbie and Ken Meet Sherlock Holmes

Derham Groves

Introduction

As an architect and crime fiction fan, I am always looking for connections between these two areas. While at first glance they may appear to be unrelated, architecture and crime fiction do have a number of things in common. One is an interest in murder. Every crime novel worthy of that name has at least one dead body, but most people have forgotten that, once upon a time, important buildings had their hidden corpses too. In the days when architecture was a black art—not so long ago—a human sacrifice was thought to be necessary when choosing a site, laying a foundation, constructing a roof, and moving in, otherwise mischievous spirits might cause the new building to collapse. Thus architects and builders were often cold-blooded murderers and the buildings they designed and constructed were the scenes of dreadful crimes. Take laying a foundation for example. Around the world, people—especially children—were customarily buried in the foundations of bridges, churches, fortifications, and houses: the Dayaks of Borneo used to suspend the main house post above a deep hole, throw a young girl in the hole, cut the rope holding the post, and crush the girl to death; while surprisingly like-minded stonemasons from Copenhagen walled-up a little girl inside a city rampart at the same time as loud music drowned out her pitiful cries for help.

In *Builders' Rites and Ceremonies* (1893) G.W. Speth neatly summarizes the evolution and meaning of this grisly practice: 'Our forefathers . . . buried a living human sacrifice in the [foundations] to ensure the stability of the structure; their sons substituted an animal; their sons again a mere effigy or other symbol; and we, their children, still immure a substitute, coins bearing the effigy

. . . of the one person to whom we all are most loyal, and whom we all most love, our Gracious Queen [Victoria]. I do not assert that one in a hundred is conscious of what he is doing . . . but the fact remains that unconsciously we are following the customs of our fathers, and symbolically providing a soul for the structure.'

Architecture and crime fiction are also interested in place. The scene of the crime is essential to crime fiction, just as place making is fundamental to architecture. However, I believe that architects can learn a lot from crime writers like Sir Arthur Conan Doyle, a particular favourite of mine, who was a master at depicting houses that conveyed the personalities of the people who occupied them. Thus from time to time I have given my first- and second-year architecture students at the University of Melbourne (Australia), where I teach, design projects based on Conan Doyle's Sherlock Holmes stories. One project involved the students designing a house for a villain or a victim in a Holmes story. It was called 'Better Holmes and Gardens'. Another project required the students to design a boutique hotel for the eccentric members of the Baker Street Irregulars, the world's oldest Holmes appreciation society. It was called 'Holmes Away From Home'.

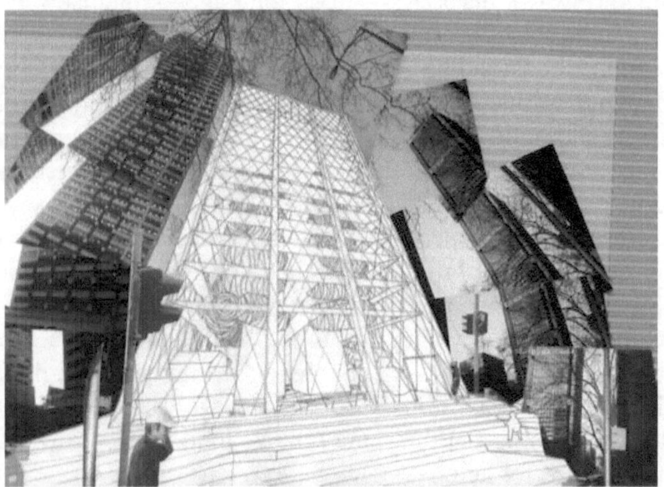

Fig. 1: Baker Street Irregulars' Hotel by Matt Choot.

I have also explored the idea of place in Australian crime fiction. In 2002 I curated *Crime Scenes,* a three-part exhibition at Monash Gallery of Art in Glen Waverley (Australia). For part one, seven local contemporary crime writers—Marshall Brown, Peter

Corris, Michael Jorgensen (who is also an architect), Barry Maitland (who is also an urban designer), Shane Maloney, Mary-Rose MacColl (whose 'detective' Harriet Darling is an architect), and Peter Temple—each described a crime scene in 500 words or less. For part two, a like-number of local artists and architects—Mark Galea, Sharon Goodwin, David Harris, Christopher Langton, Lyons, Nat and Ali, and Sally Smart—each depicted one of the seven crime scenes in the gallery. And for part three, a team of detectives from Victoria Police was asked to report on the artists' crime scenes, but without the benefit of first reading the crime fiction writers' descriptions.

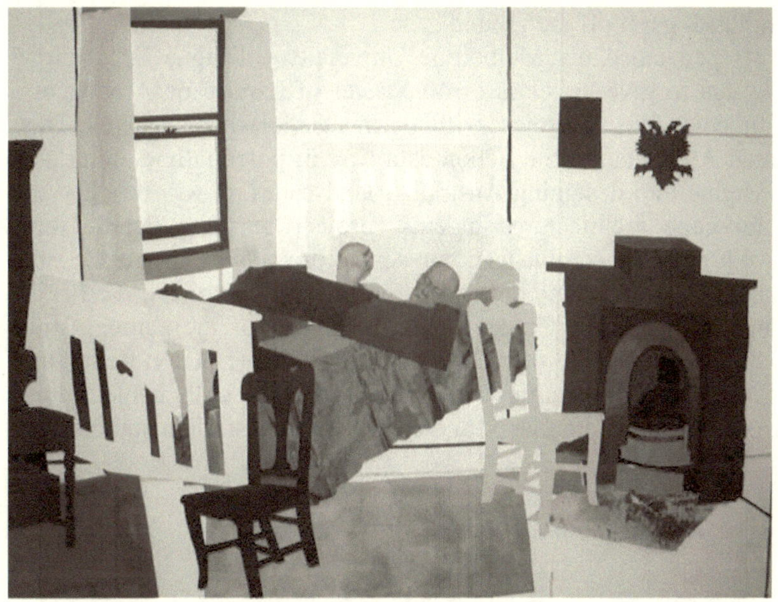

Fig. 2: A crime scene described by Michael Jorgensen and depicted by Sally Smart.

More recently, I have been reading novels written by several mid-twentieth century Australian crime writers, including Berridge Allerton, Otto Beeby, Carter Brown (Alan Yates), Sydney Bunce, Jon Cleary, Sidney Hobson Courtier, Pat Flower, Geoff de Fraga, Ian Hamilton, Helen Mace, A.E. Martin, Margot Neville (sisters Anne and Margaret Goyder), Eric North (Bernard Cronin), Bant Singer (Charles Shaw), Arthur Upfield, and June Wright. The fact that Australia has so many good crime writers is worth celebrating, which gave me an idea for another design project in 2008. The 80 third-year architecture students in my group designed a Centre for Australian Crime Fiction—consisting of a library, some galleries for exhibitions, a lecture theatre, a bookshop, a café, an outdoor courtyard, and two apartments for writers-in-residence—on the grounds of the University of Melbourne. While this was merely an exercise, a real Centre for Australian Crime Fiction could be a focus for research and teaching; a headquarters for the Crime Writers Association of Australia, the professional body for Australian crime writers; a meeting place for crime fiction societies, such as Sisters in Crime; a repository for crime fiction writing; and a venue for exhibitions, lectures and crime writers' festivals. All that is needed are the funds to get it off the ground!

I persuaded my Melbourne University colleague Dr. Andrew Saniga to give his class of 40 Master of Landscape Architecture students a design project with a crime fiction theme as well. They read Australian crime fiction as a way of potentially gaining new insights into designing Australian landscapes. (I will describe the landscape architecture students' project in more detail later.) Andrew and I commenced our design projects by introducing the students to the crime fiction of four interesting writers: the British author Sir Arthur Conan Doyle, a pioneer of the genre; Arthur Upfield, arguably Australia's best known crime fiction writer; and Sidney Hobson Courtier and June Wright, two sadly neglected but nonetheless accomplished and entertaining Australian authors.

Sir Arthur Conan Doyle

Many crime writers have a good sense of place because solving a mystery usually depends on the detective (closely followed by the reader) knowing exactly where everyone and everything were when the crime was committed. But Sir Arthur Conan Doyle may have inherited his highly developed sense of place from his father, who was an architect. Little is known about Charles Altamont Doyle's career: he joined the Scottish Office of Works in 1849 and designed the fountain at Holyrood Palace in Edinburgh, the British Royal Family's official Scottish residence, as well as one of the large stained-glass windows in Glasgow Cathedral. One of Charles' sketchbooks came to light in 1977 and was published the following year as *The Doyle Diary: The Last Great Conan Doyle*

Mystery (1978). It indicates that he was a skillful draughtsman with a vivid architectural imagination. Despite fighting a losing battle with alcoholism, Charles had a positive influence on his son's life and work: he illustrated the second edition of Conan Doyle's first Sherlock Holmes novel *A Study in Scarlet* (1887); 'many remarkable pictures' by Charles were hanging in Conan Doyle's study reported the *Strand Magazine* journalist Harry How in 'A Day With Dr. Conan Doyle' (1892), an article written while Conan Doyle was still pursuing careers in medicine and writing; and in Conan Doyle's short story 'His Last Bow' (1917) Holmes poses as an Irish-American spy named Altamont (Charles' middle name).

No doubt due to his father's influence, Conan Doyle empathized with architects his entire life. Most significantly perhaps, he pictured himself as an architect when summing up his life's work in the second edition of his autobiography *Memories and Adventures* (1930): 'When an author is in failing health and has passed his seventieth year he feels, as he surveys the line of his works, like some architect or builder who, having laboured long to complete his edifice, finally stands back to survey it in its entirety. I can only hope to add some little attic or cupola here or there. It is a modest enough structure, no doubt, and yet as I survey it I feel that I could do no better and that any powers which Providence has given me have found their full expression.'

Furthermore, I believe that Conan Doyle appreciated architecture's dark past and the parallels between entombing a person in the foundations of a building to placate the forces of Nature on one hand, and concealing a murder on the other. In the Sherlock Holmes story 'The Musgrave Ritual' (1893)—incidentally, published the same year as *Builders' Rites and Ceremonies*—Richard Brunton, the butler at Hurlstone Manor, discovers the ancient crown of the Kings of England along with several old coins in a squat wooden box in a hole seven feet deep and four feet square under the cellar floor. It was probably Sir Ralph Musgrave, a prominent Cavalier and supporter of King Charles II, who placed them there for safekeeping. But why was the hole so deep if just for a squat wooden box? That it was originally dug to bury conceal a human sacrifice in the foundations is one possible explanation. Sir Ralph may have found the hole and its ghastly contents when Hurlstone was being renovated, nobly removed the body to a cemetery, and later hid the box containing the crown and coins in the hole. As Speth explained, royal symbols eventually replaced human sacrifices. Perhaps this fact even prompted Sir Ralph to remember the hole when he was searching for a hiding place for the crown and coins. Ironically, the original grisly purpose of the hole was reinstated when Rachel Howells, Brunton's insanely jealous ex-lover, trapped him in the hole and condemned the butler to a horrible slow death.

While the architecture students were in the early stages of designing a Centre for Australian Crime Fiction, I gave them two warm-up exercises to do. The first was called 'Barbie and Ken Meet Sherlock Holmes'. Each student had to read a Holmes story and then portray the victim or villain in that story by changing the appearance of a Barbie or Ken doll. They produced a horrifying collection of dolls that had been bludgeoned, garroted, hanged, mauled, poisoned, scared, shot, stabbed, and strangled (images of these dolls appear later in this book). I have since discovered that many people enjoy doing all sorts of terrible things to poor Barbie and Ken (see www.alteredbarbie.com), however I originally got the idea for this exercise from the 'Nutshell Studies of Unexplained Death', a series of dollhouse-sized crime scenes made by International Harvester heiress Frances Glessner Lee during the 1940s.

'Barbie and Ken Meet Sherlock Holmes' not only recalled architecture's murderous history, but also encouraged the architecture students to take an equally violent approach to designing a Centre for Australian Crime Fiction, since architects confuse good taste for good design far too often in my view. To illustrate how the students might achieve this kind of edginess in their buildings, I introduced them to the work of the American 'anti-architect' and artist Gordon Matta-Clark. In *Object To Be Destroyed: The Works of Gordon Matta-Clark* (2000) art historian and author Pamela M. Lee wrote of Matta-Clark's work: 'Cutting, shattering, fragmenting, dissecting, mutilating, even decapitating: to consider the reception of Matta-Clark's art is to survey a language riven by violence—of gestures at once trenchant and brutalizing.'

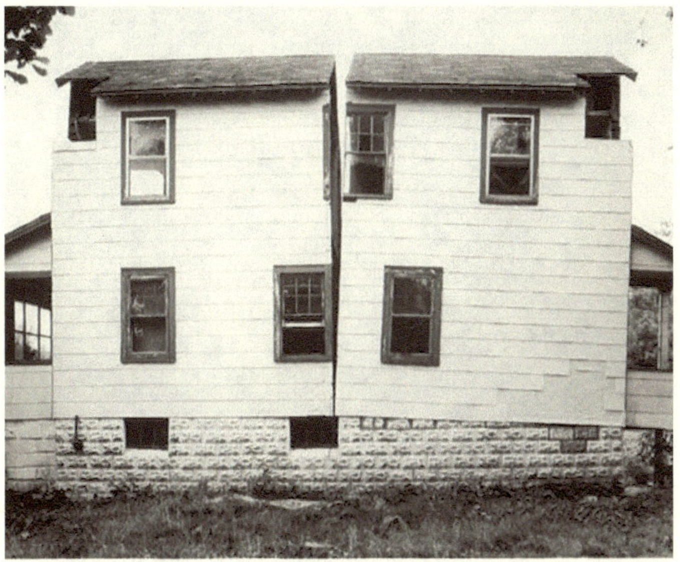

Fig. 3: 'Splitting' (1974) by Gordon Matta-Clark.

June Wright

June Wright (née Healy) is not as well known as either Arthur Upfield or S.H. Courtier, the other two Australian crime writers Andrew Saniga and I talked about, although she wrote six very successful crime novels between 1948 and 1966. She was born in 1919 in Malvern (Australia), and educated at Kildara College, Loreto College and Mandeville Hall, three exclusive catholic girls' schools in Melbourne (Australia). After leaving school and briefly studying commercial art, Wright got a job as a telephonist at the central telephone exchange in Melbourne. In 1941 she married Stewart Wright, an accountant. They had six children: Patrick, Rosemary, Nicholas, Anthony, Brenda, and Stephen. Wright's inspiring ability to juggle crime writing and motherhood was the subject of several newspaper and magazine articles about her, such as 'Wrote Thriller with Her Baby on Her Knee' (1948) and 'Books Between Babies' (1948).

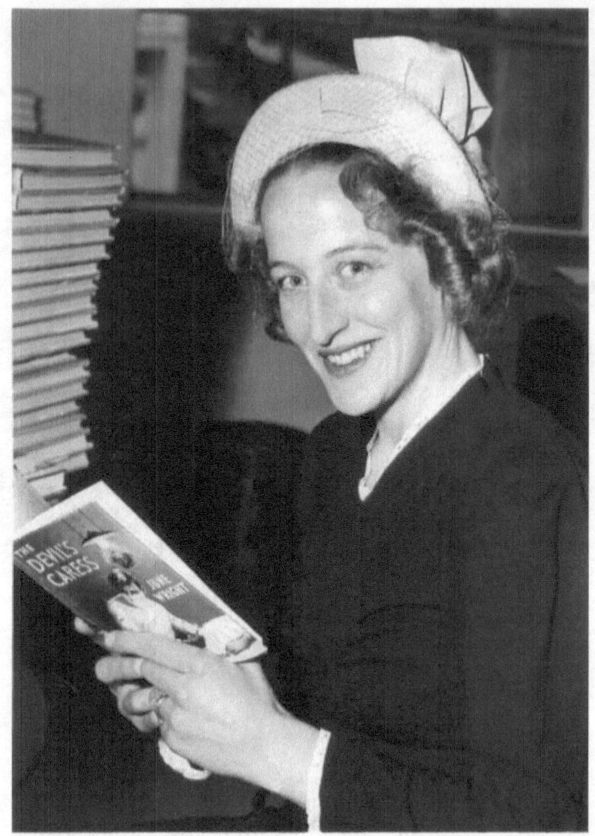

Fig. 4: June Wright.

When Wright's first child Patrick was one year old, she began writing *Murder in the Telephone Exchange* (1948), a Dorothy L. Sayers-style whodunit set in Wright's former workplace. Sarah Compton, a supervisor at the exchange, is bashed to death with a 'buttinski', a gadget used by telephone operators to interrupt telephone conversations. The story is narrated by a spirited young telephonist named Maggie Byrnes who Wright denies she modelled on herself (but I am unconvinced).

While wrapping-up vegetable scraps in a newspaper, Wright happened to see an advertisement for an international literary competition run by the London publisher Hutchinson. She entered *Murder in the Telephone Exchange,* and although it did not win the competition, it was accepted for publication. Most critics praised Wright's debut crime novel. For example, one local newspaper reviewer wrote: 'Perhaps it was the Melbourne setting that gave a new freshness to the form. (One almost expected to meet the characters walking down the streets, to hear their voices over the phone.) But I think there were other factors, too. The atmosphere, the plot, the characterization, all are good.' With the royalties that Wright earned from *Murder in the Telephone Exchange* she bought herself a fur coat and remodelled her kitchen.

In Wright's second novel *So Bad a Death* (1949), Maggie Byrnes and her husband John Matheson, a police inspector who investigated Sarah Compton's death in *Murder in the Telephone Exchange,* are frustrated by the post-Second World War housing shortage in Australia until they finally rent 'Dower House' in the outer Melbourne suburb of 'Middleburn'. Despite its genteel appearance, Middleburn turns out to be a hotbed of murderers, who Maggie eventually helps bring to justice. The crime fiction reviewer for the *Daily Telegraph* Dr. Watson Junior (a.k.a. Richard Hughes, the famous Australian China-watcher) considered *So Bad a Death* noteworthy 'as perhaps the First Australian Will Murder'.

Wright's next crime novel *The Devil's Caress* (1952) is set in the little coastal town of 'Matthews' on the Mornington Peninsula, south of Melbourne. Marsh Mowbray, an up and coming young female physician, is invited to spend a few days at the summer residence of Katherine and Kingsley Waring, two of Melbourne's leading doctors. But Marsh discovers that the Warings have some very dark secrets they will do almost anything to keep. One critic said *The Devil's Caress* made Wright's first two books 'read like bedtime stories'.

For her fourth crime novel *Reservation for Murder* (1958), Wright created the unassuming but strong willed Catholic nun-detective Mother Mary St. Paul of the Cross, or Mother Paul for short, who runs a business girls' hostel just outside of Melbourne. She is the female equivalent of G.K. Chesterton's Catholic priest-detective Father Brown. Mother Paul also appears in Wright's fifth and sixth crime novels *Faculty of Murder* (1961) and *Make-up for Murder* (1966). She is in charge of a women's university college in the earlier book and a girls' boarding school in the other. Mother Paul was based on Mother Mary Dorothea Devine, a Sister of Charity who headed the maternity ward at St. Vincent's Hospital in Melbourne when Wright gave birth to twins there during the 1940s.

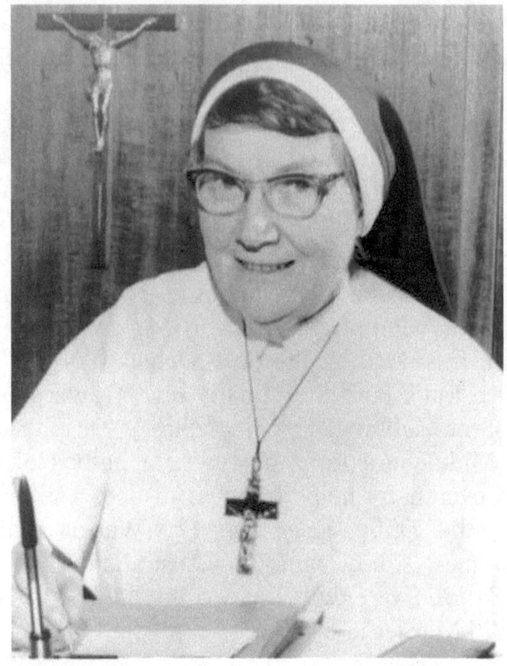

Fig. 5: Mother Dorothea Devine.

Interesting local settings, feisty female protagonists, and credible social situations characterize Wright's six crime novels. Unfortunately, she stopped writing crime fiction altogether when her husband suddenly became ill and could not work, and she had to earn a regular salary. Wright lives in Glen Waverley with her son Anthony.

'You *Can* Judge a Book by its Cover' was the name of the second warm-up exercise I gave the architecture students. It involved each student designing a dust jacket for a new edition of Wright's novel *Faculty of Murder*. The setting for this story is Melbourne University's 'Brigit Moore Hall', a Catholic women's college, and its male counterpart next-door 'Manning College'. While the original dust jacket by William Randell shows the famous gothic clock tower of Ormond College, a Presbyterian college, it seems more likely that Wright modelled Brigit Moore Hall on St. Mary's College and Manning College on Newman College, two Catholic colleges. Therefore, the students had to include some architectural elements from either St Mary's or

Newman in their dust jacket designs, which somehow expressed a sense of horror, mystery or terror. Furthermore, one of the galleries in the Centre for Australian Crime Fiction was to be named after June Wright, which prompted the students to represent the often-sinister urban places in Wright's novels in their designs.

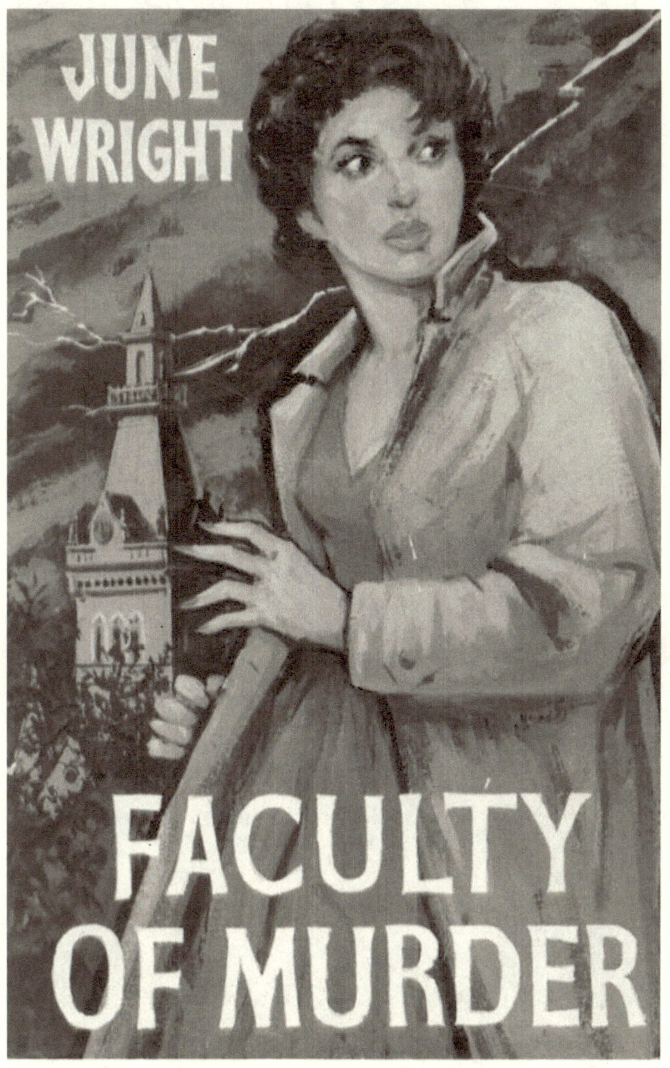

Fig. 6: Original dust jacket by William Randell for Faculty of Murder.

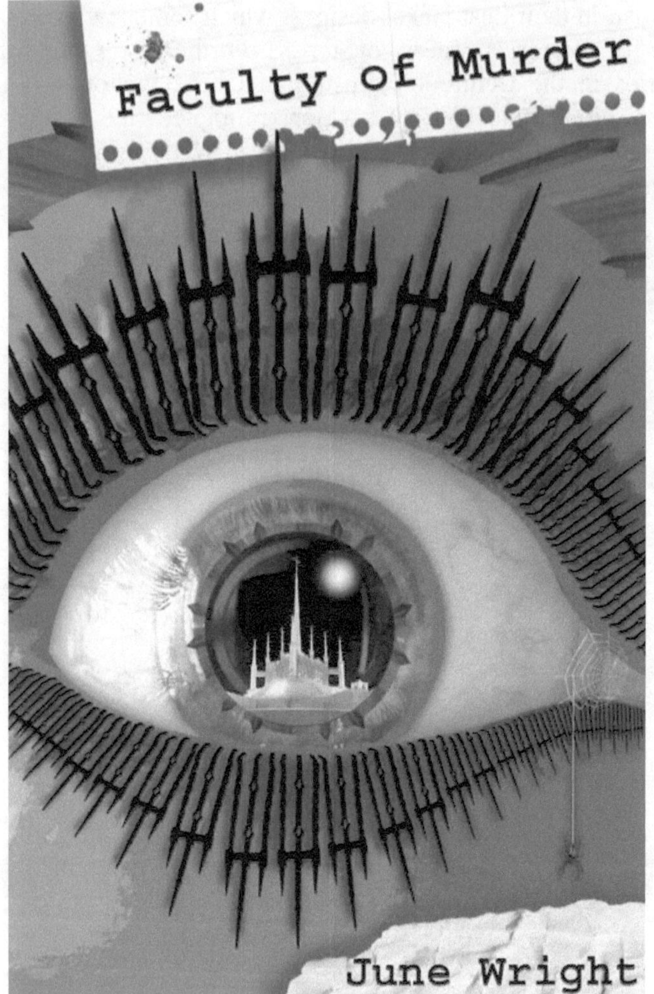

Fig. 7: New dust jacket by Audrey Zerafa for Faculty of Murder.

Arthur Upfield

Arthur Upfield was born in 1890 at Gosport in Hampshire, England. After he failed to qualify as a real estate agent (yet another crime writer with an architectural background) his father, a well-to-do draper, sent him to Australia in 1910. Upfield roamed Australia doing various odd jobs, such as boundary rider, cook and cowhand. He enlisted in the Australian Imperial Force at the start of the First World War, fighting in Turkey at Gallipoli, France and Egypt. In 1915 he married Anne Douglas, an Australian nurse. Following the war the Upfields lived in England where their only child James was born in 1920. They moved to Australia in 1921, and once again Upfield wandered the countryside in search of work. He finally settled down in Melbourne in 1931 and wrote feature articles for the *Herald* newspaper. After Upfield and Anne separated in 1946, he lived with Jessica Hawke, who later wrote his rather unreliable biography *Follow My Dust!* (1957).

While employed as a cook on an isolated property in New South Wales, Upfield began writing crime fiction in his spare time. His second crime novel *The Barrakee Mystery* (1929) featured Detective Inspector Napoleon Bonaparte, or Bony for short, the son of a white man and an Aboriginal woman, who combines the best attributes of both cultures to solve the most puzzling crimes. As the story goes, Bony was only two weeks old when he was found under a tree beside his dead mother in a remote part of Queensland and brought to an orphanage. When the matron saw him trying to eat a biography of Napoleon Bonaparte, she named him after the great French emperor. Bony proved highly intelligent, eventually graduating from the University of Queensland with a Master of Arts and joining the Queensland Police Force. Upfield loosely modelled Bony on Leon Wood, a mixed-blood Aboriginal police tracker who he met on his travels.

Upfield's novels were critically acclaimed overseas. *Cake in the Hat Box* (1955), the nineteenth Bony novel, was a runner-up for the British Crime Writers' Association's Gold Dagger Award in 1956. *Bony Buys a Woman* (1957) (titled *The Bushman Who Came Back* in the USA), the twenty-second Bony novel, was named the Book of the Year by *Ellery Queen Mystery Magazine* in 1957, and also nominated for the Mystery Writers of America's Edgar Award for Best Mystery Novel in 1958. In addition, Upfield was the first foreigner to achieve full membership of the Mystery Writers of America. However, what he really desired was recognition from the Australian literati. When it did not come, Upfield vented his spleen in the eleventh Bony novel *An Author Bites the Dust* (1948)—one of the few set in the suburbs and not the bush—in which a snobbish literary critic from Melbourne is mysteriously murdered.

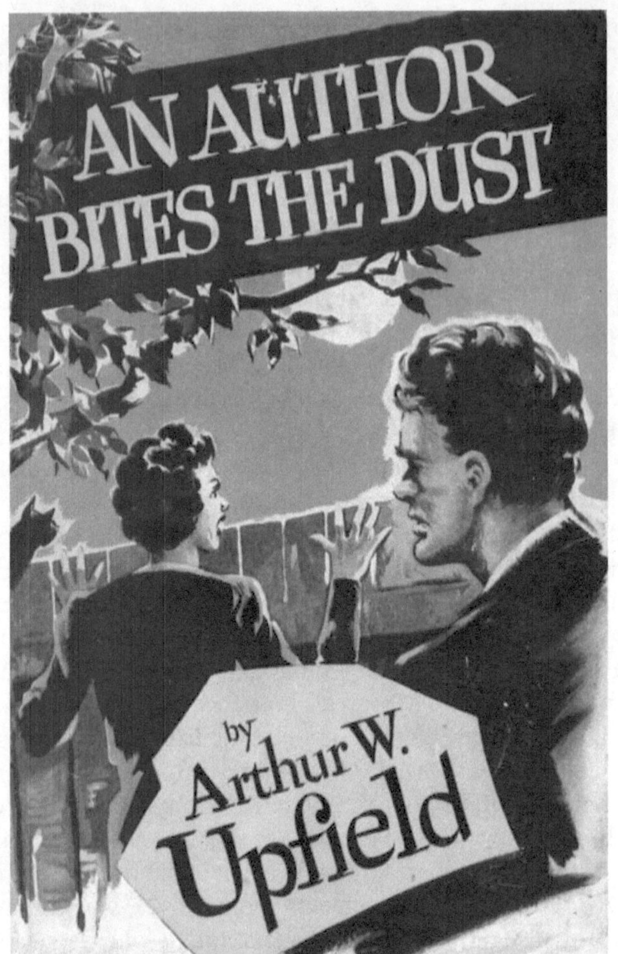

Fig. 8: An Author Bites the Dust by Arthur Upfield.

Upfield wrote 29 Bony novels that are still very popular both here and abroad, due in large part to his vivid descriptions of the 'exotic' Australian bush, which help to create an atmosphere of mystery, a fear of the unknown, a feeling of isolation, and a sense of place. The novels' equally 'exotic' Aboriginal detective is a major factor too. While some people have criticized Upfield for thoughtlessly appropriating Aboriginal culture, others have praised him for presenting a positive image of Aborigines at a time when none existed in Australian popular culture. Upfield died in 1964 at Bowral in New South Wales.

The Arthur Upfield collection at the University of Melbourne proved to be an invaluable resource for many students, Andrew Saniga and me. It contains some impressive items, including the author's albums of press cuttings, his correspondence, his manuscripts, and even his typewriter. Also, the Centre for Australian Crime Fiction's outdoor courtyard was named in Upfield's honour, so that many architecture students designed it to reflect the Australian outback settings of his Bony novels.

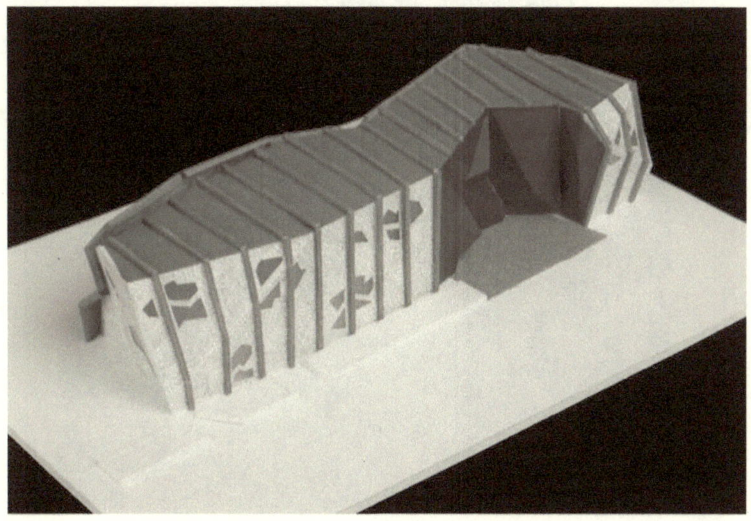

Fig. 9: The Centre for Australian Crime Fiction designed by architecture student Priscilla Finn was heavily influenced by Arthur Upfield's crime fiction.

S. H. Courtier

S. (Sidney) H. (Hobson) Courtier should be a lot better known than he is today. He wrote 24 crime novels, and even though they unfold just as dramatically in just as atmospheric Australian bush settings as Arthur Upfield's—if not more so—by comparison they have been largely forgotten. Courtier created two detectives: the debonair and handsome Superintendent Ambrose Mahon, who features in six crime novels, and Inspector C.J. 'Digger' Haig, a chain-smoking 'rough diamond', who appears in seven.

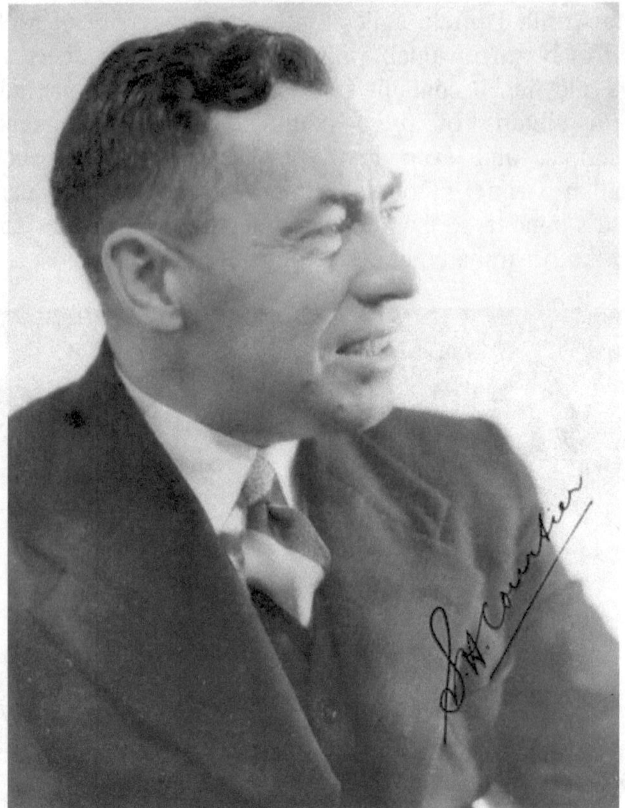

Fig. 10: Sidney Hobson Courtier.

Courtier was born in 1904 at Kangaroo Flat in the central goldfields of Victoria. He attended school in nearby Bendigo, where his father was a mine manager. This district clearly captured Courtier's imagination, because several of his crime fiction crooks hide out in abandoned mineshafts or underground lairs, such as in *Come Back to Murder* (1957), *Murder's Burning* (1967) and *See Who's Dying* (1967).

Courtier was a full-time schoolteacher who taught in many small towns in Victoria (Australia), including Belgrave South, Bolwarra, Carlsruhe, Lake Boga, Mernda, St. James, Tarra Valley, Turoar, and Yallourn, and drew heavily upon these places as settings for his novels. For example, *A Shroud for Unlac* (1958) takes place on a sheep station, *Gently Dust the Corpse* (1960) in a country pub, *Let the Man Die* (1961) in a bush nursing hospital and *The Ringnecker* (1965) in an alpine motel. His selection of unusual, yet convincing, Australian locations undoubtedly helped to make his crime novels popular in America, England, France, and Germany.

In 1933 Courtier married Audrey George. A newspaper report of their wedding also noted that 'Mr. Courtier is well known as a writer of fiction and is the author of "Underground", a story at present appearing in the *Argus,* and also of other stories appearing in Australian periodicals.' Indeed, writing as 'Sidney Belgrave', 'Rui Chestor', 'Sidney Hobson', 'Colin Kingman', 'Raorut', and 'Turoar', he wrote over 200 articles and short stories for magazines and newspapers, including *Argosy* and *Short Stories* in the USA, and the *Australian Journal* and the *Bulletin* in Australia. The Courtiers had three children: Colin, Brian and Lynne.

Between 1942 and 1944 Courtier served in the army in the Northern Territory (Australia), where he became interested in Aboriginal culture. This is reflected in his first two crime novels *The Glass Spear* (1950) and *One Cried Murder* (1954). Later he took long service leave from teaching to visit Queensland (Australia) to do research for *Now Seek My Bones* (1957) and *Death in Dream Time* (1959), two more crime novels with references to native culture. However, unlike Arthur Upfield's Inspector Napoleon Bonaparte, Courtier's Aboriginal characters generally play minor roles in his novels.

Courtier was a member of International PEN, the world association of writers. In a letter to his brother-in-law Alan George, he recalled a funny incident at one of its meetings in Melbourne, which reflected his quirky sense of humour: 'One night at PEN, just before I became President of that august body, I had Nell and Ian Langlands as my guests and they were both interested in the various "famous" writers. Ian asked me who was the talkative lady with the stocking fallen down around her ankle. I looked and, heavens, it was Nettie Palmer. Vance, her husband, was nearby but apparently he didn't notice, and it would seem nobody else noticed—except Ian. The stocking was still draped around her ankle when the meeting ended, which amazed Ian. The stocking really took his mind off the pearls of wisdom uttered during the evening. We concluded that *that* was one stocking we didn't want to hang up. That's really a Christmas story.'

In 1967 Courtier suffered a devastating stroke that robbed him of speech and some movement, however he doggedly taught himself to speak again using a series of speech exercises that he devised himself. (Later he tried unsuccessfully to have these published.) Significantly, he wrote about sensory loss in four of his subsequent crime novels—the loss of movement in *No Obelisk for Emily* (1970), the loss of memory in *Dead If I Remember* (1972), the loss of hearing in *Into the Silence* (1973), and the loss of sanity in *The Smiling Trip* (1975). The last two books straddle crime fiction and science fiction. Courtier died in 1974 at Safety Beach in Victoria.

Twenty landscape architecture students read *See Who's Dying* by S.H. Courtier—a Cold War spy thriller that begins in Melbourne, moves to Canberra and ends in 'Tulladoon', a deserted mining town on the edge of the desert in outback Queensland—before visiting the old rocket range and satellite tracking station in the desert near Woomera in South Australia. While the other 20 students read another of Courtier's books *Murder's Burning*—a whodunit set in the abandoned East Gippsland hamlet of 'Paladin Valley', which was totally destroyed in a suspicious fire—before visiting the abandoned school and quarry sites at Stony Creek near Talbot in Victoria. It was impossible to get exact matches, but the idea was that Courtier's two novels would inform the two places chosen by Andrew Saniga for the students to investigate. 'Courtier's fiction . . . helped explain and define many of the physical things that we saw, and even served to implicate the people whom we met,' commented Andrew Saniga.

Each landscape architecture student designed a new dust jacket for whichever of the two books by Courtier he or she read, a poster advertising a film adaptation of the book, a stage prop or set for use in the film, and an outdoor performance space based on the stage prop or set. In addition, one of the galleries in the Centre for Australian Crime Fiction was named after Courtier, which prompted the architecture students to explore a variety of his most popular themes in their designs, including bush fires, camouflage, caves, death, decay, desert landscapes, espionage, ruin, and travel.

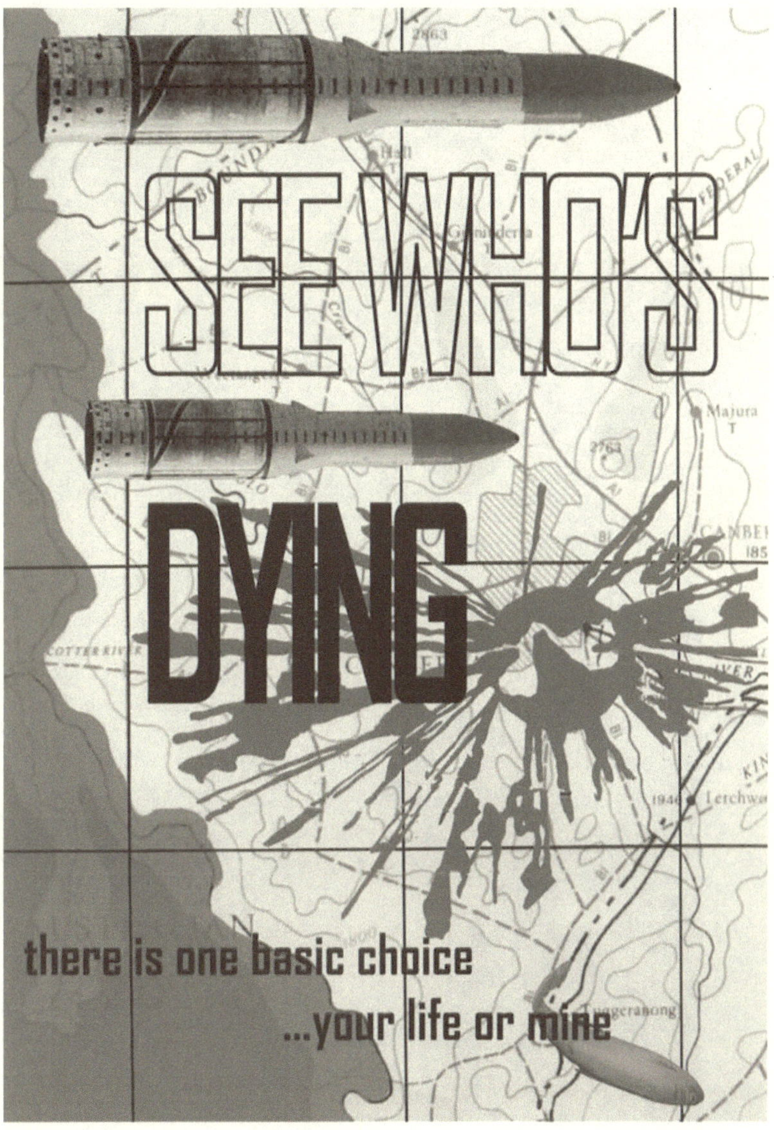

Fig. 11: Poster for a film version of S.H. Courtier's novel See Who's Dying, designed by landscape architecture student Robin Tregenza.

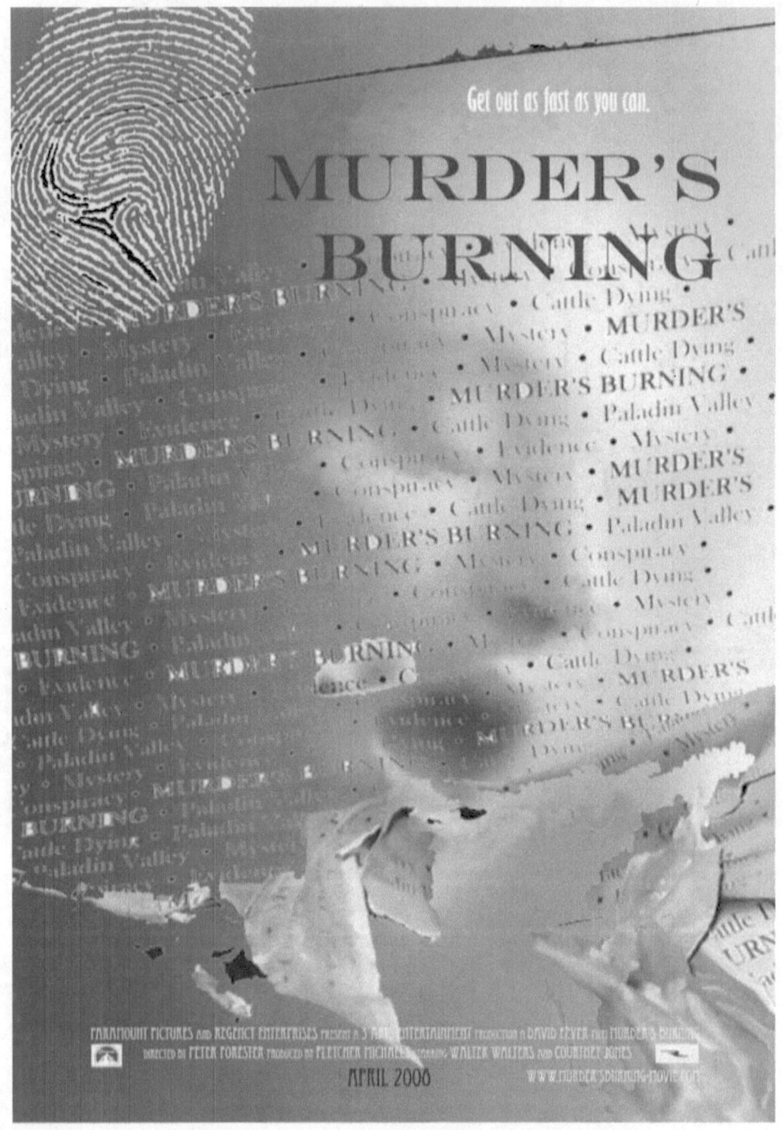

Fig. 12: Poster for a film version of S.H. Courtier's novel Murder's Burning, designed by landscape architecture student Carla Low.

Conclusion

The architecture and landscape architecture students tackled their designs in a number of different ways. Many began with a 'pure' form, such as a square or a circle, to represent everyday life, and then 'violated' it in some way to symbolize crime. For example, some gouged chunks out of it; some ripped it apart; some shattered it to pieces; some stabbed it through the middle, and some tore strips off it. One student even used fresh and rotten fruit to symbolize good and evil.

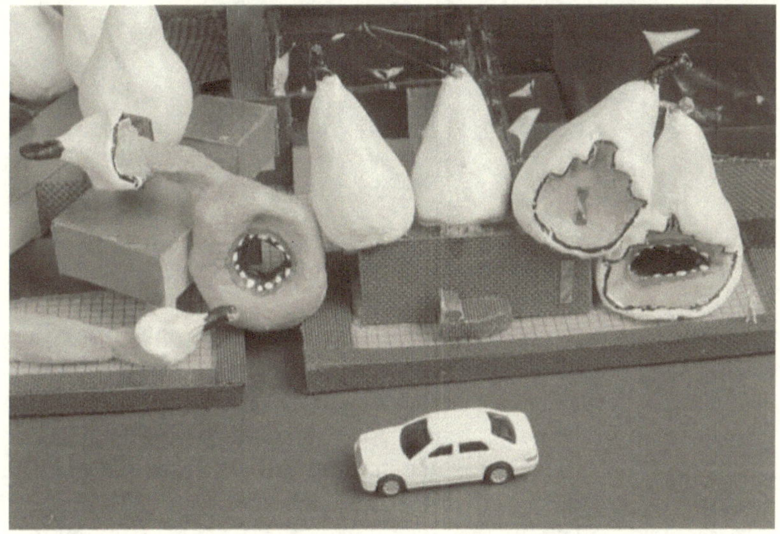

Fig. 13: Lavanya Arulanandam's Centre for Australian Crime Fiction design was based on rotting fruit.

Many students turned their design into a crime scene. Several thought of it as a murder victim, spread-eagling the 'body' over the site or burying it underground. A number of students covered the site with evidence of crime, including bloodstains, bullet-holes, fingerprints, footprints, guns, knives, and shattered glass. In a few cases these 'clues' were manifested in the building form, but more often they appeared as interesting details. A couple of students also recognized that a house is commonly the scene of the crime and designed a Centre for Australian Crime Fiction with a domestic theme.

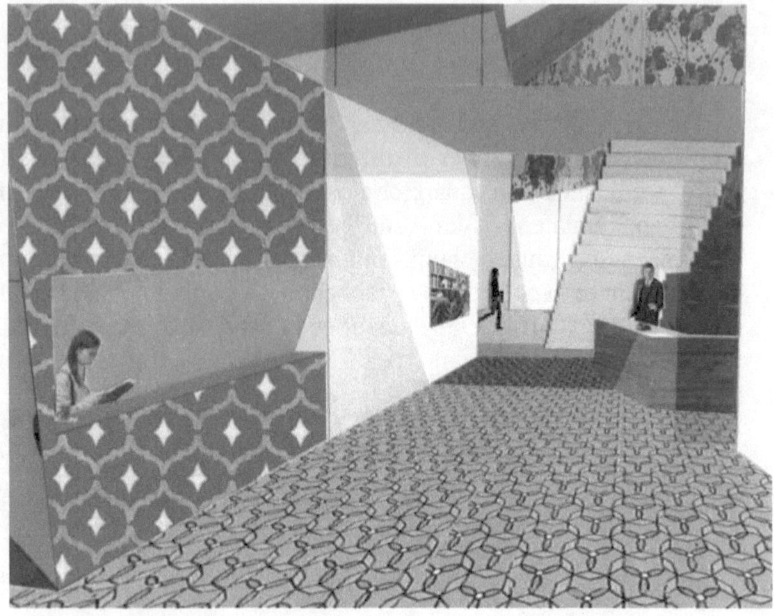

Fig. 14: Centre for Australian Crime Fiction by architecture student Melissa Spencer.

A lot of students drew inspiration for their designs from Sidney Hobson Courtier's subterranean locations, Arthur Upfield's outback scenes and June Wright's urban settings. Several responded to the eye-catching cover graphics of 1950s pulp crime novels. A number of students' designs represented the usual suspects of crime fiction—the criminal, the detective, the detective's sidekick, the eyewitness, the 'suspiciously innocent' person and the victim. And a few even wrote their own detective stories. (31)

The idea that buildings and landscapes can tell stories underpinned these design projects. In the design field, narrative is often used to assemble elements and determine form. If implemented skilfully, the outcomes can elicit powerful memories and create strong bonds between people and place. But in less capable hands the results can be clichéd, puerile and shallow. Overall, the students' work was extremely engaging. It was driven by ideas. It told a good story. And it focused on place. However, books have the power to impart new information, whereas buildings and landscapes can evoke only what is already known—albeit in a new and perhaps more profound way. That is why reading 'place' requires a lot more speculative imagination than reading a book.

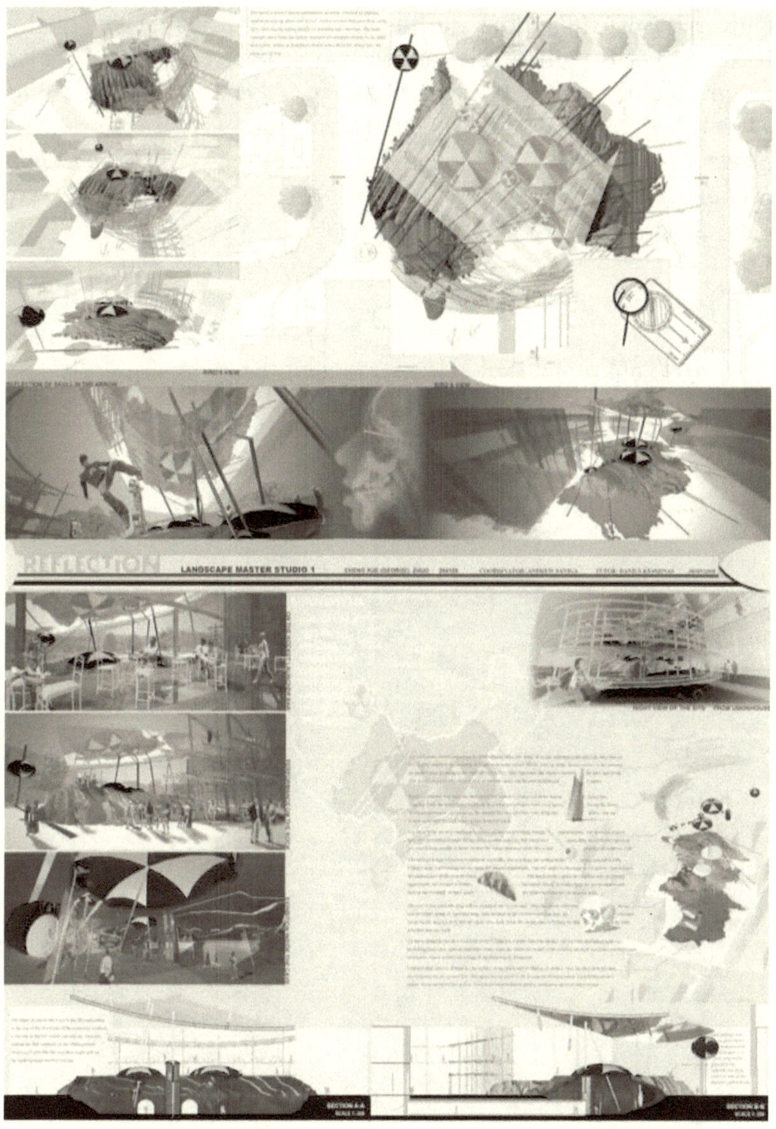

Fig. 15: Outdoor-performance space designed by landscape architecture student George Zhuo Cheng Xue.

Biography

Dr. Derham Groves is a Senior Lecturer in Architecture at the University of Melbourne and the first Australian member of the Baker Street Irregulars. He has written several books on popular culture including *You Bastard Moriarty* (1996), *In the Privacy of Their Own Holmes* (2004) with David Harris, and *There's No Place Like Holmes: Exploring Sense of Place Through Crime Fiction* (2008).

Gum Tree Gumshoes:
Role-Playing Narratives in Australian Landscape Architecture

Andrew Saniga

Woomera

Melbourne artist and musician Danius Kesminas and I led the landscape architecture students in a design project based on Dr. Derham Groves' research into Australian crime fiction. I asked the students to design an outdoor entertainment space on the north side of Melbourne University's Union Building, to correspond with the site for the Centre for Australian Crime Fiction being designed by Derham's architecture students. This space currently supports a range of student activities, but it is small and cramped. With plans afoot to remove the existing car parking facilities that take up much of the site, the university's Property and Grounds Committee wanted a robust space that was able to accommodate everything from beer sculling to jewellery stalls. At the same time, they also wanted a highly distinctive space that might be showcased, say, in future marketing brochures. The committee's instruction to me and thus also to my students was: 'BE CREATIVE!'

By decree of the landscape architecture curriculum, the design project that I offer to Masters of Landscape Architecture students is supposed to use history as a strategy for generating design ideas. I could see the potential of using S.H. Courtier's novels *See Who's Dying* and *Murder's Burning*, which are both set in the late 1960s, as a window on the post-World War II era. These novels contain a rich array of sensorial and cultural associations that underpin people and place through Courtier's vivid descriptions of buildings, landscapes, objects, and all kinds of ephemeral social rituals. The author's lucidity acted as a portal to a different time. I wanted the landscape architecture students to get a handle on this by returning to the scene of the crime, so we initiated an engagement with ruins and relics and called the project 'Design in Reverse'. This endeavour brought two worlds into one: the literary and visual narratives of Courtier's time, and our own physical presence in the kinds of locations that clearly inspired him in the first place. Our bodies became the conduit for interpreting past customs and behaviours in the real world. The potential for role-playing was rife.

See Who's Dying explores the impact of the Cold War in Australia. The James Bond-like plot is thick with espionage, double agents, defection, and anagrams. It starts with a nail being shot into a person's skull (one is reminded of the architecture students' delightfully gruesome Barbie and Ken dolls). Then the novel's leading man drives to arid central Queensland where he descends a deep shaft into the earth and discovers that Communist China is installing underground missiles aimed at Australia's capital cities plus Woomera, an isolated town approximately 500 kilometres northwest of Adelaide in the heart of the South Australian desert. Woomera was founded in 1947 to house and service the defence and civilian personnel associated with the Long Range Weapons Project, but it subsequently provided the infrastructure for other top-secret military projects, such as testing British nuclear bombs and launching Australia's first satellite. In Woomera's heyday, during the 1960s, more than 6,000 people lived there and the town's social and cultural life bloomed. With the help of massive government spending, the barren Australian desert was made to sustain life.

With *See Who's Dying* firmly in our minds, 13 landscape architecture students, Danius Kesminas and I hit the road to Woomera. Upon arrival we were confronted by the realisation that the whole of the little town—including its ruins—is symbolic of the excesses of the Cold War. Many relics from this period are in a state of decay but defy erasure, like the ELDO launch pad, a concrete structure so massive that even the military could not blow it up. Other Cold War relics have been appropriated for different uses. For example, we camped next to a three-metre by six-metre prefabricated structure that once housed defence personnel out in the extreme desert heat, but today it is an air-conditioned bar complete with a pool table and even a crazy paving patio. The latter was designed and constructed by Latvian John Rasnacs, another Cold War relic. He and his family were displaced from their homeland after World War II and ended up in the Australian desert building Woomera's infrastructure as part of the process of becoming Australian. As the students started to physically sift through and identify these and other links to the past, the salience of Courtier's fiction became more and more real. It helped explain and define many of the physical things that we saw, and continually served to implicate the people who we met. What's more, the cryptic elements in Courtier's storytelling helped conjure our own antics on tour.

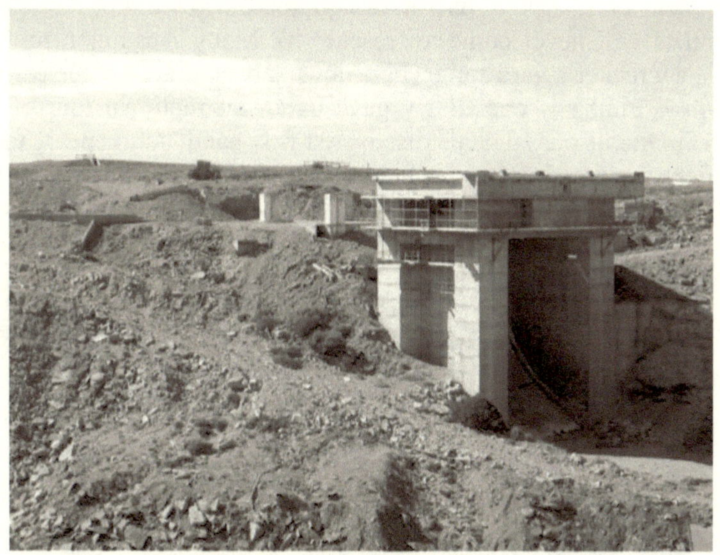

Fig. 16: Launch Pad at the Woomera Rocket Range, Woomera Prohibited Area, 2006.

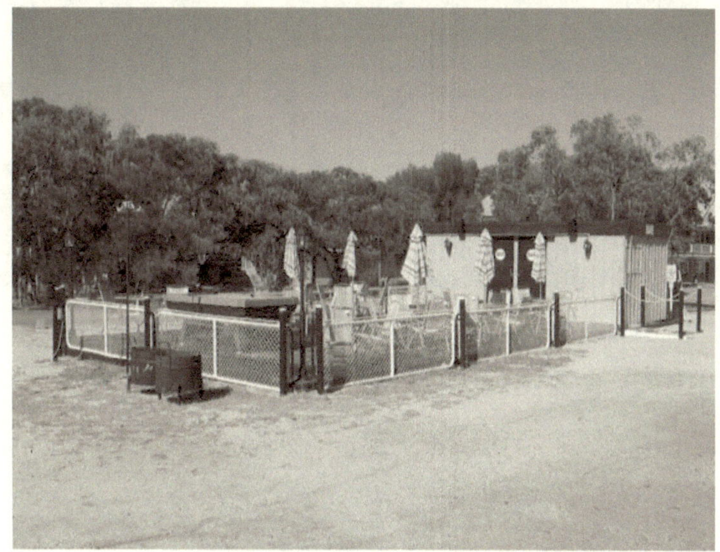

Fig. 17: Public Bar, Woomera Traveller's Village and Caravan Park, 2008.

On the first day in the field we visited Barry Hancock at the Woomera Sewerage Treatment Plant. He has been in Woomera from its earliest days, but lives five kilometres away in Pimba, the complete antithesis of urban design (and with any luck, town planners will never come to 'rescue' it). Many Australian towns have a wrecker's yard somewhere down a back road, but the entire town of Pimba *is* one. Barry gave us an instructional tour of—SHIT! One of our students discovered first-hand, so to speak, that it sticks to your shoes and is hard to get off. But *Barry* could get it off, and after engaging us in a totally freewheeling conversation, he left us with a final thought: 'Where I work is where all of us is equal. We all end up the same.'

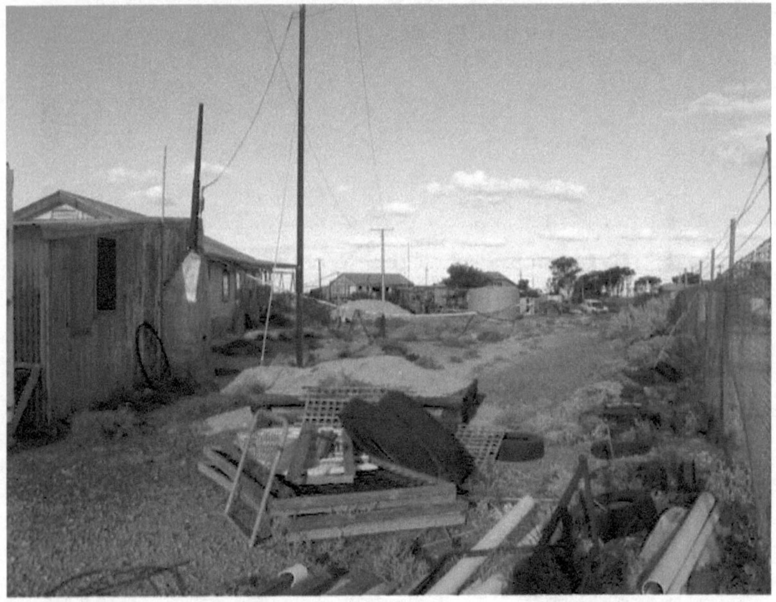

Fig. 18: The streets of Pimba, South Australia.

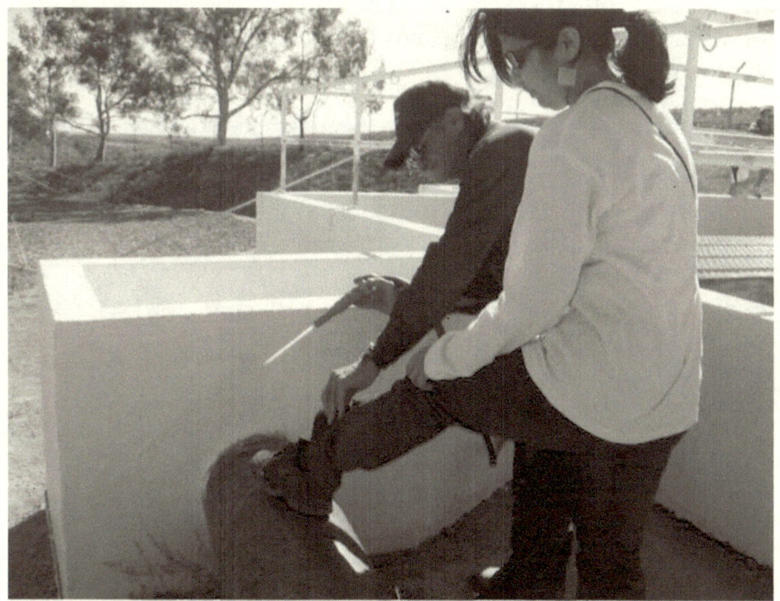

Fig. 19: Barry Hancock and Shveta Khaneja at Woomera Sewerage Treatment Plant.

The days were filled with conversations like this and other revealing experiences. We spent a day at the Eucolo Creek Engraving Site with Andrew Starkey, an Aboriginal Liaison Officer for the Department of Defence, who had a fantastic sense of humour. He had no idea what we were doing in Woomera, nor could he have cared less. Andrew introduced us to the art and culture of the local Aboriginals, many of whom were displaced in more recent times by nuclear tests and other government activities. It was pretty heavy stuff and served to remind us of the kitsch use of Aboriginal culture in *See Who's Dying,* like when a spy camouflages himself as an Aboriginal using black boot polish, which was very much a part of Courtier's day. An indistinguishable chord was struck as a result of engaging with the persona of Andrew Starkey. The weight of history was upon us as we began to retrace Courtier's literary steps.

We had long sessions at the Sportsman's Bar and the bar at the Woomera Golf Club with the likes of Charlie Payne, a local identity from Coolaroo Street, who quickly cottoned onto one of Danius's many pranks. It involved Charlie pretending to be a roaming academic sent by the university to surreptitiously monitor the students' progress. One student actually bought it! And then off we'd go again, plunging into open-ended narratives invented on the spot.

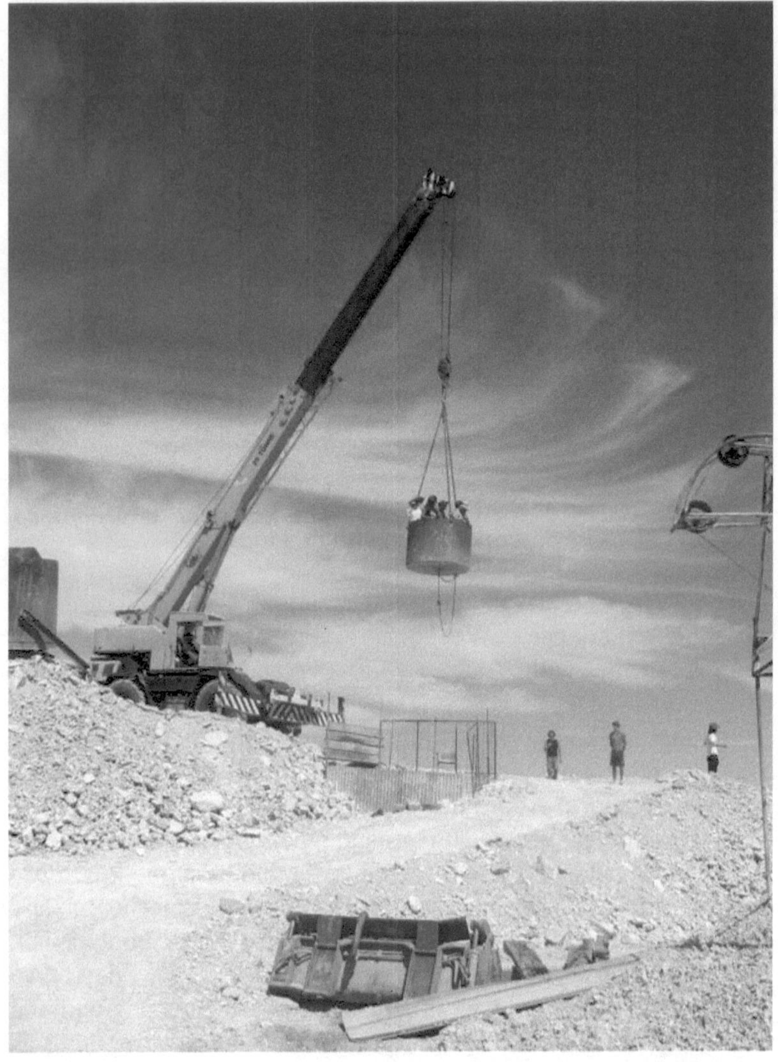

Fig 20: Descending the Hansen Brothers' opal mine, Andamooka, 2008.

In the neighbouring town of Andamooka, we hooked up with the three Hansen brothers—Eric, Ingo and Peter—who lowered us into an 18-metre deep mining shaft, three at a time in a rusted metal bucket, using an antiquated crane, another Cold War relic. With the help of a black light, we sought out opal veins as if they were invisible ink within the chalky sediment—yet another convoluted reference to the genre of crime fiction, and one potentially translatable into landscape design.

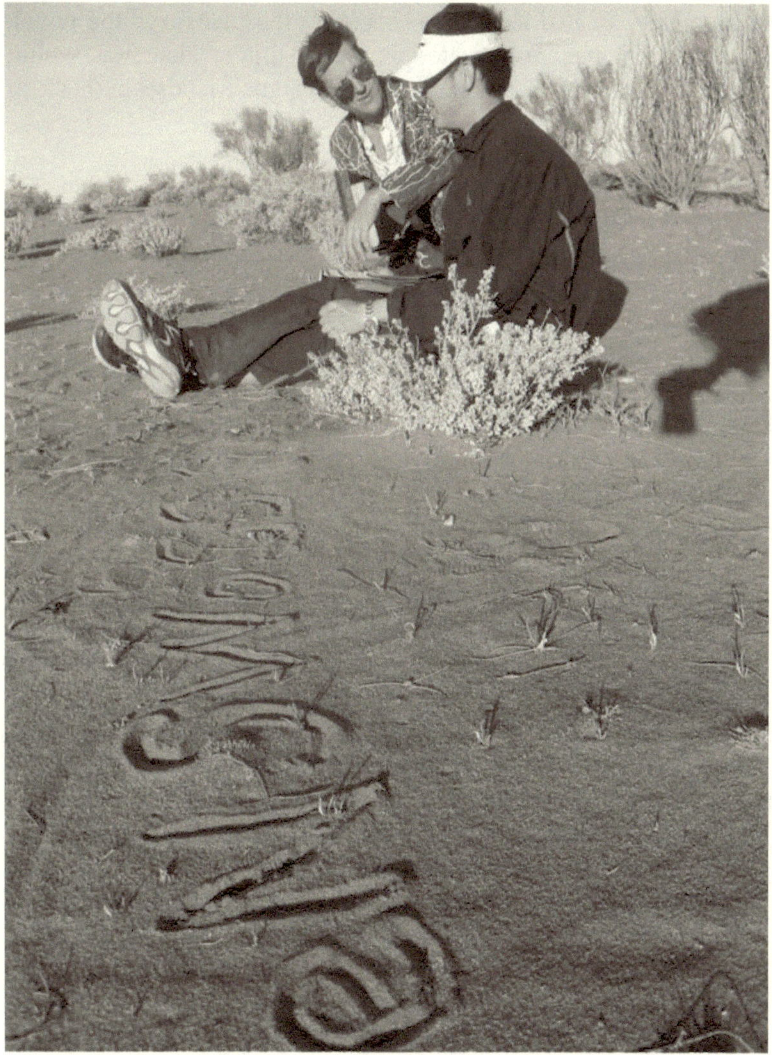

Fig. 21: Danius Kesminas talking to Cheng Xue (George) Zhuo during the painting class.

On the last day, Danius ran a painting class using *See Who's Dying* as the actual canvas. Each of the 13 students did a watercolour sketch of the Woomera landscape on a photocopy of one of the book's 13 chapters (only then did we realize the coincidence between the number of students and chapters). Such was the immediacy of all of our experiences on this trip that it seemed like we had started to 'become' the place *and* the novel. This formed the raw material for a drama that we would eventually attempt to translate into a designed landscape back in Melbourne.

Stony Creek

The other landscape architecture students read S.H. Courtier's novel *Murder's Burning.* It is set in 'Paladin Valley', a fictitious hamlet in East Gippsland, Victoria, which was destroyed by bushfire and subsequently abandoned. The lead character visits the burnt out and deserted small town to solve the mystery of his friend's death. Danius and I took the students to the Stony Creek, a small town north of Ballarat in western Victoria, to visit the ruins of a burned out and deserted quarry. Travelling to Stony Creek was a disorientating experience. It is extremely difficult to find, because it is un-signposted and located in a State Forest. To make matters worse, it was over 40 degrees Celsius and a day of Total Fire Ban. This made working in the field tough. It was also stressful for me, because I didn't know whether the quarry was owned privately or by the State. As twilight approached, I prepared smoked sausage, Israeli pickled cucumbers and beer for the students. Returning from a bush walk, they said a local farmer had stopped and questioned them. Within moments that man, Warren, was marching toward us, so I marched right up to him, ready to start explaining our situation. Despite initially fearing that we were arsonists, he turned out to be friendly and good-humoured. He was also incredibly knowledgeable and told us about bushfires that he had seen move in a matter of hours from the mountains on the horizon to the very spot where we were picnicking.

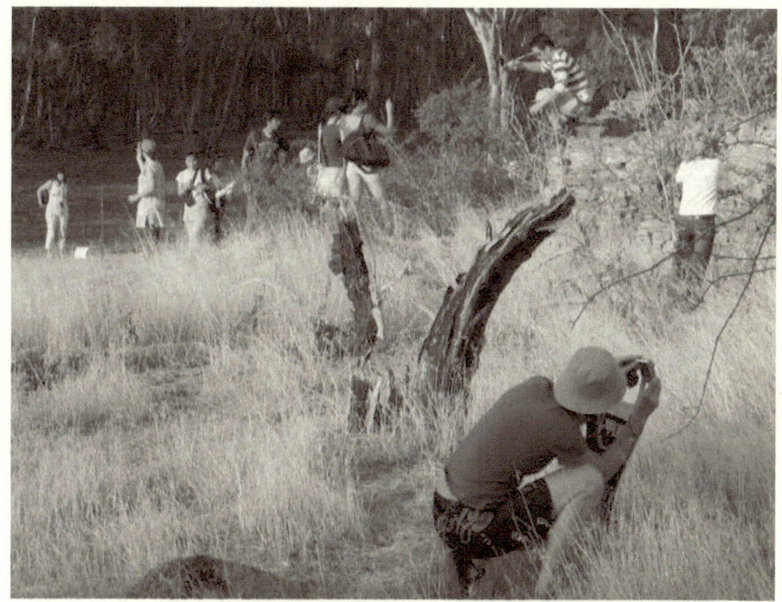

Fig. 22: Students at Stony Creek Quarry, Stony Creek.

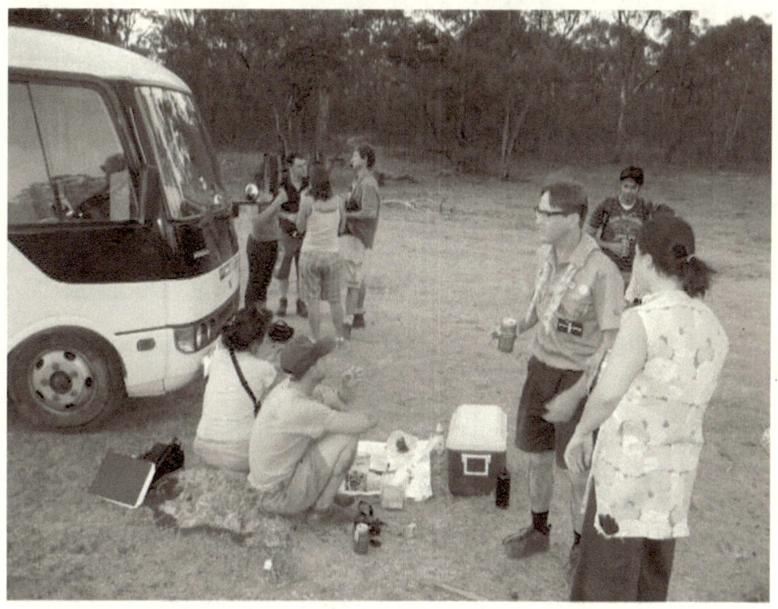

Fig. 23: Picnicking at Stony Creek Quarry, Stony Creek.

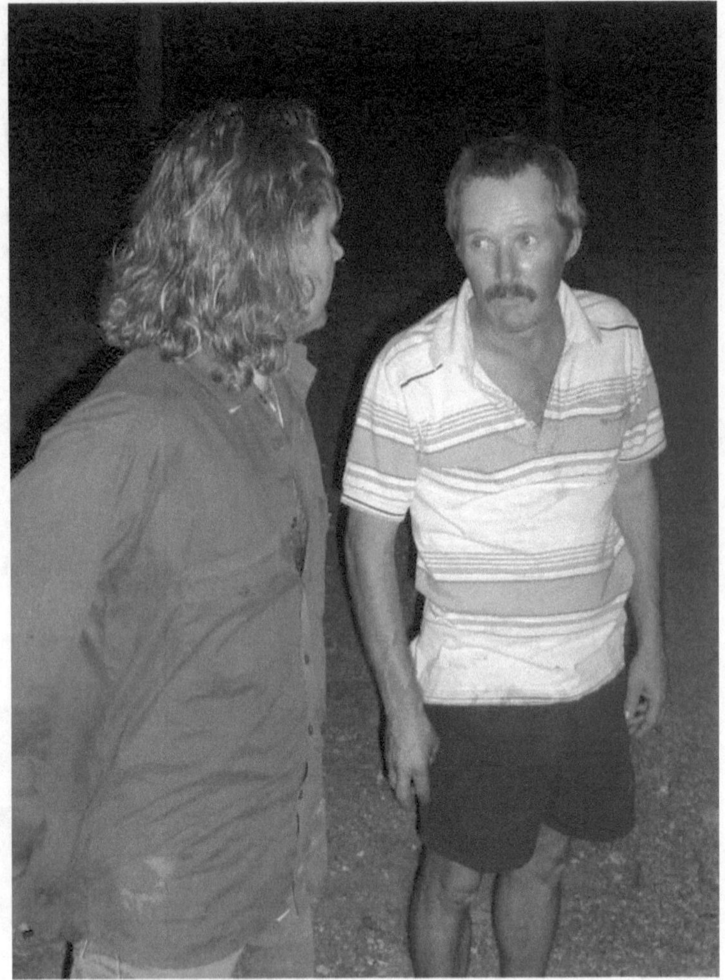

Fig. 24: Andrew Saniga and Warren at an unmarked intersection near Stony Creek.

By sunset everyone felt exhilarated, but also a little nervous about getting out of there safely. We had a 10-kilometre drive through thick tinder-dry bush just to get onto the highway home. I drove a bus with 24 students onboard, and two cars followed me. The track was rough and dusty and complicated to navigate. After a while I discovered that no cars were behind me anymore. They must have taken a wrong turn in the dust and darkness. With no maps or knowledge of the area, and no mobile phone coverage, the situation looked grim. After turning back and searching various tracks, we eventually found one of the cars, but the other containing a female student was nowhere to be seen. We stopped to assess the situation. It is safe to say there was a fair degree of panic in the air, especially given that everyone was on edge with all of the talk about bushfires that day, and the temperature was still over 30 degrees and stifling hot. To add to our mounting troubles, we discovered that the bus's radiator was leaking. All of this elevated the teaching of 'site analysis' to a new level: we had read of fear in Courtier's book, now we were experiencing it ourselves. Then a beam of light suddenly emerged through the trees and two cars appeared over a rise. Our lost student was driving the second car and Warren, the local farmer we had met earlier that day, was leading the way in the first. There was great relief. Warren took us to get some water to fill the radiator, and after some good-natured banter we drove away from Stony Creek, the conversation in the bus filled with Courtier—and Warren. We felt as if we had endured the Paladin Valley fire and just scraped through the dust jacket back to the real world, almost as battered and bruised as the architecture students' dolls.

Some weeks after the fieldtrips to Woomera and Stony Creek, I invited Geoff Tulloch, a retired member of Victoria Police Force, to talk to the landscape architecture students about the daily life of a Melbourne police detective during the 1960s, the decade when *See Who's Dying* and *Murder's Burning* were written. He described the primitive nature of detective work back then, and the humour of his stories—like many of our experiences on the fieldtrips—soon began to permeate the students' work. Their final designs were highly distinctive, and the details of what they proposed truly captured the various sentiments gained from working in the field. I see this not only as a fitting product of landscape architecture, but also as representative of the persuasiveness of using the narrative approach in design education. For as well as becoming an instrument for generating ideas based on, of all things, crime fiction, using S.H. Courtier's narratives allowed new and dynamic readings of broader cultural history.

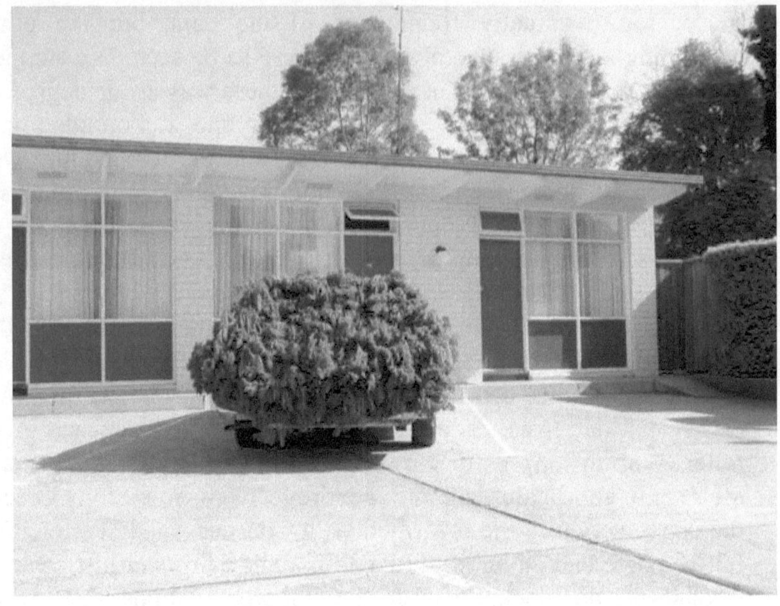

Fig. 25: See Who's Dying 'Treemobile' by Mary Sullivan.

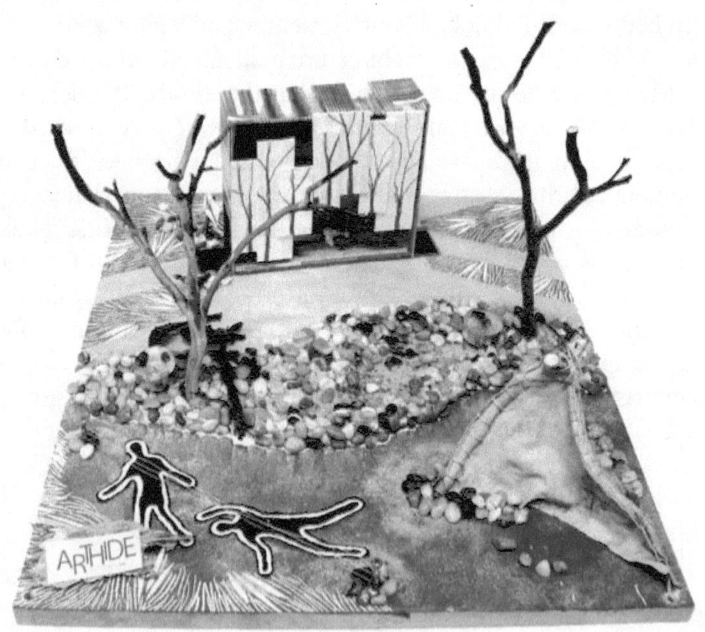

Fig. 26: Murder's Burning performance space by Flora Lau

Biography

Dr. Andrew Saniga is a Senior Lecturer in landscape architecture at the University of Melbourne. In 2004 he completed his doctoral thesis titled 'An Uneasy Profession: defining the landscape architect in Australia, 1912-1972', which explained the emergence of the profession of landscape architecture in Australia. He is currently writing a history of landscape architecture in Australia.

Shooting Barbie and Ken

Lee McRae

My sister had a collection of dolls, and like any girl at that age; she was besotted with them all. Her favourites were a 'walking' doll and another dressed in a pink lacy frock. She also had a collection of Barbies complete with a bag of accessories: tiny shoes, sports clothing and even a doll-sized set of golf clubs. Another was a Japanese doll with real human hair, cold black eyes, and a realistic face. I was terrified of it. Was it Japanese folklore, family myth, or my imagination that I recall that particular doll having the ability to move around the house on its own and to cry blood? For most of the time it was stored in the bottom of my mother's wardrobe and I was quite happy to not see it. But older sisters being as they are, she would sometimes bring it out and leave it in our room, and then ask how it got there. Needless to say, my doll collection consisted of one single doll and the rest were teddy bears.

I've been working at the University of Melbourne for almost 13 years. As a photographer there, I am not attached to any one faculty, so the work is varied and interesting. Through work I have travelled to the Middle East and worked on an archaeological-dig. I've gained access to buildings and spaces that most wouldn't. I've photographed amazing artworks, prints, decorative arts, furniture, sculpture, magnificent rare books, and historical relics. Every day is different and I never know what I'm going to be asked to photograph. Basically, I love my job!

Derham Groves, Senior Lecturer in Architecture, is a client of mine. When I answer the door and see Derham standing there my immediate thought is: 'So what is he going to ask me to shoot today? This should be interesting.'

A few years ago he asked me to photograph two 'Gerry Gee Junior' ventriloquist dolls from the 1960s. They were both in immaculate condition and we both agreed that this was probably because the children they belonged to were too frightened to play with them. They were left in my studio for a week or so. Initially sitting on the bench, I had to move them out of sight and store them in a cupboard, as their beady eyes would follow me around the studio. And did I see one move once? I was slightly unnerved by them both. I couldn't wait for Derham to come and collect them. He loved the shots—he even has them as a screen saver on his computer!

Last year Derham paid me a visit with the prospect of a new photographic project. 'Can you come to my office?' he asked. Inside, tucked away on bookshelves and in the drawers of filing cabinets, were the dolls from the 'Barbie and Ken Meet Sherlock Holmes' student project. Hardly recognisable as dolls at all, let alone ones intended for children to play with. They were amazing. Each labelled with the name and title of the victim or villain. Over a series of weeks, Derham would trolley over a box full of dolls. After each boxful was photographed, he would take them away and return with another load.

I thought they were fabulous. The detail and effort that went into them were incredible. Burned, cut, bloody, mutilated, scarred, maimed, disfigured murder victims. And not one of them bothered me in the slightest. So thank you Derham—I think you may have cured me of my fear of dolls.

Biography

Lee McRae's interest in photography began when at age 11 her mother bought her a camera for Christmas. She has worked as a professional photographer for close to three decades. Lee is completely self-taught and strongly believes making your own mistakes is the best way to learn. 'I learn something new every day. After all isn't that what life's about?'

THE VALLEY OF THE DOLLS

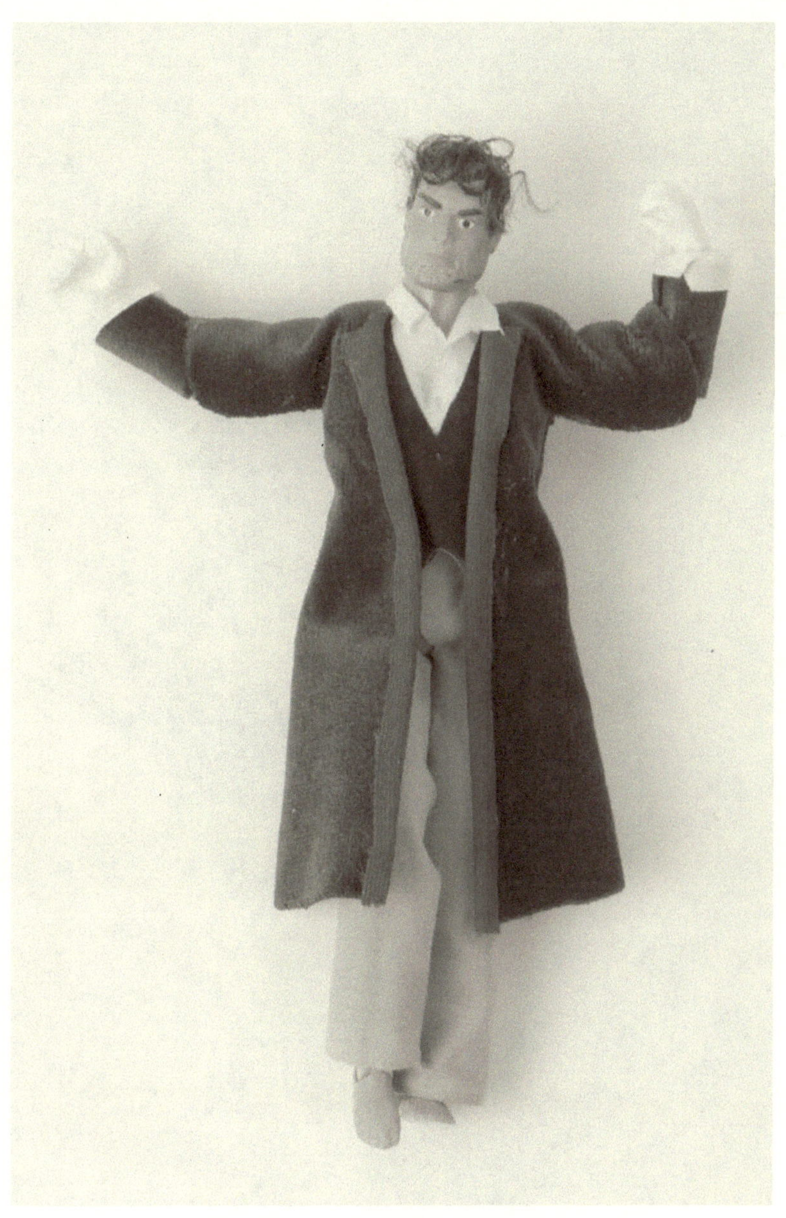

001
Enoch Drebber
from A Study in Scarlet
Lucy Hayward

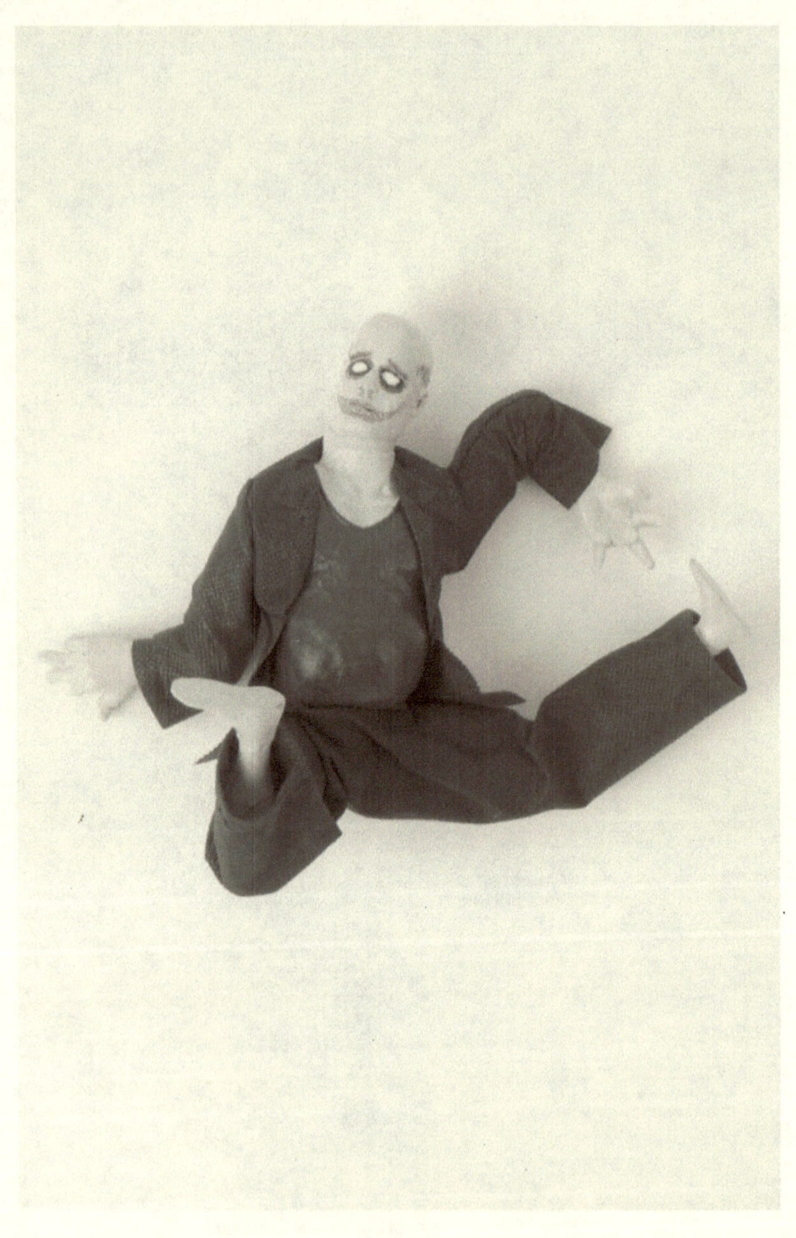

002
Bartholomew Sholto
from The Sign of Four
Cheryl Heap

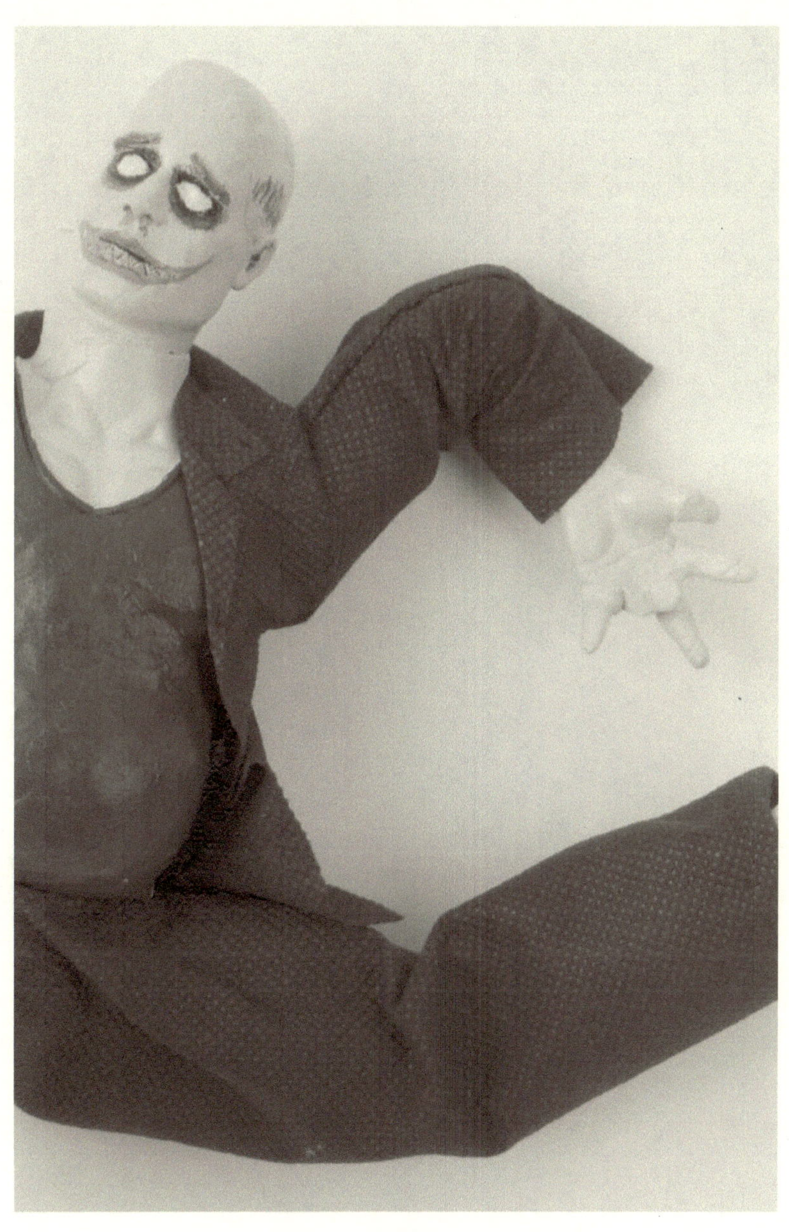

003
Bartholomew Sholto
from The Sign of Four
Cheryl Heap

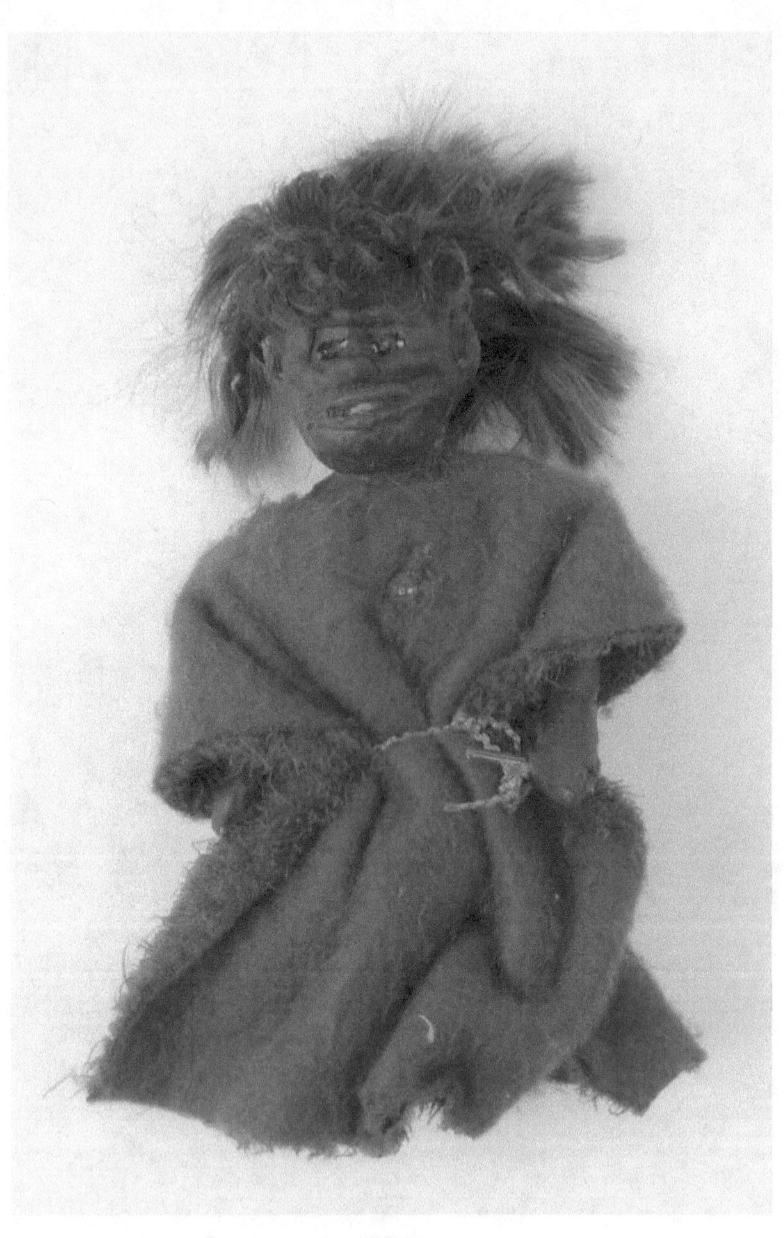

004
Tonga
from The Sign of Four
Georgina Harvey

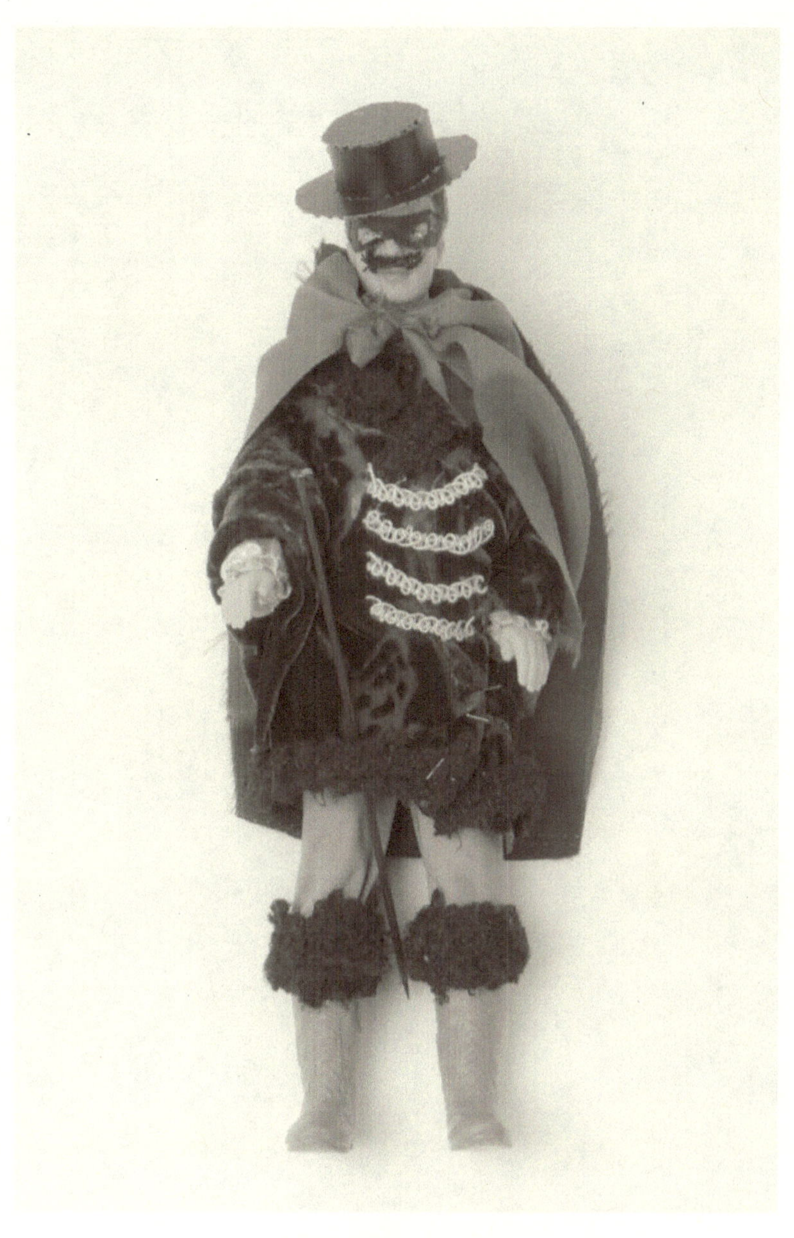

005
The King of Bohemia
from "A Scandal in Bohemia"
En Yee Tee

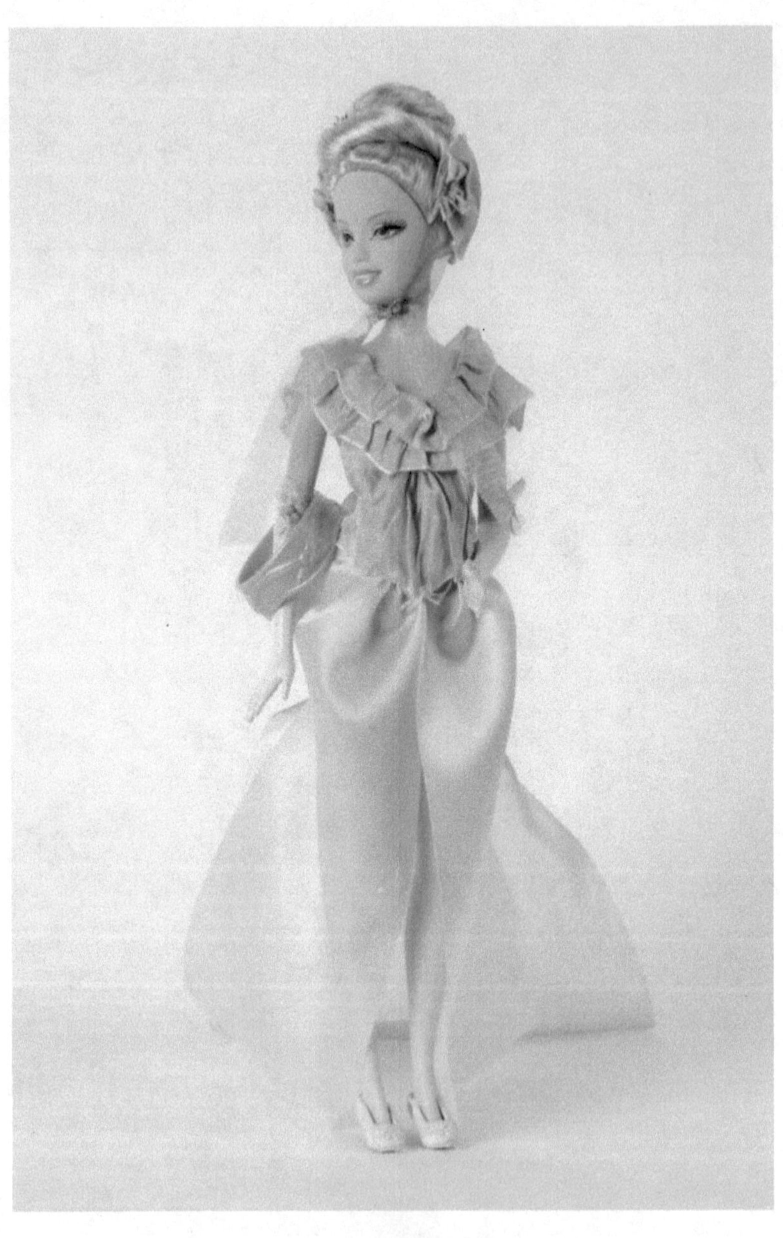

006
Irene Adler
from "A Scandal in Bohemia"
Lee Lih Jiunn

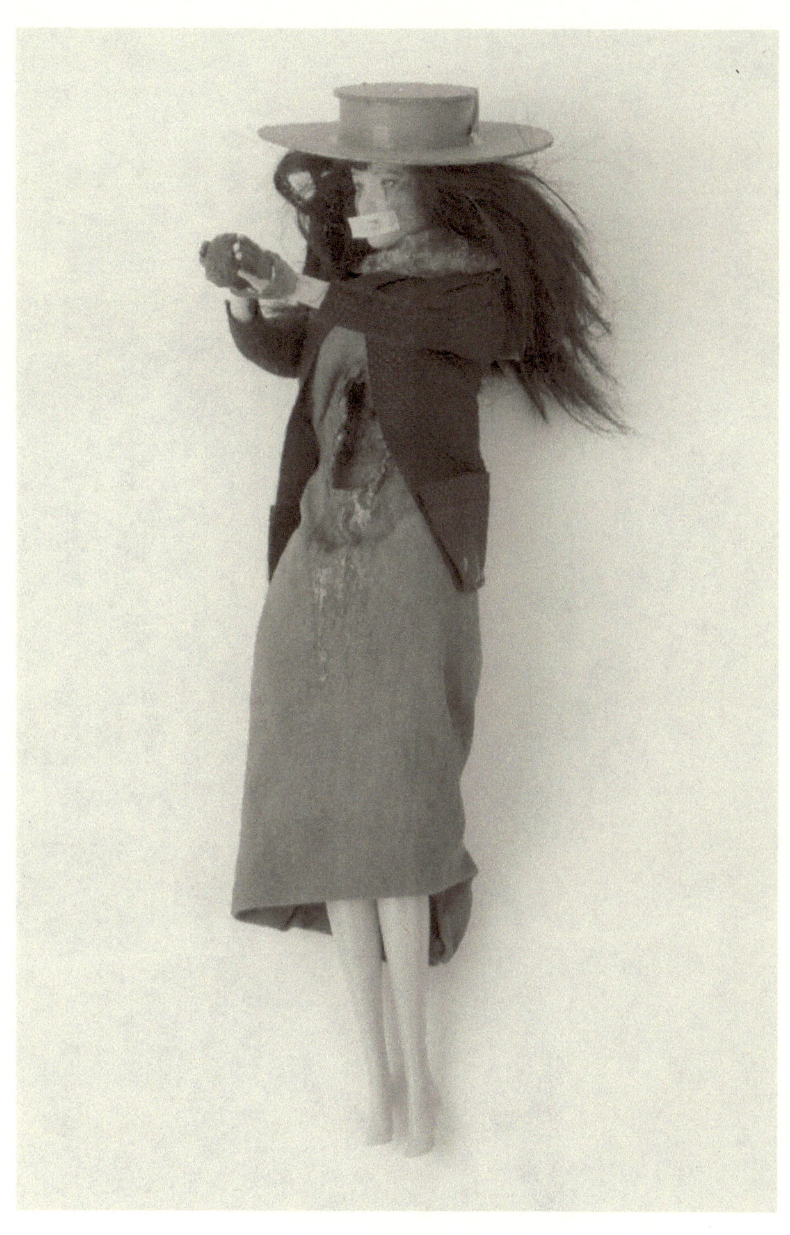

007
Mary Sutherland
from "A Case of Identity"
Gerardo Deguzman

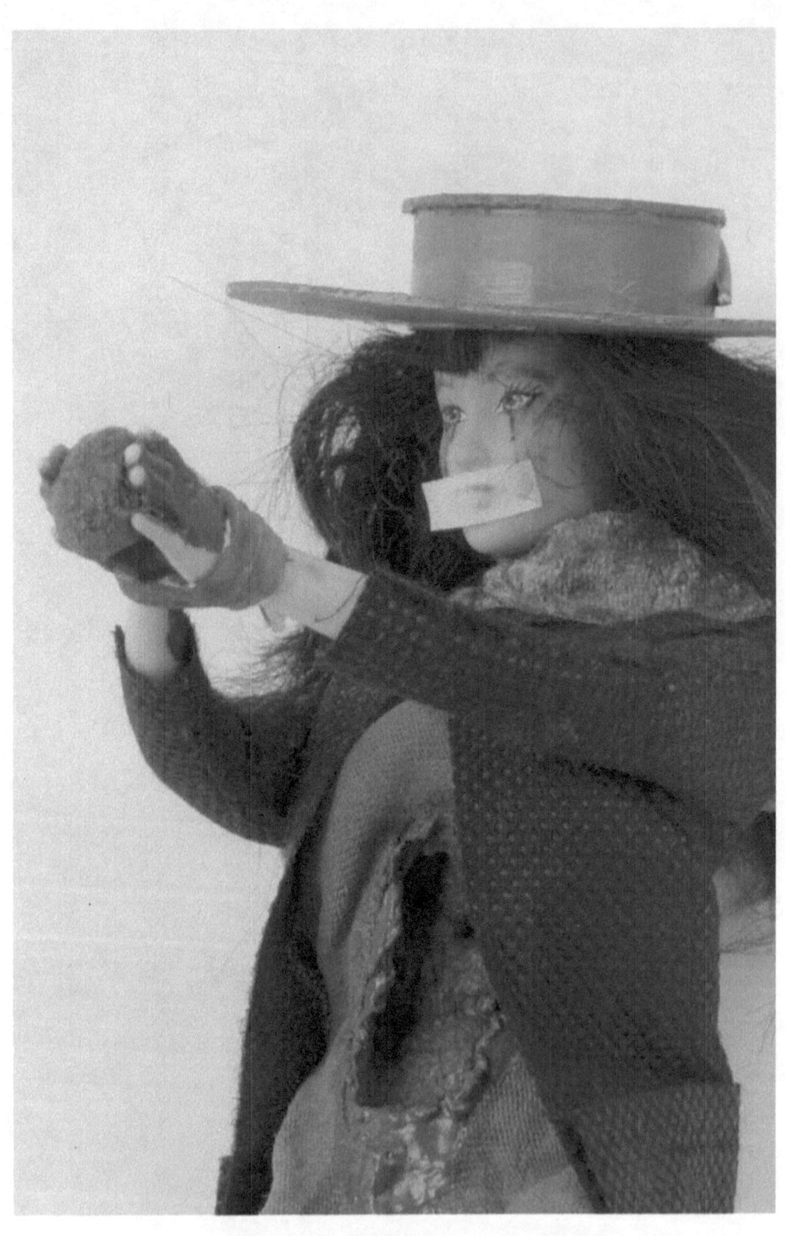

008
Mary Sutherland
from "A Case of Identity"
Gerardo Deguzman

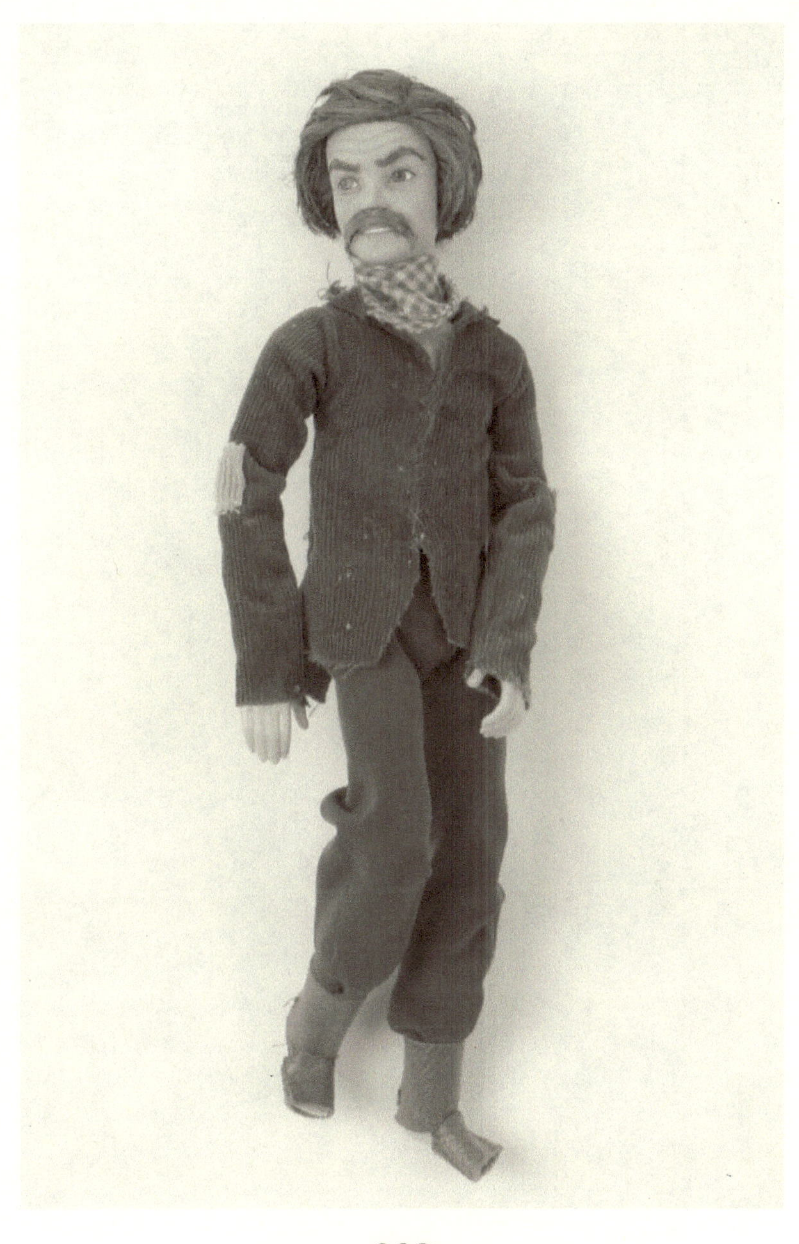

009
Charles McCarthy
from "The Boscombe Valley Mystery"
Priscilla Finn

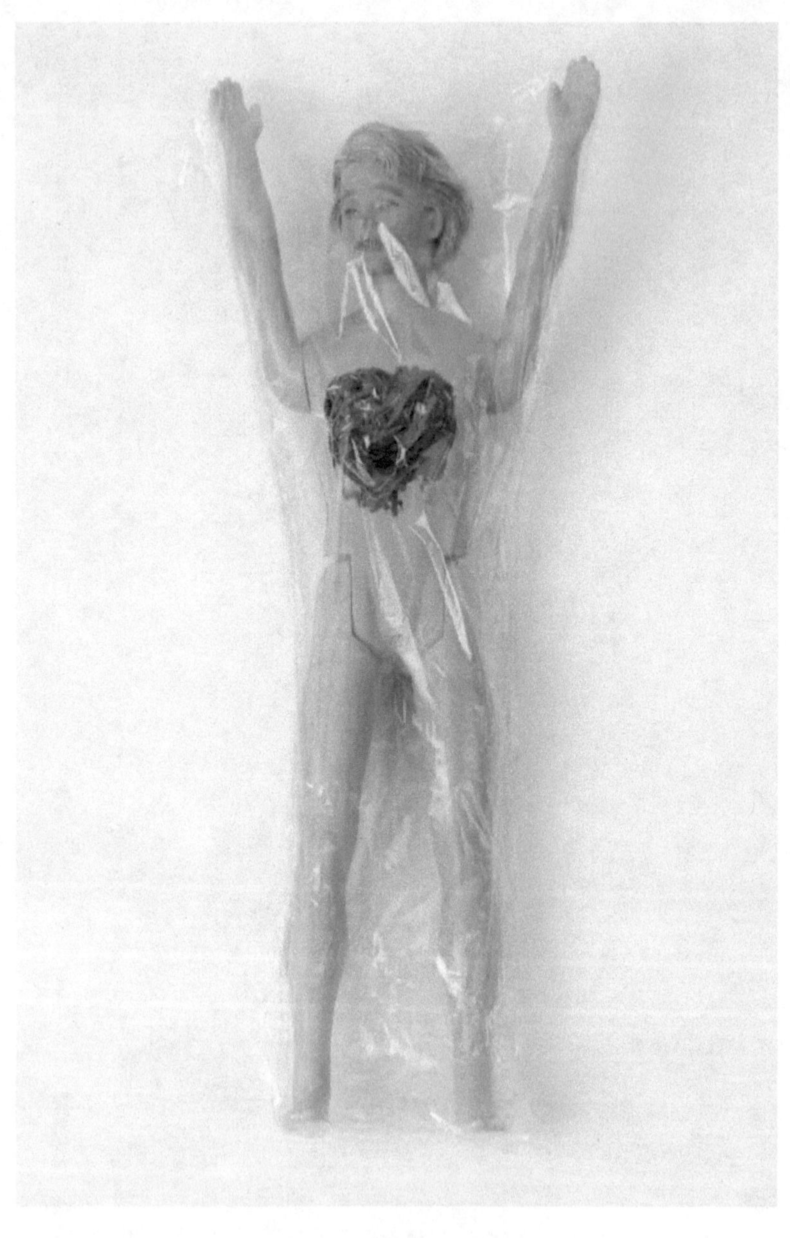

010
John Openshaw
from "The Five Orange Pips"
Jennifer Sumia

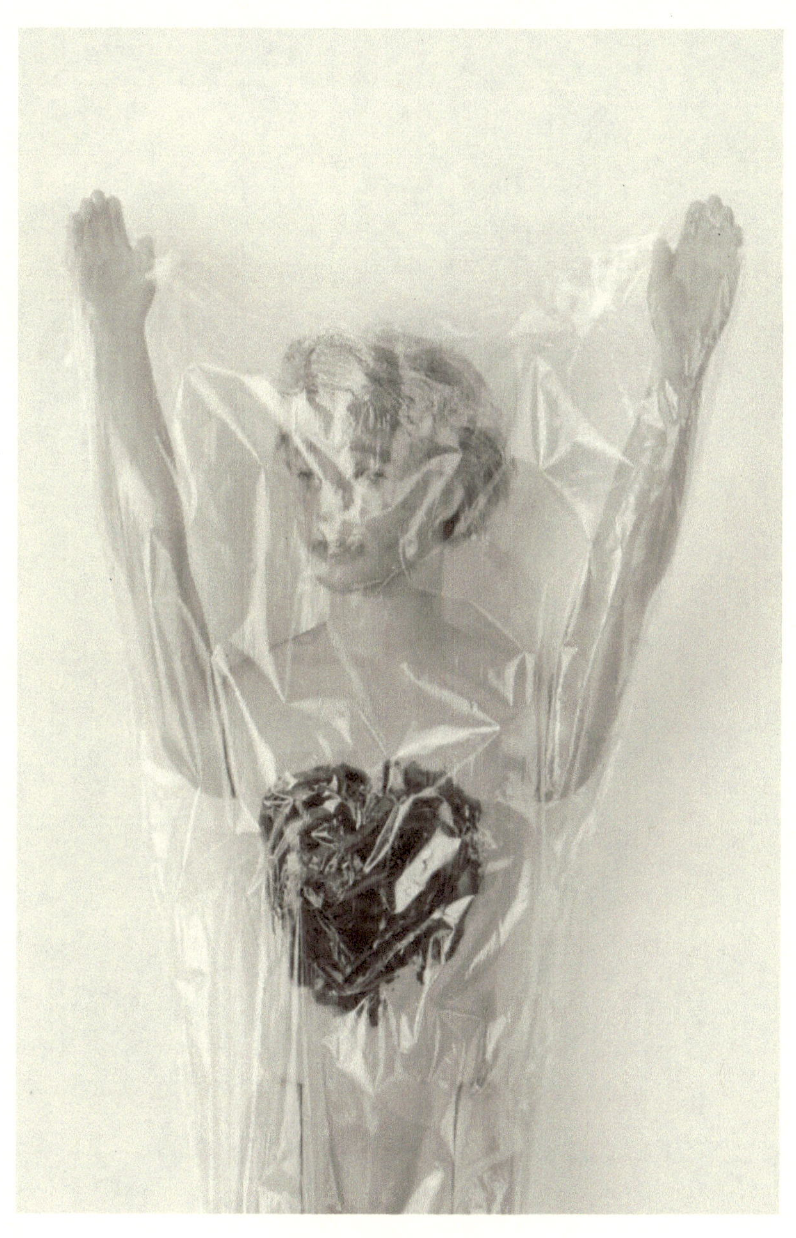

011
John Openshaw
from "The Five Orange Pips"
Jennifer Sumia

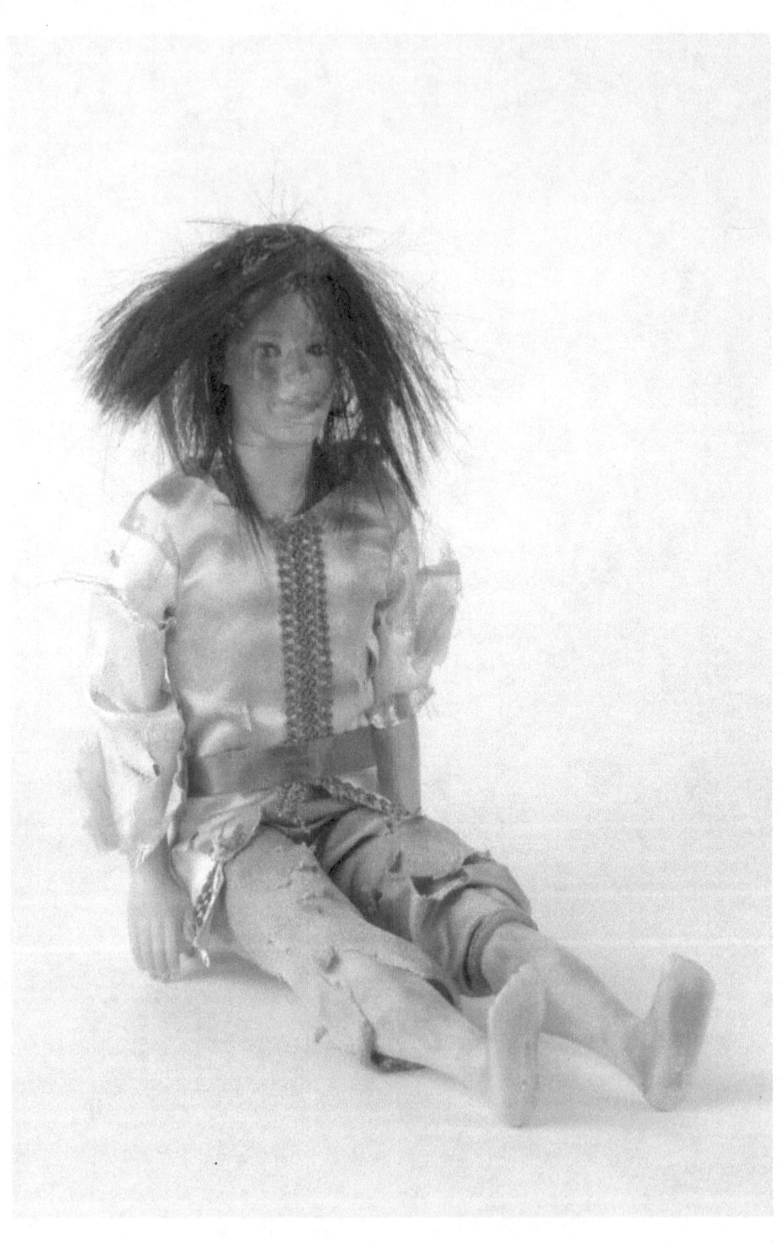

012
Hugh Boone (a.k.a. Neville St. Claire)
from "The Man with the Twisted Lip"
Jasmine Heo

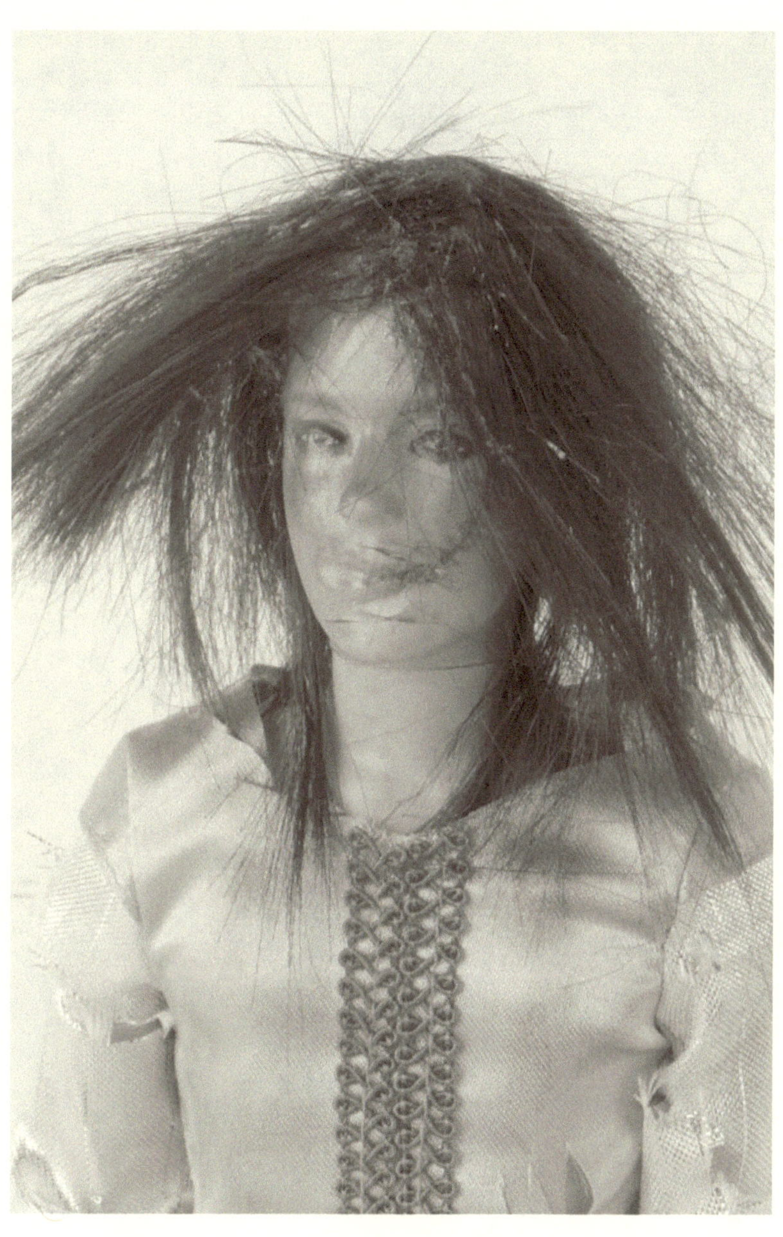

013
Hugh Boone (a.k.a. Neville St. Claire)
from "The Man with the Twisted Lip"
Jasmine Heo

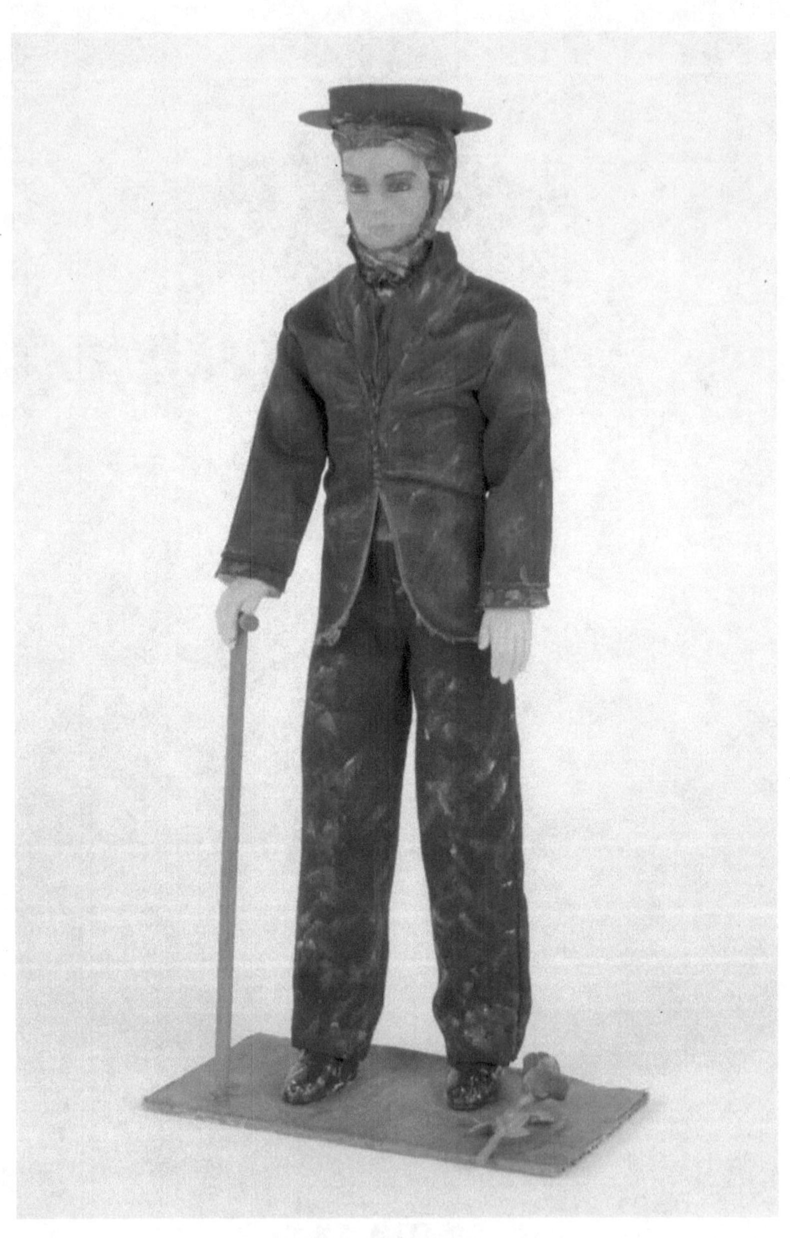

014
Henry Baker
from "The Blue Carbuncle"
Silvia Lesmana

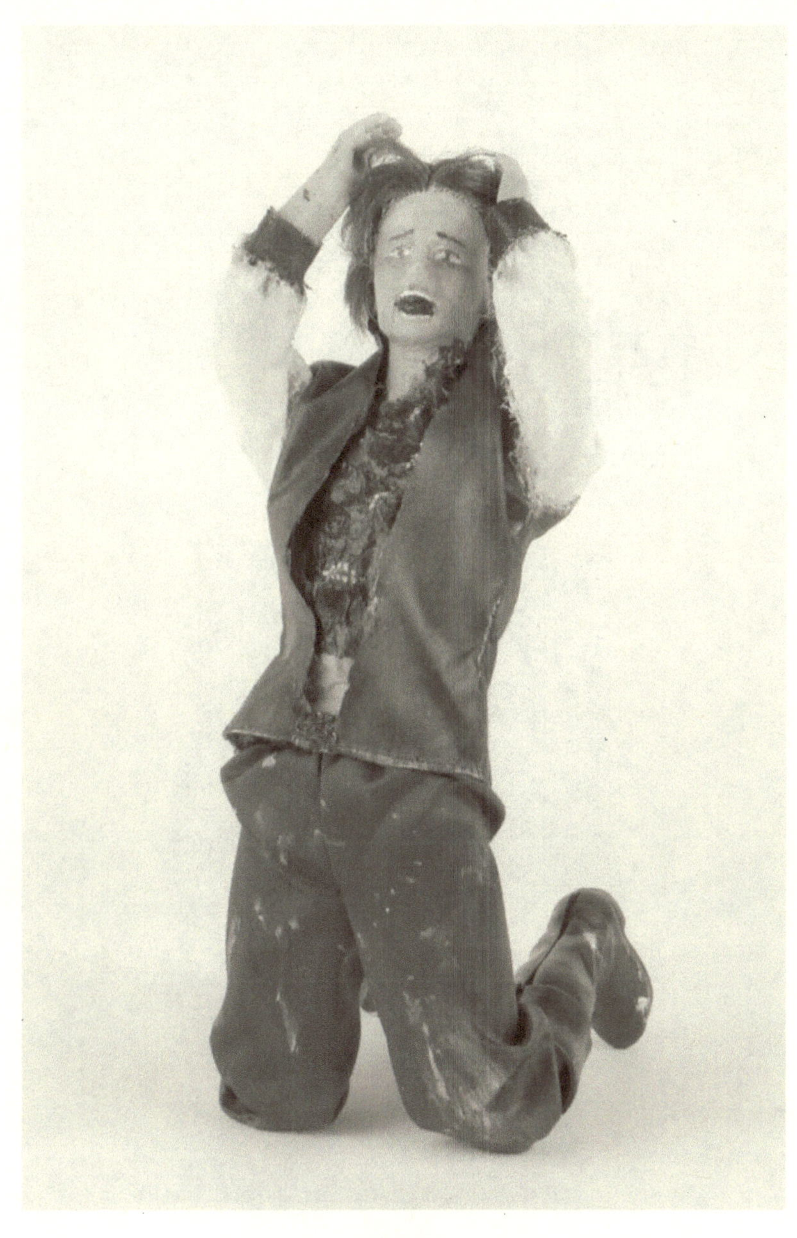

015
James Ryder
from “The Blue Carbuncle”
Lee Yin Ling

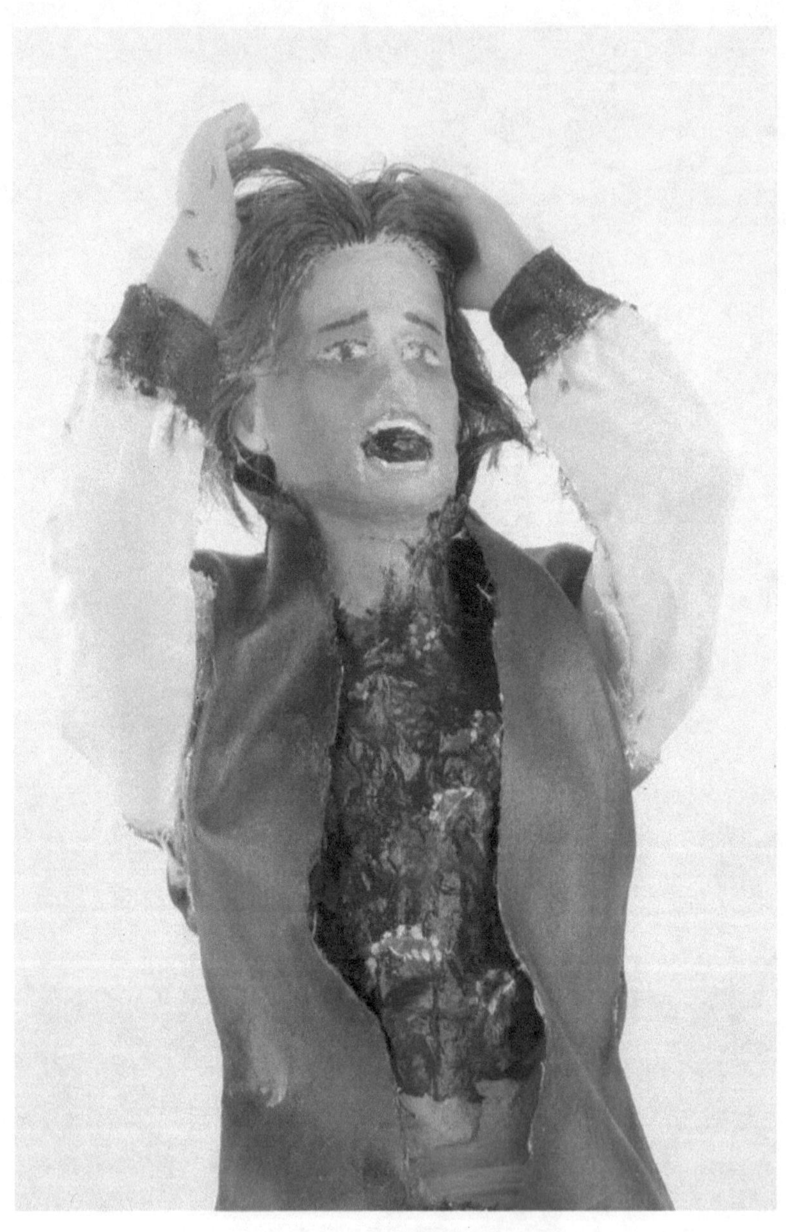

016
James Ryder
from "The Blue Carbuncle"
Lee Yin Ling

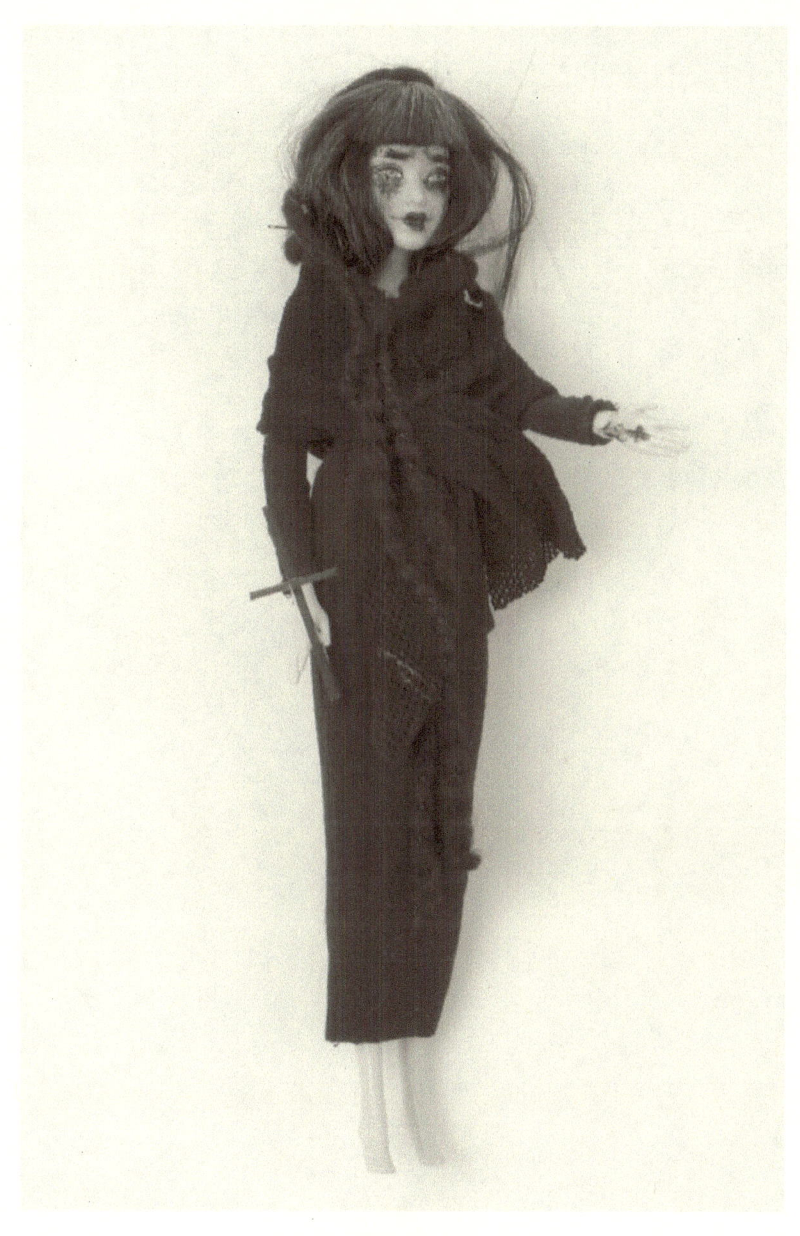

017
Helen Stoner
from "The Speckled Band"
Ho Swen Yung

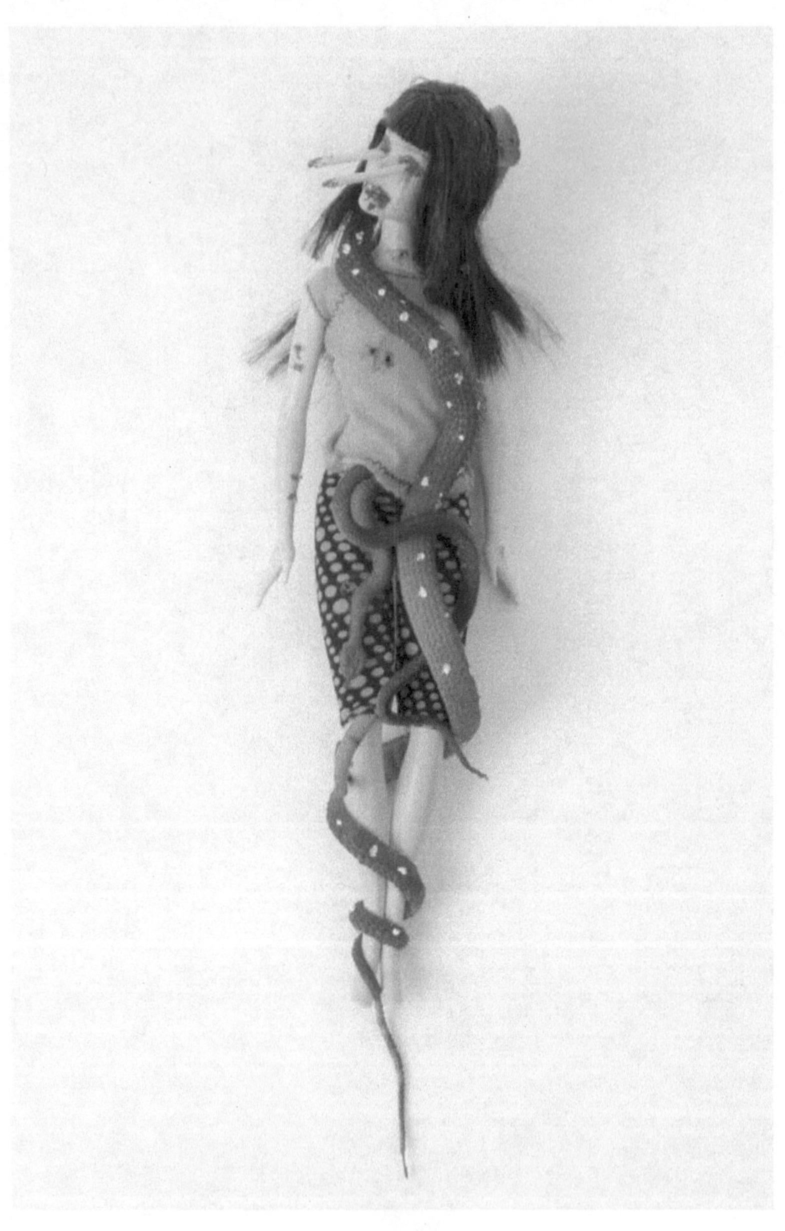

018
Julia Stoner
from "The Speckled Band"
Hayley Brivik

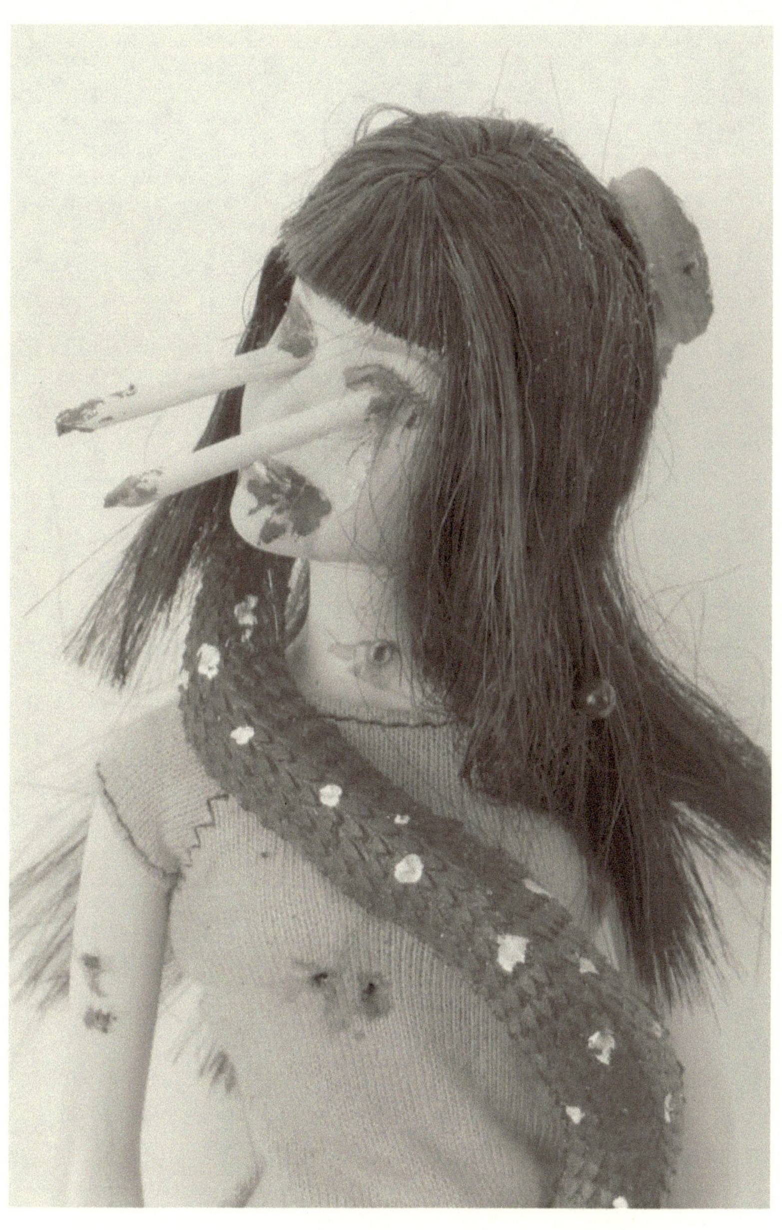

019
Julia Stoner
from "The Speckled Band"
Hayley Brivik

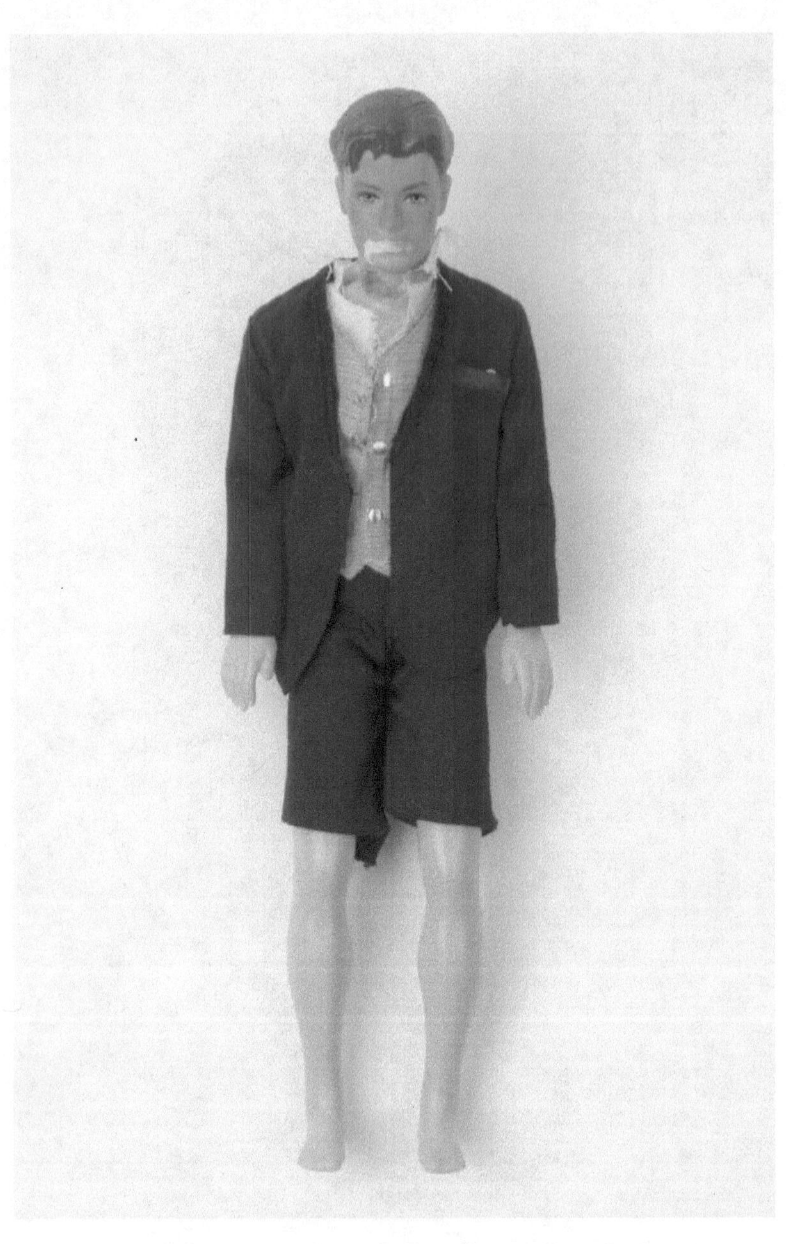

020
Dr. Grimesby Roylott
from "The Speckled Band"
Lee Yin Hsuan

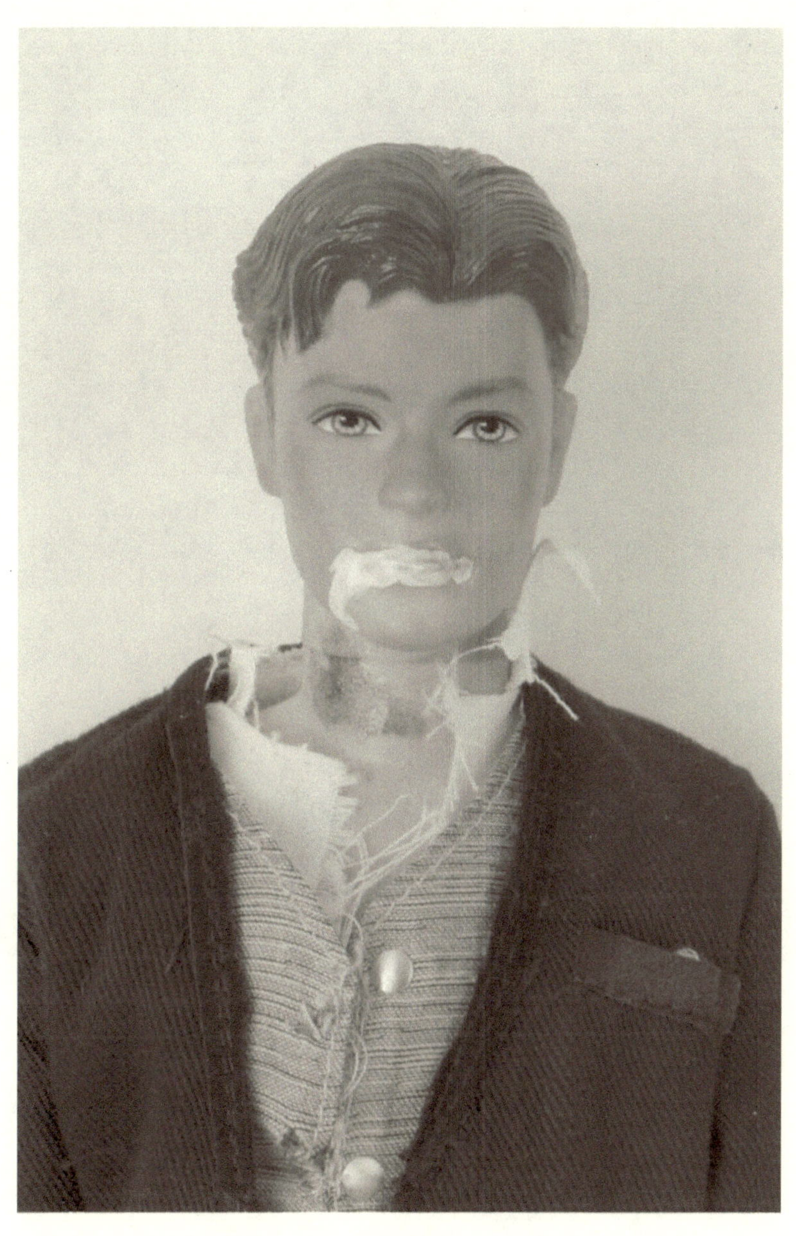

021
Dr. Grimesby Roylott
from "The Speckled Band"
Lee Yin Hsuan

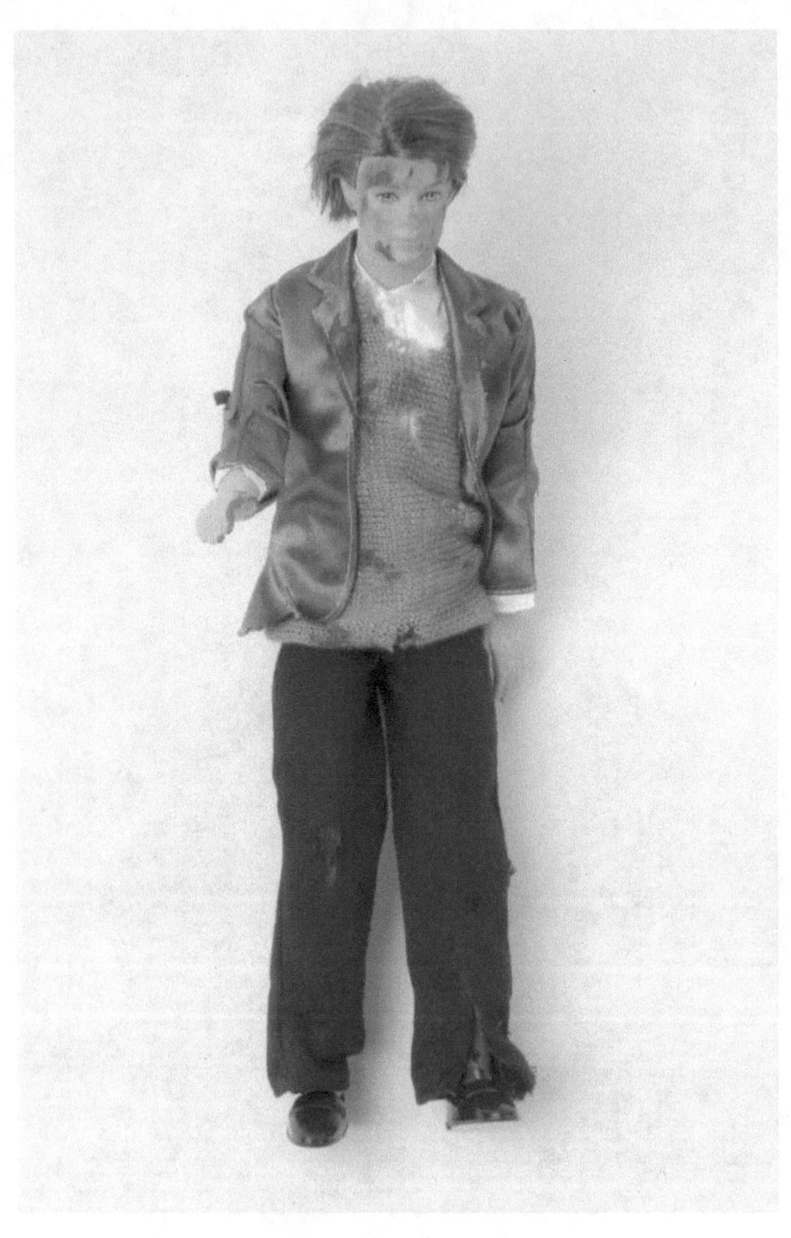

022
Victor Hatherley
from "The Engineer's Thumb"
Carol Chau

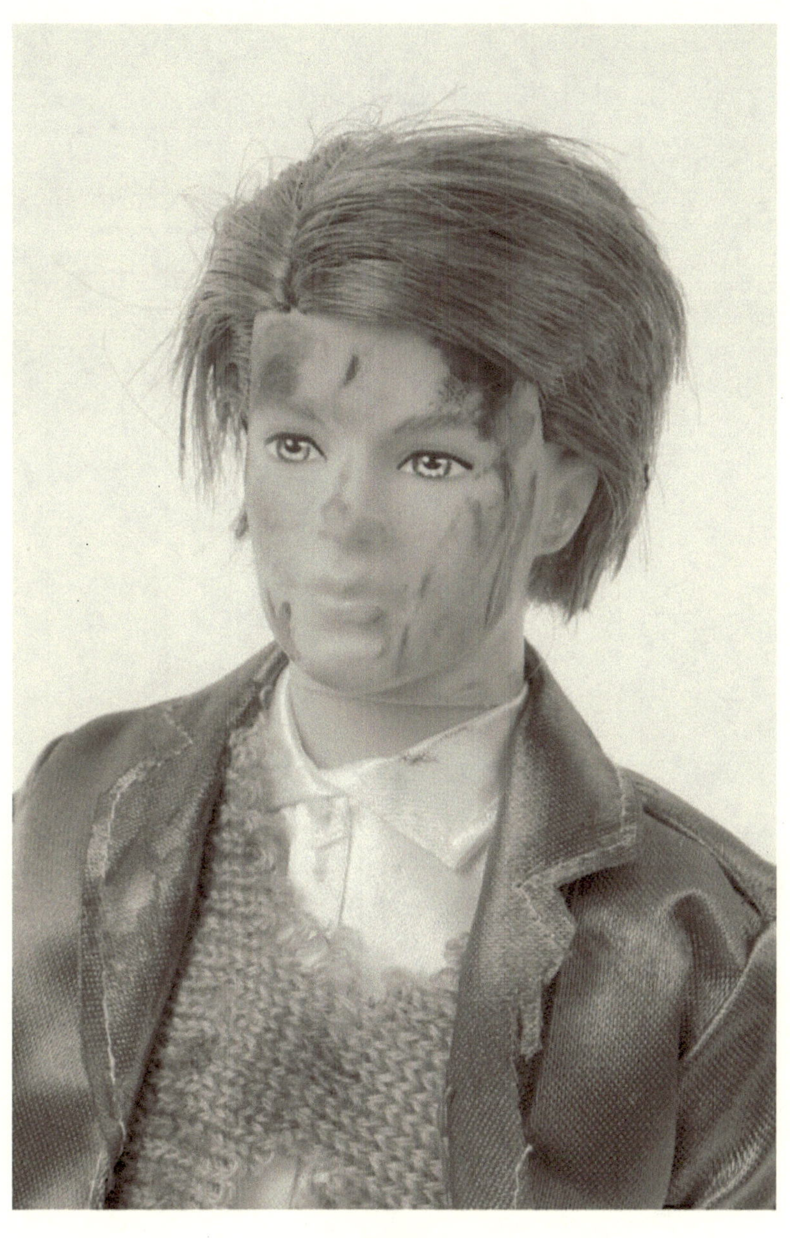

023
Victor Hatherley
from "The Engineer's Thumb"
Carol Chau

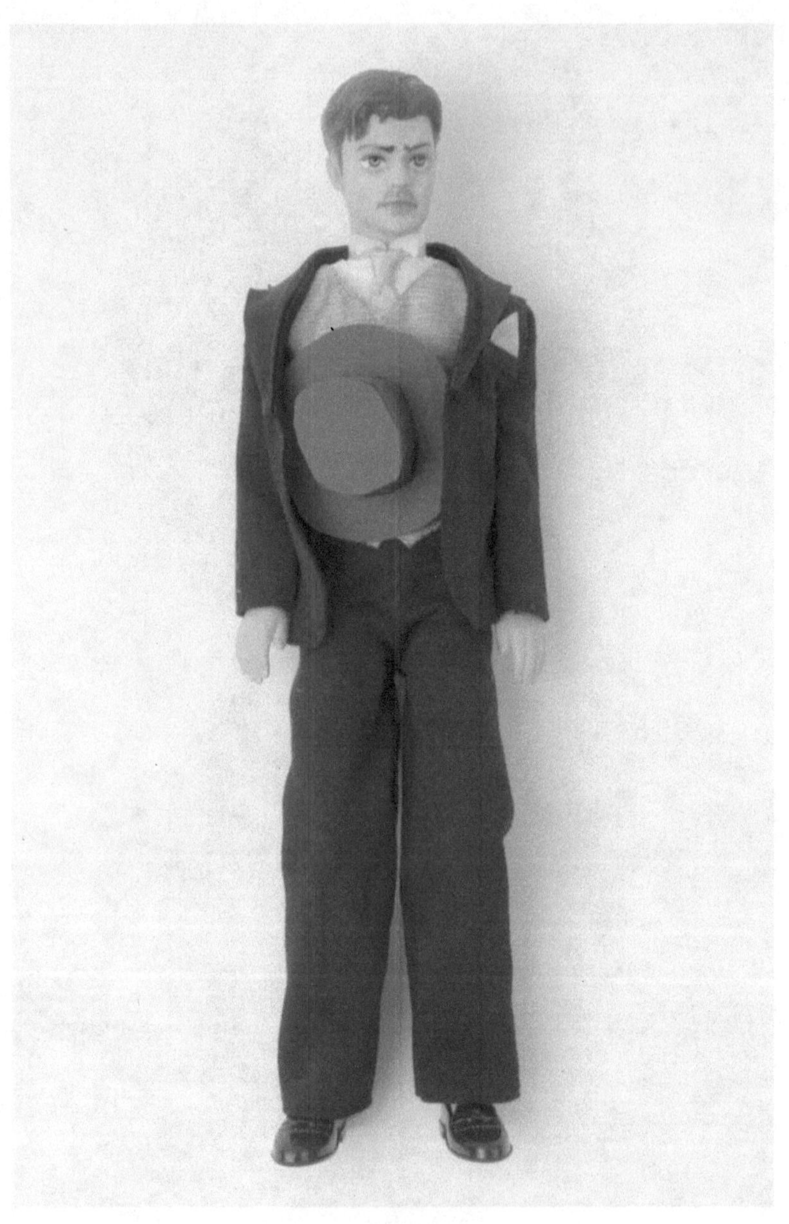

024
Lord St. Simon
from "The Noble Bachelor"
Annie Shao

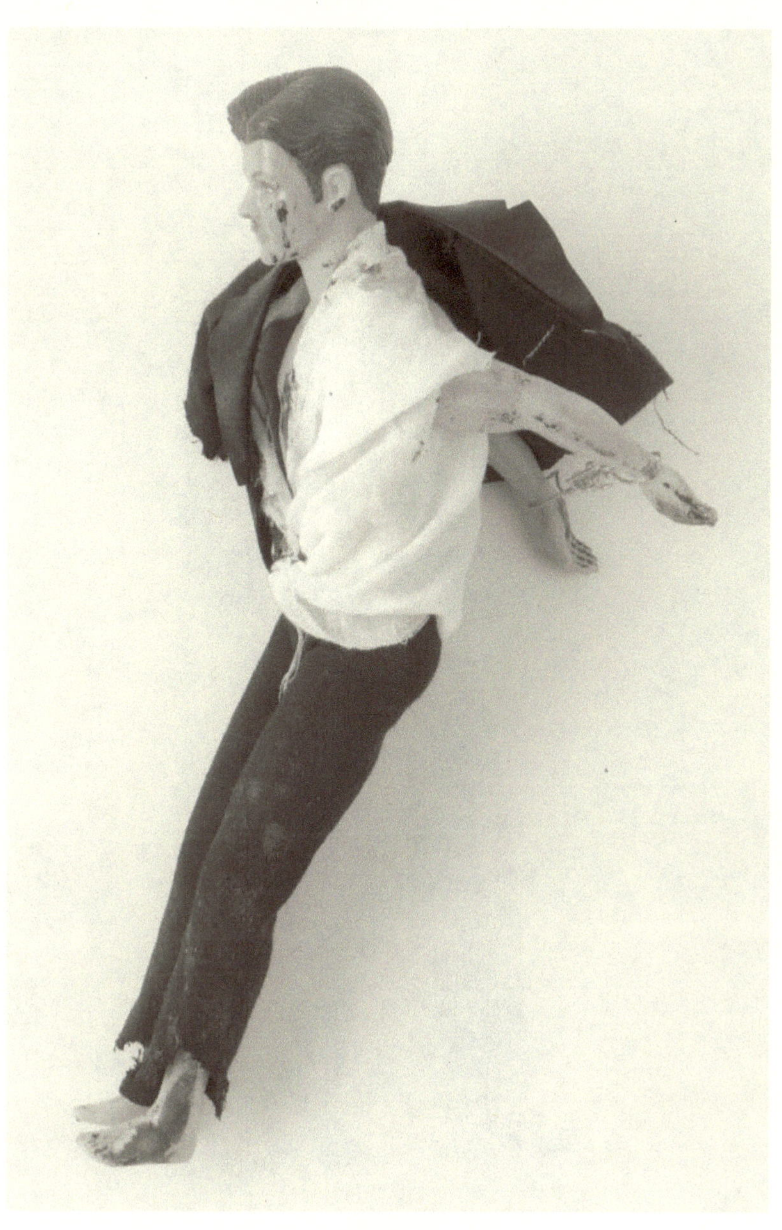

025
Arthur Holder
from "The Beryl Coronet"
Conglin Cai

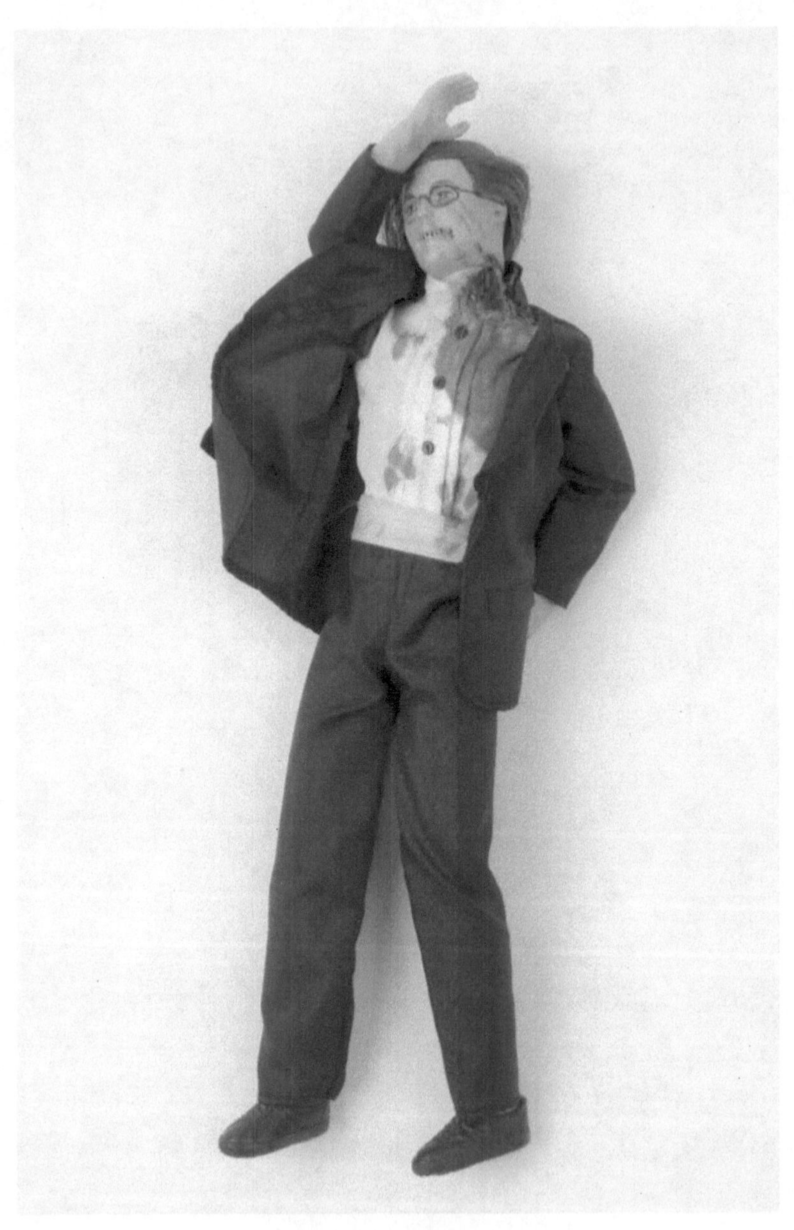

026
Jephro Rucastle
from "The Copper Beeches"
David Wegman

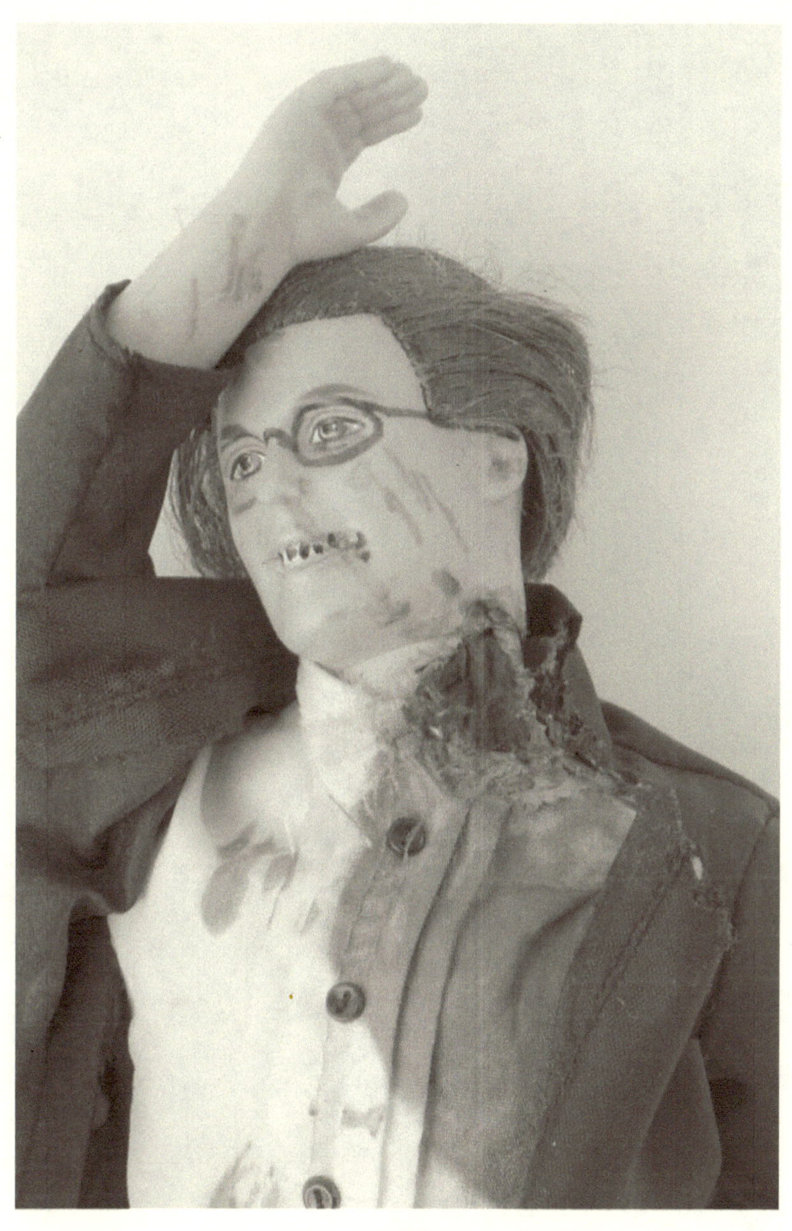

027
Jephro Rucastle
from "The Copper Beeches"
David Wegman

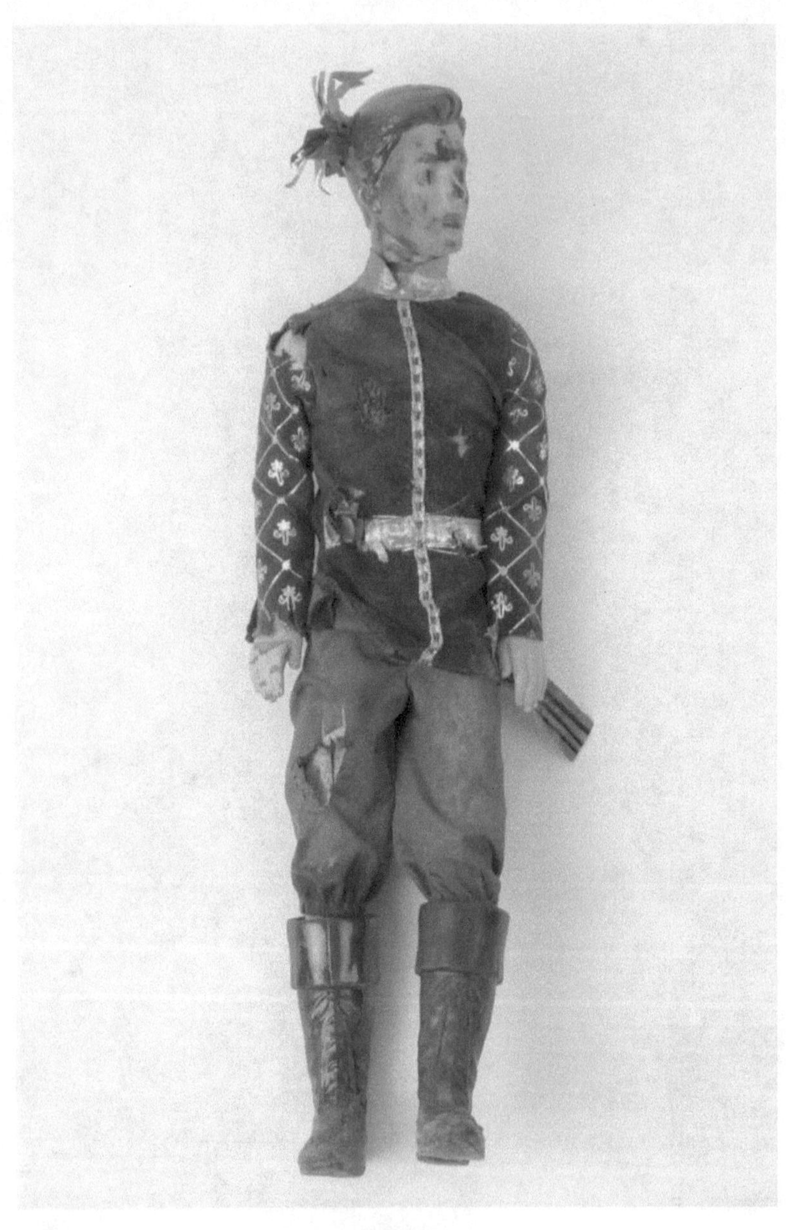

028
John Straker
from "Silver Blaze"
Akshay Rajan

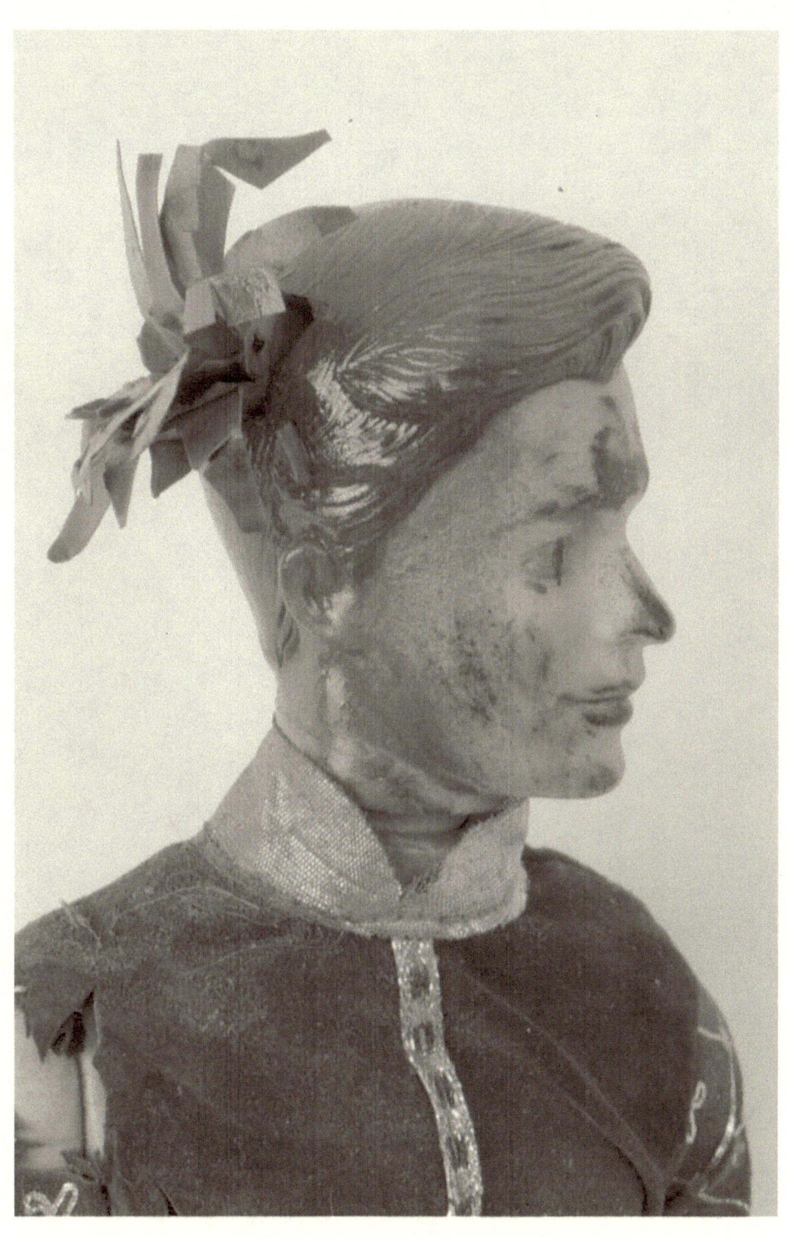

029
John Straker
from "Silver Blaze"
Akshay Rajan

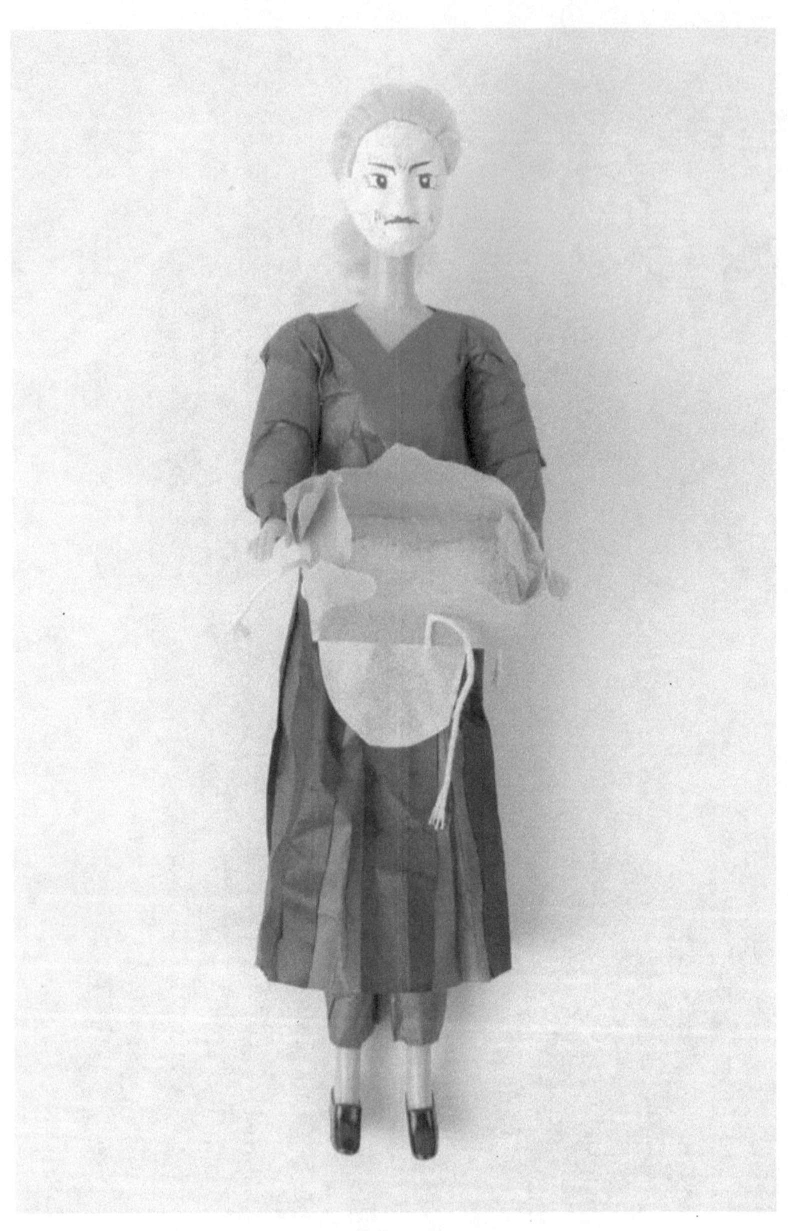

030
Susan Cushing
from "The Cardboard Box"
Joo Yung Koag

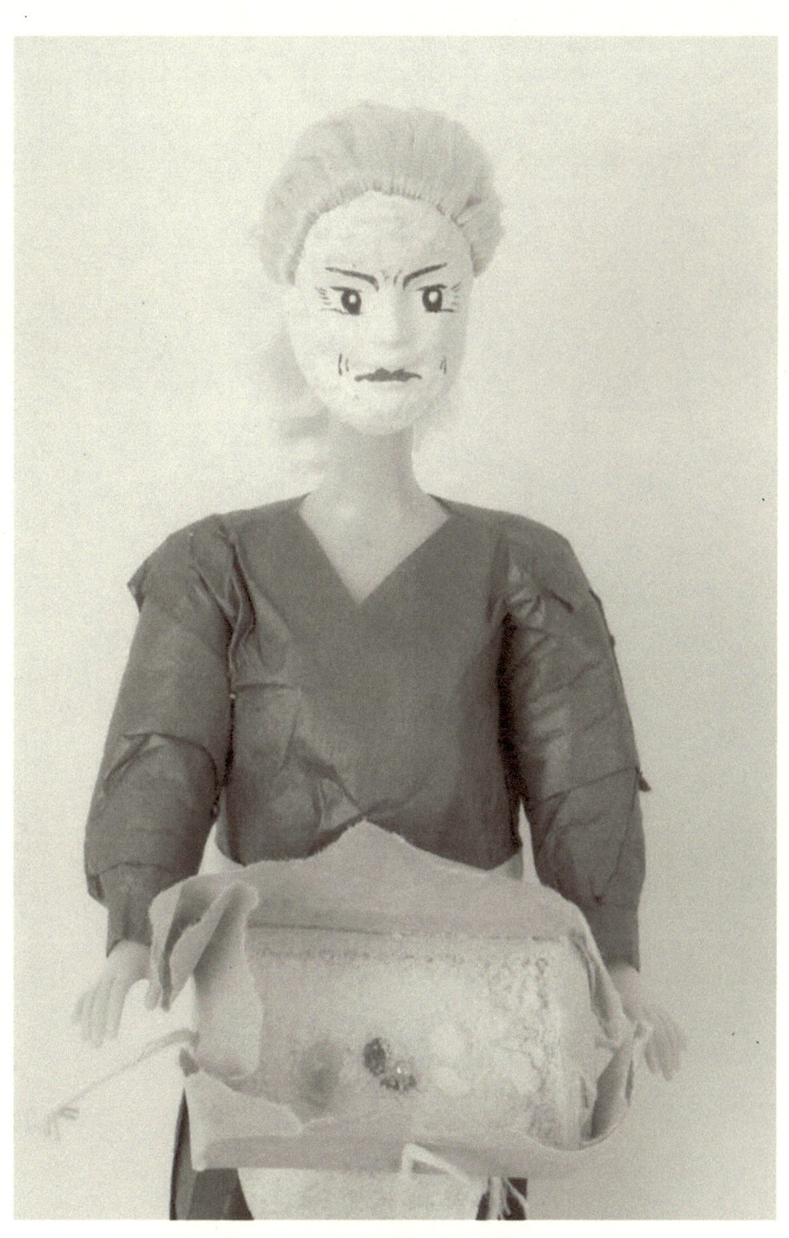

031
Susan Cushing
from "The Cardboard Box"
Joo Yung Koag

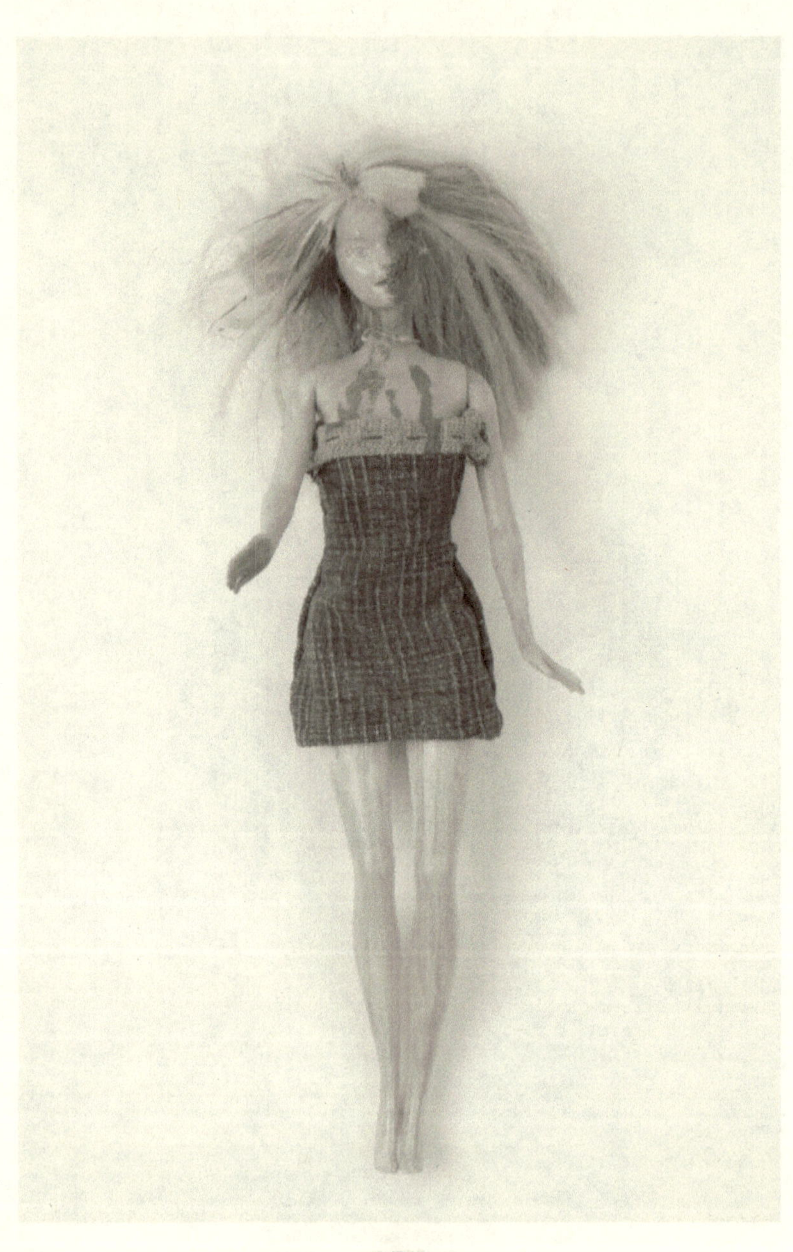

032
Mary Cushing
from "The Cardboard Box"
Alana Gelbart

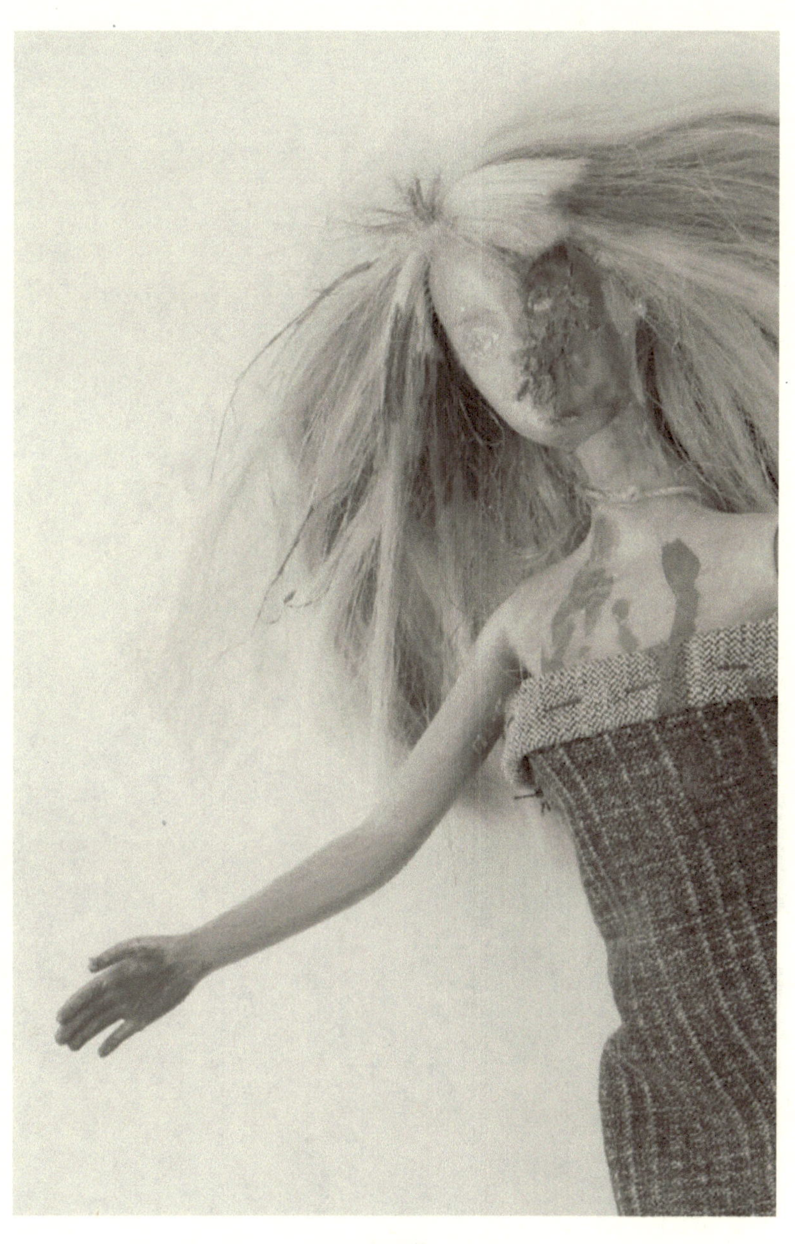

033
Mary Cushing
from "The Cardboard Box"
Alana Gelbart

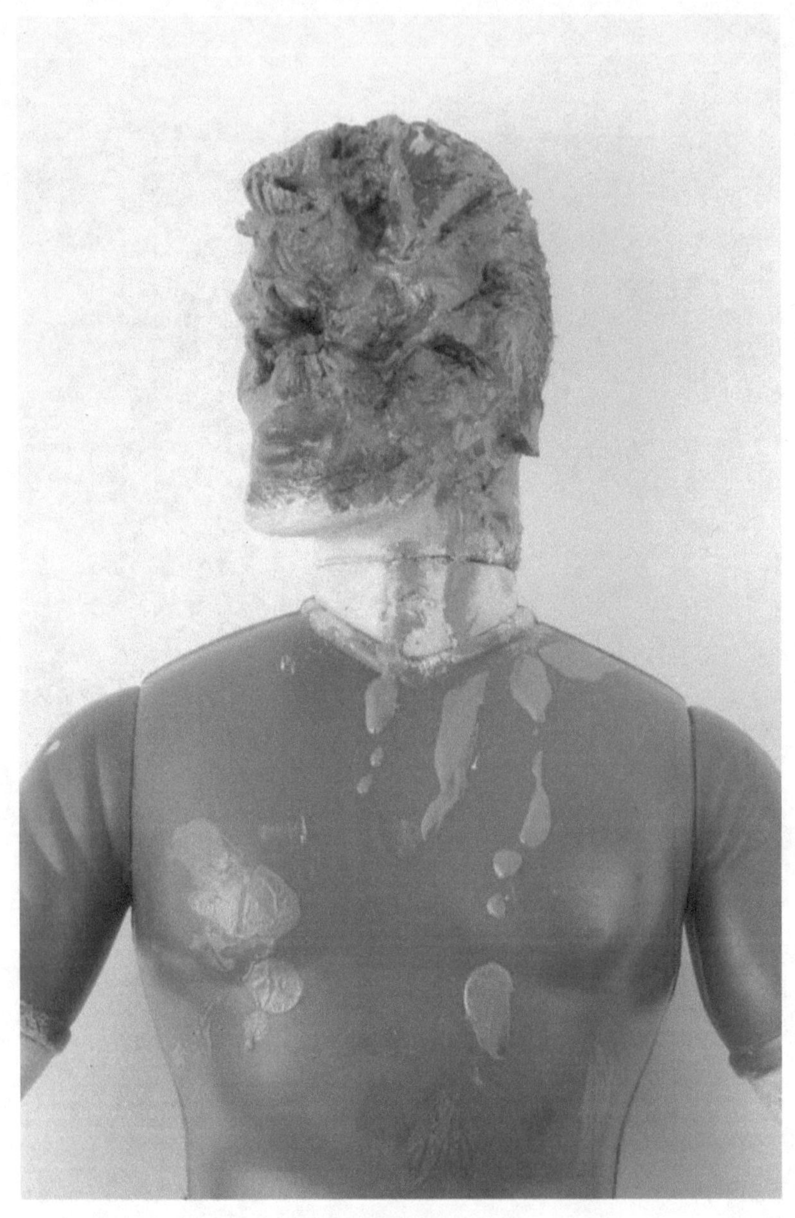

034
Alec Fairbairn
from "The Cardboard Box"
Hui Yin Low

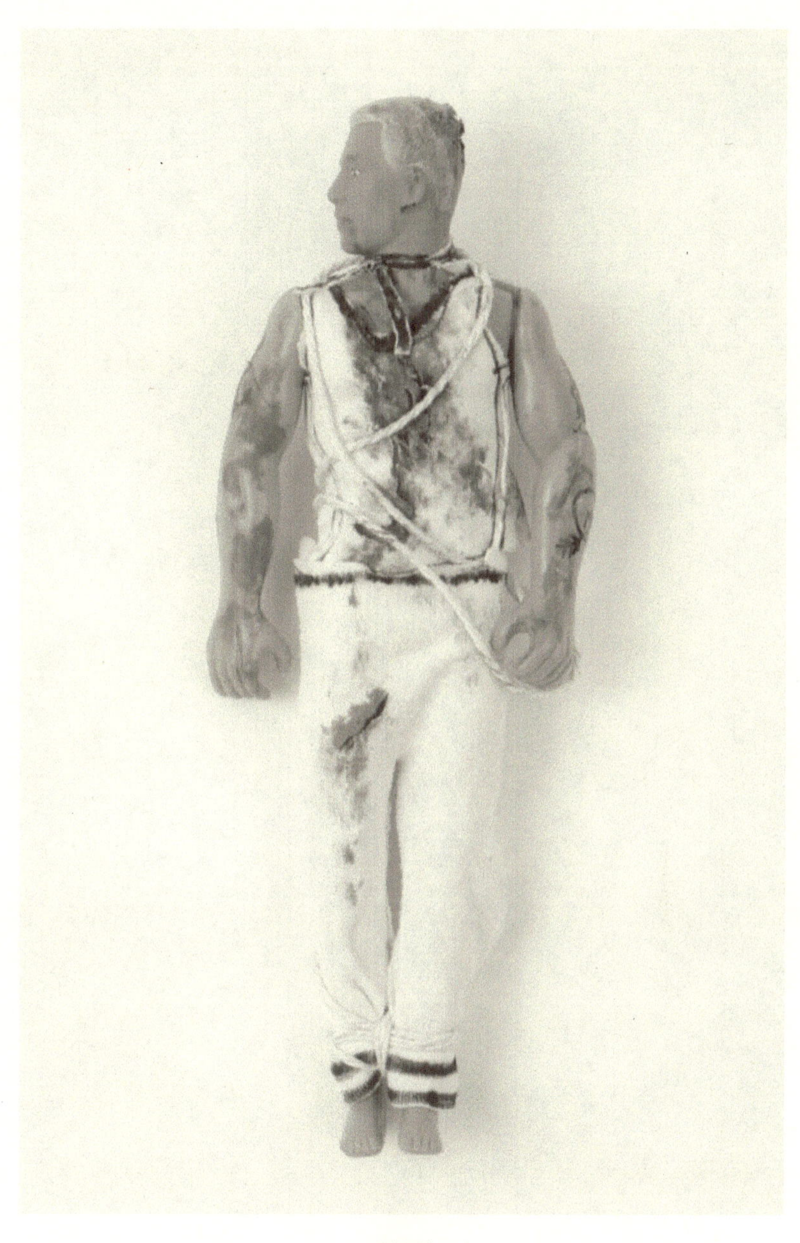

035
James Browner
from "The Cardboard Box"
Alexandra Wall

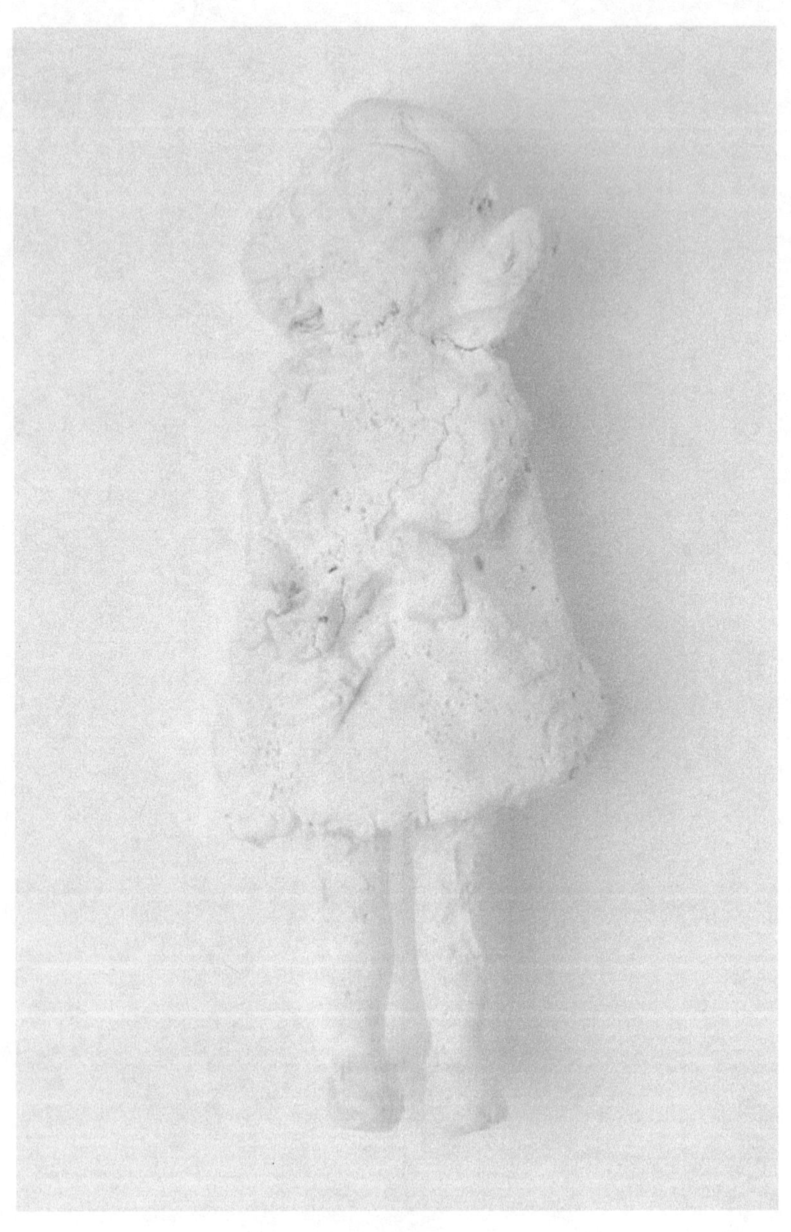

036
Lucy Hebron
from "The Yellow Face"
Stephanie Jacobs

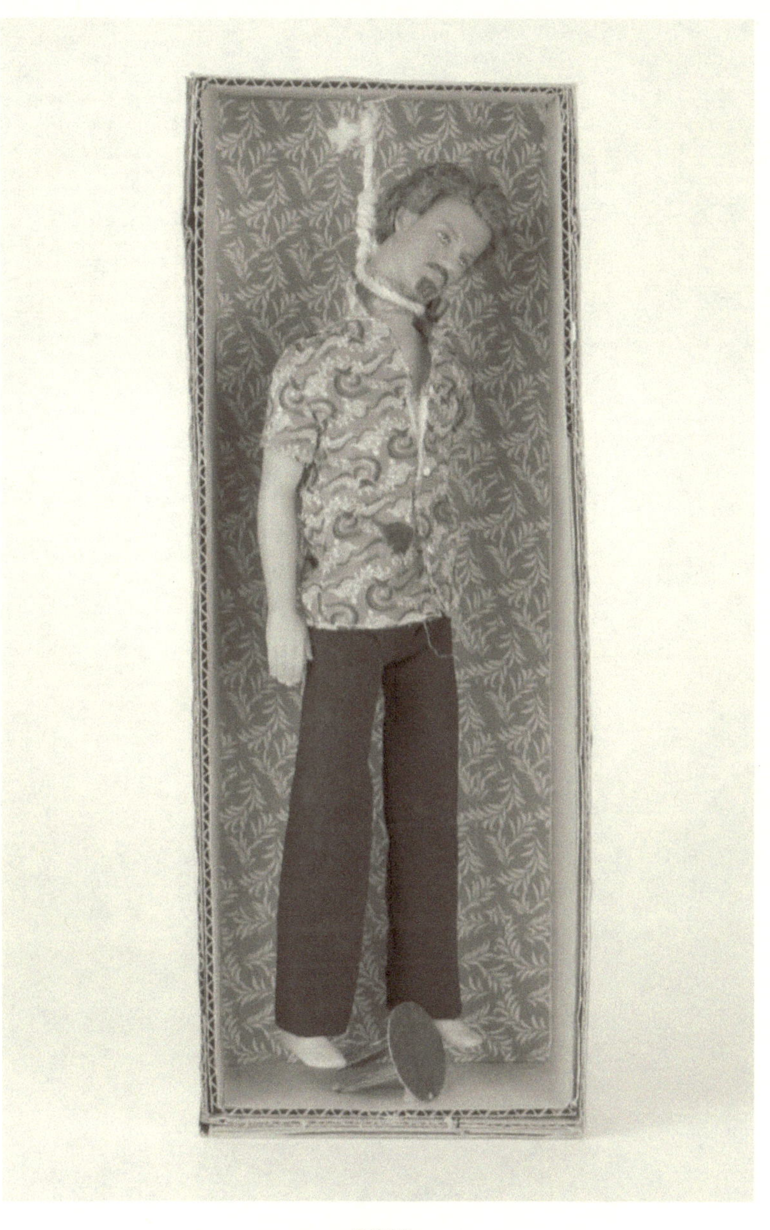

037
Arthur Pinner
from, "The Stockbroker's Clerk"
Mahsa Rahmanimahdiabadi

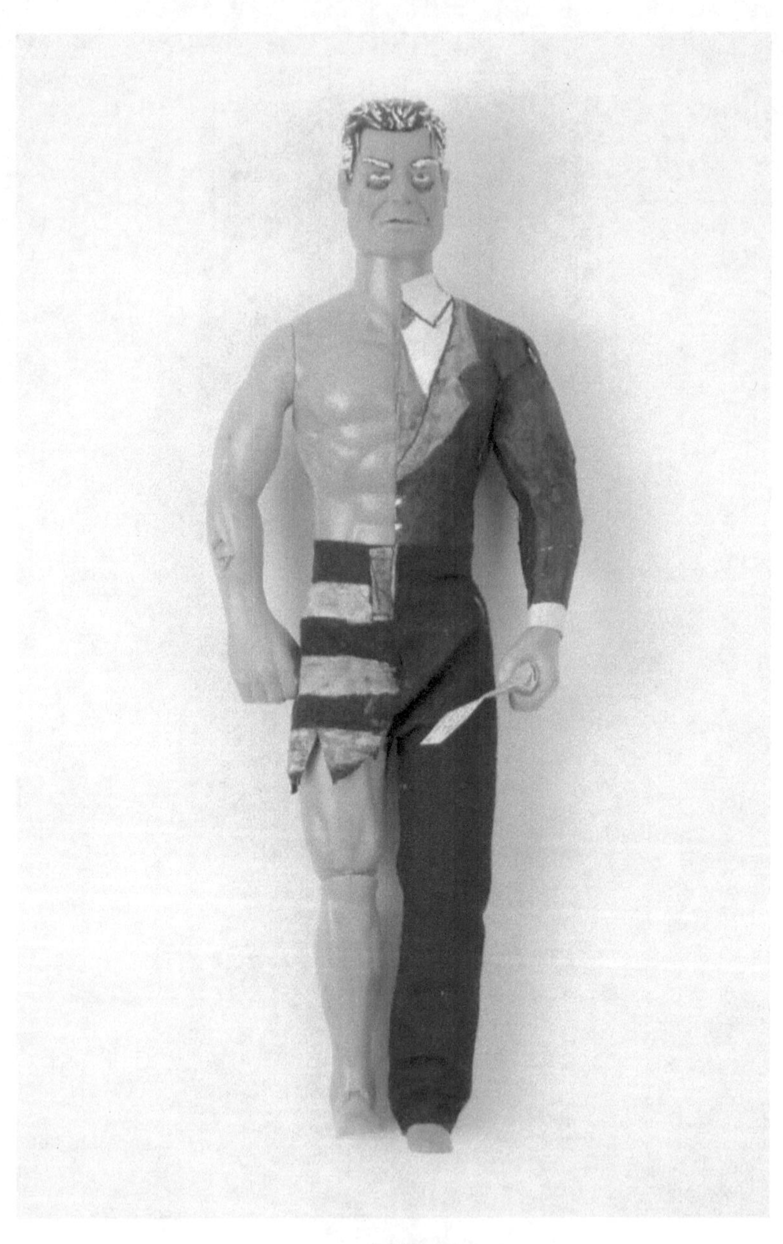

038
Old Trevor
from "The Gloria Scott"
Ivan Kwan

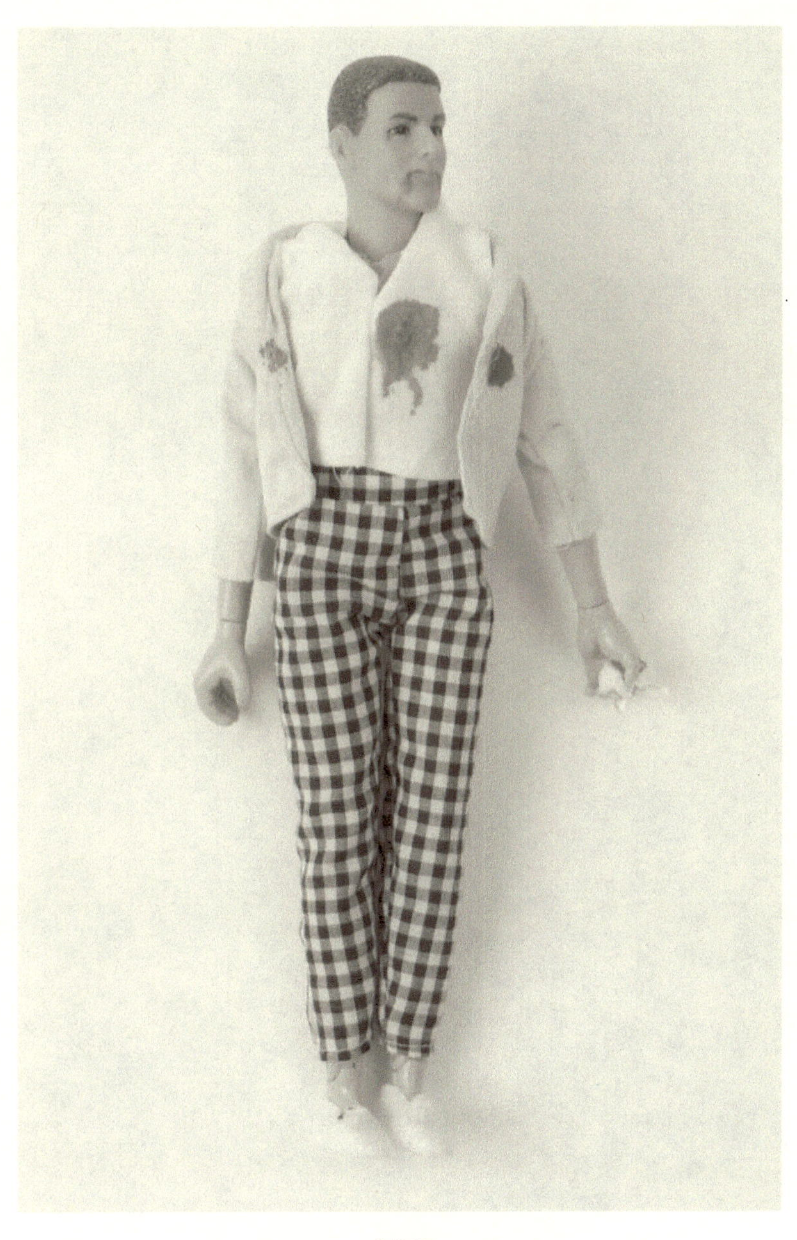

039
William the coachman
from "The Reigate Squire"
Graham Bennett

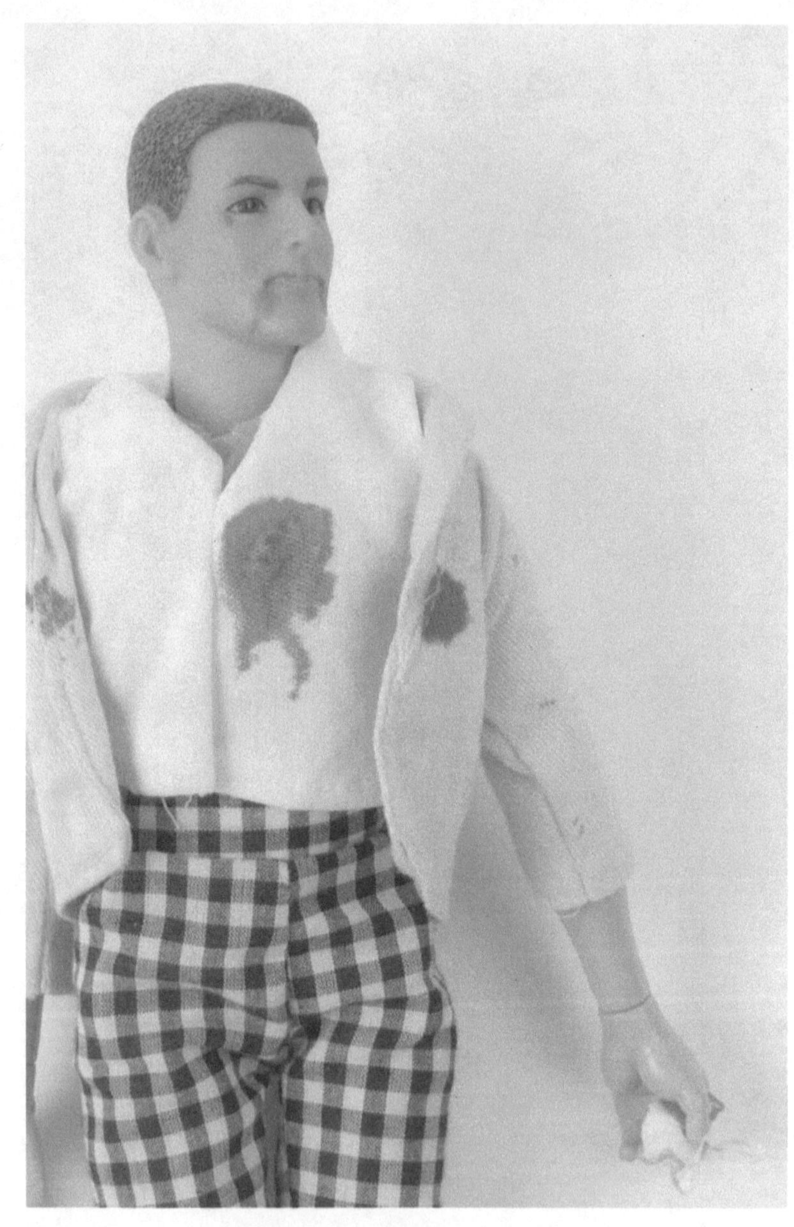

040
William the coachman
from "The Reigate Squire"
Graham Bennett

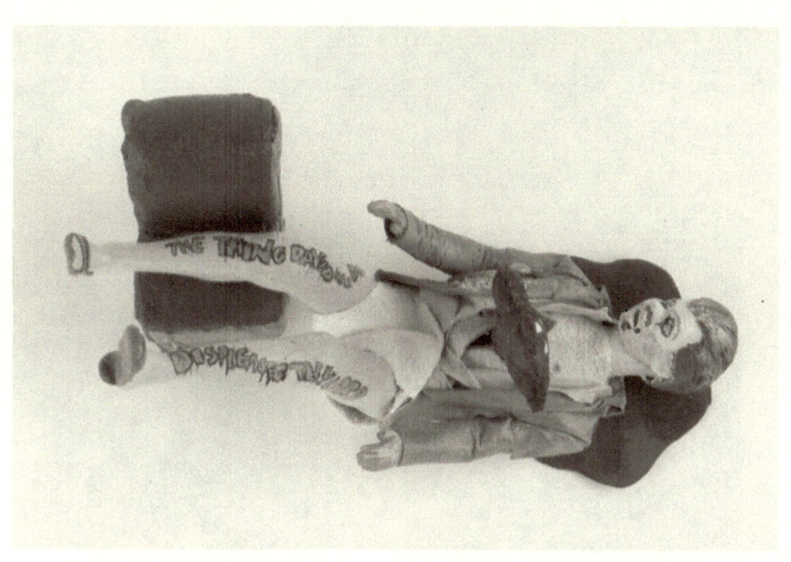

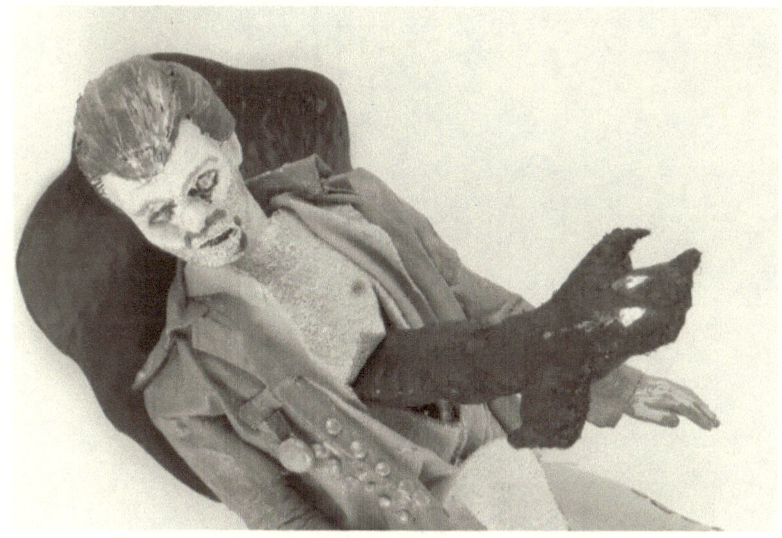

041 & 042
Colonel James Barclay
from "The Crooked Man"
Lavanya Arulanandam

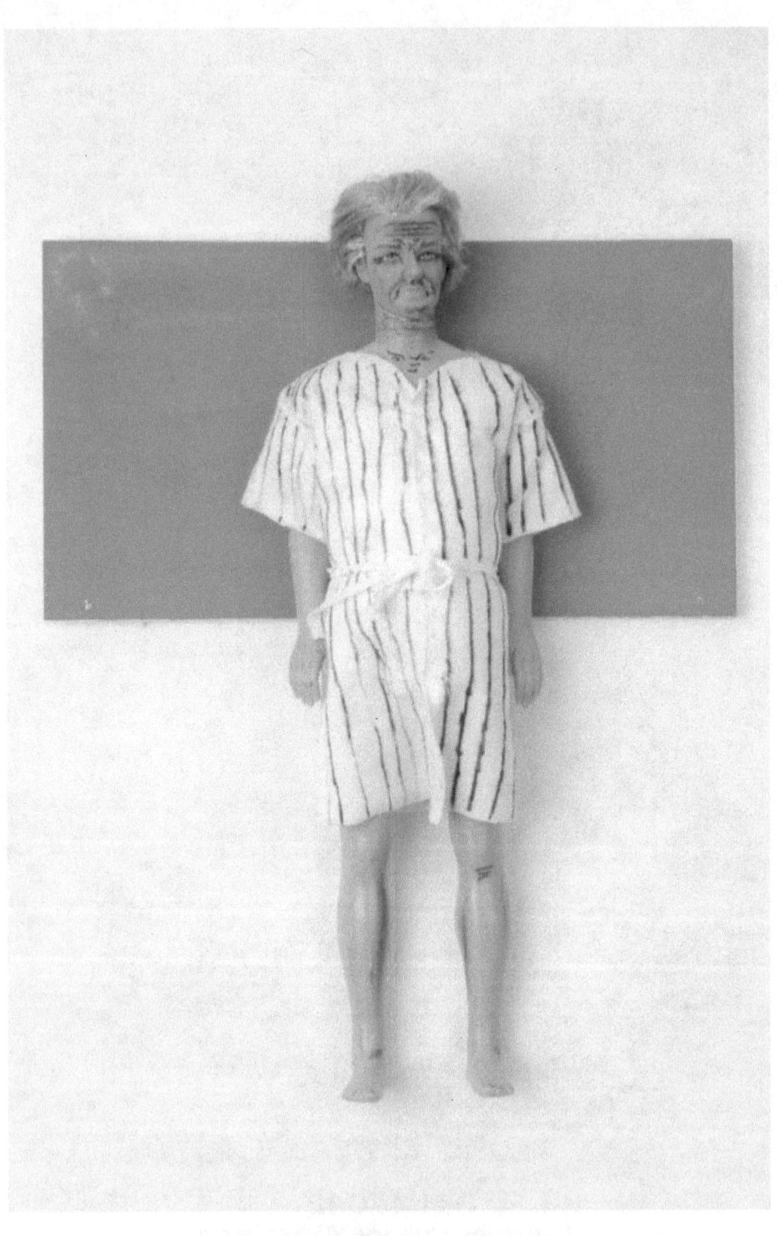

043
Blessington (a.k.a. Sutton)
from "The Resident Patient"
Kathy Wu

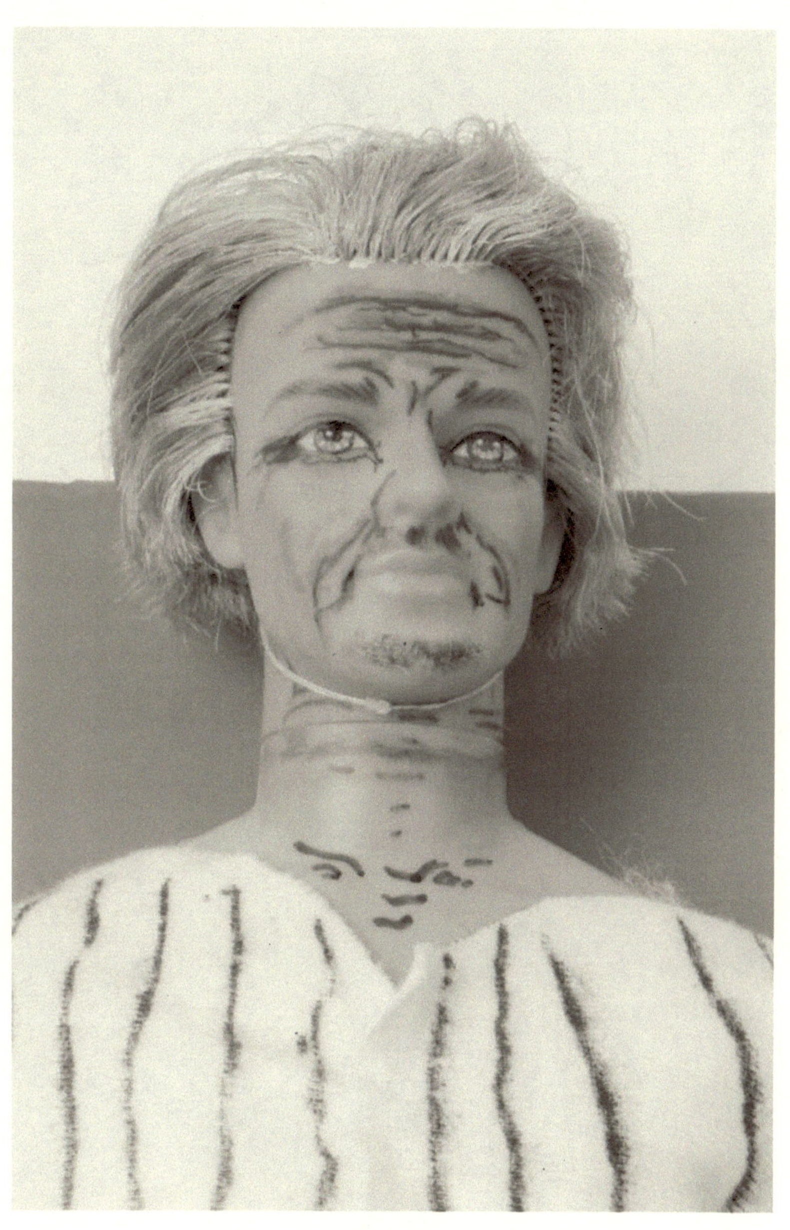

044
Blessington (a.k.a. Sutton)
from "The Resident Patient"
Kathy Wu

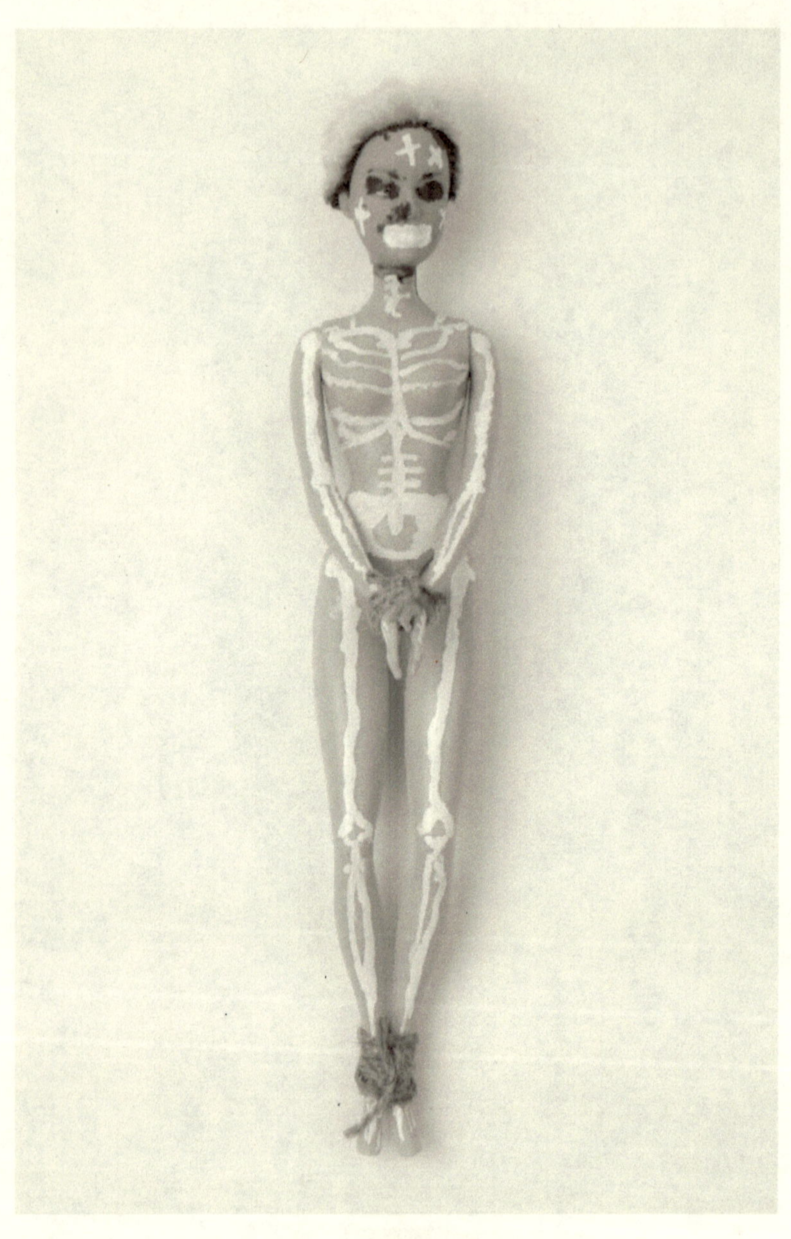

045
Paul Kratides
from "The Greek Interpreter"
Stella Bao

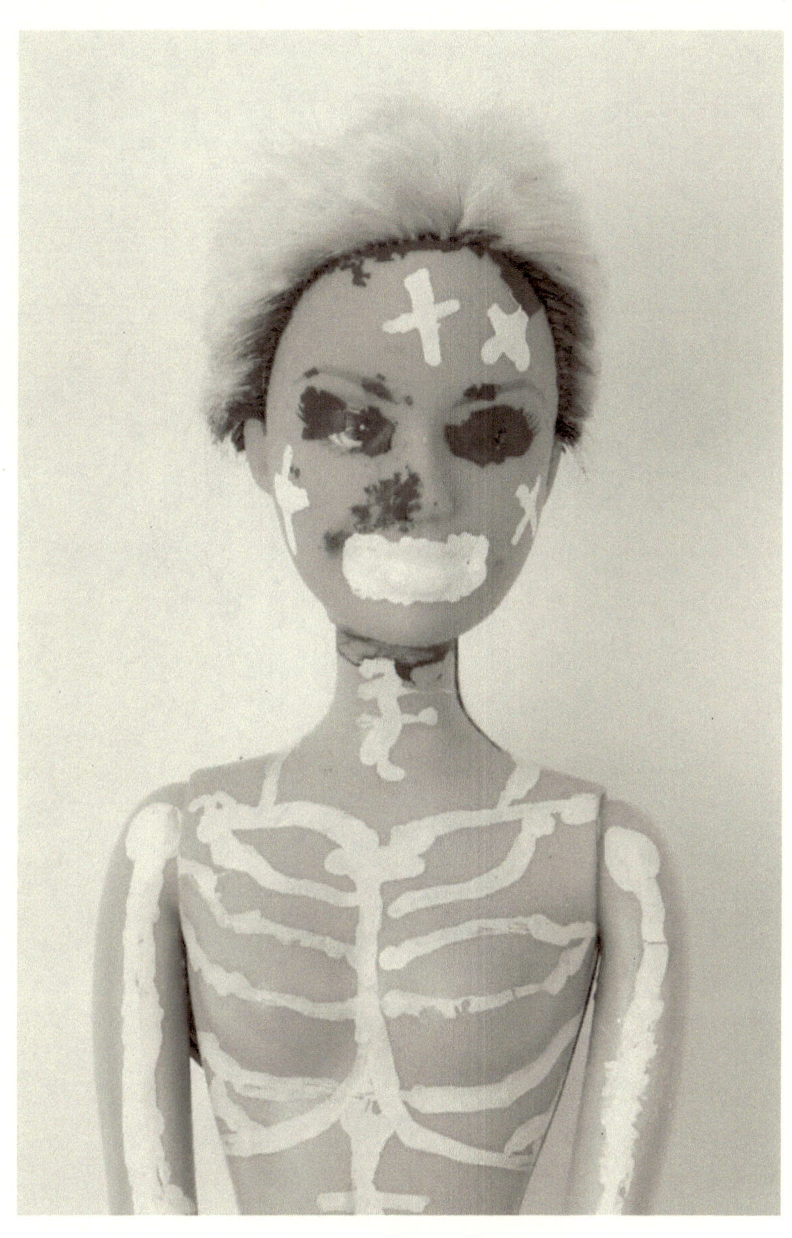

046
Paul Kratides
from "The Greek Interpreter"
Stella Bao

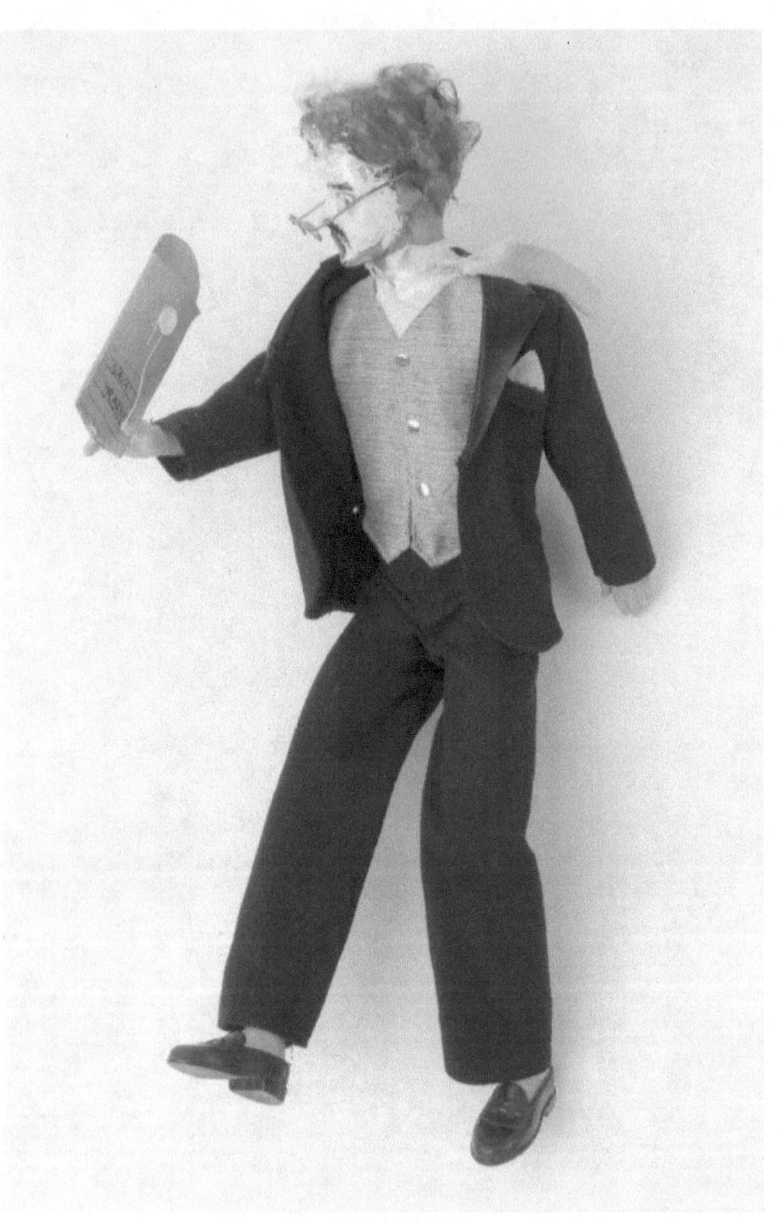

047
Percy Phelps
from "The Naval Treaty"
Vincent Sun

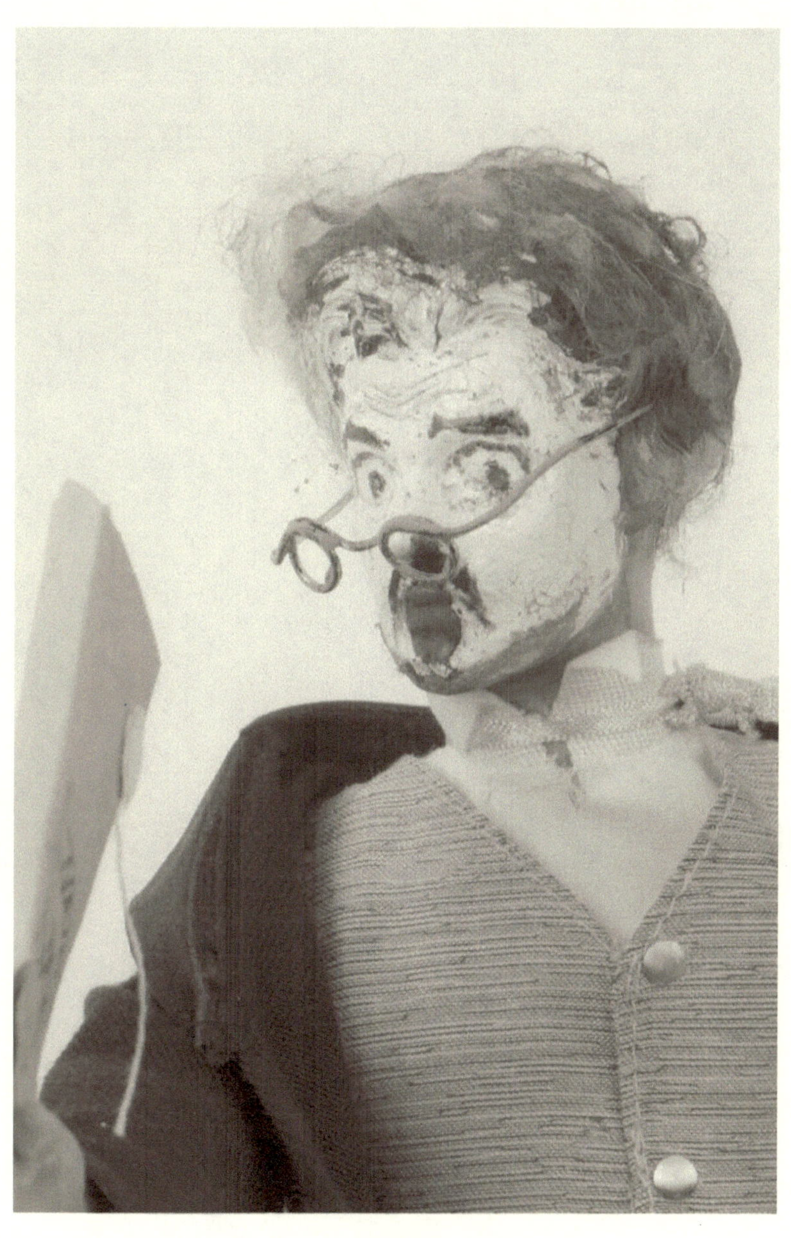

048
Percy Phelps
from "The Naval Treaty"
Vincent Sun

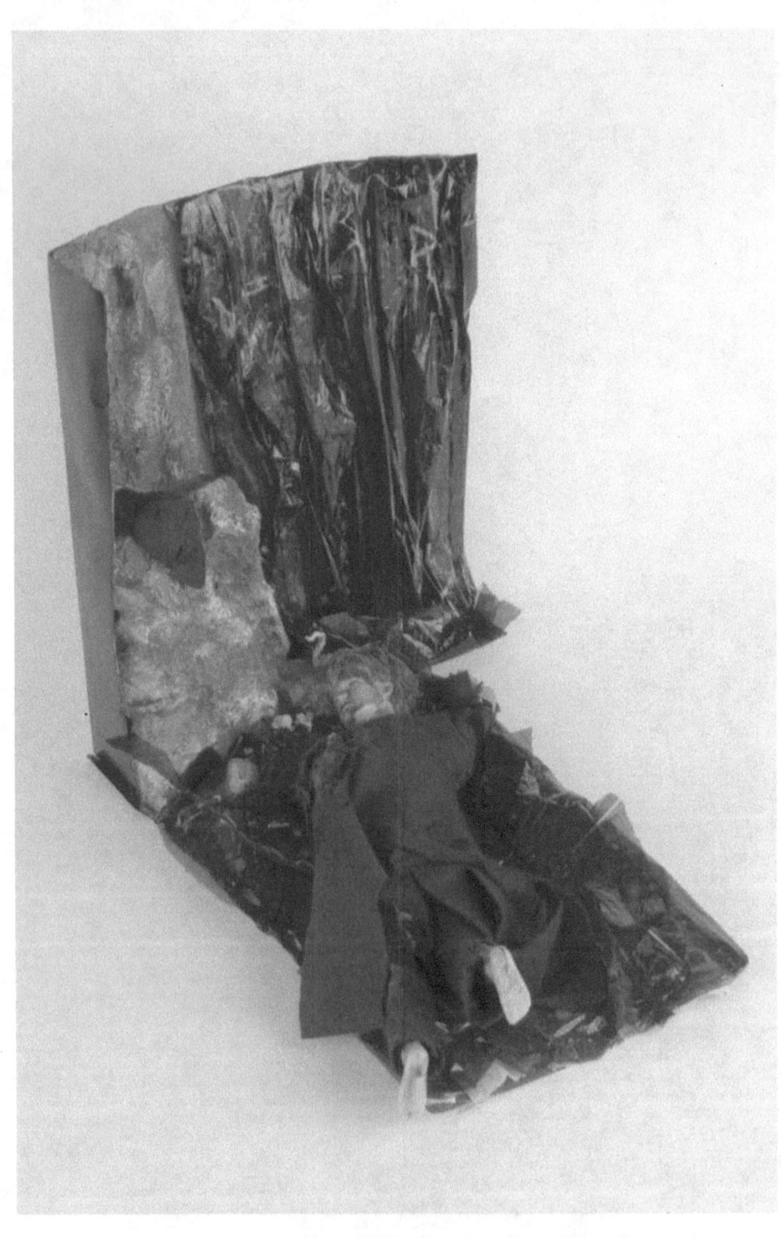

049
Sherlock Holmes
from "The Final Problem"
Morsaleena Moytree Paruque

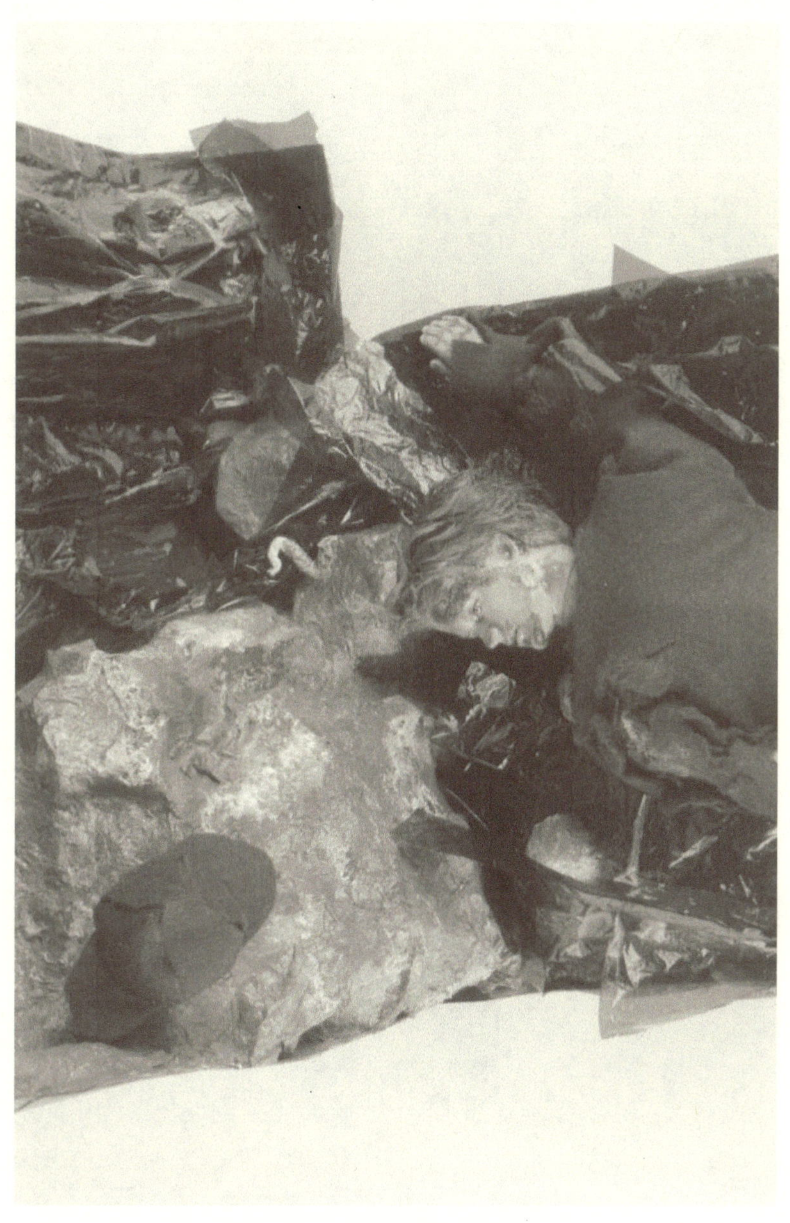

050
Sherlock Holmes
from "The Final Problem"
Morsaleena Moytree Paruque

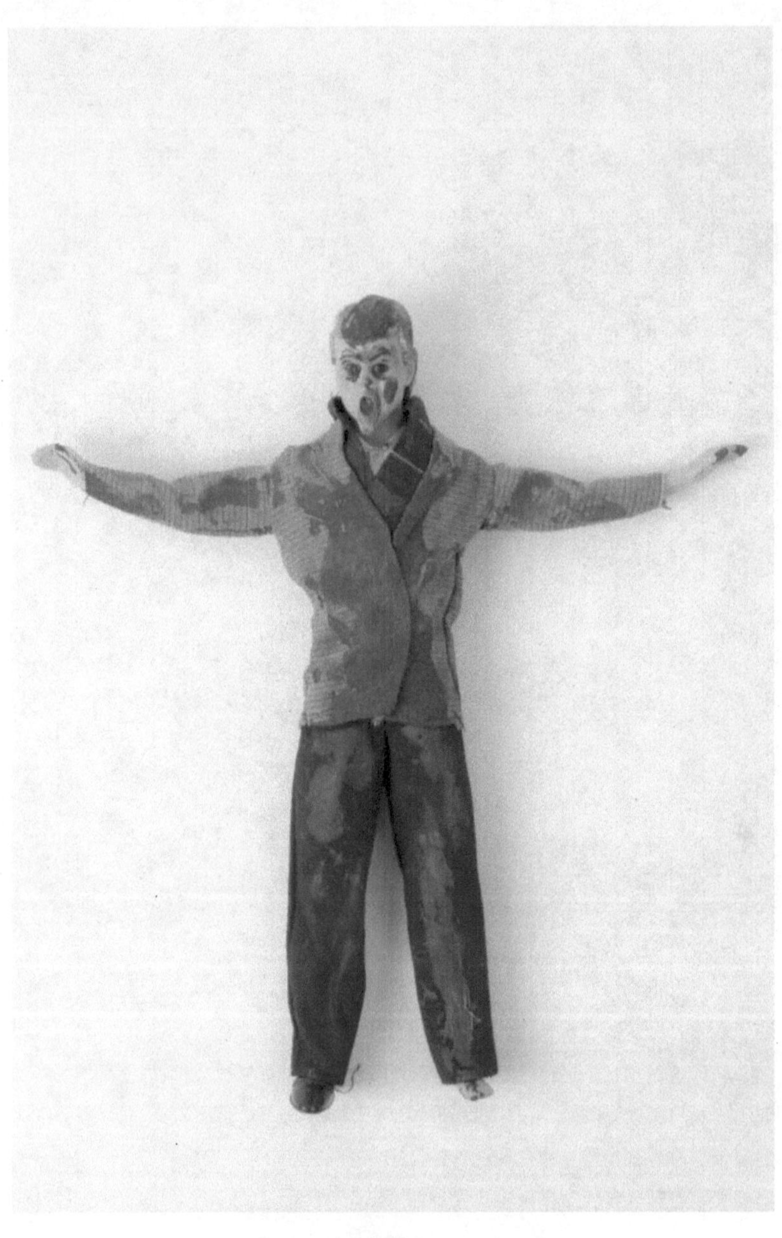

051
Sir Charles Baskerville
from The Hound of the Baskervilles
Adriana Neculai

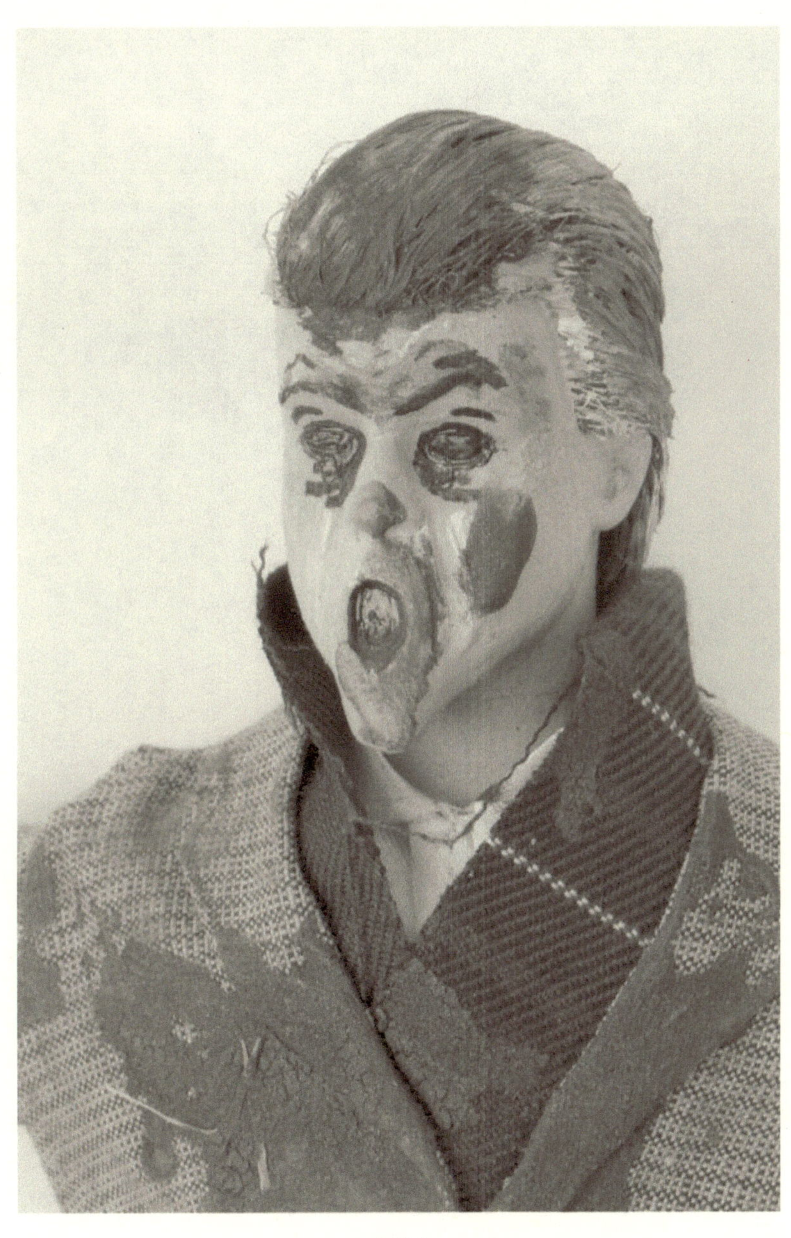

051
Sir Charles Baskerville
from The Hound of the Baskervilles
Adriana Neculai

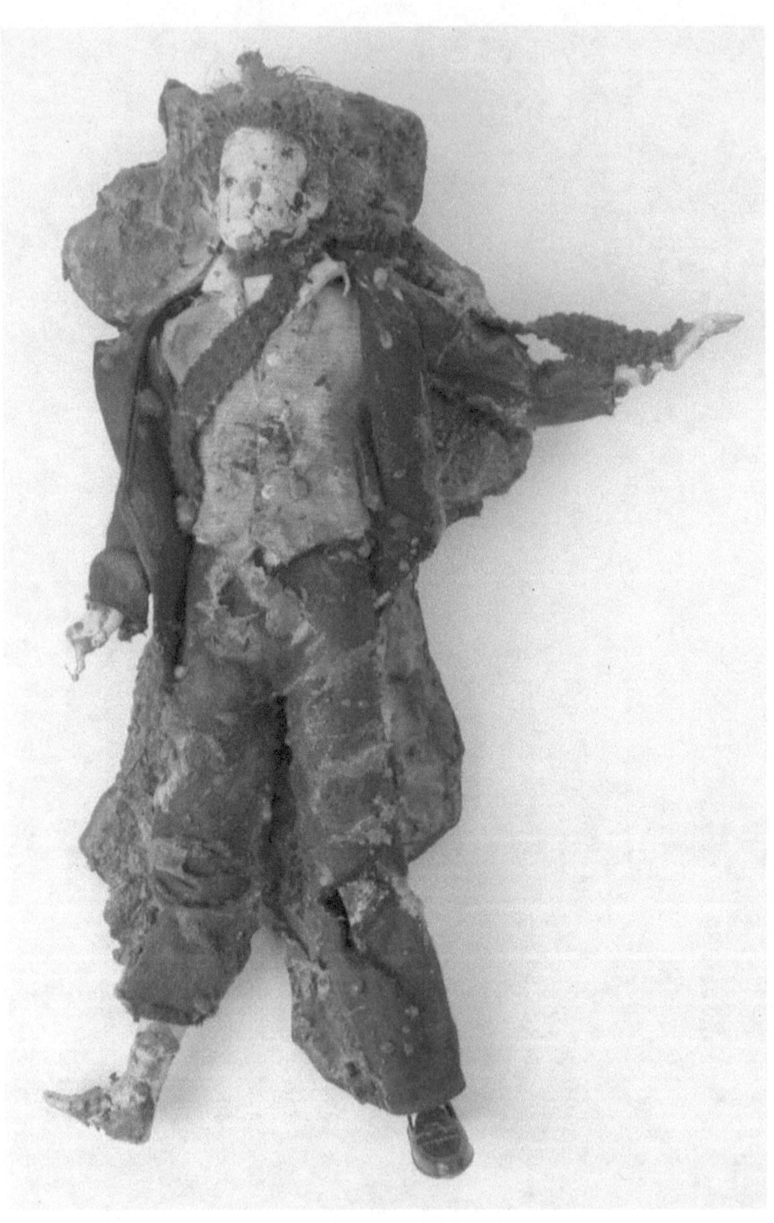

053
Jack Stapleton
from The Hound of the Baskervilles
Katherine Brice

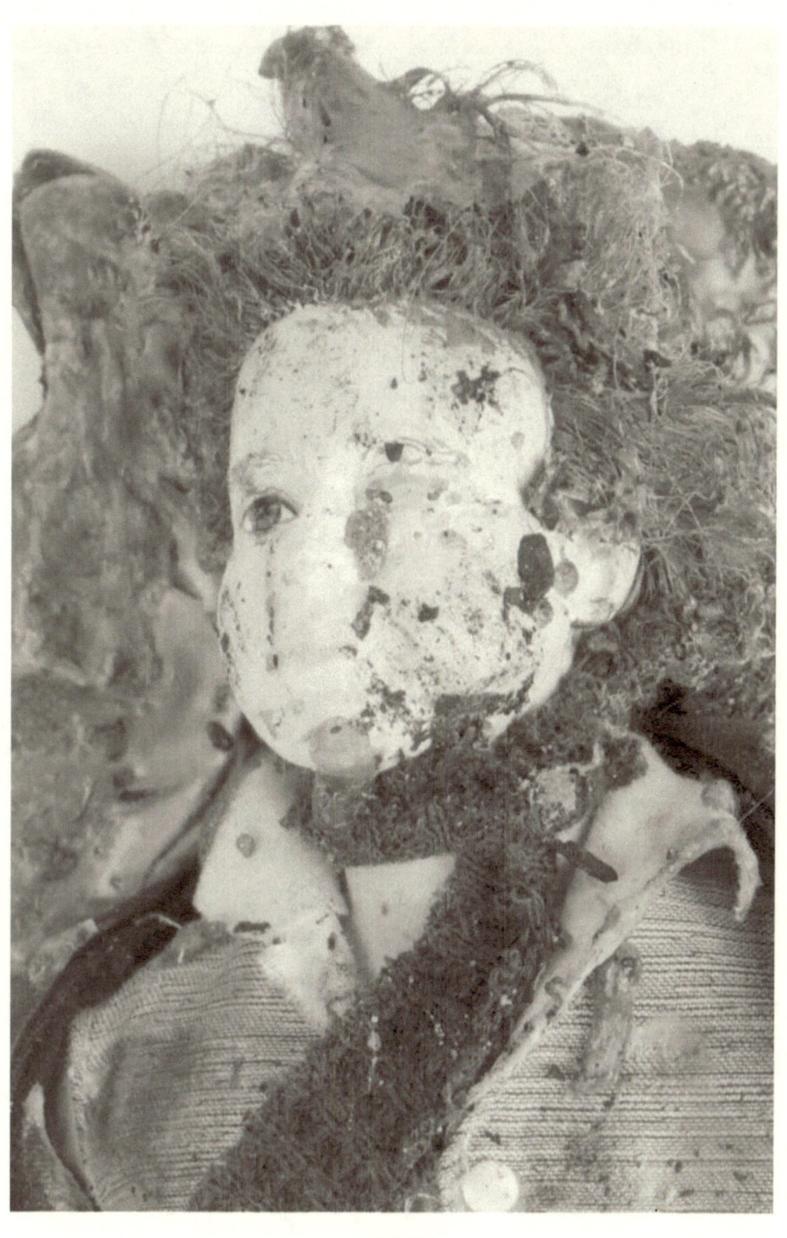

054
Jack Stapleton
from The Hound of the Baskervilles
Katherine Brice

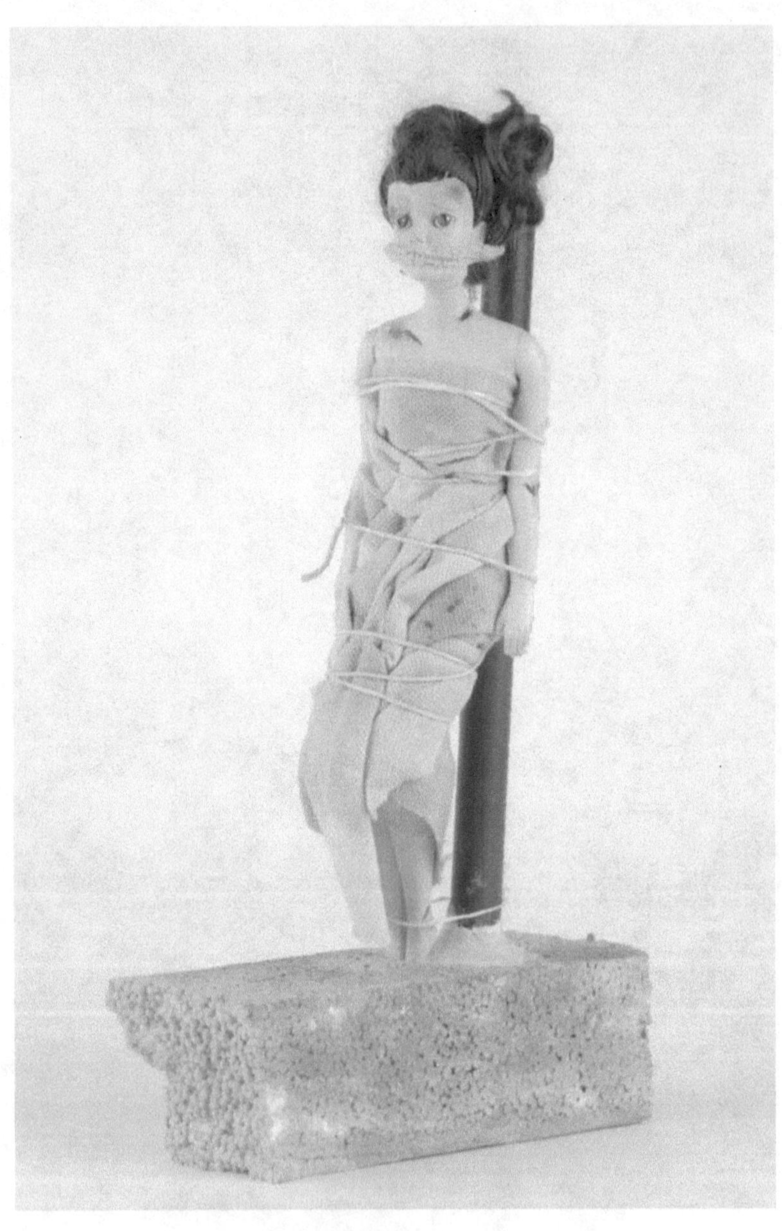

055
Beryl Stapleton
from The Hound of the Baskervilles
Rosemary Giles

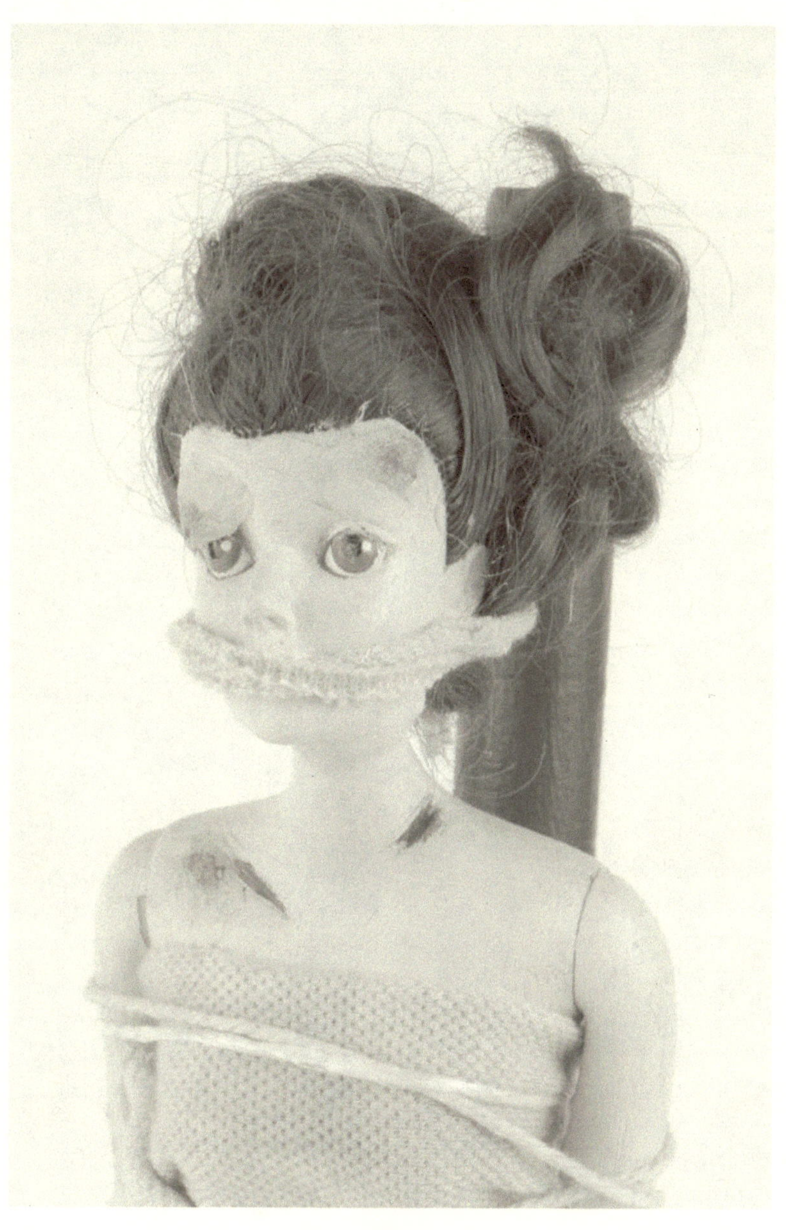

056
Beryl Stapleton
from The Hound of the Baskervilles
Rosemary Giles

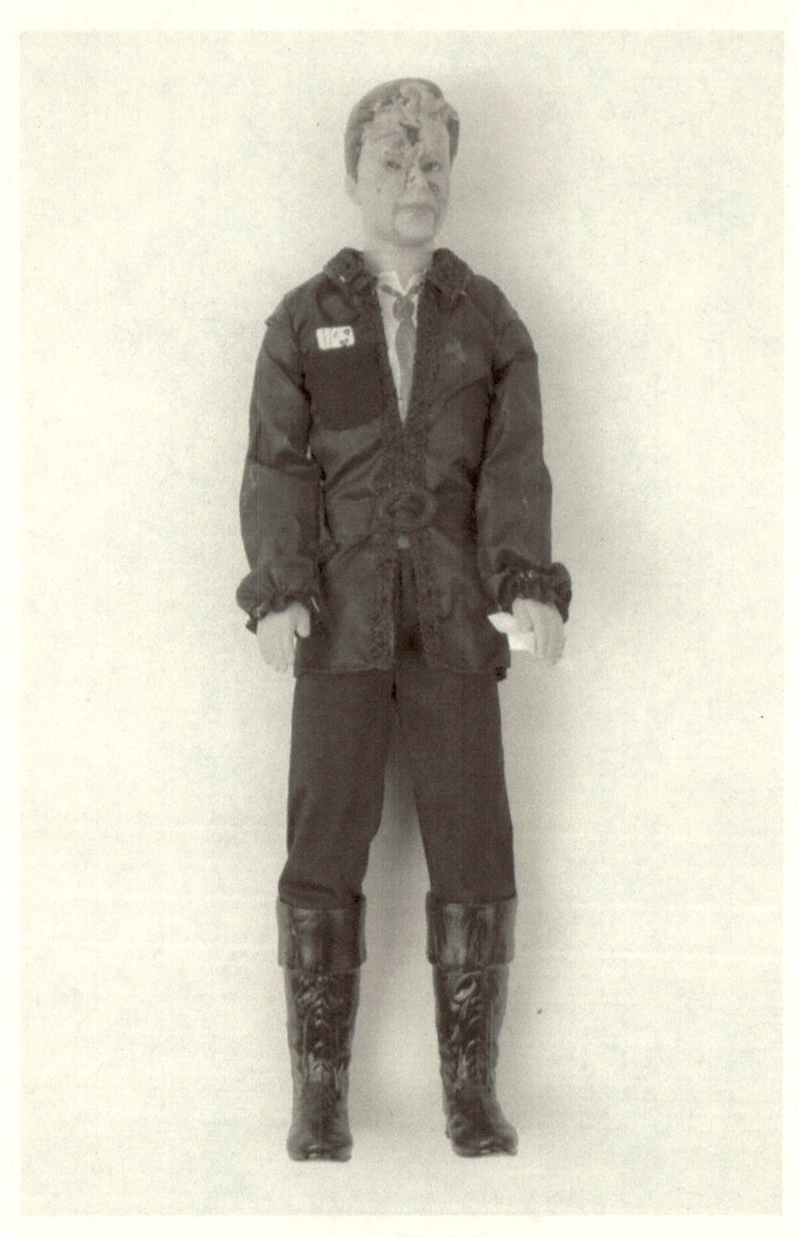

057
The Honourable Ronald Adair
from "The Empty House"
Irma Harambasic

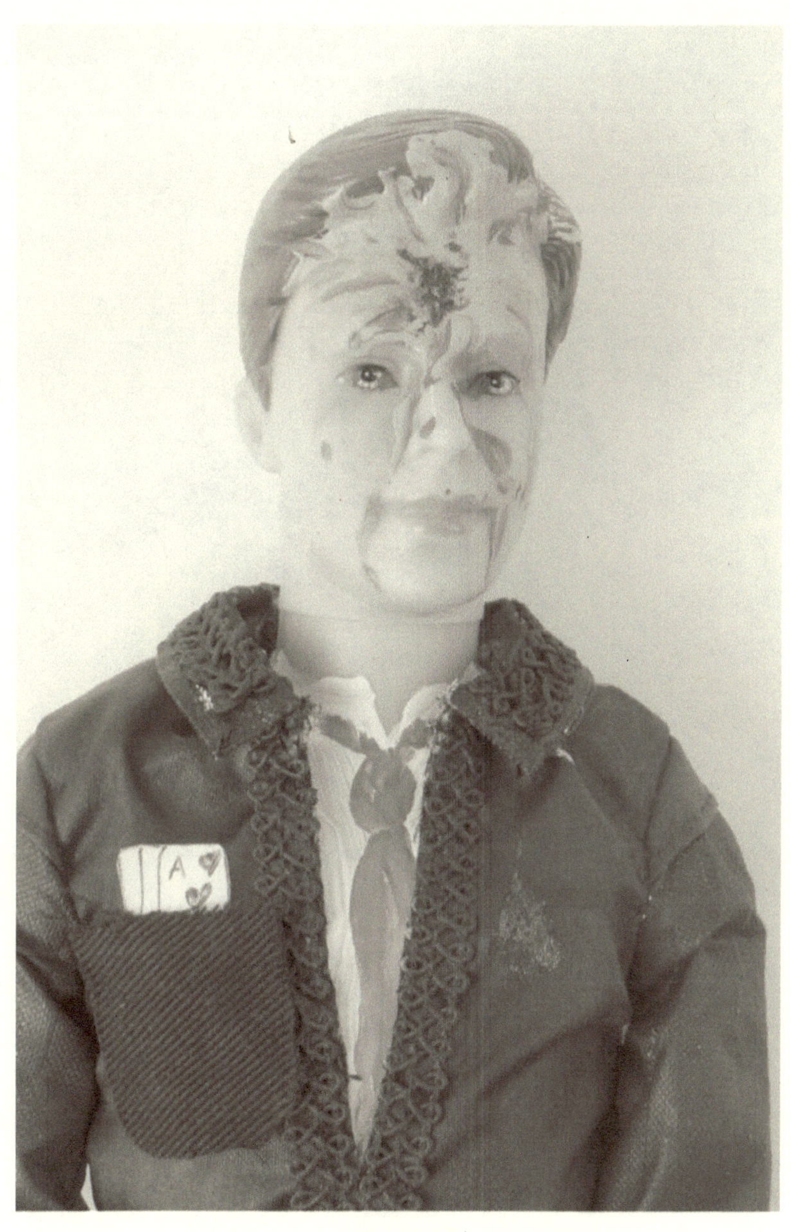

058
The Honourable Ronald Adair
from "The Empty House"
Irma Harambasic

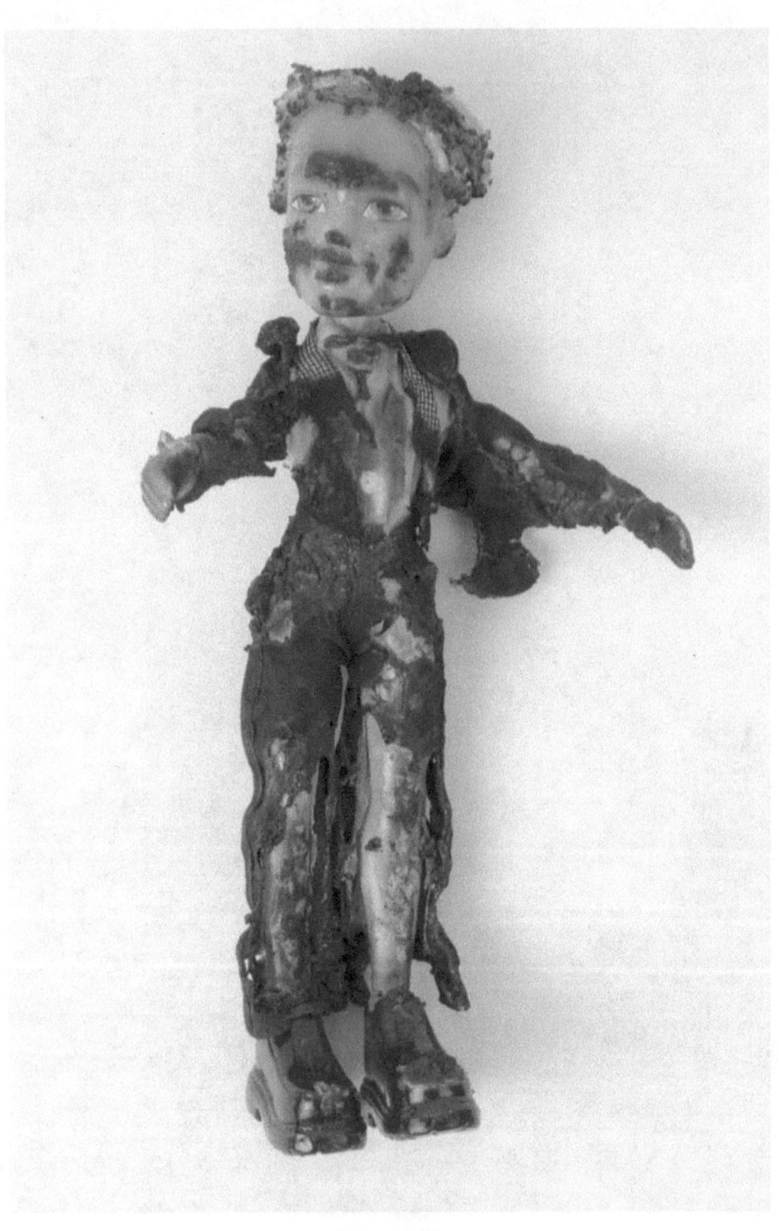

059
Jonas Oldachre
from "The Norwood Builder"
Jana Helal

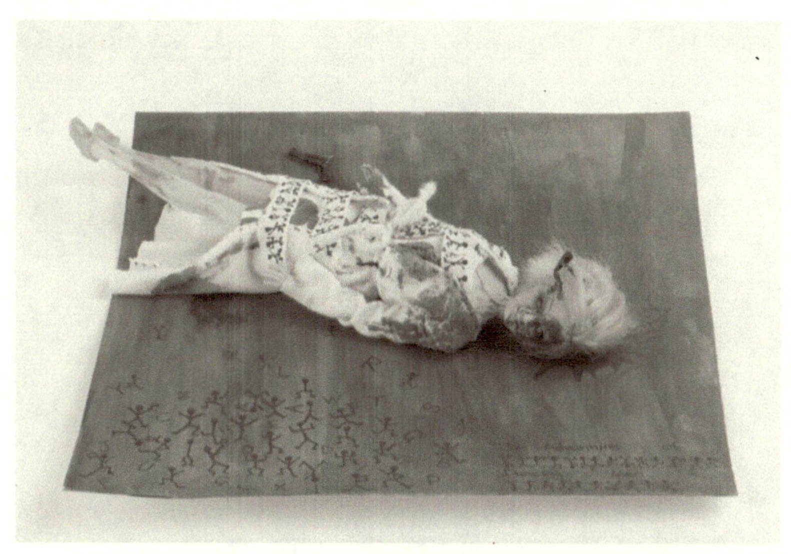

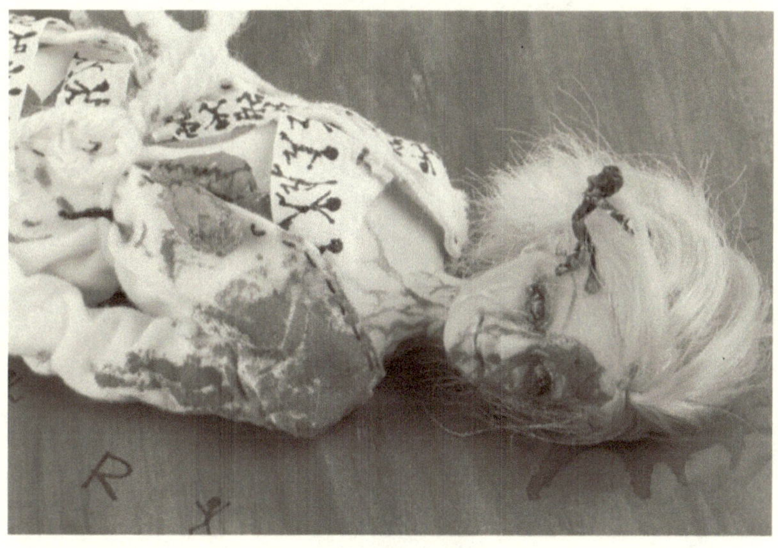

060 & 061
Elsie Cubitt
from "The Dancing Men"
Qiaoshu Wu

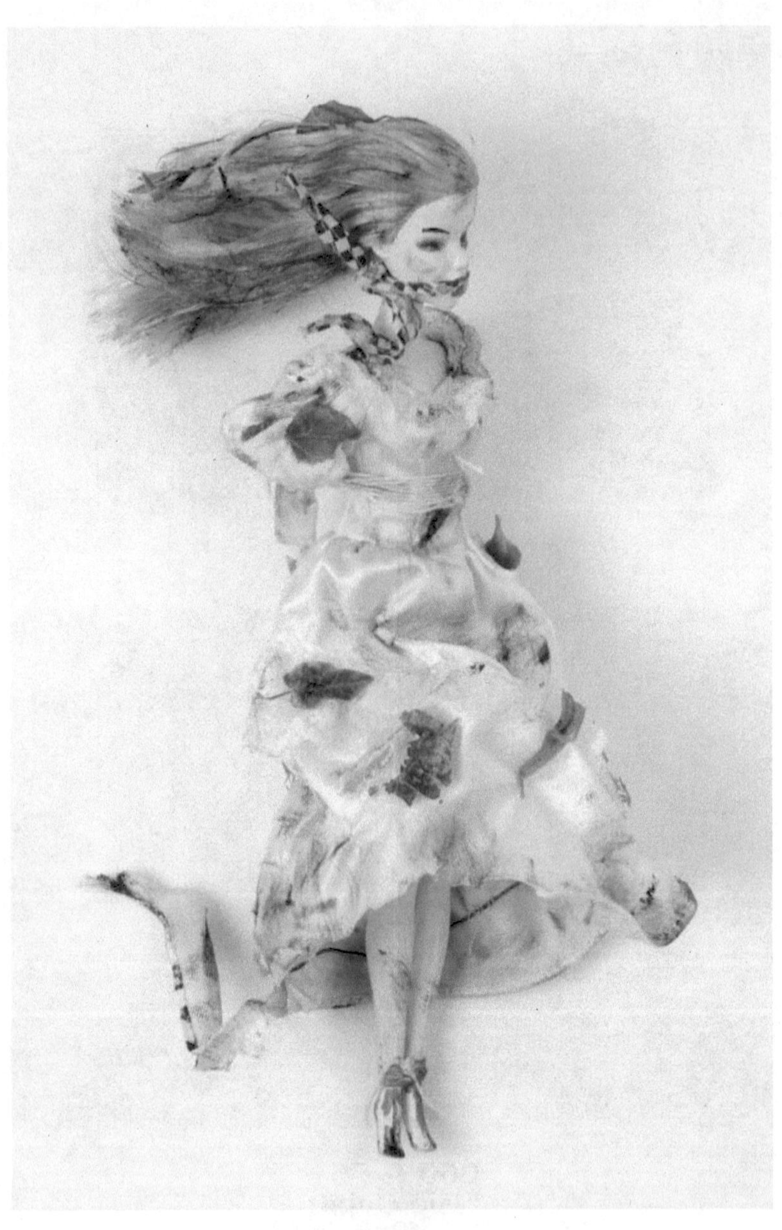

062
Violet Smith
from "The Solitary Cyclist"
Madeleine Beart

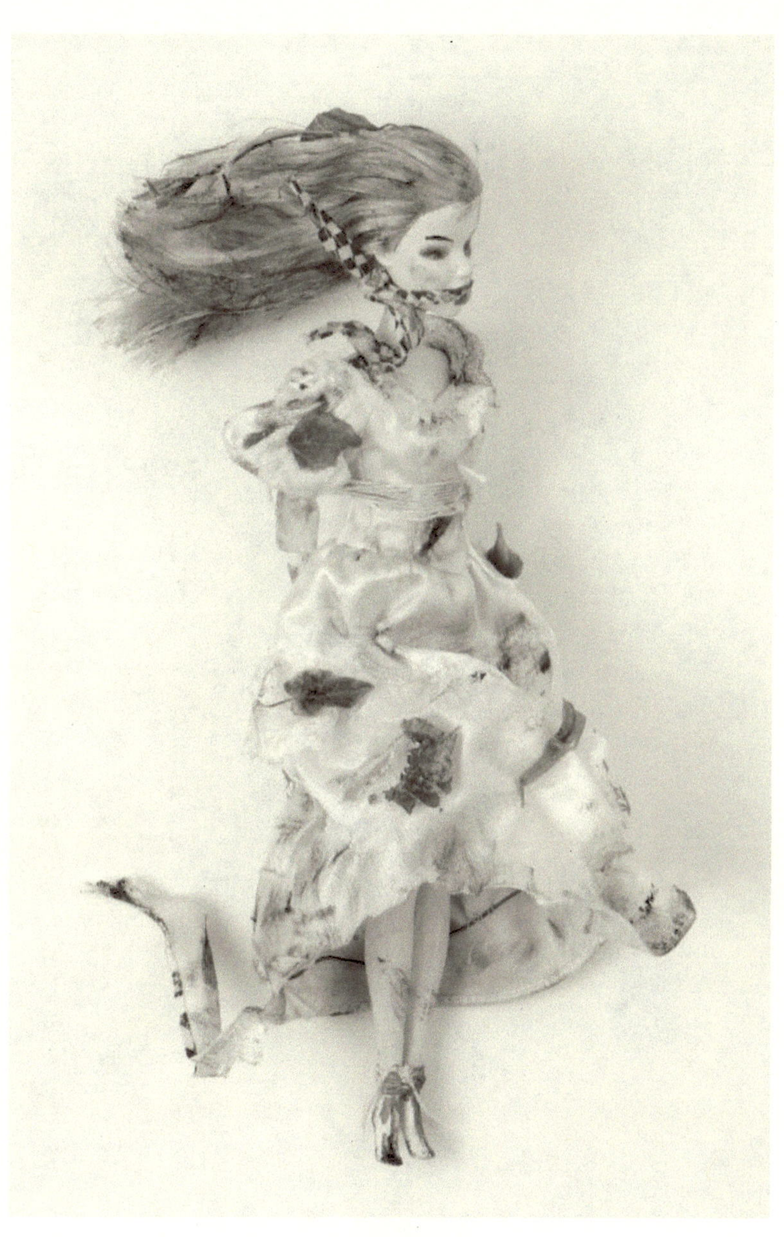

063
Violet Smith
from "The Solitary Cyclist"
Madeleine Beart

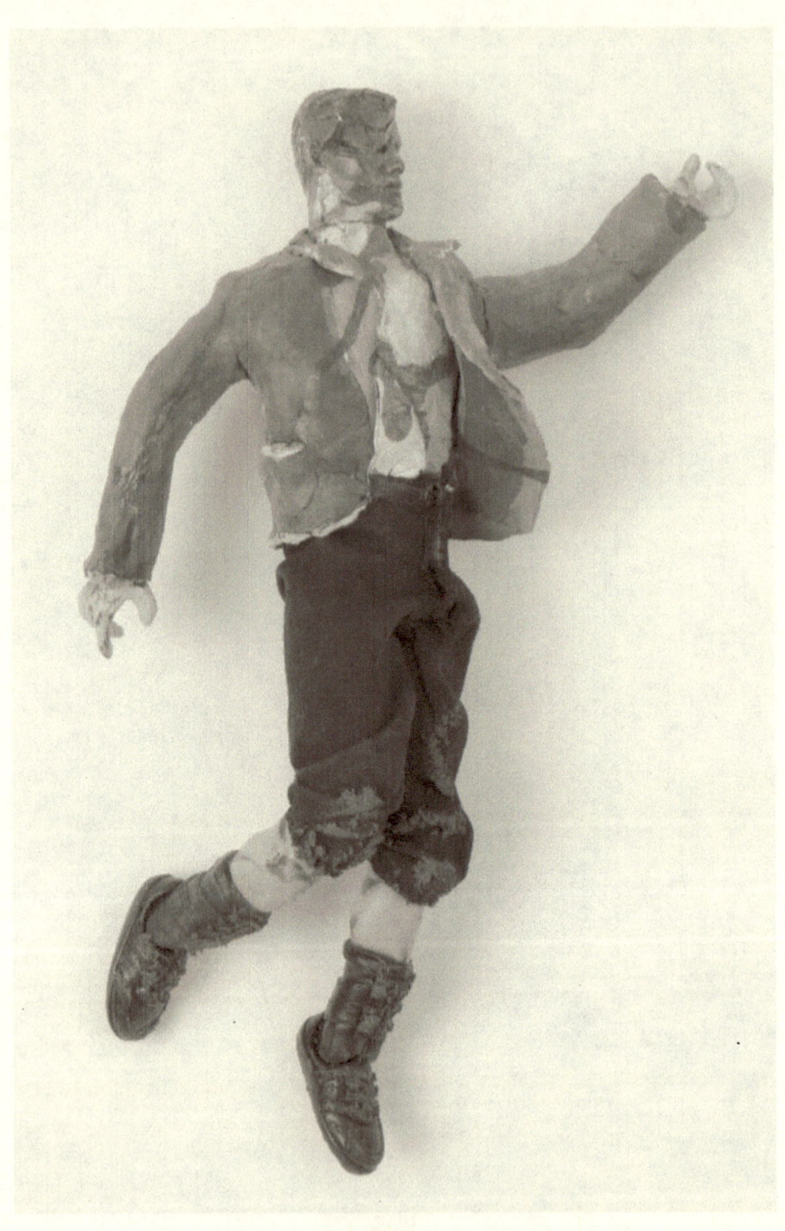

064
Heidegger the German master
from "The Priory School
Andrew Volkman

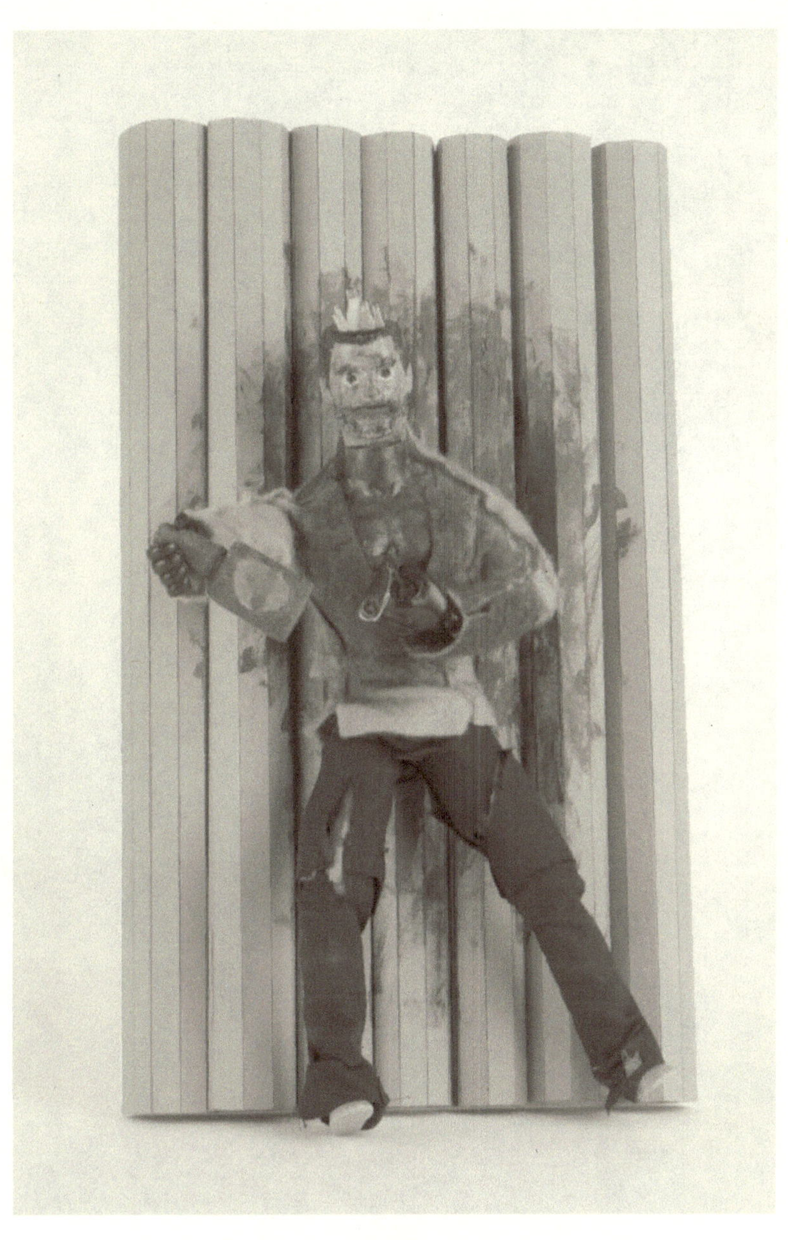

065
Peter Carey (a.k.a. Black Peter)
from "Black Peter"
Beatrice Toh

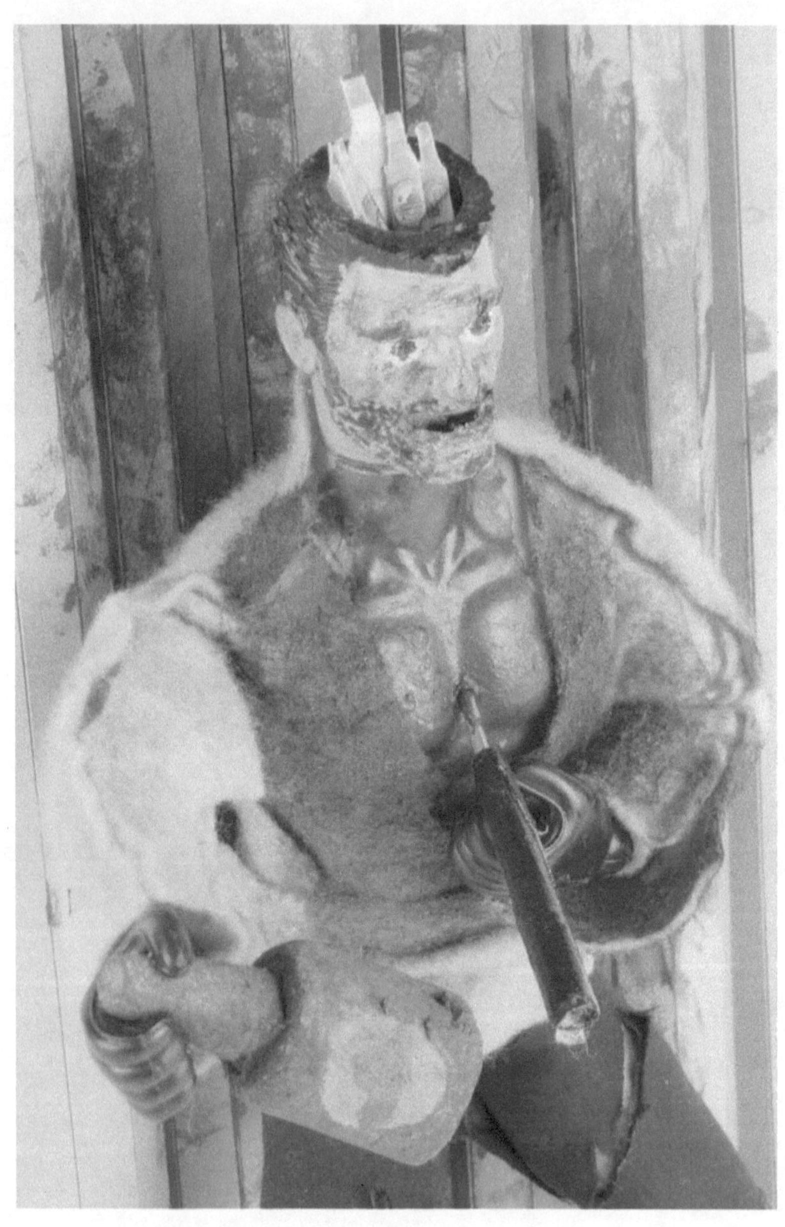

066
Peter Carey (a.k.a. Black Peter)
from "Black Peter"
Beatrice Toh

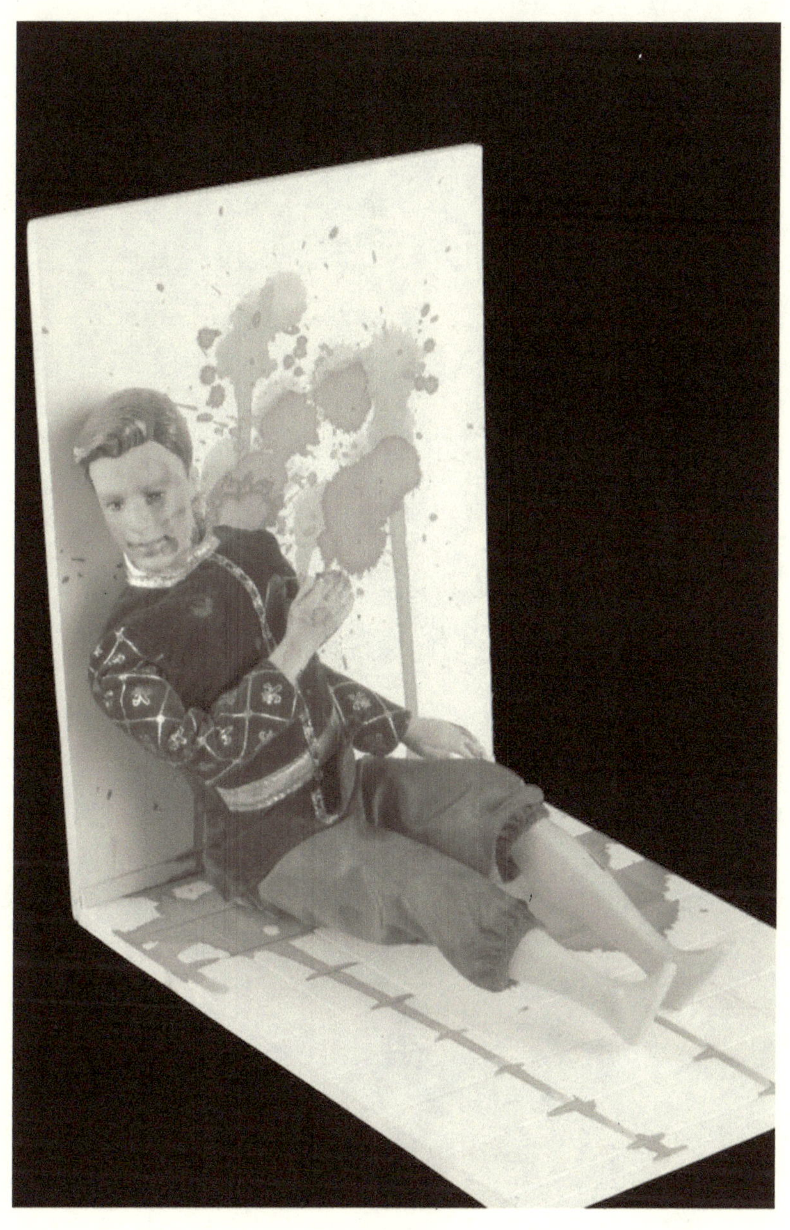

067
Charles Augustus Milverton
from "Charles Augustus Milverton
Craig Noyce

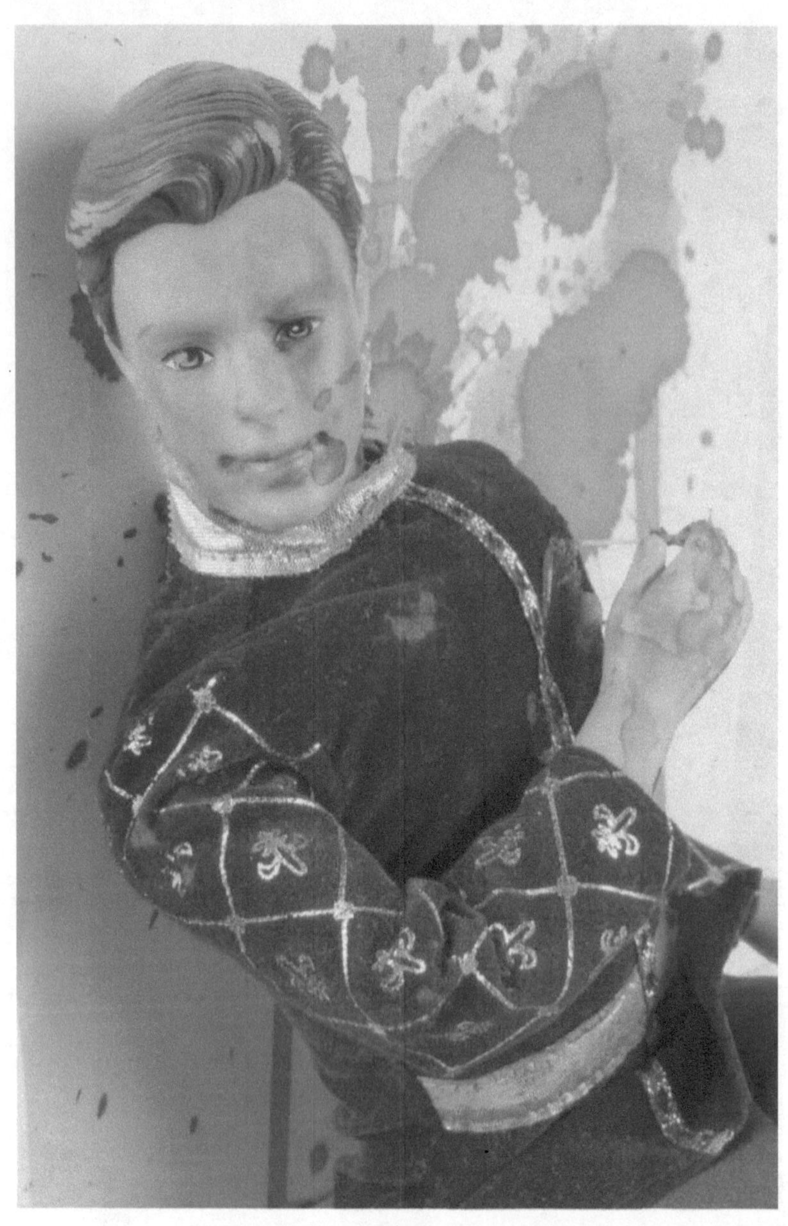

068
Charles Augustus Milverton
from "Charles Augustus Milverton
Craig Noyce

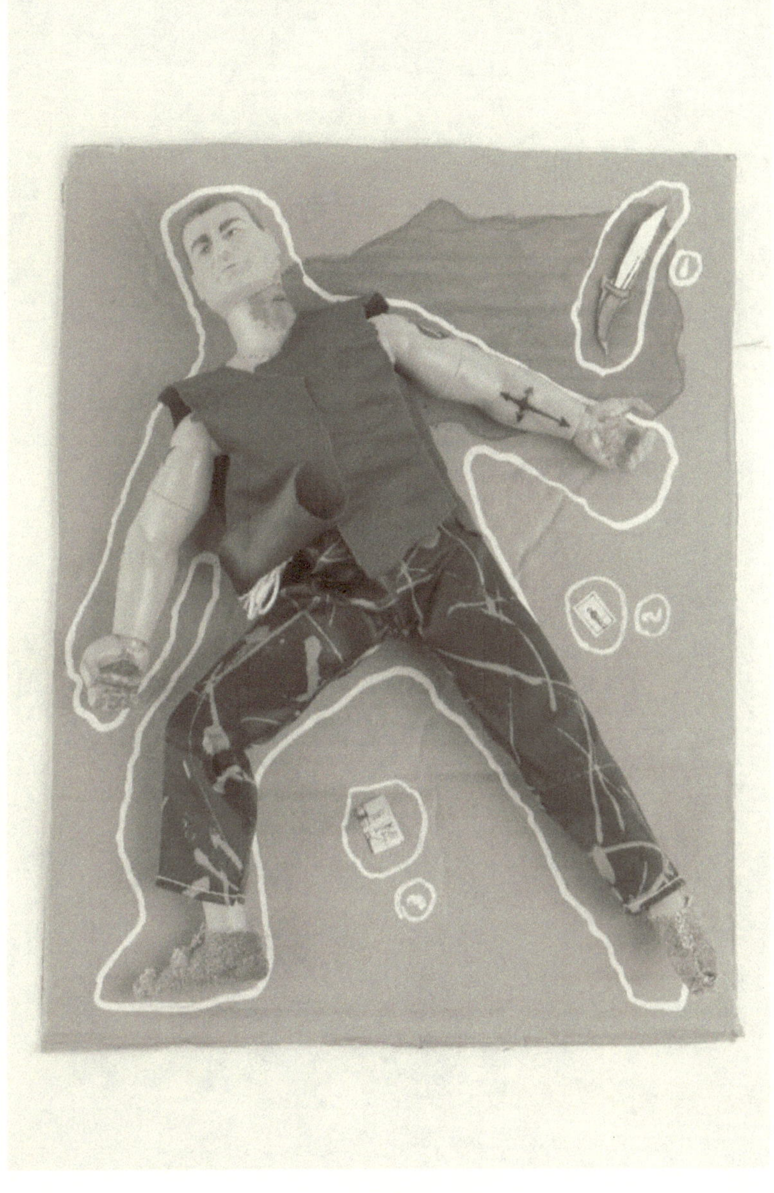

069
Pietro Venucci
from "The Six Napoleons"
Ng Yee Chung

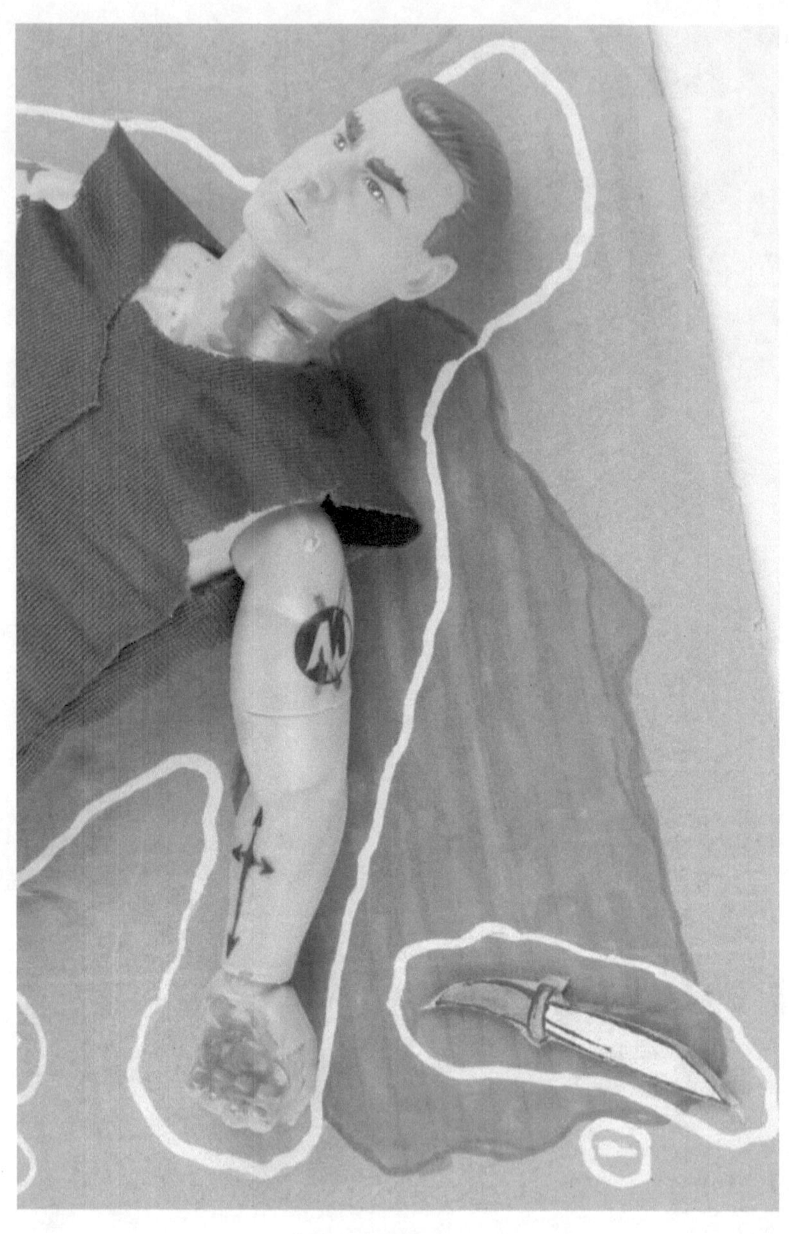

070
Pietro Venucci
from "The Six Napoleons"
Ng Yee Chung

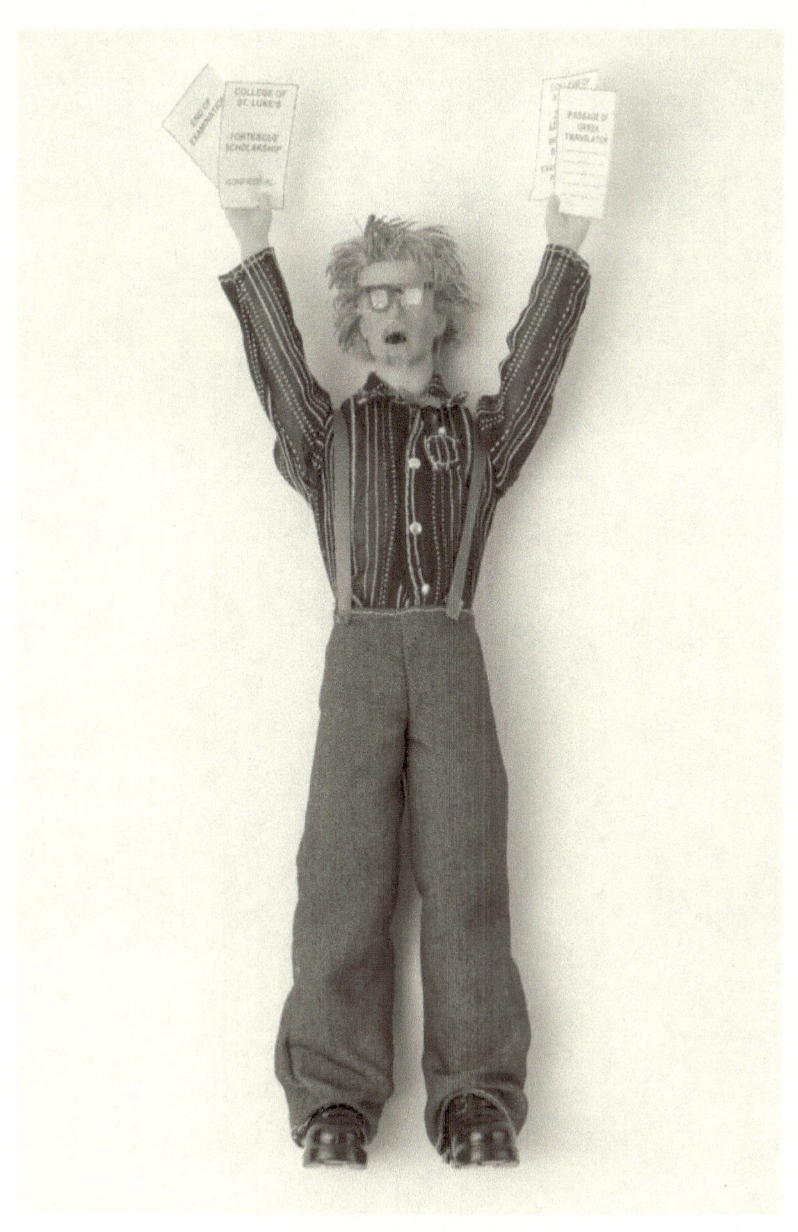

071
Hilton Soames
from "The Three Students"
Katie Miller

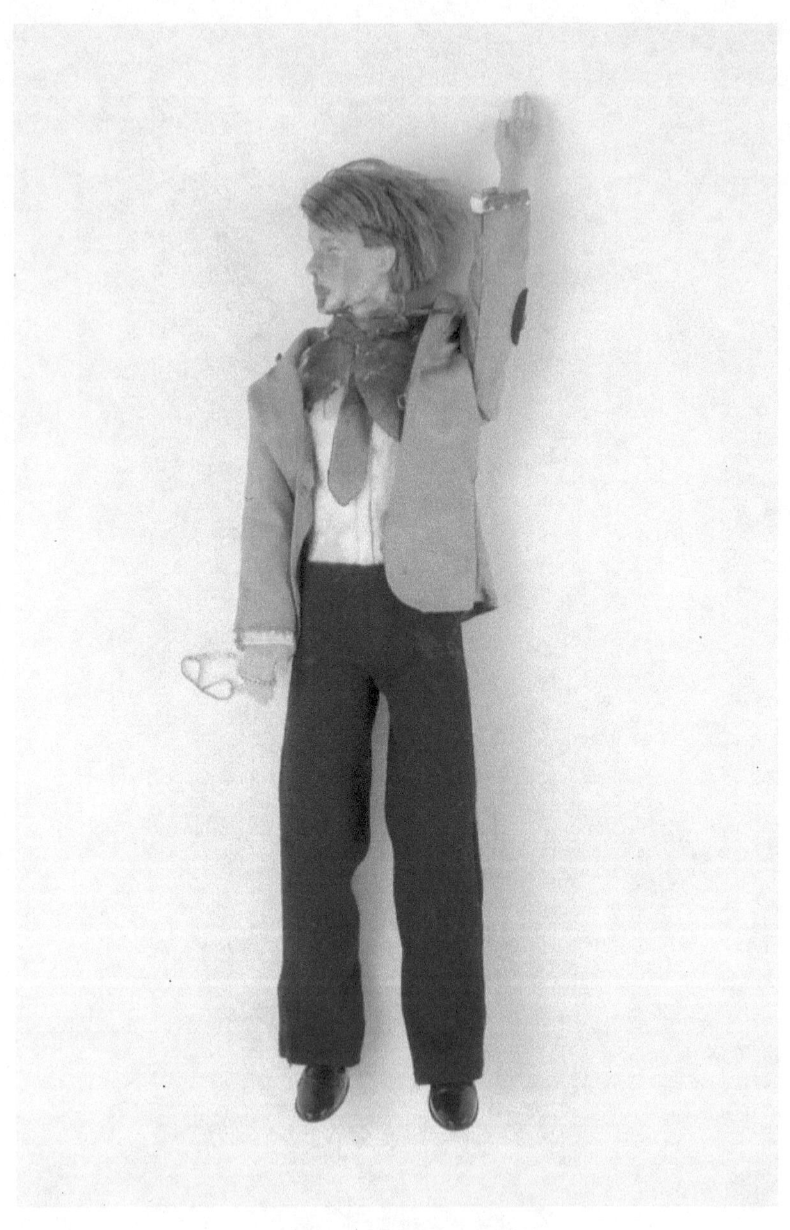

072
Willoughby Smith
from "The Golden Pince-Nez"
David Lazzarotto

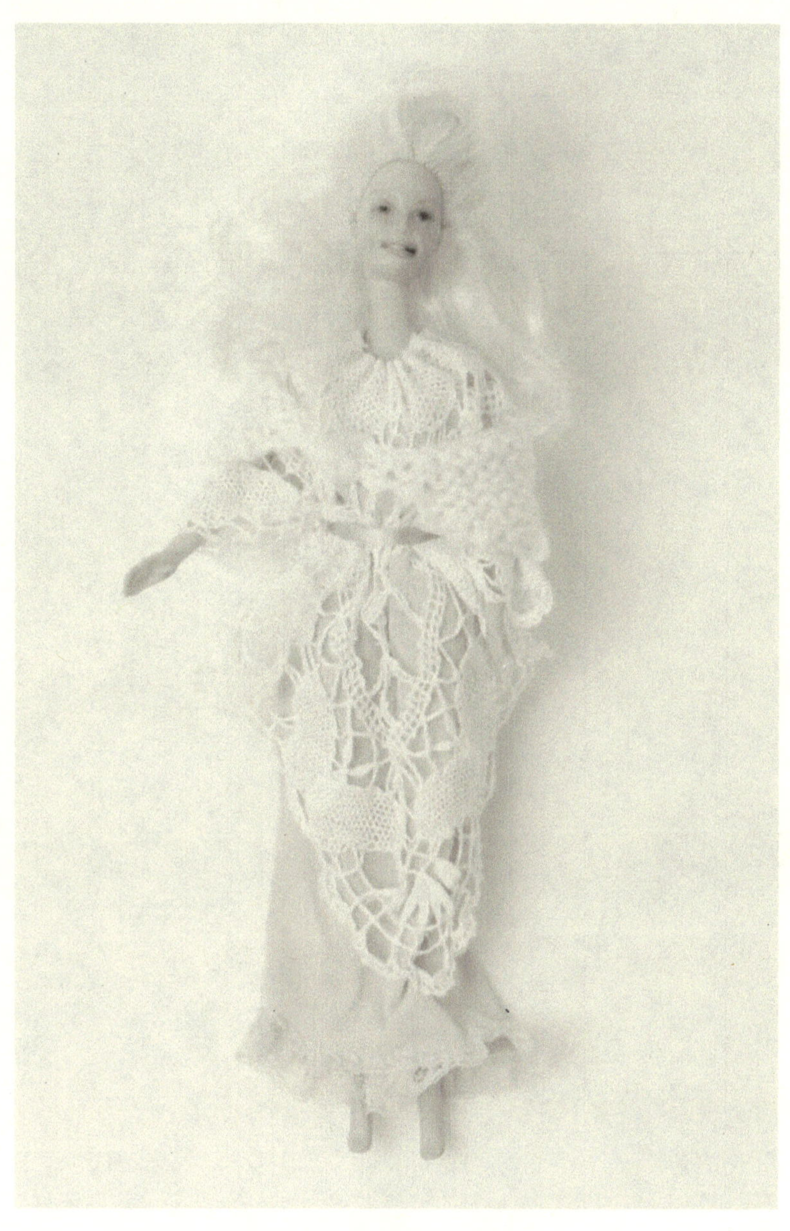

073
Mrs. Godfrey Staunton
from "The Missing Three-Quarter"
Kirilly Barnett

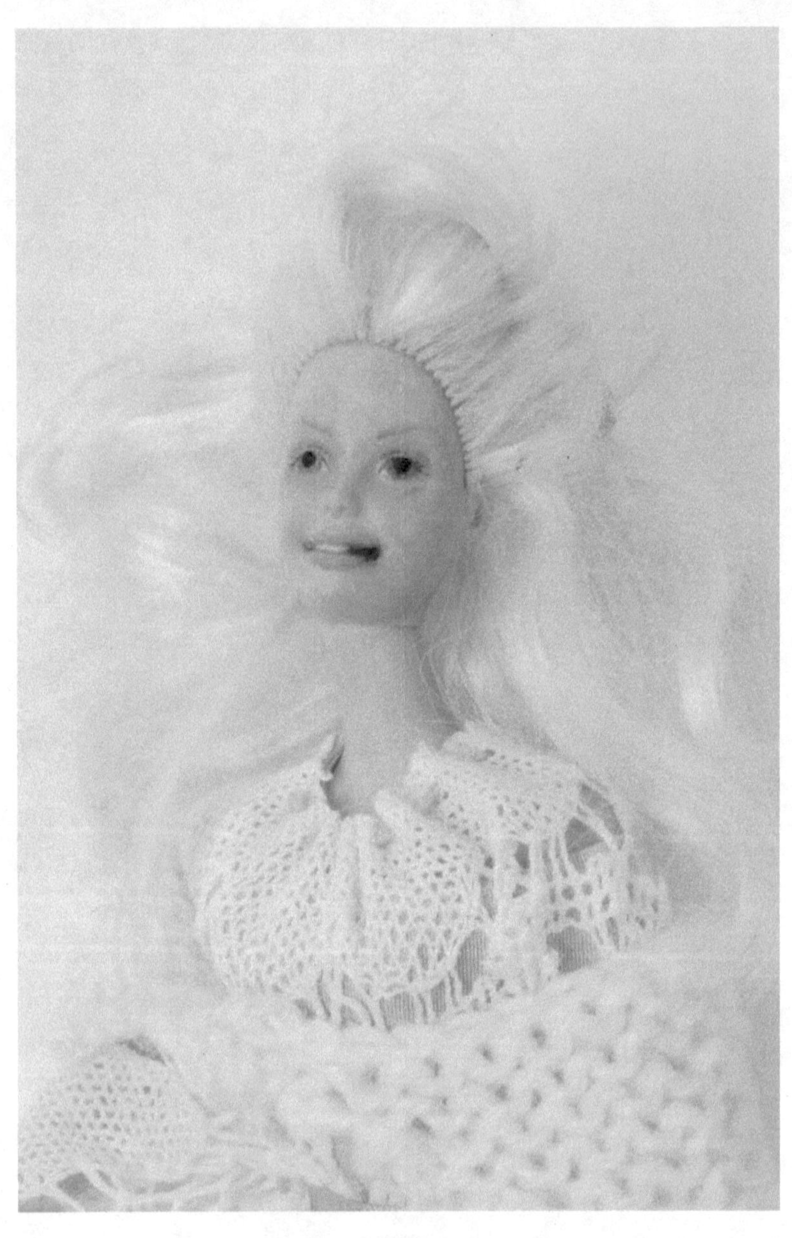

074
Mrs. Godfrey Staunton
from "The Missing Three-Quarter"
Kirilly Barnett

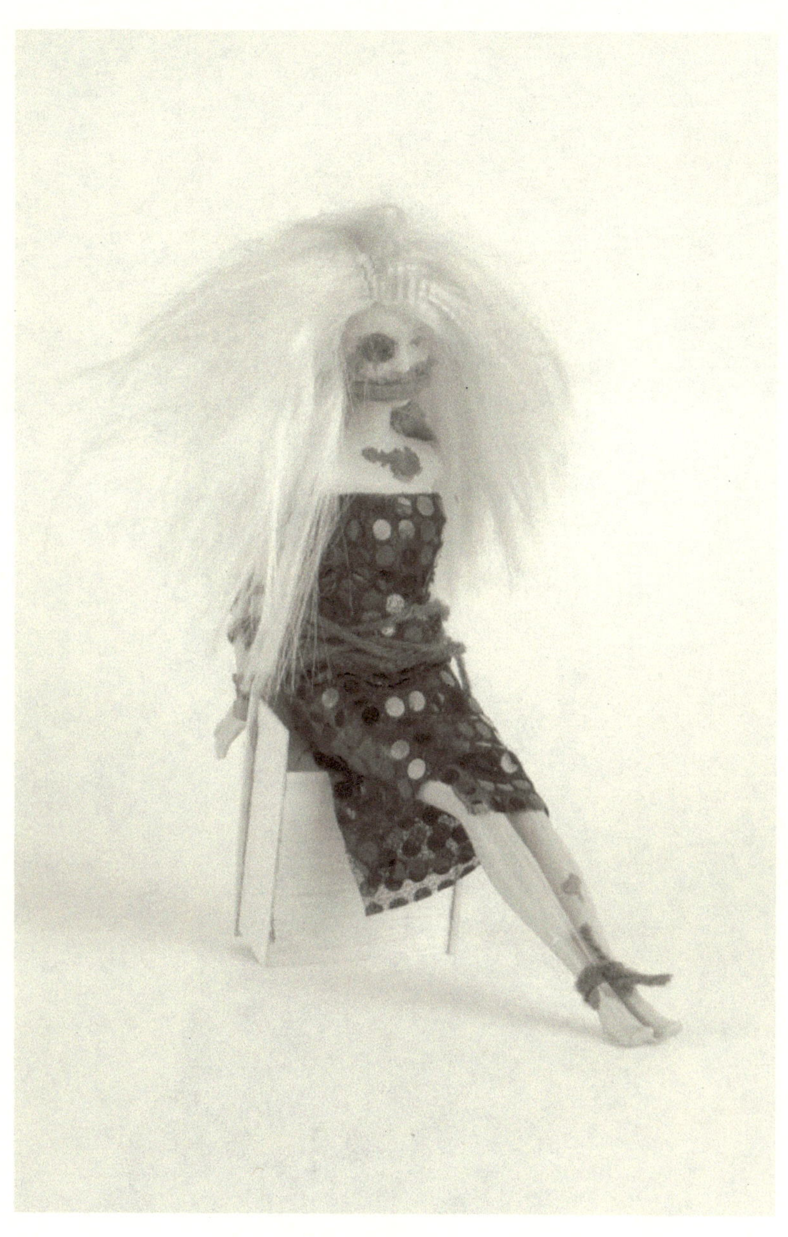

075
Lady Mary Brackenstall
from "The Abbey Grange"
Emily Stubbe

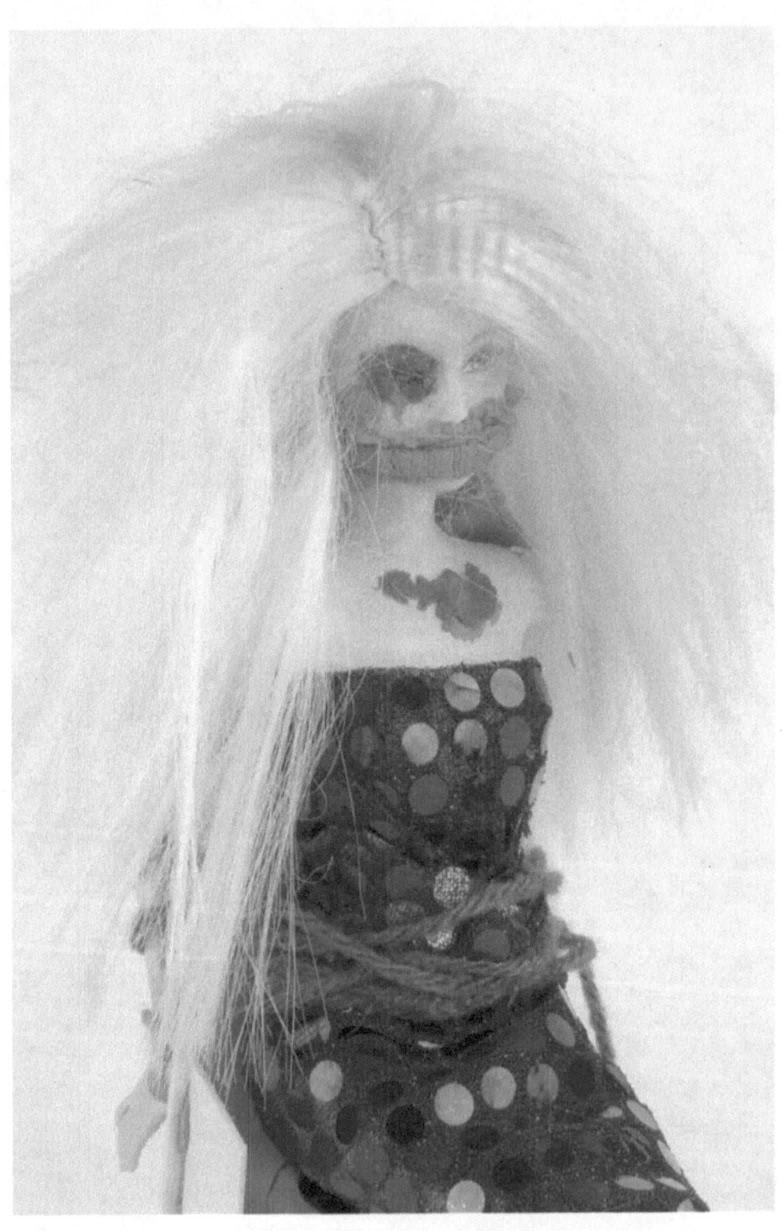

076
Lady Mary Brackenstall
from "The Abbey Grange"
Emily Stubbe

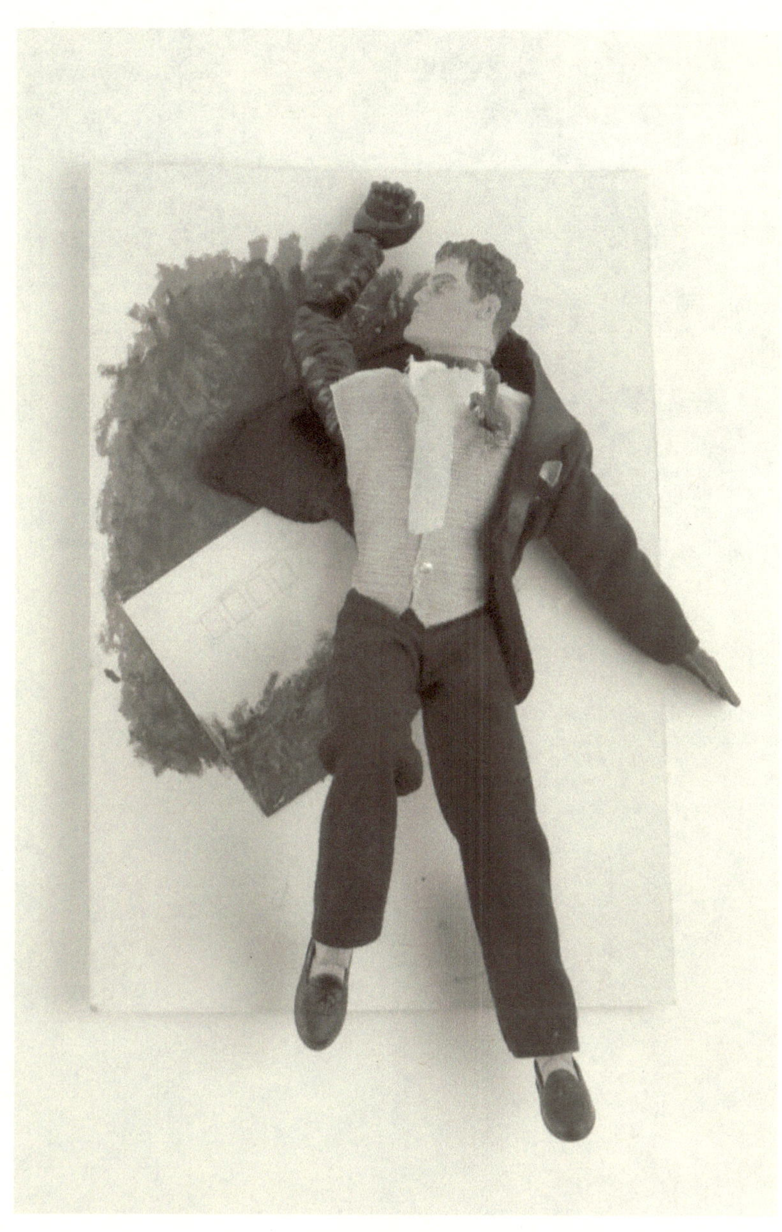

077
Eduardo Lucas
from "The Second Stain"
Naomi Clarke

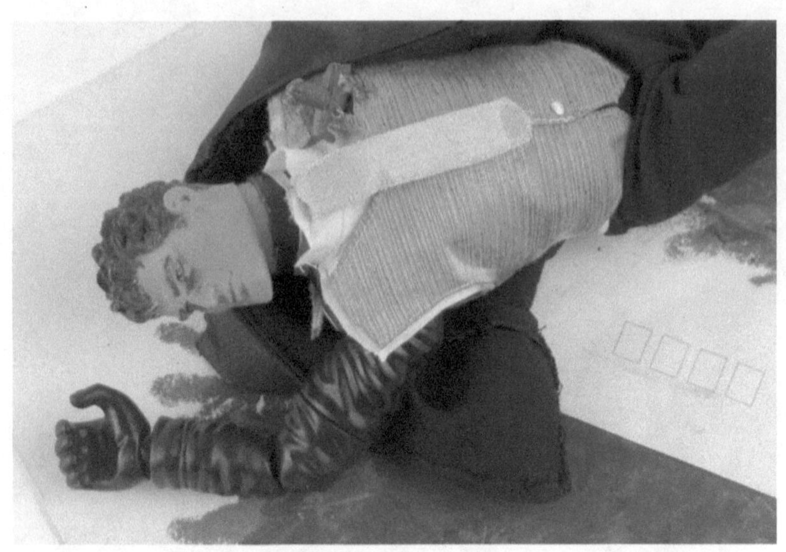

078
Eduardo Lucas
from "The Second Stain"
Naomi Clarke

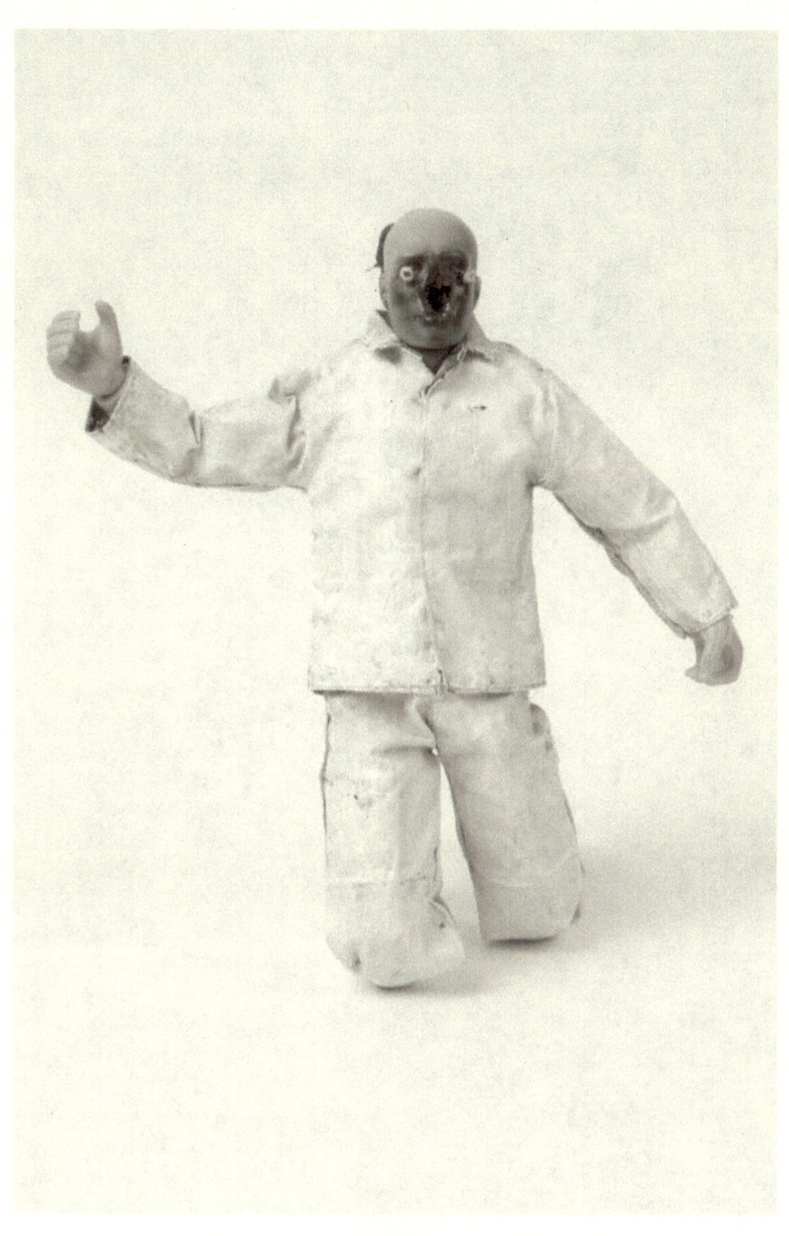

079
John Douglas
from The Valley of Fear
Harrison Wraight

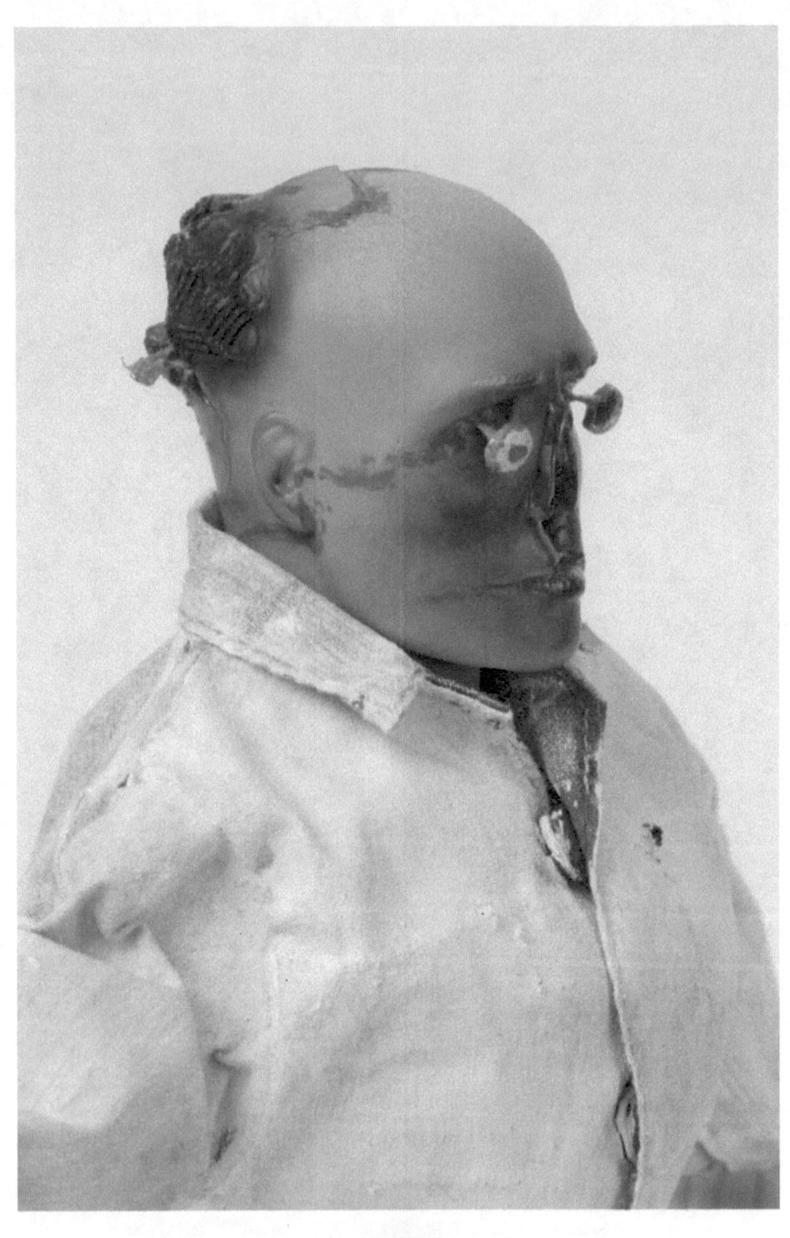

080
John Douglas
from The Valley of Fear
Harrison Wraight

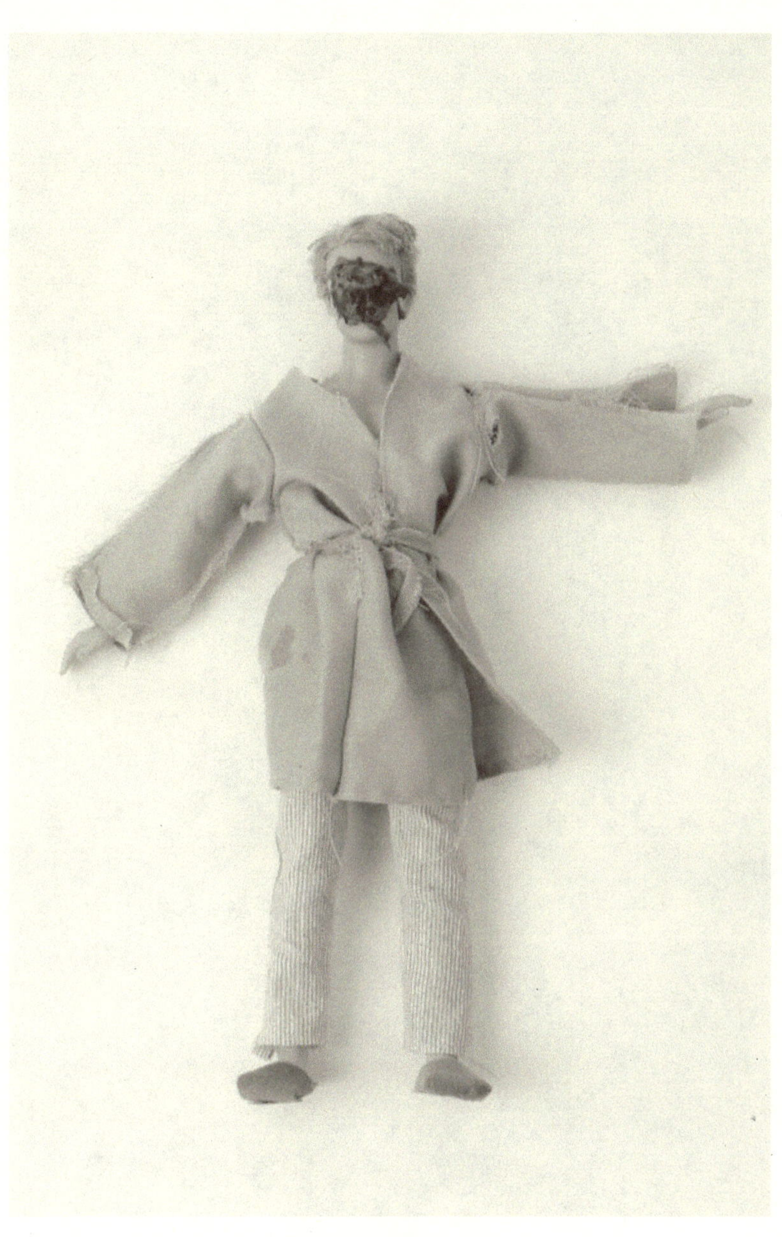

081
John Douglas
from The Valley of Fear
Alexandra Kennedy

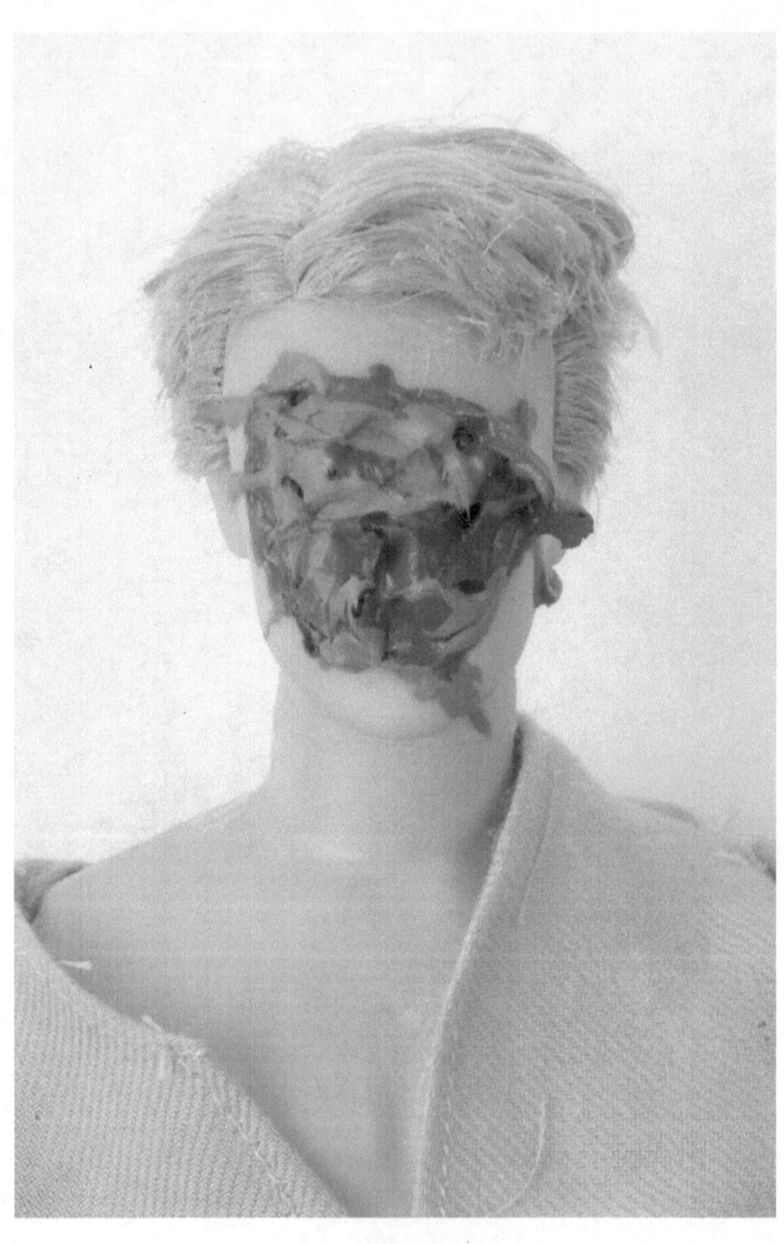

081
John Douglas
from The Valley of Fear
Alexandra Kennedy

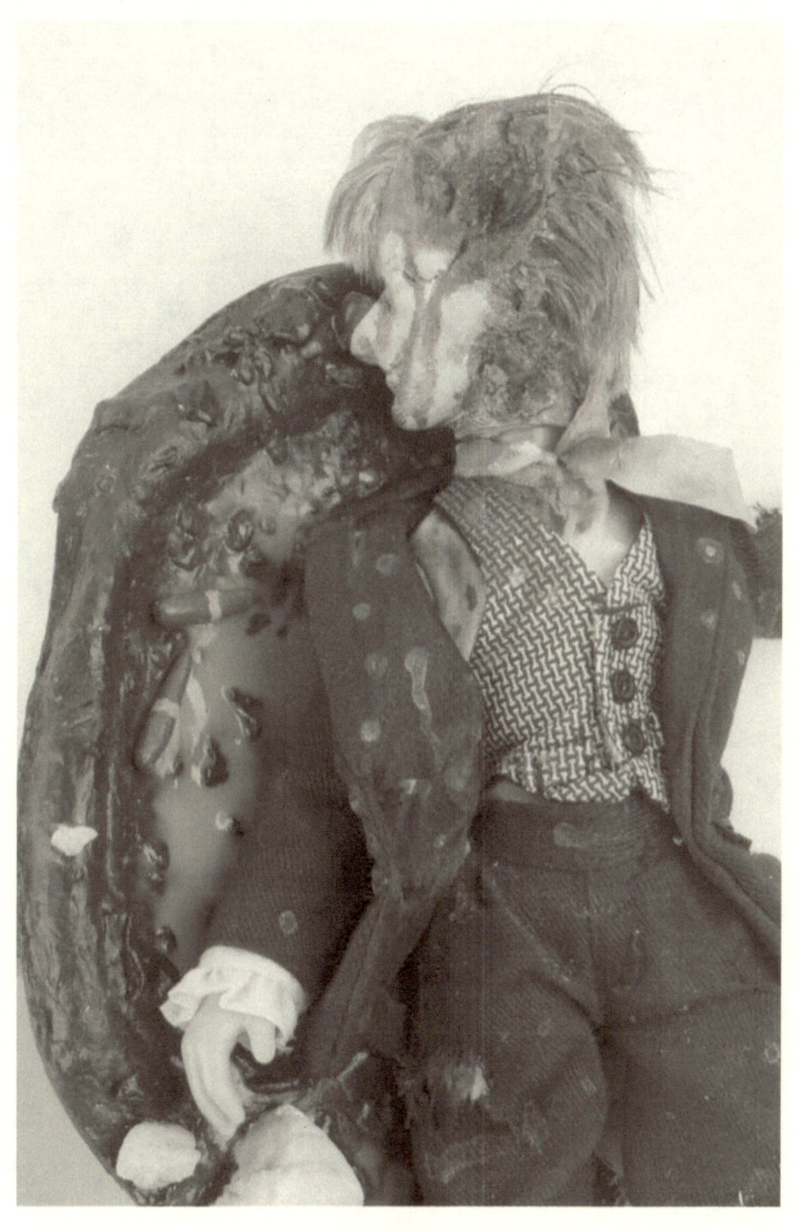

083
Aloysius Garcia
from "Wisteria Lodge"
Rachel Jones

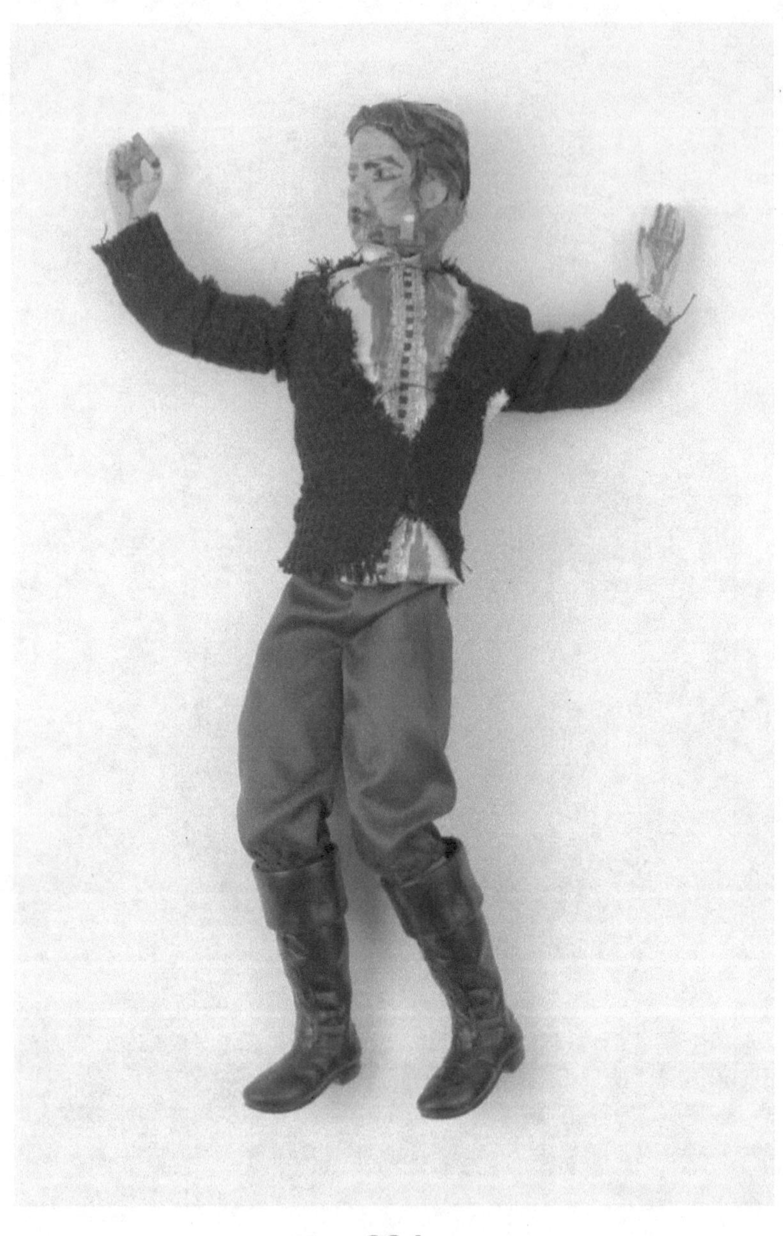

084
Giuseppe Gorgiano (a.k.a. Black Gorgiano)
from "The Red Circle"
Esther Lau Der Lyn

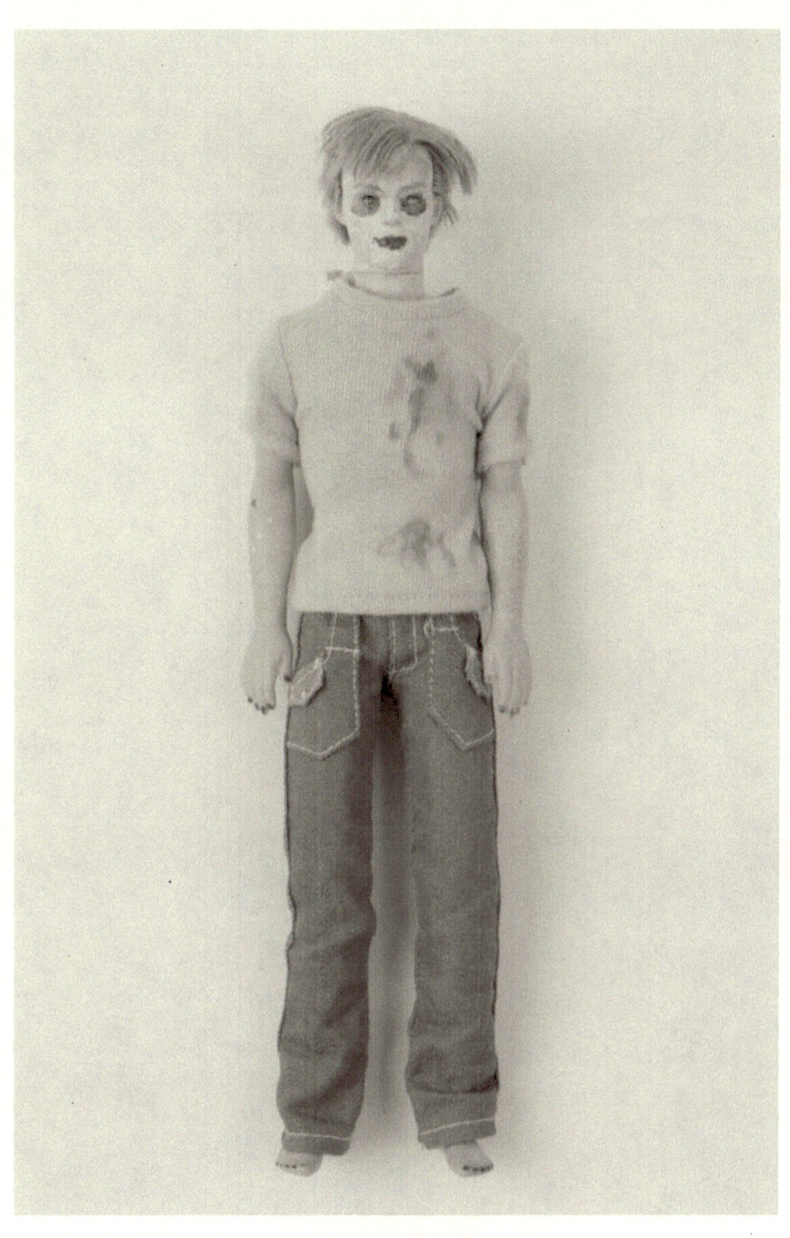

085
Sherlock Holmes
from "The Dying Detective"
Lee Fong Chin

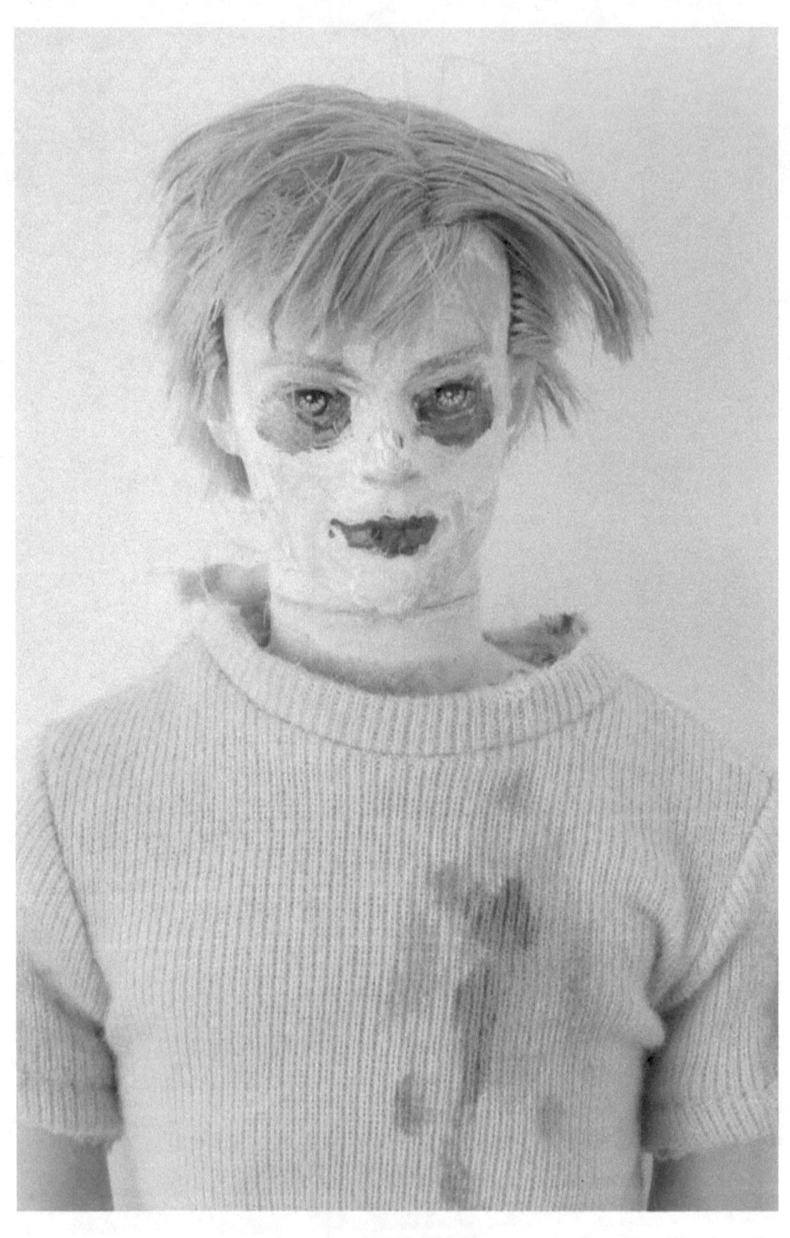

086
Sherlock Holmes
from "The Dying Detective"
Lee Fong Chin

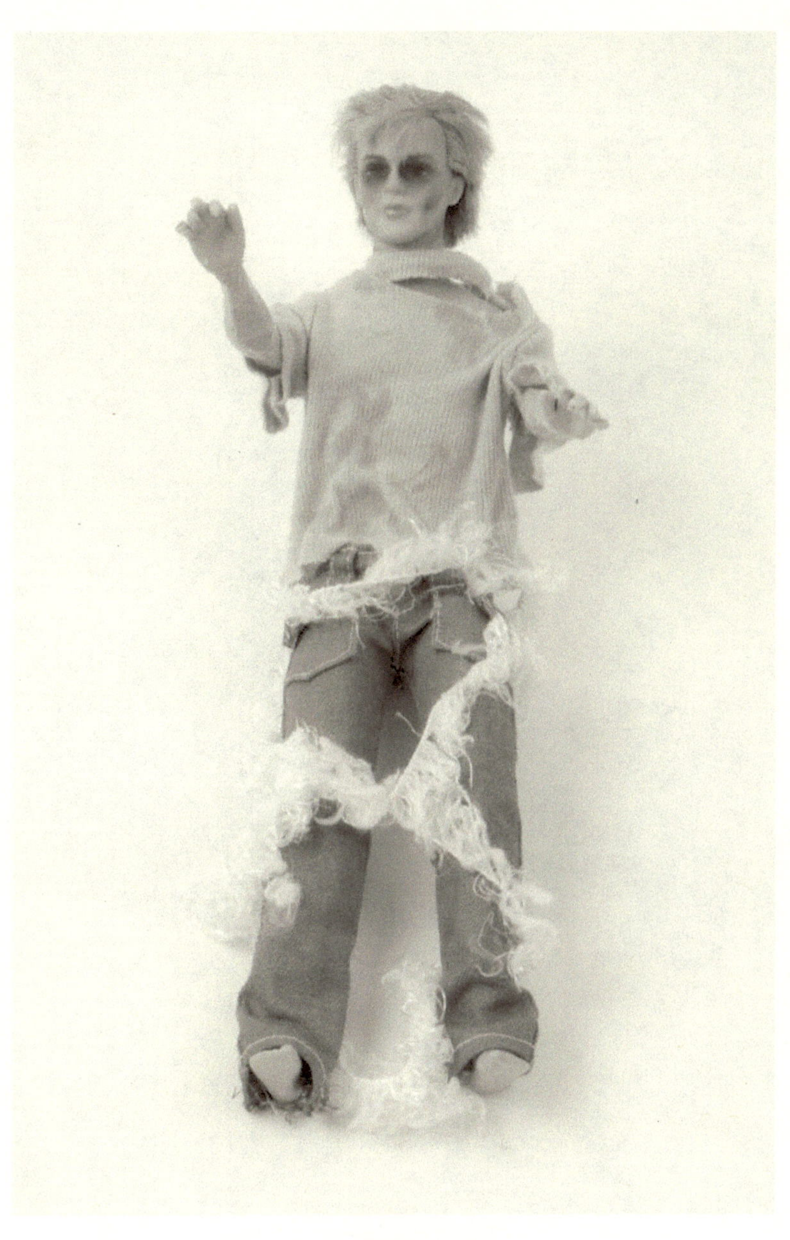

087
Victor Smith
from "The Dying Detective"
Frankie Siu

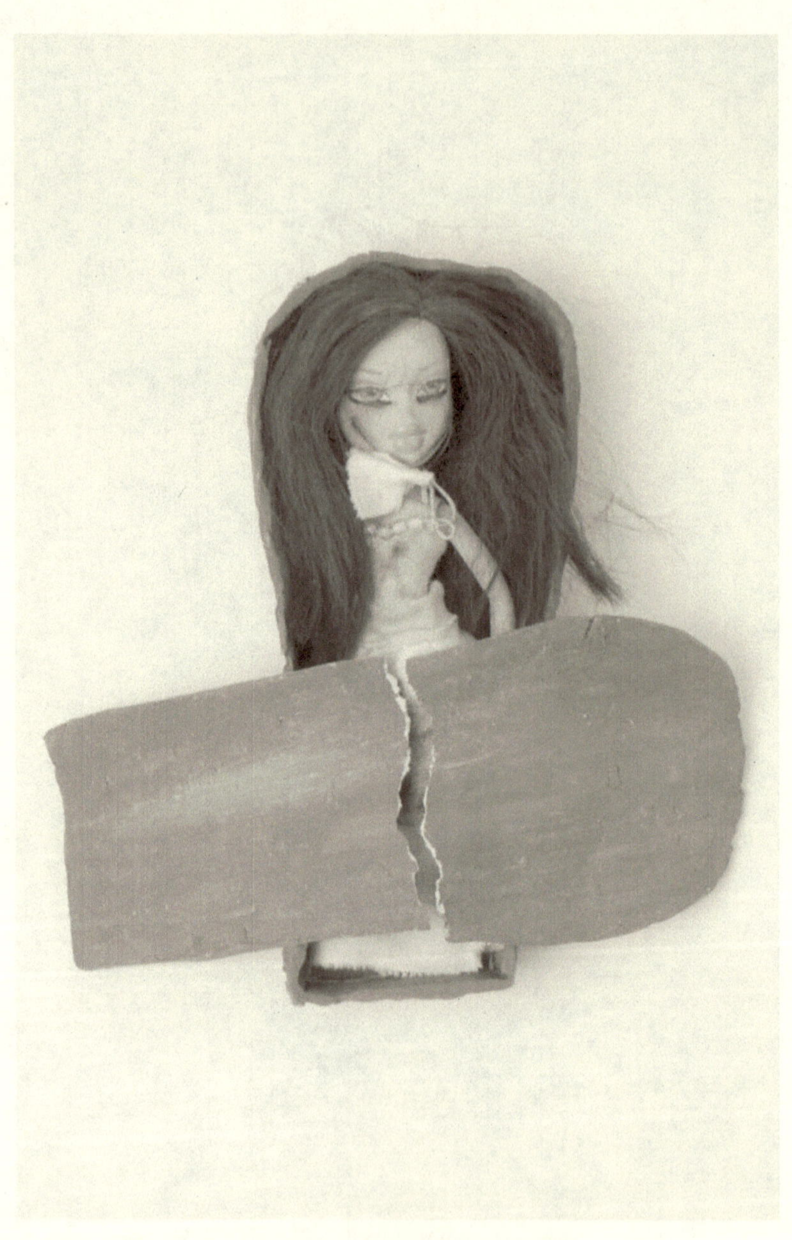

088
Lady Frances Carfax
from "The Disappearance
of Lady Frances Carfax
Chin Siong Ong

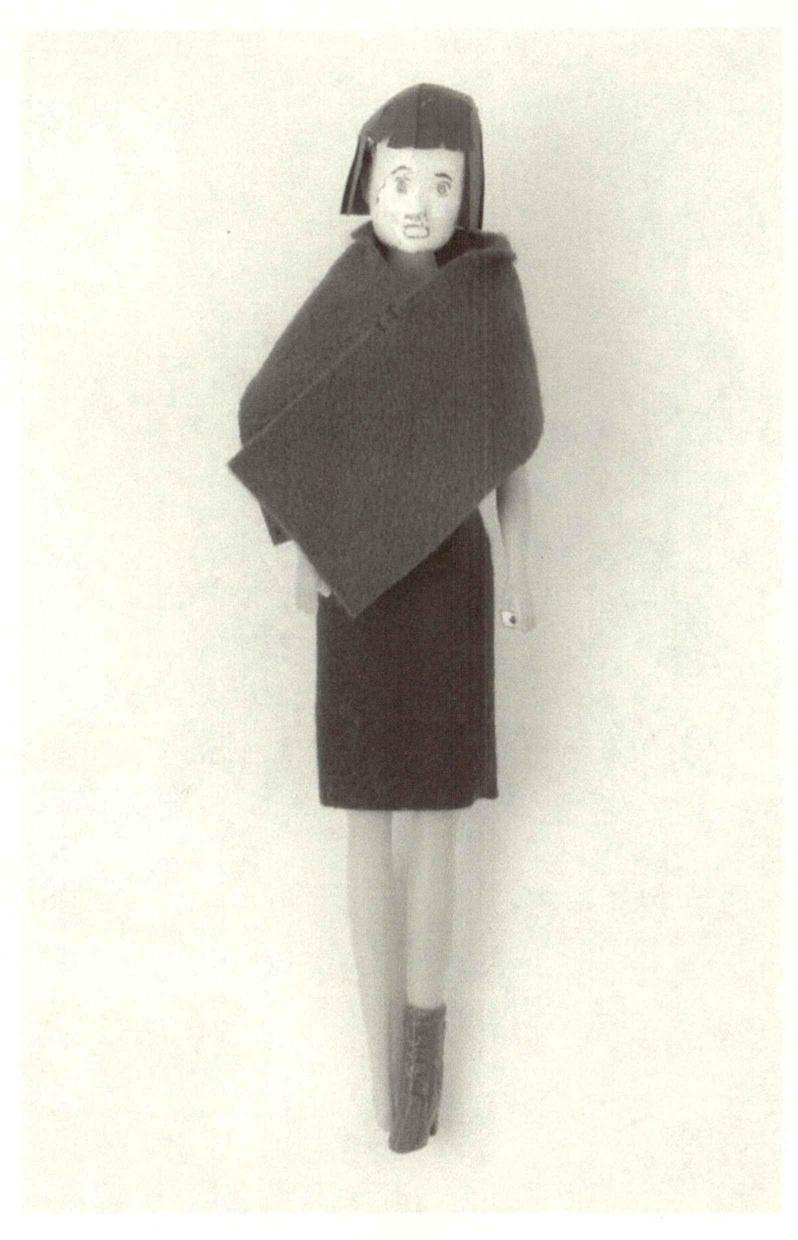

089
Brenda Tregennis
from "The Devil's Foot"
Daveen Ma

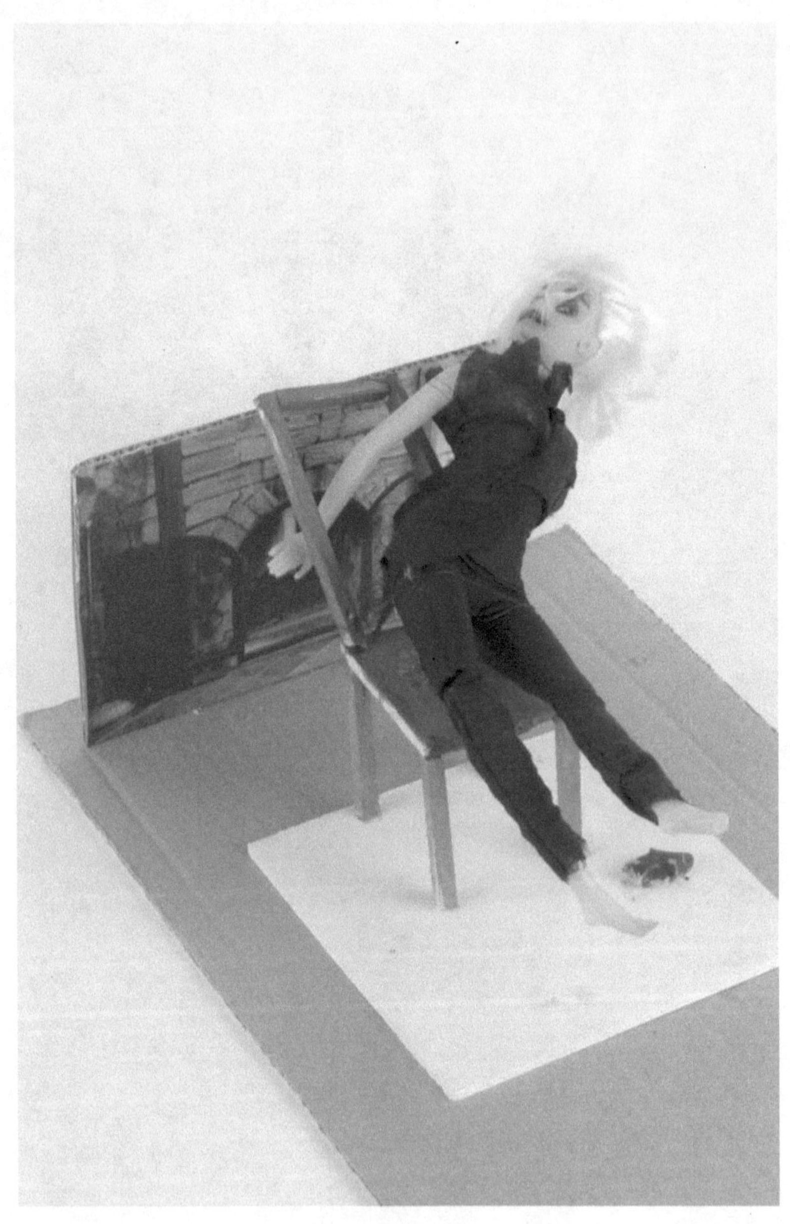

090
Brenda Tregennis
from "The Devil's Foot"
Fay Gong

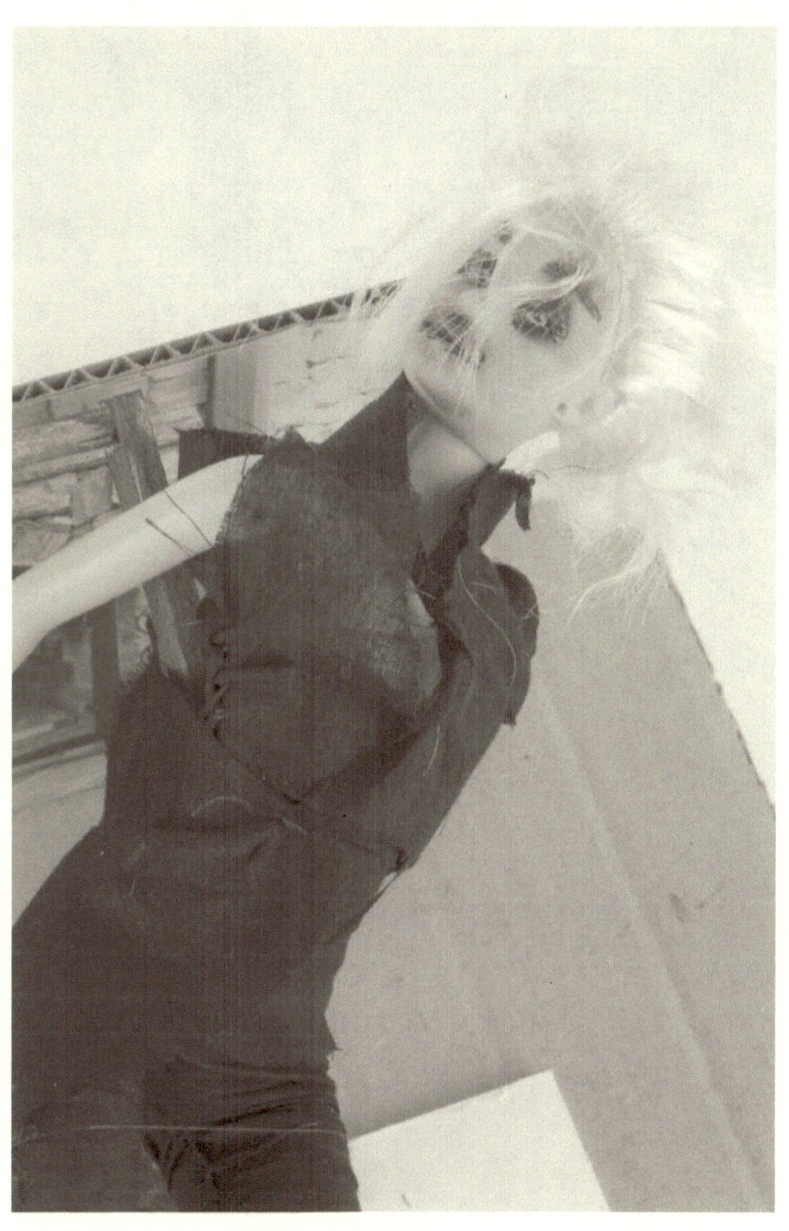

090
Brenda Tregennis
from "The Devil's Foot"
Fay Gong

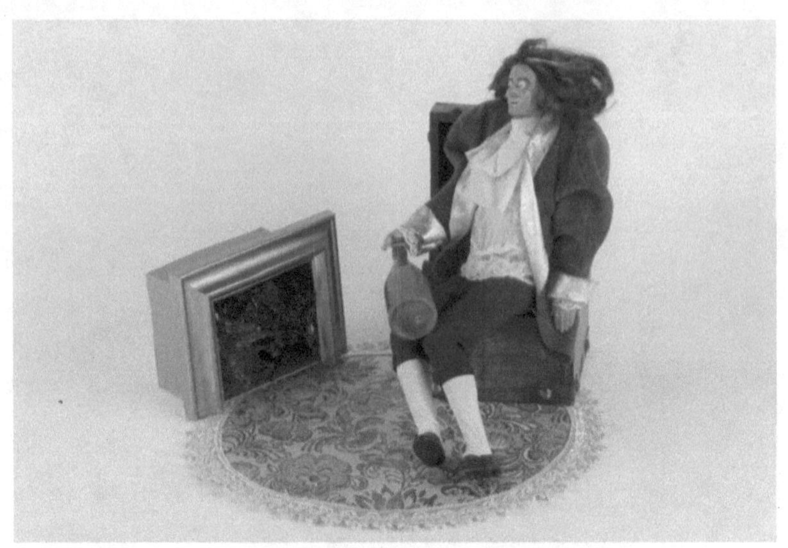

092
George Tregennis
from "The Devil's Foot"
Nicholas Antoniou

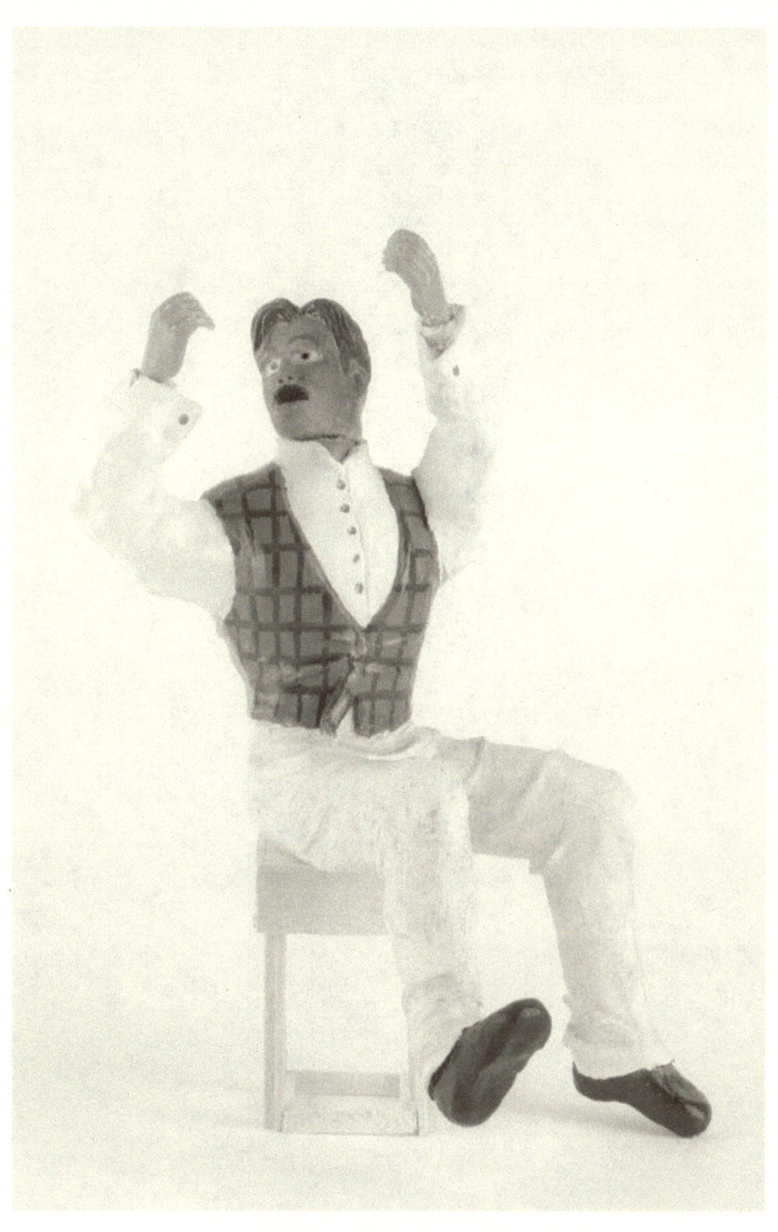

093
Mortimer Tregennis
from "The Devil's Foot"
Rayman Chung

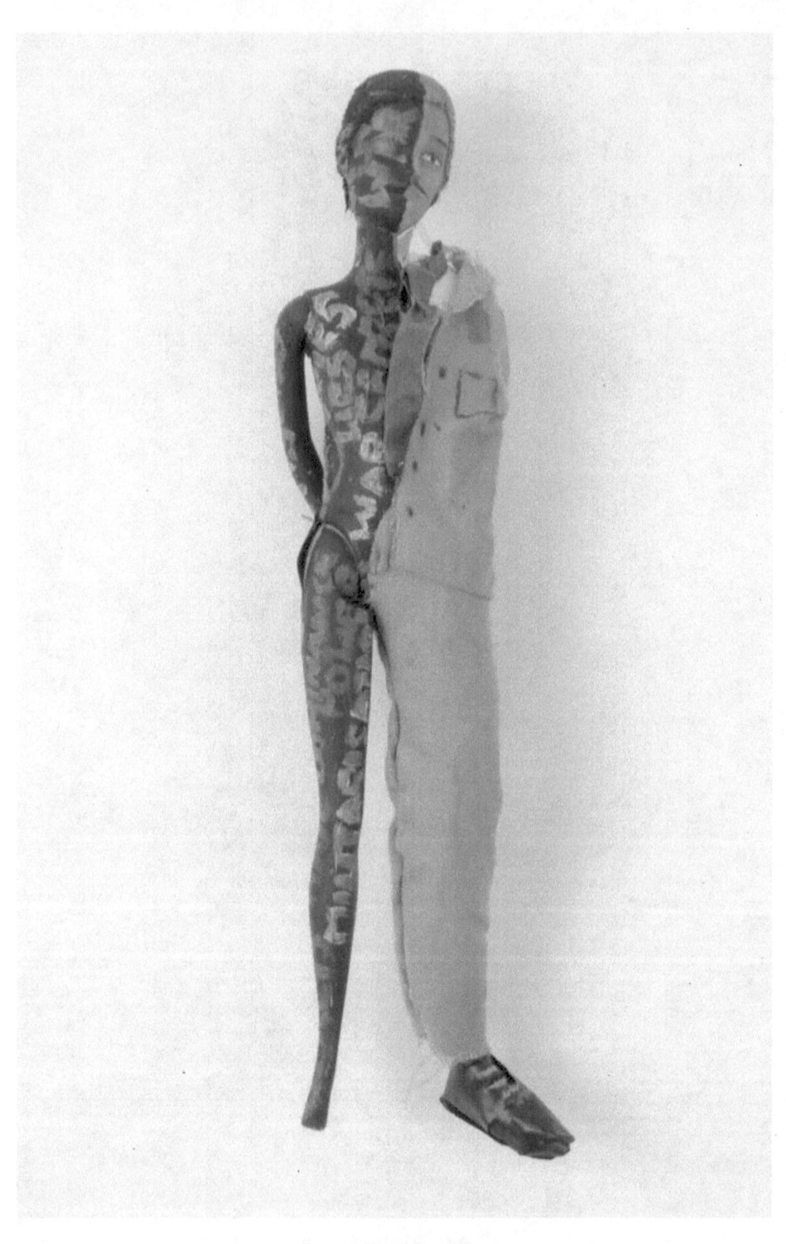

094
Von Bork
"His Last Bow"
Claire Welsh

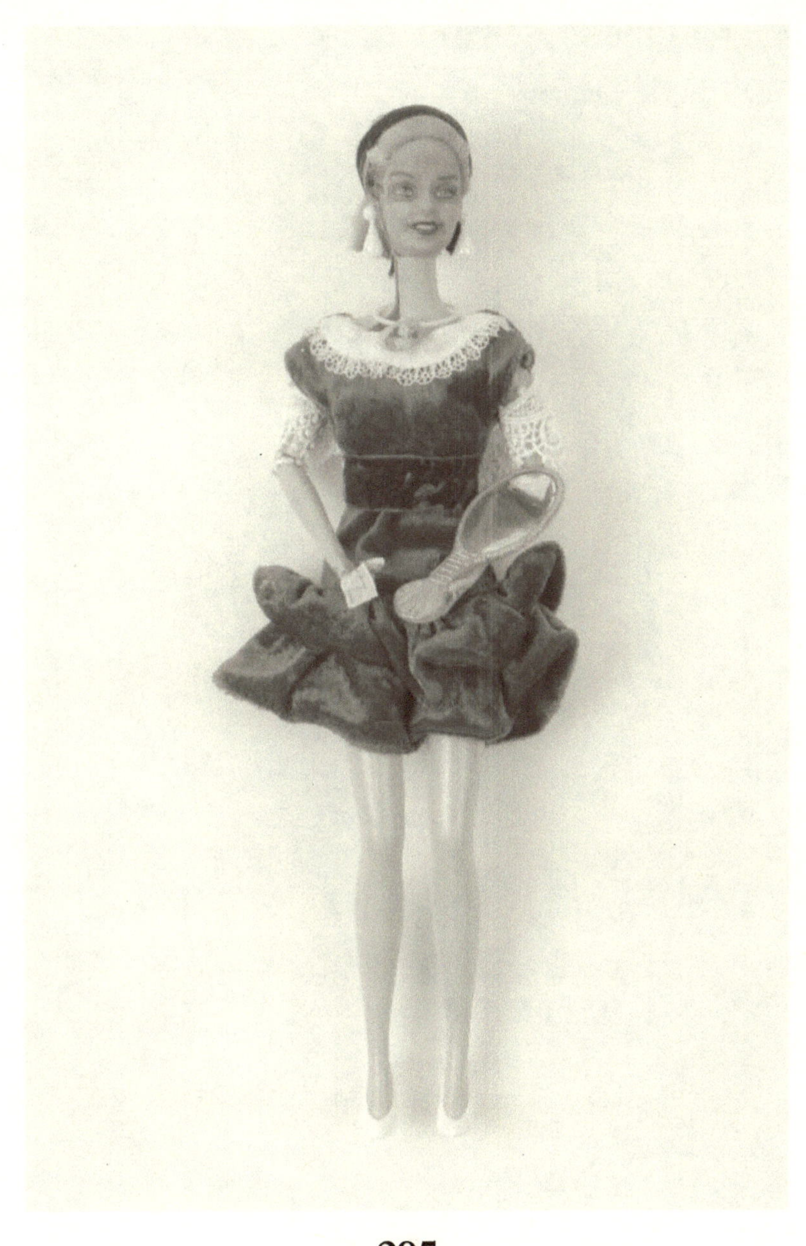

095
Maria Pinto
from "The Problem of Thor Bridge"
Tahlee Bruch

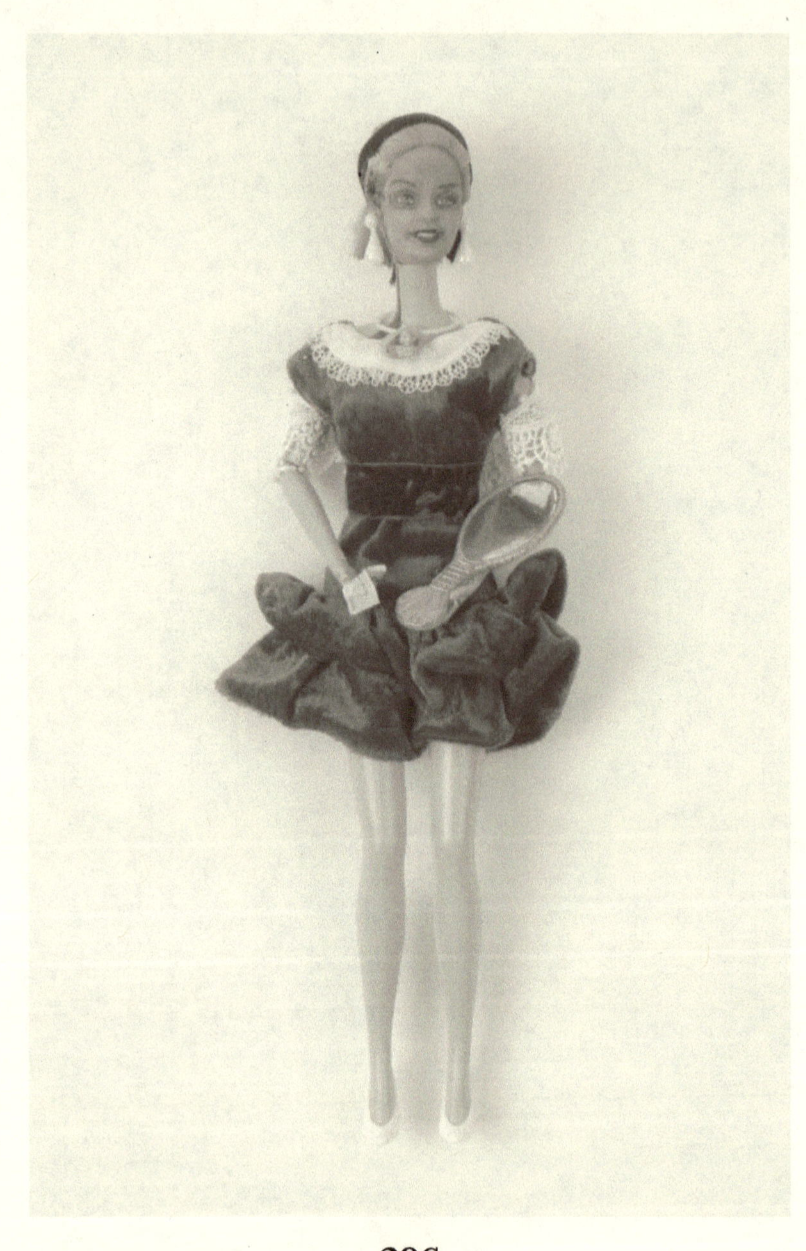

096
Maria Pinto
from "The Problem of Thor Bridge"
Tahlee Bruch

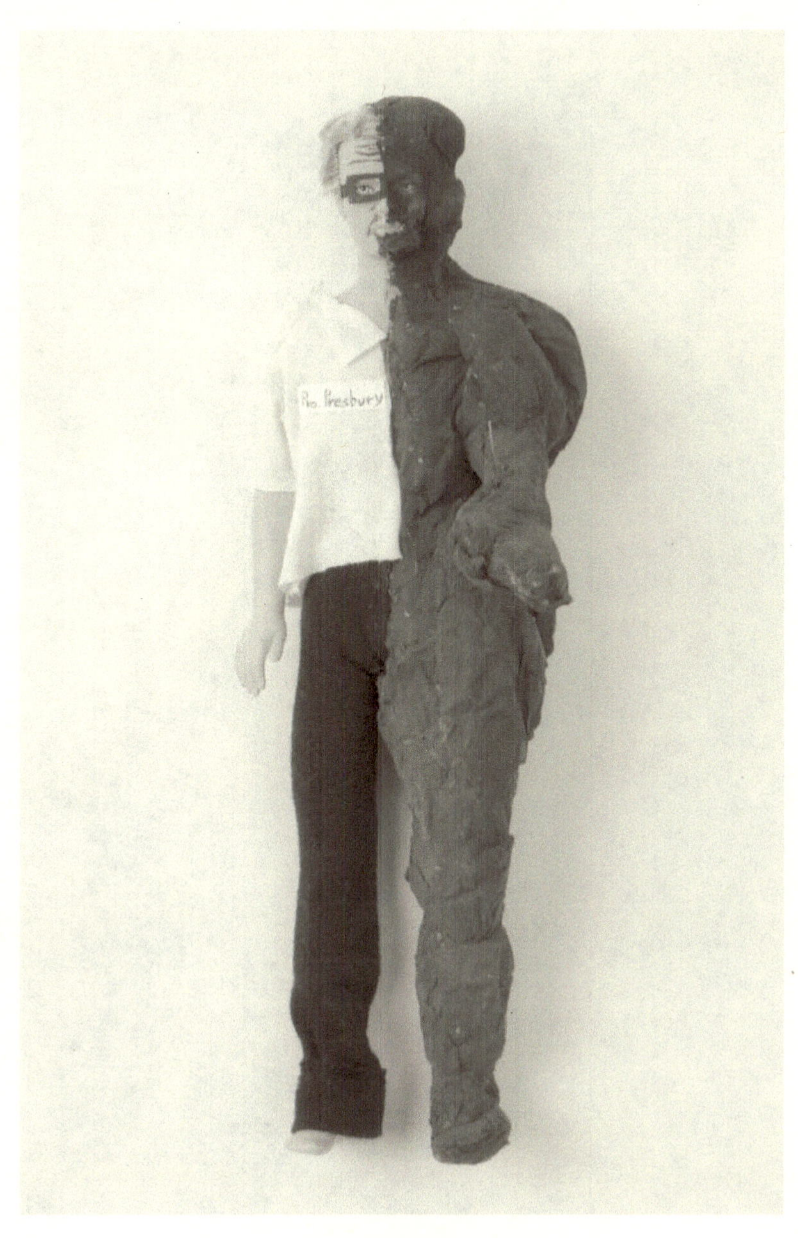

097
Professor Presbury
from "The Creeping Man"
Fung Hin Mang

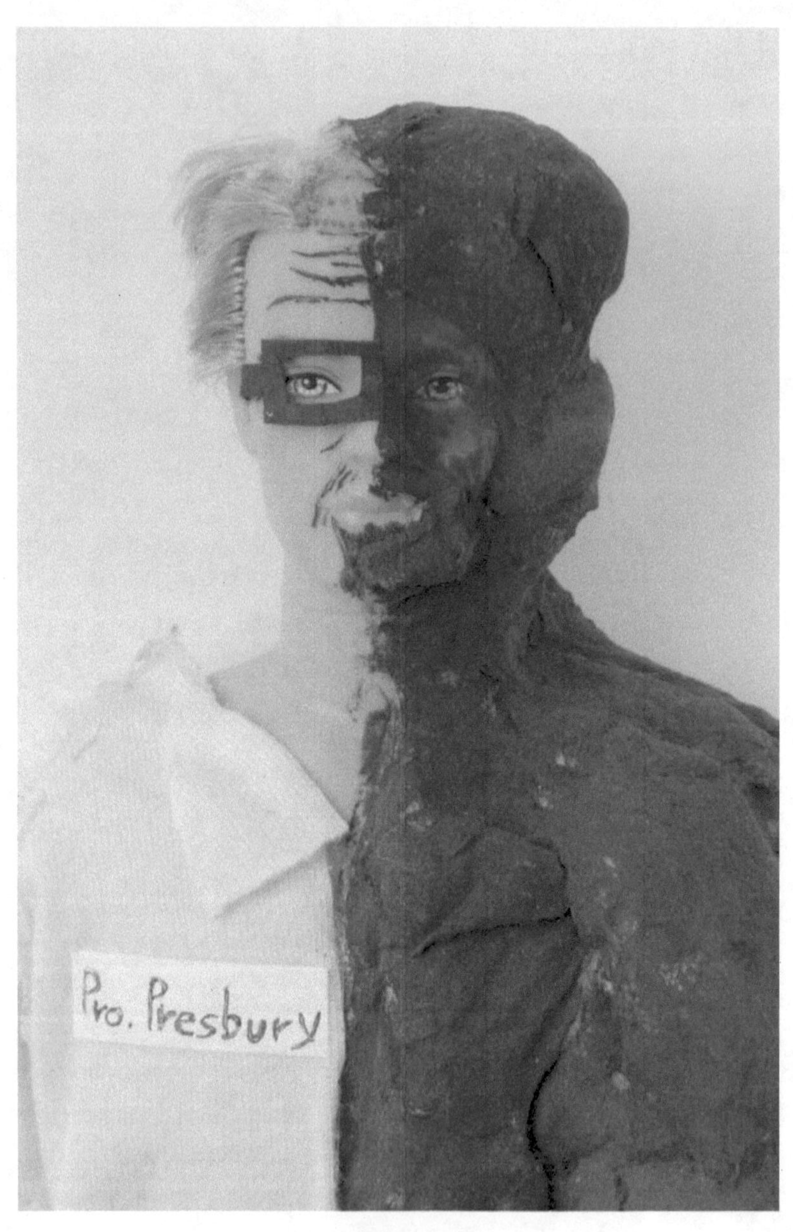

098
Professor Presbury
from "The Creeping Man"
Fung Hin Mang

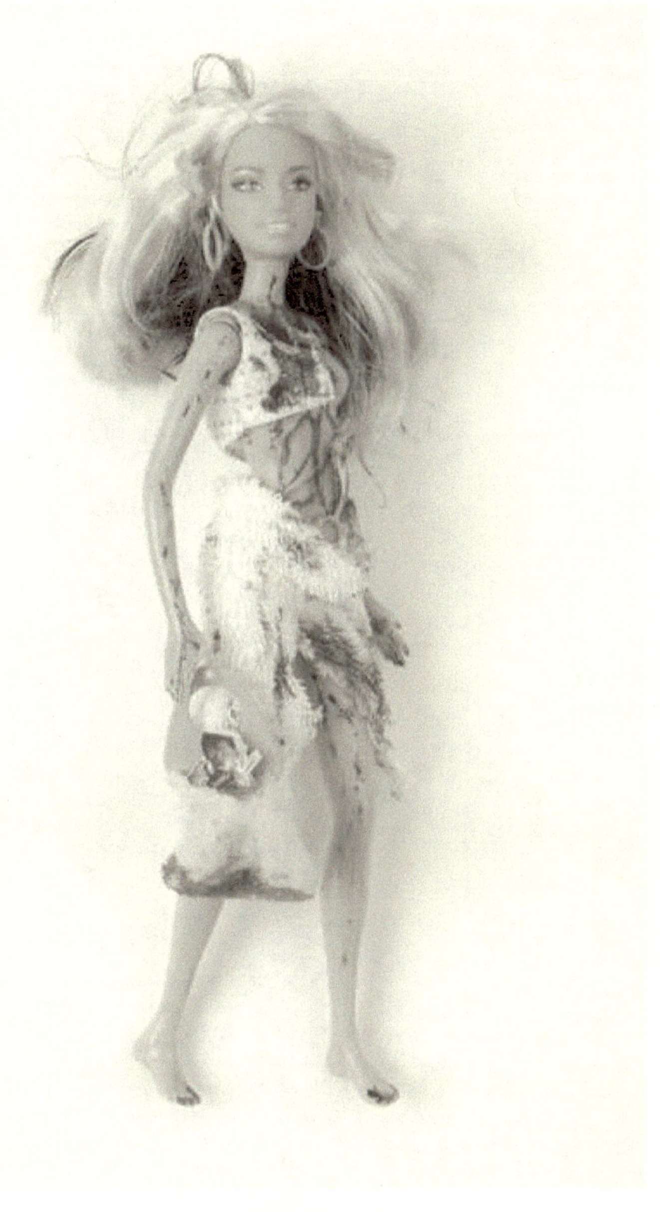

099
Mrs. Fergusson
from "The Sussex Vampire"
Koe Hock Chuan

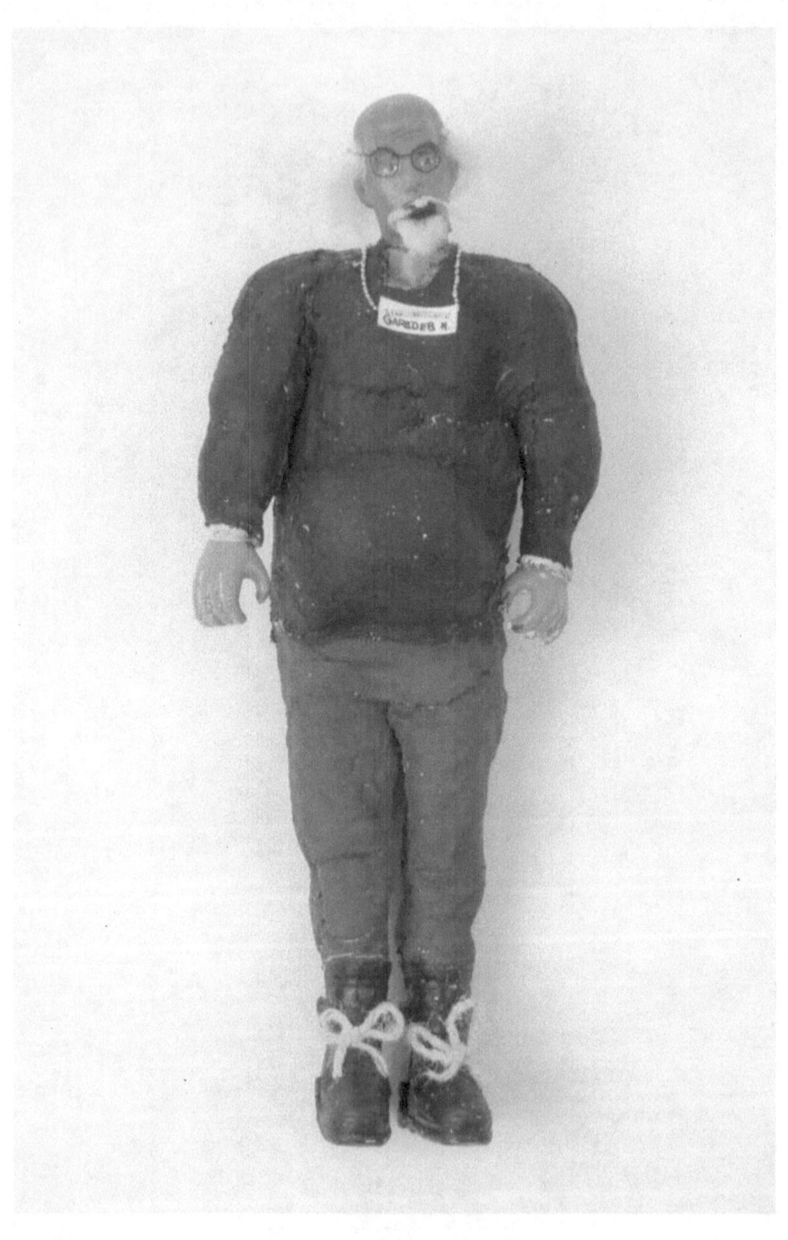

100
Nathan Garrideb
from "The Three Garridebs"
Dana Shandler

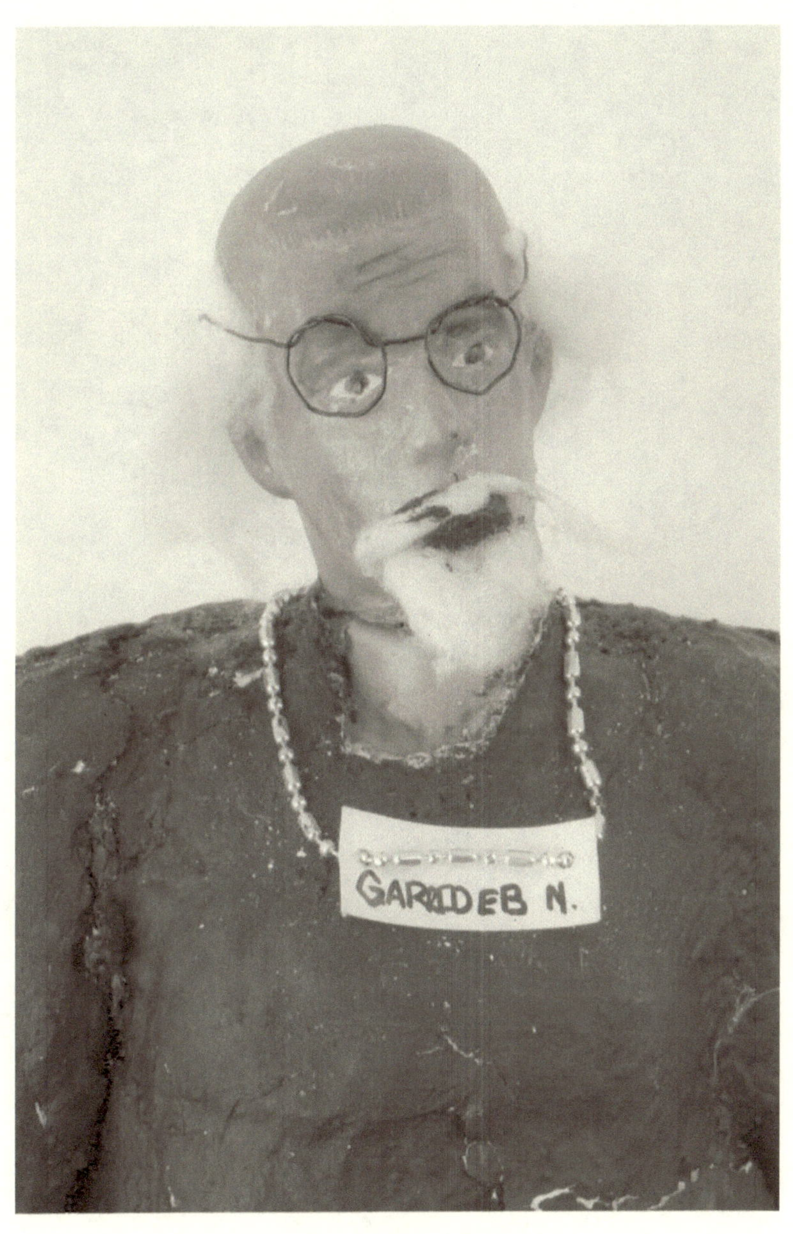

101
Nathan Garrideb
from "The Three Garridebs"
Dana Shandler

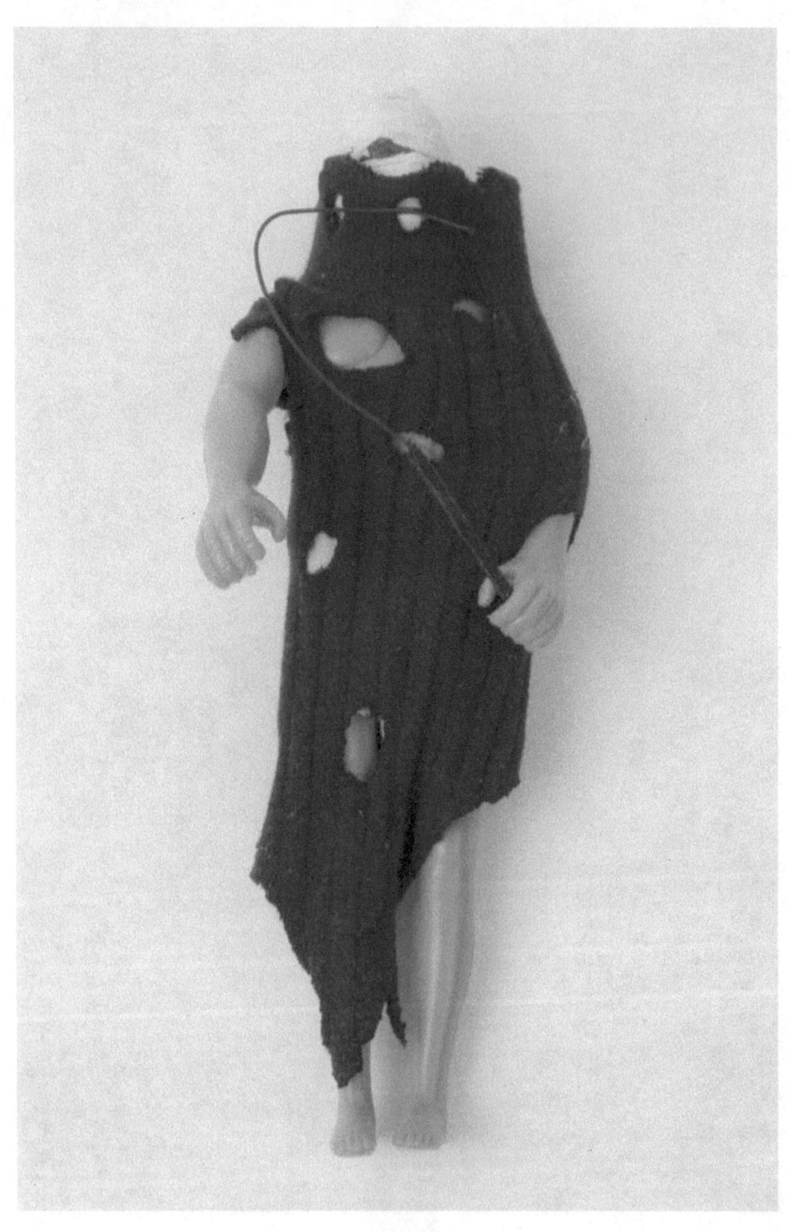

102
Baron Adelbert Gruner
from "The Illustrious Client"
Gong Chen

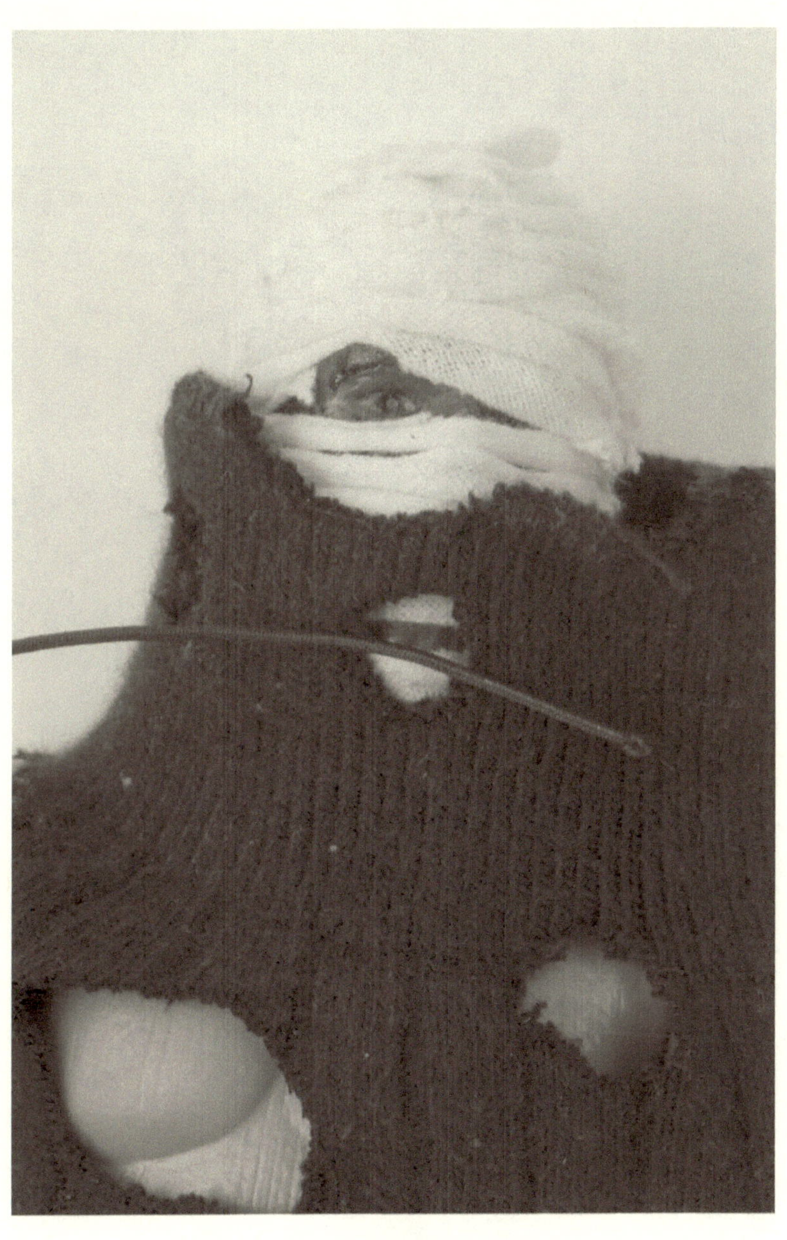

103
Baron Adelbert Gruner
from "The Illustrious Client"
Gong Chen

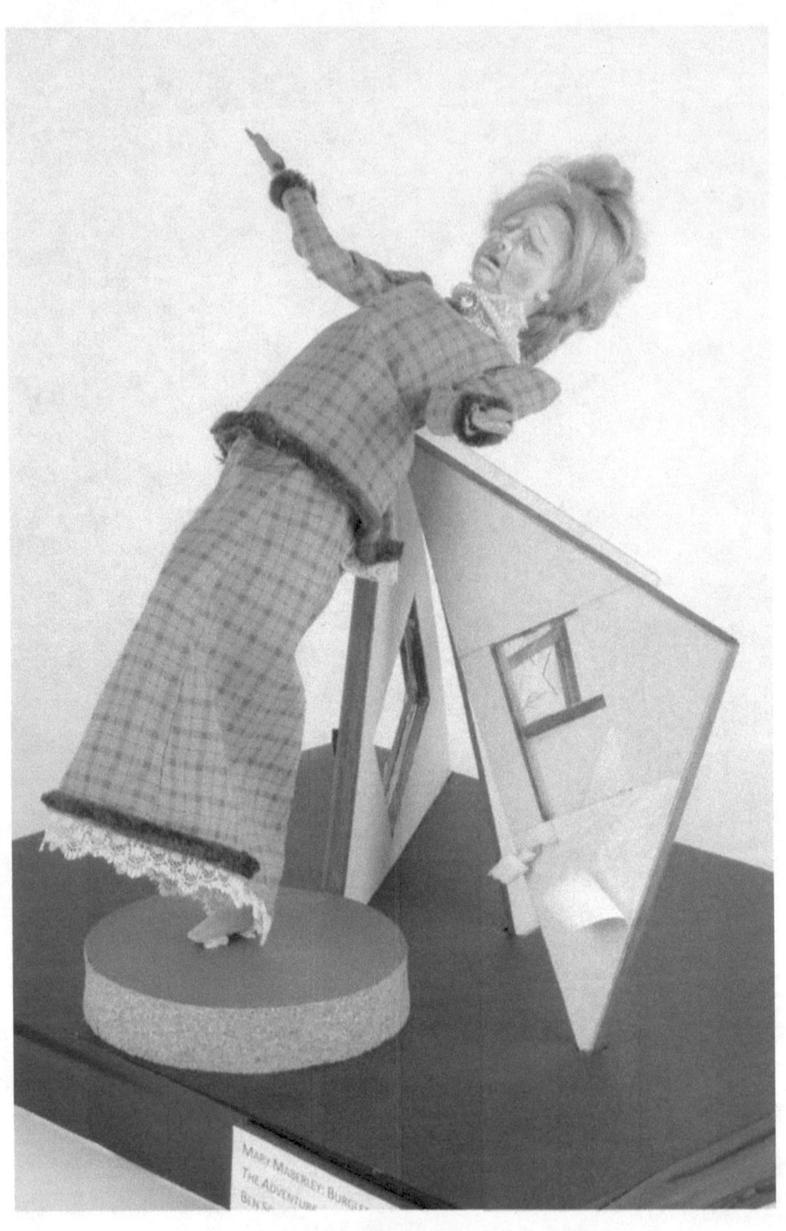

104
Mary Maberley
from "The Three Gables"
Ben Schmideg

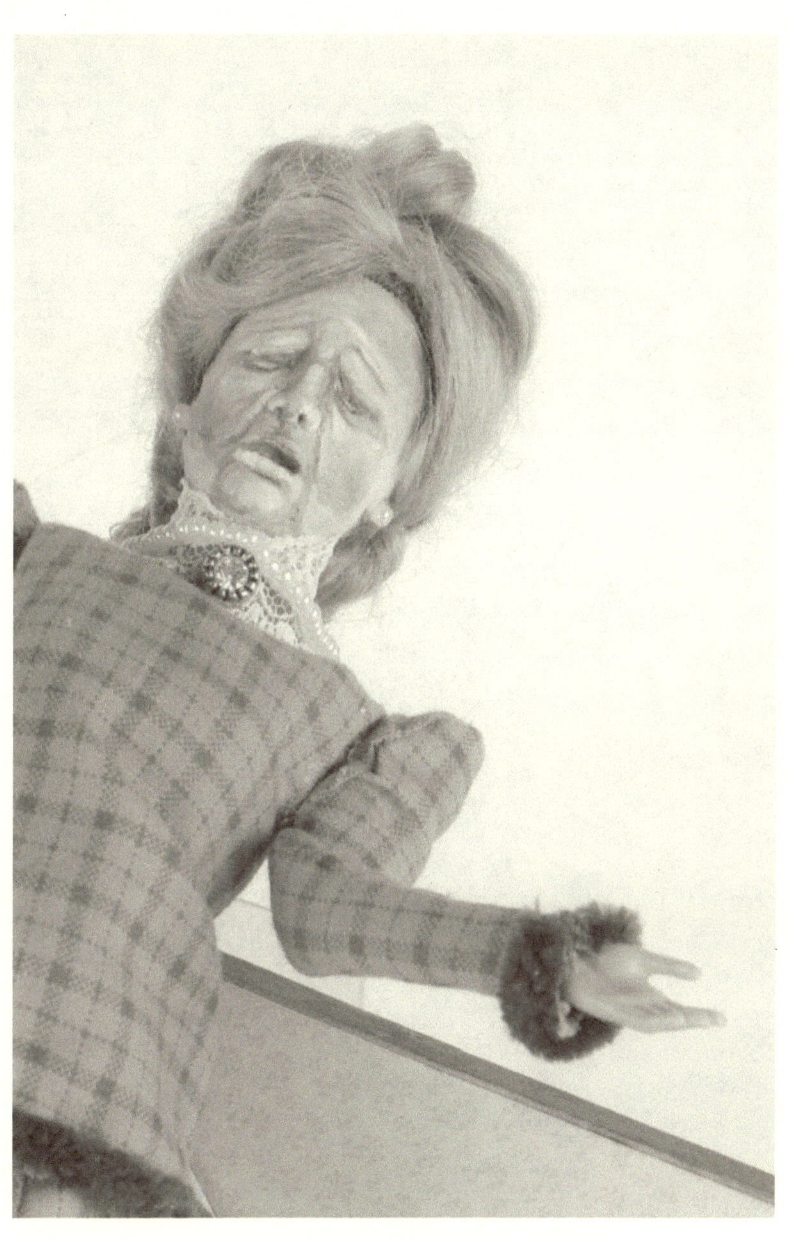

105
Mary Maberley
from "The Three Gables"
Ben Schmideg

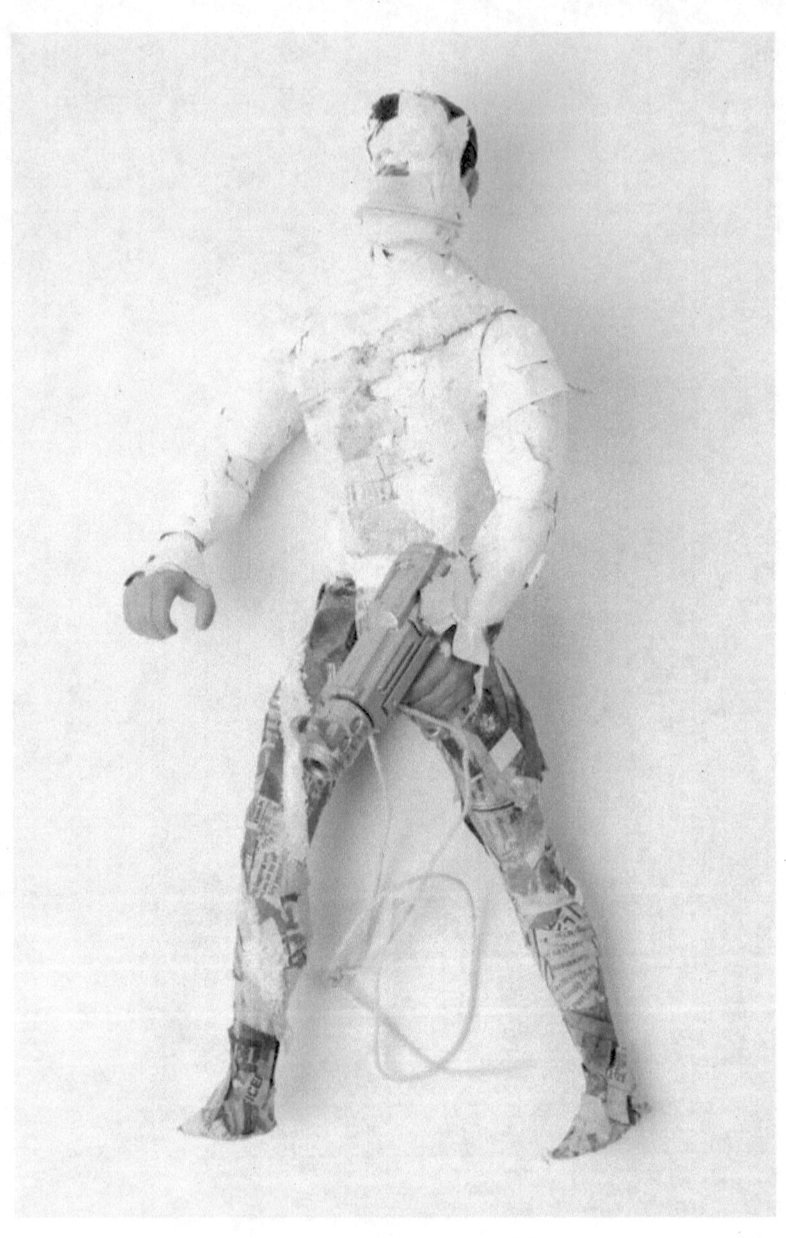

106
Godfrey Emsworth
from "The Blanched Soldier"
Yeung Hiu Lei

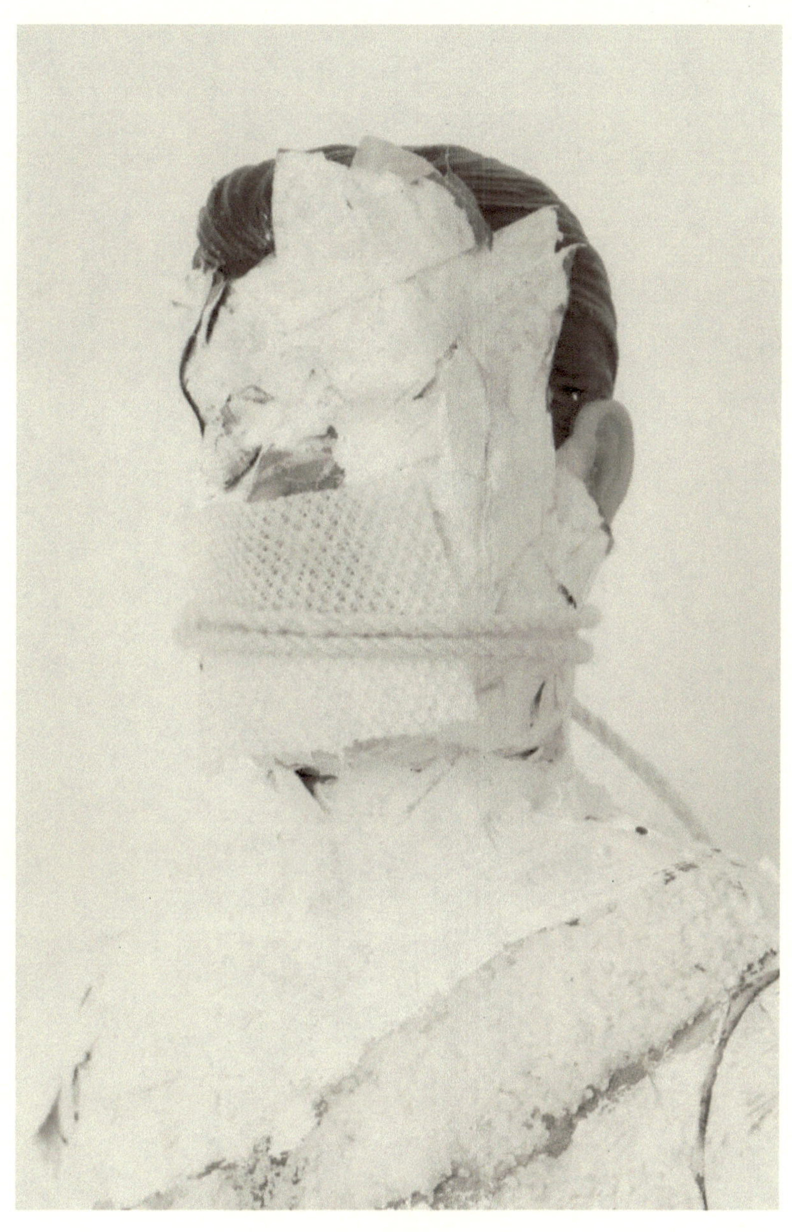

107
Godfrey Emsworth
from "The Blanched Soldier"
Yeung Hiu Lei

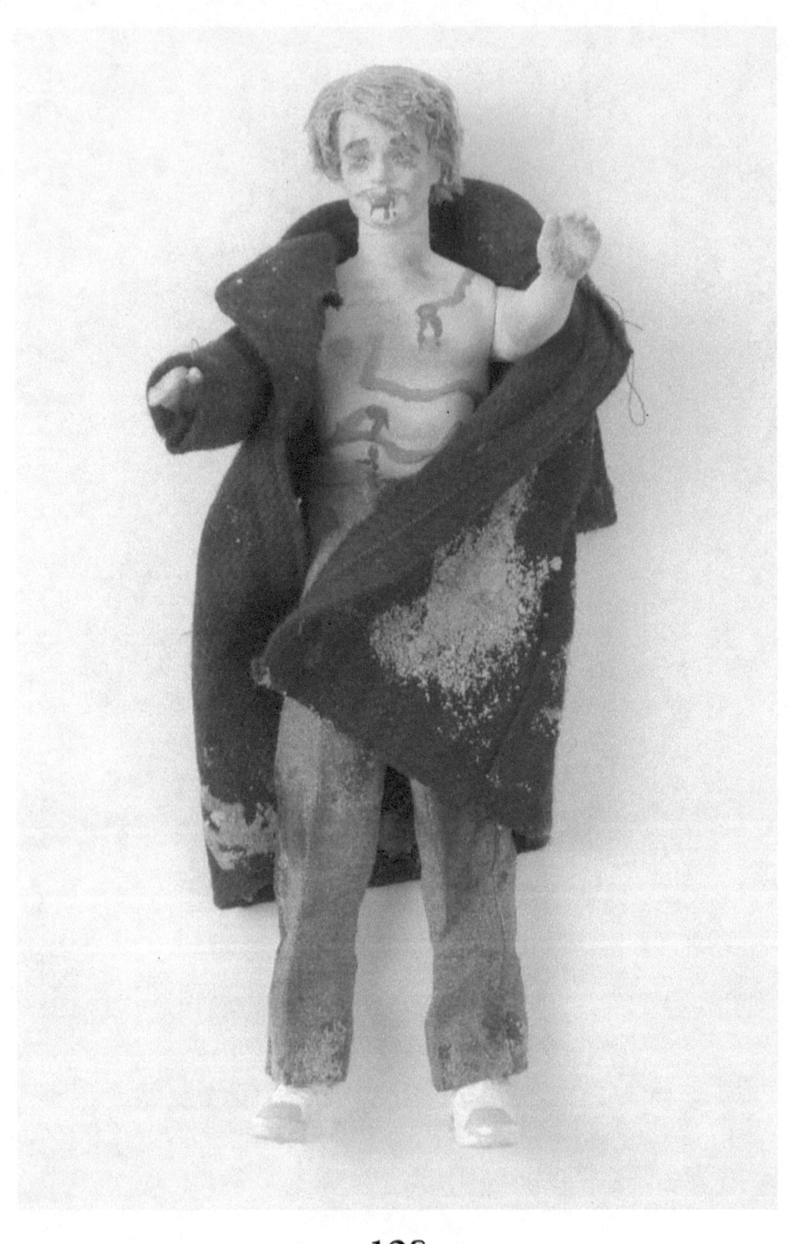

108
Fitzroy McPherson
from "The Lion"s Mane"
Audrey Zerafa

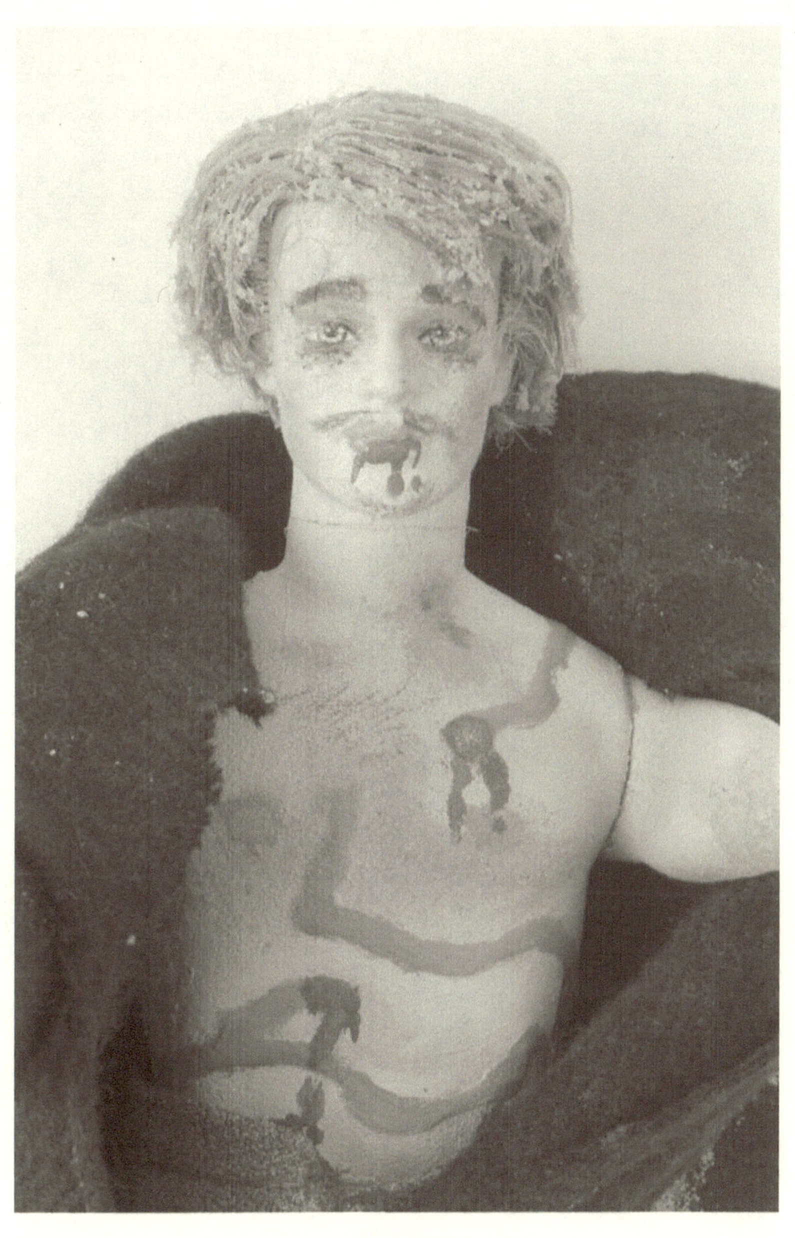

109
Fitzroy McPherson
from "The Lion"s Mane"
Audrey Zerafa

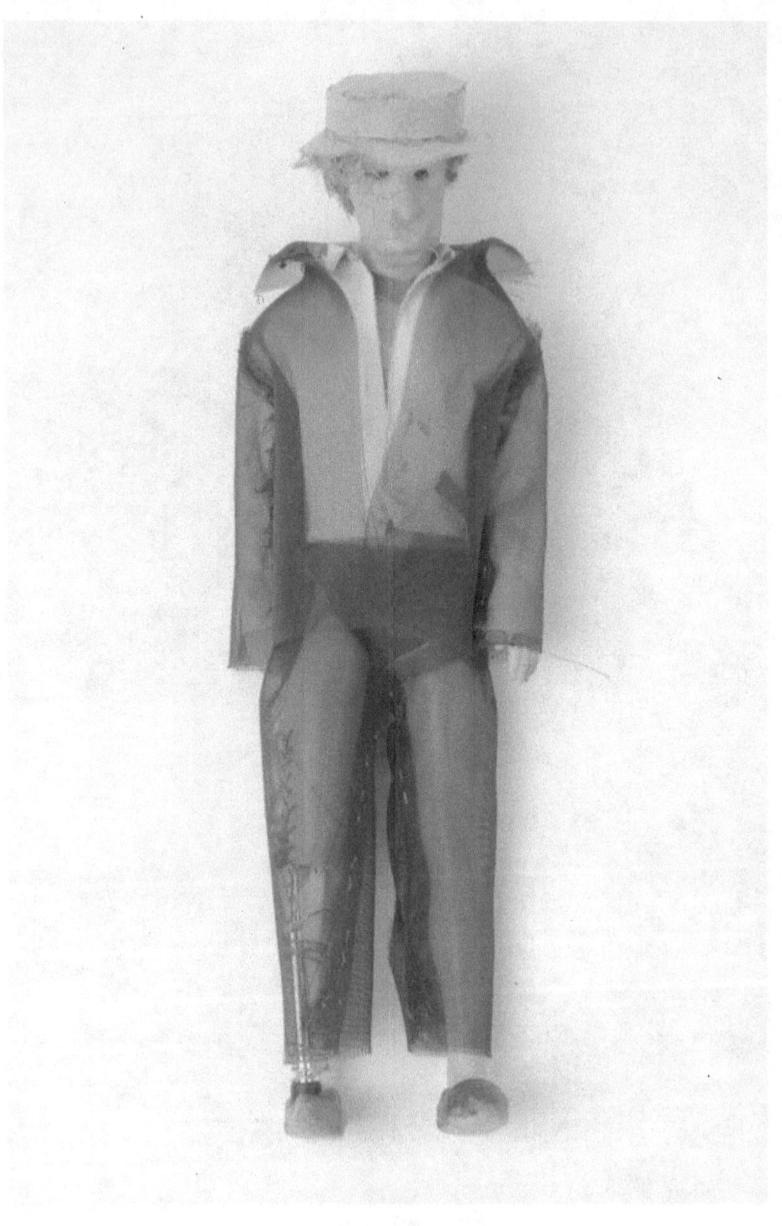

110
Josiah Amberley
from "The Retired Colourman"
Meijing Gui

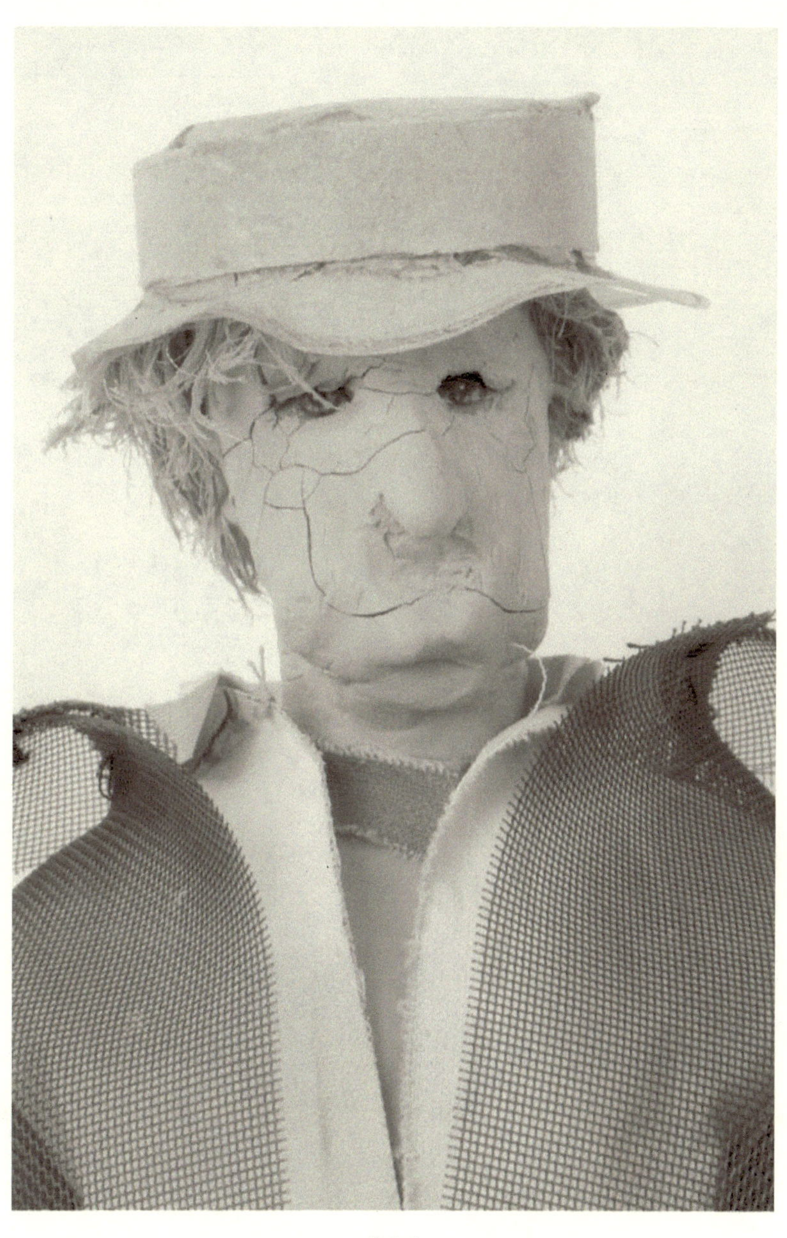

111
Josiah Amberley
from "The Retired Colourman"
Meijing Cui

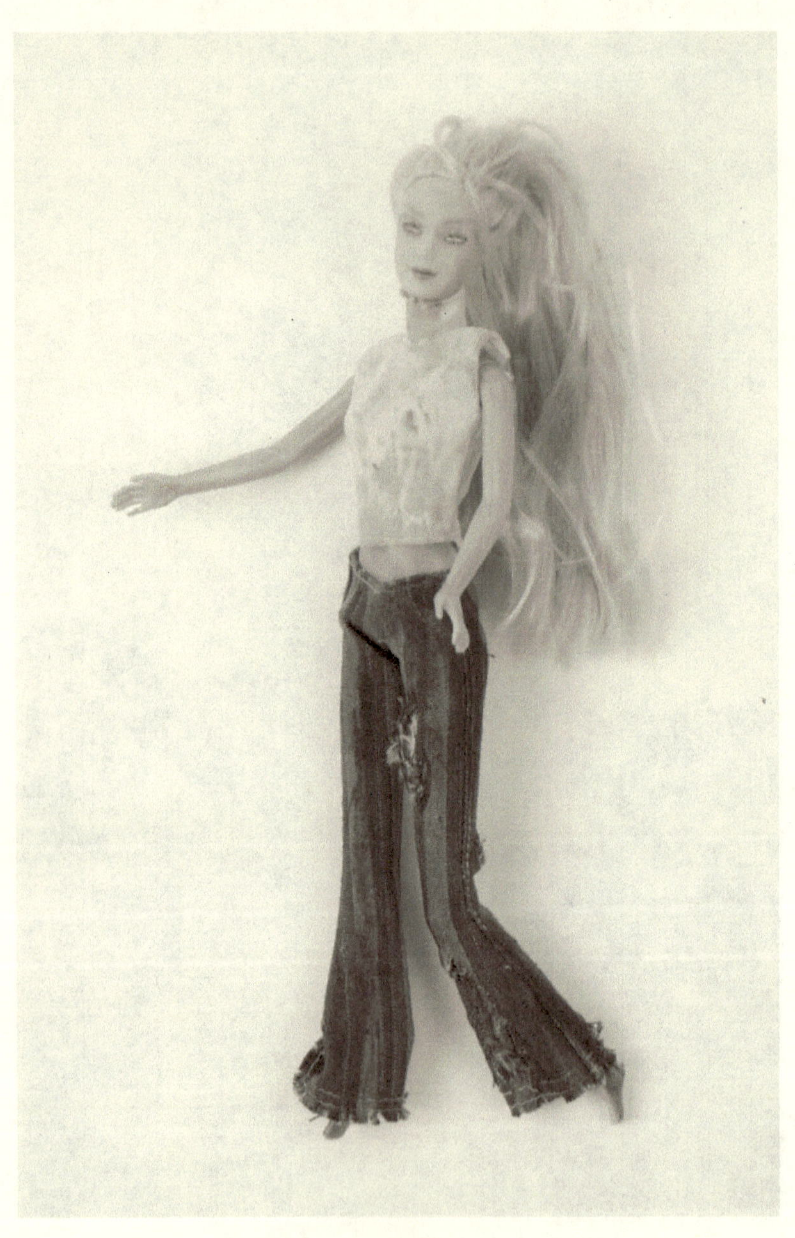

112
Mrs. Amberley
from "The Retired Colourman"
Chong Chik Yin

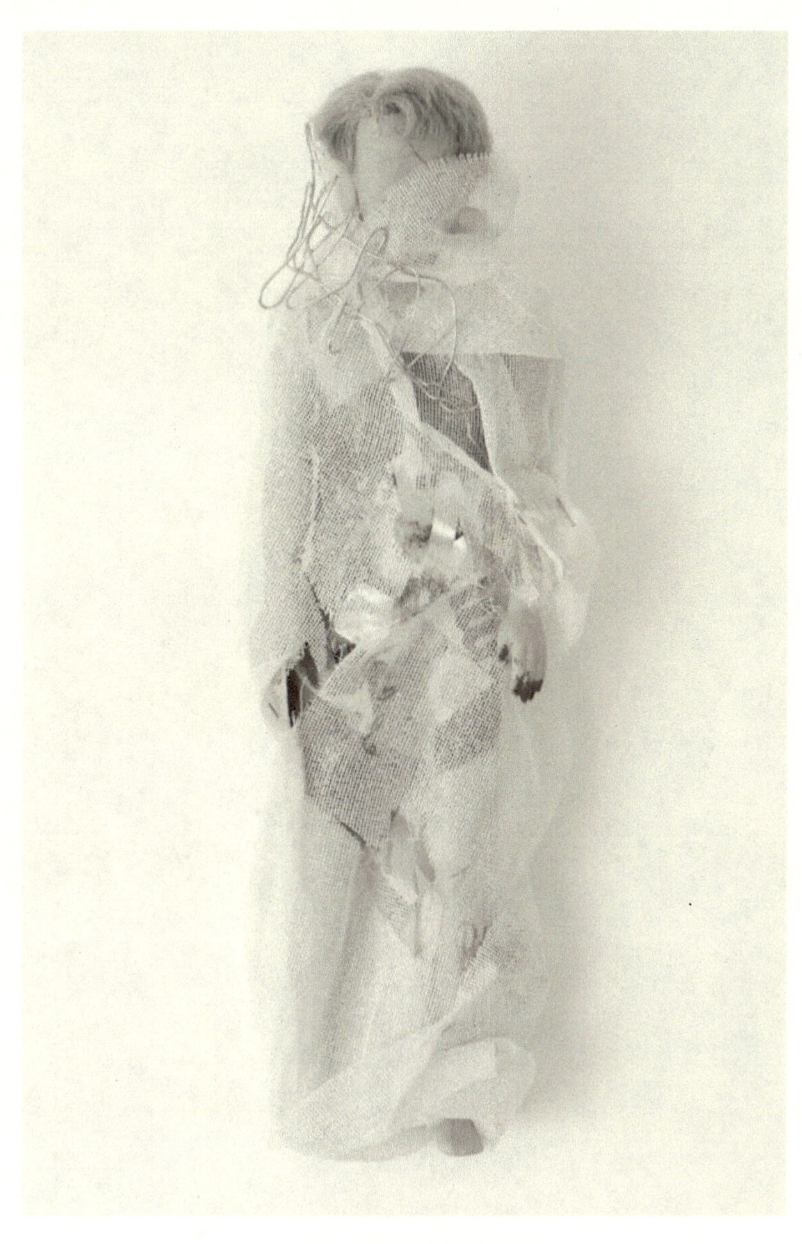

113
Dr. Ray Ernest
from "The Retired Colourman"
Zhao Le

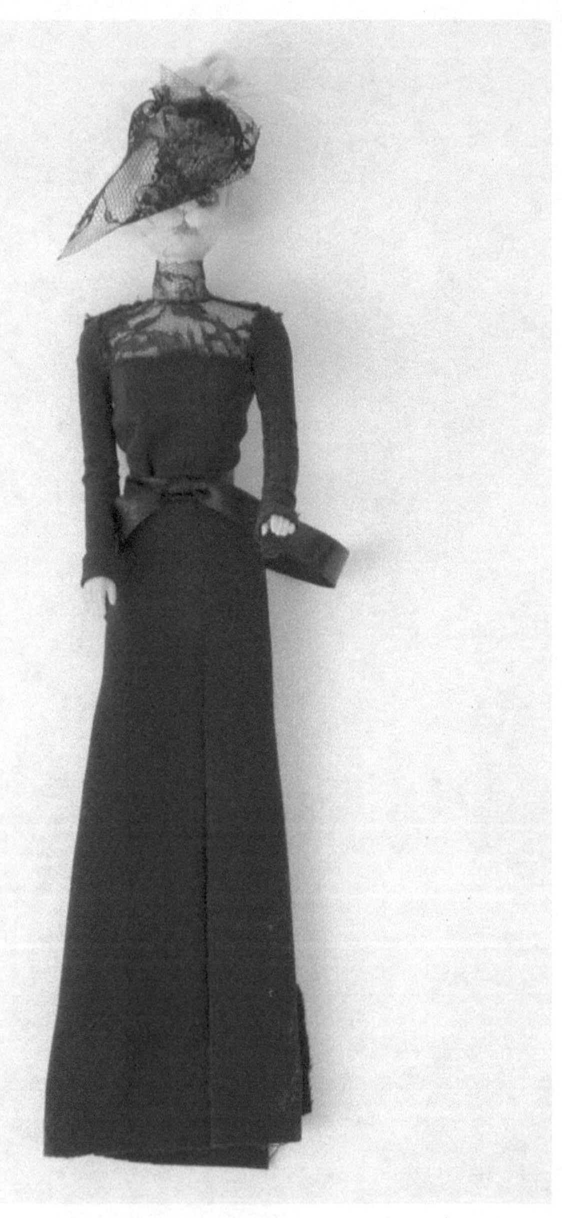

114
Eugenia Ronder
from "The Veiled Lodger"
Melissa Spencer

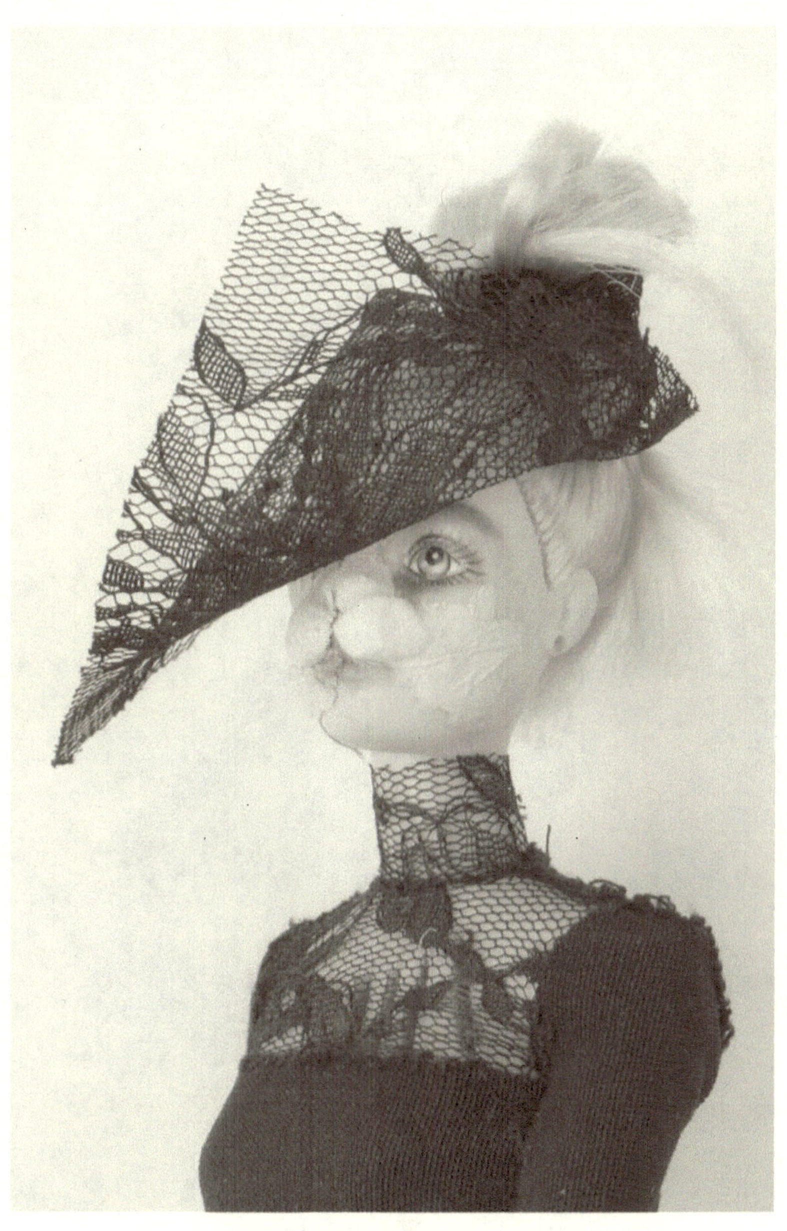

115
Eugenia Ronder
from "The Veiled Lodger"
Melissa Spencer

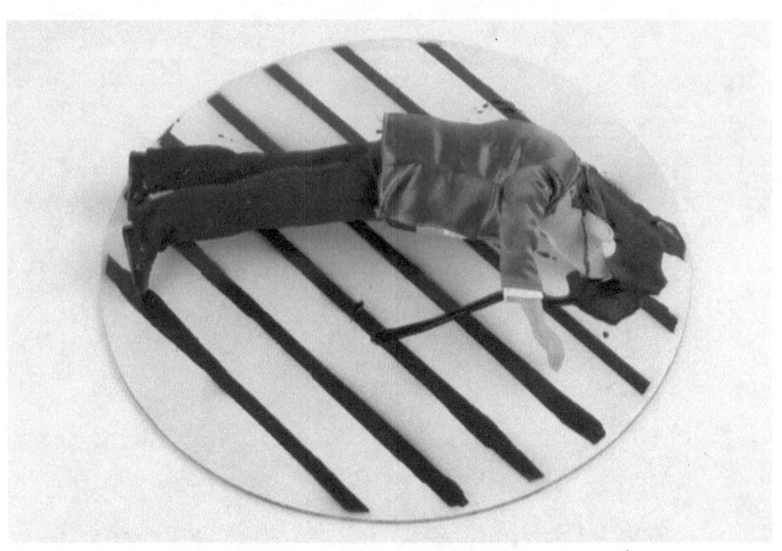

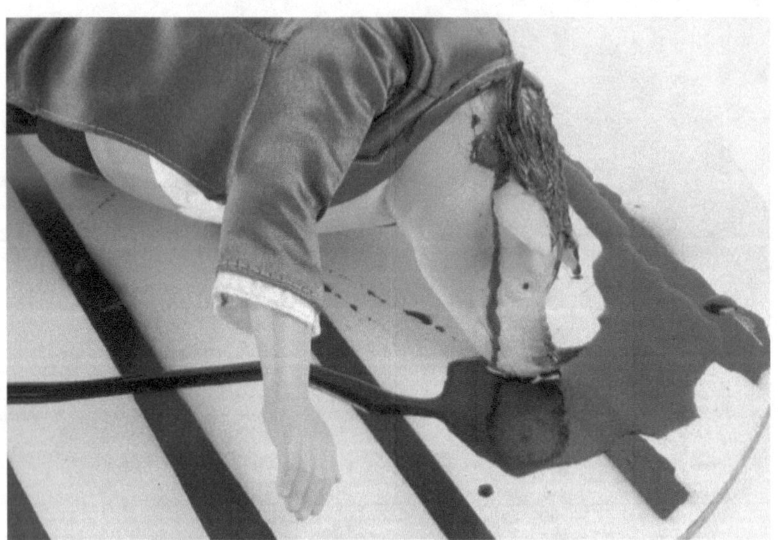

116 & 117
Ronder the circus owner
from "The Veiled Lodger"
Ben Grollo

Select Bibliography

Botz, Corinne May, *The Nutshell Studies of Unexplained Death,* New York: The Monacelli Press, 2004.

Browne, Ray B., *The Spirit of Australia: The Crime Fiction of Arthur W. Upfield,* Bowling Green: Bowling Green State University Popular Press, 1988.

Courtier, S.H., *Murder's Burning,* London: Hammond, 1967.

Courtier, S.H., *See Who's Dying,* London: Hammond, 1967.

Doyle, Sir Arthur Conan, *The New Annotated Sherlock Holmes* volumes I & II (edited by Leslie L. Klinger), New York: W.W. Norton, 2005.

Doyle, Sir Arthur Conan, *The New Annotated Sherlock Holmes* volume III (edited by Leslie L. Klinger), New York: W.W. Norton, 2006.

Groves, Derham, *Feng-Shui and Western Building Ceremonies.* Singapore: Graham Brash, 1991.

Groves, Derham, *There's No Place Like Holmes: Exploring Sense of Space Through Crime Fiction,* North Carlton: Black Jack Press, 2008.

Groves, Derham, 'Holmes Is Where the Art Is: Architectural Design Projects' in *Murder 101: Essays on the Teaching of Detective Fiction* (edited by Edward J. Rielly), Jefferson, North Carolina: McFarland, 2009, pp.61 – 69.

Johnson-Woods, Toni, *Pulp: A Collector's Book of Australian Pulp Fiction Covers,* Canberra: National Library of Australia, 2004.

Lee, Pamela M., *Object To Be Destroyed: The Work of Gordon Matta-Clark,* Cambridge, Massachusetts: The MIT Press, 2004.

Rabaté, Jean-Michel, *Given: 1° Art 2° Crime: Modernity, Murder and Mass Culture,* Eastbourne: Sussex Academic Press, 2007.

Von Kleist, Henrich, Charles Baudelaire and Rainer Maria Rilke (translated by Idris Parry and Paul Keegan), *Essays on Dolls,* London: Syrens, 1994.

Wright, June, *Murder in the Telephone Exchange,* London: Hutchinson, n.d.

Wright, June, *Faculty of Murder,* London: John Long, 1961.

RAMBLE HOUSE's

HARRY STEPHEN KEELER WEBWORK MYSTERIES

(RH) indicates the title is available ONLY in the **RAMBLE HOUSE** edition

The Ace of Spades Murder
The Affair of the Bottled Deuce (RH)
The Amazing Web
The Barking Clock
Behind That Mask
The Book with the Orange Leaves
The Bottle with the Green Wax Seal
The Box from Japan
The Case of the Canny Killer
The Case of the Crazy Corpse (RH)
The Case of the Flying Hands (RH)
The Case of the Ivory Arrow
The Case of the Jeweled Ragpicker
The Case of the Lavender Gripsack
The Case of the Mysterious Moll
The Case of the 16 Beans
The Case of the Transparent Nude (RH)
The Case of the Transposed Legs
The Case of the Two-Headed Idiot (RH)
The Case of the Two Strange Ladies
The Circus Stealers (RH)
Cleopatra's Tears
A Copy of Beowulf (RH)
The Crimson Cube (RH)
The Face of the Man From Saturn
Find the Clock
The Five Silver Buddhas
The 4th King
The Gallows Waits, My Lord! (RH)
The Green Jade Hand
Finger! Finger!
Hangman's Nights (RH)
I, Chameleon (RH)
I Killed Lincoln at 10:13! (RH)
The Iron Ring
The Man Who Changed His Skin (RH)
The Man with the Crimson Box
The Man with the Magic Eardrums
The Man with the Wooden Spectacles
The Marceau Case
The Matilda Hunter Murder
The Monocled Monster
The Murder of London Lew
The Murdered Mathematician
The Mysterious Card (RH)
The Mysterious Ivory Ball of Wong Shing Li (RH)
The Mystery of the Fiddling Cracksman
The Peacock Fan
The Photo of Lady X (RH)
The Portrait of Jirjohn Cobb
Report on Vanessa Hewstone (RH)
Riddle of the Travelling Skull
Riddle of the Wooden Parrakeet (RH)
The Scarlet Mummy (RH)
The Search for X-Y-Z
The Sharkskin Book
Sing Sing Nights
The Six From Nowhere (RH)
The Skull of the Waltzing Clown
The Spectacles of Mr. Cagliostro
Stand By—London Calling!
The Steeltown Strangler
The Stolen Gravestone (RH)
Strange Journey (RH)
The Strange Will
The Straw Hat Murders (RH)
The Street of 1000 Eyes (RH)
Thieves' Nights
Three Novellos (RH)
The Tiger Snake
The Trap (RH)
Vagabond Nights (Defrauded Yeggman)
Vagabond Nights 2 (10 Hours)
The Vanishing Gold Truck
The Voice of the Seven Sparrows
The Washington Square Enigma
When Thief Meets Thief
The White Circle (RH)
The Wonderful Scheme of Mr. Christopher Thorne
X. Jones—of Scotland Yard
Y. Cheung, Business Detective

Keeler Related Works

A To Izzard: A Harry Stephen Keeler Companion by Fender Tucker — Articles and stories about Harry, by Harry, and in his style. Included is a compleat bibliography.

Wild About Harry: Reviews of Keeler Novels — Edited by Richard Polt & Fender Tucker — 22 reviews of works by Harry Stephen Keeler from *Keeler News.* A perfect introduction to the author.

The Keeler Keyhole Collection: Annotated newsletter rants from Harry Stephen Keeler, edited by Francis M. Nevins. Over 400 pages of incredibly personal Keeleriana.

Fakealoo — Pastiches of the style of Harry Stephen Keeler by selected demented members of the HSK Society. Updated every year with the new winner.

RAMBLE HOUSE's OTHER LOONS

Strands of the Web: Short Stories of Harry Stephen Keeler — Edited and Introduced by Fred Cleaver
The Sam McCain Novels — Ed Gorman's terrific series includes *The Day the Music Died, Wake Up Little Susie* and *Will You Still Love Me Tomorrow?*
A Shot Rang Out — Three decades of reviews from Jon Breen
Blood Moon — The first of the Robert Payne series by Ed Gorman
The Time Armada — Fox B. Holden's 1953 SF gem.
Black River Falls — Suspense from the master, Ed Gorman
Sideslip — 1968 SF masterpiece by Ted White and Dave Van Arnam
The Triune Man — Mindscrambling science fiction from Richard A. Lupoff
Detective Duff Unravels It — Episodic mysteries by Harvey O'Higgins
Mysterious Martin, the Master of Murder — Two versions of a strange 1912 novel by Tod Robbins about a man who writes books that can kill.
The Master of Mysteries — 1912 novel of supernatural sleuthing by Gelett Burgess
Dago Red — 22 tales of dark suspense by Bill Pronzini
The Night Remembers — A 1991 Jack Walsh mystery from Ed Gorman
Rough Cut & New, Improved Murder — Ed Gorman's first two novels
Hollywood Dreams — A novel of the Depression by Richard O'Brien
Six Gelett Burgess Novels — *The Master of Mysteries, The White Cat, Two O'Clock Courage, Ladies in Boxes, Find the Woman, The Heart Line*
The Organ Reader — A huge compilation of just about everything published in the 1971-1972 radical bay-area newspaper, *THE ORGAN.*
A Clear Path to Cross — Sharon Knowles short mystery stories by Ed Lynskey
Old Times' Sake — Short stories by James Reasoner from Mike Shayne Magazine
Freaks and Fantasies — Eerie tales by Tod Robbins, collaborator of Tod Browning on the film FREAKS.
Five Jim Harmon Sleaze Double Novels — *Vixen Hollow/Celluloid Scandal, The Man Who Made Maniacs/Silent Siren, Ape Rape/Wanton Witch, Sex Burns Like Fire/Twist Session*, and *Sudden Lust/Passion Strip.* More doubles to come!
Marblehead: A Novel of H.P. Lovecraft — A long-lost masterpiece from Richard A. Lupoff. Published for the first time!
The Compleat Ova Hamlet — Parodies of SF authors by Richard A. Lupoff - New edition!
The Secret Adventures of Sherlock Holmes — Three Sherlockian pastiches by the Brooklyn author/publisher, Gary Lovisi.
The Universal Holmes — Richard A. Lupoff's 2007 collection of five Holmesian pastiches and a recipe for giant rat stew.
Four Joel Townsley Rogers Novels — By the author of *The Red Right Hand: Once In a Red Moon, Lady With the Dice, The Stopped Clock, Never Leave My Bed*
Two Joel Townsley Rogers Story Collections — Night of Horror and Killing Time
Twenty Norman Berrow Novels — *The Bishop's Sword, Ghost House, Don't Go Out After Dark, Claws of the Cougar, The Smokers of Hashish, The Secret Dancer, Don't Jump Mr. Boland!, The Footprints of Satan, Fingers for Ransom, The Three Tiers of Fantasy, The Spaniard's Thumb, The Eleventh Plague, Words Have Wings, One Thrilling Night, The Lady's in Danger, It Howls at Night, The Terror in the Fog, Oil Under the Window, Murder in the Melody, The Singing Room*
The N. R. De Mexico Novels — Robert Bragg presents *Marijuana Girl, Madman on a Drum, Private Chauffeur* in one volume.
Four Chelsea Quinn Yarbro Novels featuring Charlie Moon — *Ogilvie, Tallant and Moon, Music When the Sweet Voice Dies, Poisonous Fruit* and *Dead Mice*
Four Walter S. Masterman Mysteries — *The Green Toad, The Flying Beast, The Yellow Mistletoe* and *The Wrong Verdict,* fantastic impossible plots. More to come.
Two Hake Talbot Novels — *Rim of the Pit, The Hangman's Handyman.* Classic locked room mysteries.
Two Alexander Laing Novels — *The Motives of Nicholas Holtz* and *Dr. Scarlett*, stories of medical mayhem and intrigue from the 30s.
Four David Hume Novels — *Corpses Never Argue, Cemetery First Stop, Make Way for the Mourners, Eternity Here I Come*, and more to come.
Three Wade Wright Novels — *Echo of Fear, Death At Nostalgia Street* and *It Leads to Murder*, with more to come!

Six Rupert Penny Novels — *Policeman's Holiday, Policeman's Evidence, Lucky Policeman, Policeman in Armour, Sealed Room Murder, Sweet Poison,* classic mysteries.

Five Jack Mann Novels — Strange murder in the English countryside. *Gees' First Case, Nightmare Farm, Grey Shapes, The Ninth Life, The Glass Too Many.*

Seven Max Afford Novels — *Owl of Darkness, Death's Mannikins, Blood on His Hands, The Dead Are Blind, The Sheep and the Wolves, Sinners in Paradise* and *Two Locked Room Mysteries and a Ripping Yarn* by one of Australia's finest novelists.

Five Joseph Shallit Novels — *The Case of the Billion Dollar Body, Lady Don't Die on My Doorstep, Kiss the Killer, Yell Bloody Murder, Take Your Last Look.* One of America's best 50's authors.

Two Crimson Clown Novels — By Johnston McCulley, author of the Zorro novels, *The Crimson Clown* and *The Crimson Clown Again.*

The Best of 10-Story Book — edited by Chris Mikul, over 35 stories from the literary magazine Harry Stephen Keeler edited.

A Young Man's Heart — A forgotten early classic by Cornell Woolrich

The Anthony Boucher Chronicles — edited by Francis M. Nevins
Book reviews by Anthony Boucher written for the *San Francisco Chronicle,* 1942 - 1947. Essential and fascinating reading.

Muddled Mind: Complete Works of Ed Wood, Jr. — David Hayes and Hayden Davis deconstruct the life and works of a mad genius.

Gadsby — A lipogram (a novel without the letter E). Ernest Vincent Wright's last work, published in 1939 right before his death.

My First Time: The One Experience You Never Forget — Michael Birchwood — 64 true first-person narratives of how they lost it.

Automaton — Brilliant treatise on robotics: 1928-style! By H. Stafford Hatfield

The Incredible Adventures of Rowland Hern — Rousing 1928 impossible crimes by Nicholas Olde.

Slammer Days — Two full-length prison memoirs: *Men into Beasts* (1952) by George Sylvester Viereck and *Home Away From Home* (1962) by Jack Woodford

Murder in Black and White — 1931 classic tennis whodunit by Evelyn Elder

Killer's Caress — Cary Moran's 1936 hardboiled thriller

The Golden Dagger — 1951 Scotland Yard yarn by E. R. Punshon

Beat Books #1 — Two beatnik classics, *A Sea of Thighs* by Ray Kainen and *Village Hipster* by J.X. Williams

A Smell of Smoke — 1951 English countryside thriller by Miles Burton

Ruled By Radio — 1925 futuristic novel by Robert L. Hadfield & Frank E. Farncombe

Murder in Silk — A 1937 Yellow Peril novel of the silk trade by Ralph Trevor

The Case of the Withered Hand — 1936 potboiler by John G. Brandon

Finger-prints Never Lie — A 1939 classic detective novel by John G. Brandon

Inclination to Murder — 1966 thriller by New Zealand's Harriet Hunter

Invaders from the Dark — Classic werewolf tale from Greye La Spina

Fatal Accident — Murder by automobile, a 1936 mystery by Cecil M. Wills

The Devil Drives — A prison and lost treasure novel by Virgil Markham

Dr. Odin — Douglas Newton's 1933 potboiler comes back to life.

The Chinese Jar Mystery — Murder in the manor by John Stephen Strange, 1934

The Julius Caesar Murder Case — A classic 1935 re-telling of the assassination by Wallace Irwin that's much more fun than the Shakespeare version

West Texas War and Other Western Stories — by Gary Lovisi

The Contested Earth and Other SF Stories — A never-before published space opera and seven short stories by Jim Harmon.

Tales of the Macabre and Ordinary — Modern twisted horror by Chris Mikul, author of the *Bizarrism* series.

The Gold Star Line — Seaboard adventure from L.T. Reade and Robert Eustace.

The Werewolf vs the Vampire Woman — Hard to believe ultraviolence by either Arthur M. Scarm or Arthur M. Scram.

Black Hogan Strikes Again — Australia's Peter Renwick pens a tale of the outback.

Don Diablo: Book of a Lost Film — Two-volume treatment of a western by Paul Landres, with diagrams. Intro by Francis M. Nevins.

The Charlie Chaplin Murder Mystery — Movie hijinks by Wes D. Gehring

The Koky Comics — A collection of all of the 1978-1981 Sunday and daily comic strips by Richard O'Brien and Mort Gerberg, in two volumes.

Suzy — Another collection of comic strips from Richard O'Brien and Bob Vojtko

Dime Novels: Ramble House's 10-Cent Books — *Knife in the Dark* by Robert Leslie Bellem, *Hot Lead* and *Song of Death* by Ed Earl Repp, *A Hashish House in New York* by H.H. Kane, and five more.

Blood in a Snap — The *Finnegan's Wake* of the 21st century, by Jim Weiler and Al Gorithm

Stakeout on Millennium Drive — Award-winning Indianapolis Noir — Ian Woollen.

Dope Tales #1 — Two dope-riddled classics; *Dope Runners* by Gerald Grantham and *Death Takes the Joystick* by Phillip Condé.

Dope Tales #2 — Two more narco-classics; *The Invisible Hand* by Rex Dark and *The Smokers of Hashish* by Norman Berrow.

Dope Tales #3 — Two enchanting novels of opium by the master, Sax Rohmer. *Dope* and *The Yellow Claw.*

Tenebrae — Ernest G. Henham's 1898 horror tale brought back.

The Singular Problem of the Stygian House-Boat — Two classic tales by John Kendrick Bangs about the denizens of Hades.

Tiresias — Psychotic modern horror novel by Jonathan M. Sweet.

The One After Snelling — Kickass modern noir from Richard O'Brien.

The Sign of the Scorpion — 1935 Edmund Snell tale of oriental evil.

The House of the Vampire — 1907 poetic thriller by George S. Viereck.

An Angel in the Street — Modern hardboiled noir by Peter Genovese.

The Devil's Mistress — Scottish gothic tale by J. W. Brodie-Innes.

The Lord of Terror — 1925 mystery with master-criminal, Fantômas.

The Lady of the Terraces — 1925 adventure by E. Charles Vivian.

My Deadly Angel — 1955 Cold War drama by John Chelton

Prose Bowl — Futuristic satire — Bill Pronzini & Barry N. Malzberg .

Satan's Den Exposed — True crime in Truth or Consequences New Mexico — Award-winning journalism by the *Desert Journal*.

The Amorous Intrigues & Adventures of Aaron Burr — by Anonymous — Hot historical action.

I Stole $16,000,000 — A true story by cracksman Herbert E. Wilson.

The Black Dark Murders — Vintage 50s college murder yarn by Milt Ozaki, writing as Robert O. Saber.

Sex Slave — Potboiler of lust in the days of Cleopatra — Dion Leclerq.

You'll Die Laughing — Bruce Elliott's 1945 novel of murder at a practical joker's English countryside manor.

The Private Journal & Diary of John H. Surratt — The memoirs of the man who conspired to assassinate President Lincoln.

Dead Man Talks Too Much — Hollywood boozer by Weed Dickenson

Red Light — History of legal prostitution in Shreveport Louisiana by Eric Brock. Includes wonderful photos of the houses and the ladies.

A Snark Selection — Lewis Carroll's *The Hunting of the Snark* with two Snarkian chapters by Harry Stephen Keeler — Illustrated by Gavin L. O'Keefe.

Ripped from the Headlines! — The Jack the Ripper story as told in the newspaper articles in the *New York* and *London Times.*

Geronimo — S. M. Barrett's 1905 autobiography of a noble American.

The White Peril in the Far East — Sidney Lewis Gulick's 1905 indictment of the West and assurance that Japan would never attack the U.S.

The Compleat Calhoon — All of Fender Tucker's works: Includes *The Totah Trilogy, Weed, Women and Song* and *Tales from the Tower,* plus a CD of all of his songs.

www.ingramcontent.com/pod-product-compliance
Lightning Source LLC
LaVergne TN
LVHW090949080826
845145LV00003B/950
9781605433387